I0666703

Words of Warfare

Songs of Sevria
Volume 2

Patrick Basil

Cover art by germancreative

Maps by Vitor Nunes

Patrick Basil

*For the Lawrence Family.
Your love and support
kept me writing during
my darkest days.*

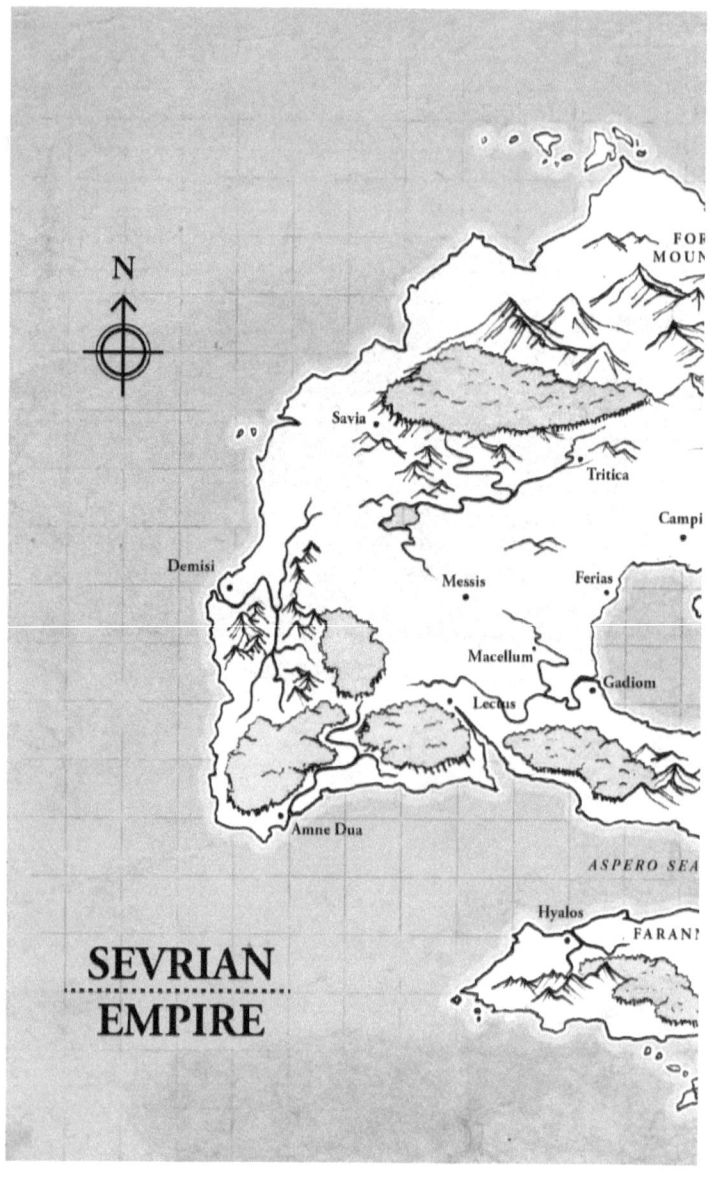

Patrick Basil

Chapter 1

W hen the forest ended at the base of the world's largest wall, Catherine was not impressed. Her whiskers hung low and her ears folded back in annoyance. She was a Margot—half feline, half human—a desert creature from the sands of Uurden Els. Her soul-sister Rinn pushed her way through the underbrush, spitting out bits of leaves.

"I think we've arrived." Rinn proclaimed as she spotted the wall. She squinted up at the imposing monstrosity that blocked out half the sky.

Cat tapped absently at the stones. "Who put this thing here?"

One by one, Rinn and Cat's friends emerged from the forest. They jokingly referred to themselves as Rinn's army. They were not much of an army: one soldier, a handful of teenagers, two dwarves, and a quarter-giant. But they were all loyal to Rinn, willing to follow her anywhere, even into the heart of a civil war.

The quarter-giant Molossus proudly placed a hand on the enormous limestone wall. "This is the Vallum, the eastern edge of the Sevrian Empire. One thousand miles of stone and engineering." Several of the teenagers whistled at the architectural marvel. It towered over Rinn's army like a cliff. At the top of the mighty rampart, miniature sentry towers dotted its lofty parapets. Rinn saw no windows nor doors, only stark, imposing wall stretching to the horizon north and south. For its size, the barrier had not been well maintained, chunks of fallen stone littered the forest floor and trees grew right up against the stones like weeds.

The traitorous redhead Sionne asked. "What now, princess?"

"Stop calling me that." Rinn chafed. Now that she was here, Rinn was unsure what to do. She spent the last half-year traveling through the Rustic Lands to the edge of the Sevrian Empire. She turned fifteen on the journey. She did not have much of a celebration, a homemade sweetbread cooked over a campfire and a round of singing. But she was surrounded by her friends and family, her favorite way to spend a birthday. In the last six months Rinn had changed. Her long blond hair was growing back. Her height had shot up so much, she was almost eye to eye with her father. Her skinny, girlish figure became more defined, her muscles tempered by daily hiking and hunting. Her friend Feena, who was close in age, had fully blossomed in the ways that turned boy's heads. Rinn's adoptive sister Catherine was even starting to show feminine curves beneath her fur. Rinn was frustratingly skinny and under-developed. She wondered if she was doomed to look like a bean-pole all her life. She set her worries aside, more important concerns were pressing, like how to get past this wall.

Rinn reached out a hand and touched the Vallum. Its yellow stones had been polished marble-smooth and pieced together without visible seams. Rinn recognized the craftsmanship—dwarven. And not just any dwarves, this wall was built by Dvalinn dwarves. When Rinn fled the Empire two years ago with her father, she had known nothing of dwarves or war or magic. Now she was coming home, well versed in all these things.

"The Dvalinn built this." Rinn observed.

Felsic and Mafic, the two dwarves accompanying her, scrutinized the colossal wall. Mafic, the more rotund and cheerful of the two, agreed. "Most certainly. Our Dvalinn cousins fit stone together so tightly not even water can pass through." The two brothers were Dverg, dwarven artisans skilled at delicate handiwork, completely unaccustomed to large scale construction.

"It's not very pretty." Felsic scoffed at the bland stone.

Rinn chuckled. With a rustling of branches, Rinn's father emerged from the forest on horseback. Last year he took an arrow to his hip and it never healed correctly. He remained in the saddle most of the time, which was challenging in the dense forests of the Rustic Lands. But he was a trained equestrian, and he navigated the wilderness with grace. Rinn asked him. "How far do you think it is to the nearest gate?"

Marshal peered down the length of the massive wall. "The gates are spaced every 50 miles. But we've been avoiding the main roads, so there's no telling how close the nearest one might be. If I could get a peek on the other side of the wall, I'd have a better chance of knowing where we were."

"I could go." Catherine raised a paw eagerly.

"I don't think that's the best idea." Molossus, the quarter giant, held up a hand to object, but Cat was already gone, vanished into the air. Margot did that—disappeared into thin air and reappeared at will. At least Catherine did that, and she was the only Margot Rinn had ever met. Rinn was not sure what other Margot were like, but in her mind they all behaved just like her sister.

"Where did she go?" Feena looked around, bewildered.

"Don't worry." Lutra reassured her. "She does that. She'll come back when she wants to."

"We'll camp here until she returns." Marshal announced. Everyone let their packs slide to the ground and plopped down to rest.

3

"I could really use a bathroom." Sionne eyed the Vallum suspiciously.

Lutra cuffed him on the back of the head. "Go find a tree."

Marshal organized a hunting party to scavenge for small game in the vicinity. He took Feena and her brother Calder along. Feena was learning how to use a bow, she had no talent for hand-to-hand combat. Her brother, however, was a natural swordsman. Lutra, the aspiring teenage bard, departed with the dwarves to forage for food. Felsic and Mafic had a knack for finding edible mushrooms, and Lutra always knew how to spot sweet, ripe berries.

Rinn stayed behind with Molo and Sionne. She was glad to have the giant and his curious rock Clive around. Sionne was a different story. She had saved him from certain death, but she did not trust him. He had betrayed her too many times in the past. He only came along because he had nowhere else to go, kicked out of his clan and shunned for life. Rinn offered him his only chance at redemption, not that he seemed to want it. Still, he had made an effort to clean up, he tossed his old threadbare clothes out in favor of a new travel outfit and he even bathed occasionally. His red hair stuck out in every direction like a bird's nest and his teeth were crooked and unwashed, but he was trying.

Rinn started digging a fire pit with a small shovel from her pack. The dwarves taught everyone how to make campfires that are invisible from afar by digging into the ground. A small side tunnel allowed air to flow under the fire and keep it burning. Dwarven fire pits did not make much smoke and were excellent for cooking. Molo ambled over as Rinn worked.

"Need any help?" The giant man offered.

Rinn wiped her sweaty brow. "I'm good. Just keep an eye out for Cat."

Molo held up Clive, his strange rock with a purple eye painted on it. He scanned the area with a frustrated grimace. "I can't see her, but she could be anywhere."

"She'll be back." Rinn promised, digging deeper into the ground. The foraging party returned with wild mushrooms and forest onions. Marshal and the hunters arrived some time later with a clutch of strange rabbits with long squirrel tails and bushy ears. The animals in the Rustic Lands always seemed peculiar to Rinn, yet most of them tasted perfectly fine.

"Any sign of Cat?" Marshal asked, dismounting with his catch.

"Not yet." Molo answered in a hushed voice. Rinn tried not to look anxious, but her sister had been gone a long time. Dinner came and went with no sign of the missing feline. As daylight faded, Rinn became seriously worried. She hugged her knees as she sat on the ground near the fire. Her father came to sit beside her.

"You can contact her, can't you?" Marshal said. The bond between Rinn and Cat went deeper than anyone suspected, but she was not ready to reveal that fact, even to her own father. Still, parents had secret ways of knowing about their children, at least that is how it seemed to Rinn.

"Yes." Rinn nodded. "I can contact her."

"I think it's time." Her father pressed.

Rinn grudgingly agreed. She rose up and cleared her head. She recalled the time Feena and two other girls from Hilltop had been kidnapped. A rescue attempt failed, and all hope seemed lost, but Cat spoke to Rinn in her mind and helped her locate the imprisoned girls. Rinn held on to that sensation as she spoke to the evening air. "Cat, can you hear me?"

Everyone watched Rinn in expectation. Several minutes passed, and Cat finally answered. Help me. I'm stuck.

A wave a relief poured over Rinn. "Cat, where are you?"

I'm on the other side of the wall. Cat moaned. It won't let me back through.

Rinn did not realize she was gesticulating wildly. Her friends could only hear one side of the conversation and they watched her curiously. "Cat, are you okay?"

I'm hungry. Cat noted.

"But are you safe?" Rinn could not see her sister, but she could feel her nod her head yes. It was unsettling knowing Cat's actions as if they were her own. She wondered how deep their magic bond ran, how closely their souls touched. "Stay put. I'll come get you." Rinn vowed. Cat sniffed and nodded again.

Lutra grabbed Rinn's hand. "Is Cat okay?"

Gently prying her hand away, Rinn answered. "She's fine. She's just trapped on the other side of the wall. For some reason she can't slip back through."

Molo wrinkled his bald head and scratched at his bristle-brush beard. "Why would anyone build a wall that lets magic in but not out?"

"They want to keep something inside." Felsic deduced.

"Or someone." Marshal furtively cast a glance at Rinn.

Oblivious to the implication, Rinn asked. "So, how do we get Cat out?"

Marshal responded. "I'll ride to the nearest gatehouse and go through."

Molo shook his head. "Too risky. Night is almost upon us and the nearest gate could be miles away." Holding Clive high above his head he scanned the wall, discovering nothing.

Lutra peered up at the Vallum soaring above him. "I don't think we have enough rope to go over."

The normally quiet Calder commented. "If you did, would you want to climb it?"

"No." Lutra admitted.

Rinn could feel Cat pacing on the opposite side of the wall, a disquieting sensation that made her feel frustrated and impatient. "We have to do something." Rinn blurted out. She stomped over to the Vallum and started to concentrate. A faint green glow emanated in the twilight, her Sigillum magic manifesting.

Marshal gimped over and covered Rinn's hands. "Whoa, what're you doing?"

Rinn tried to squirm past her father. "I'm going to pry some of these stones away, get Cat out of there."

"Hold on." He warned. "You could bring the entire wall down upon us."

Rinn threw up her arms. "What am I supposed to do? Nothing? I can't sit here and wait while Cat's stuck on the other side of that monstrosity."

Her father rested his hands on her shoulders. "Calm down. I know it's difficult, but we'll have to wait until morning."

"Actually." Molo considered. "She might have a reasonable idea." Both Rinn and Marshal turned to Molo. He outlined his reasoning. "I've seen sections of the Vallum under repair. The stone cladding is only five or ten feet thick at best. The center of the wall is backfill dirt and rubble. If Rinn could lift away a section of the stones, we might be able to tunnel through the rest."

"That would take all night." Marshal protested. "The Vallum's as thick as a stadium. We'll wait until morning and find a gatehouse."

"I'm not going to wait." Rinn insisted. She turned her attention back to the wall, selecting a section to remove.

"Hold a moment." Molo cautioned. "Let's get everyone a safe distance away, just in case. We don't all have magic shields, like you do." He winked. Rinn paused long enough for her friends to reassemble under the protective canopy of trees. Rinn touched the wall and traced the area she meant to remove. In a quiet voice she whispered a word:

"onlithe." Rinn could hear the perfectly set stones loosen, settle in place. She extended one hand and summoned her shield by speaking aloud another word: "beorgan". Her familiar green, glowing barrier appeared before her, a globe of triangles and swirls hovering in the air. It always surprised Rinn how beautiful her magic could be, she typically called upon her shield in battle when she had no time to admire it. With a smile, she pushed her barrier forward into the Vallum, forcing it through the miniscule cracks between the polished stones.

Rinn felt a sharp pain, like a pinprick. An unseen force tugged at her. She winced as she was dragged forward to the wall, her feet digging ruts in the ground. She tried to resist the force, but her shield was feeding on its magnetism, becoming denser, heavier. Rinn was bathed in blinding green light. She urged her barrier to collapse, but the energy was overwhelming. She was losing control. Her shield expanded like a sun, burning away the Vallum. The weight of the magic crushed Rinn. With outstretched hands she fought against the tidal wave of energy hurtling at her. Tears in her eyes, she twisted back to her father and the others in the trees. "Run!" She screamed. "I can't hold it any longer." In a last act of desperation, she threw herself to the ground as a section of the Vallum wall exploded outward.

Chapter 2

A violent crack of thunder echoed across the land, as the forest was showered in debris, dirt, and powdered stone. Startled animals scampered in every direction, and flocks of birds took to the wing, squawking in protest. A plume of yellow dust settled over the area. Rinn lay prostrate on the ground, alive, but covered in dirt and shards of broken rock. She was sore all over and her head throbbed fiercely. She pushed rubble away from her face and tried to sit up. She could feel the sting of hundreds of cuts and scrapes across her body.

"Hello?" Rinn coughed. "Anyone?"

Rinn spit flecks of stone and crawled out from under the blanket of debris. She wiped her eyes with hands caked in dirt. And that was when she saw it—the gaping hole in the Vallum. Childish guilt flooded over her. I need to fix this before someone sees it. Maybe, I could fill the gap with dirt. But the explosion had demolished an entire portion of the wall, opening a fissure as wide as a street. There was no hiding this. The noise alone would alert soldiers for miles. Her only chance now was to find her friends and run.

Rinn concentrated on these words in her head. "Cat, are you there?"

In her mind she could feel Cat sucking on an injured paw. Yes. But the wall-thingy doesn't look so good.

"Thanks." Rinn muttered in embarrassment. "I'm going to make sure everyone else is okay, and then I'm coming to get you."

Rinn called for her friends. The dwarves answered first, stalking out of the forest covered in dust, but otherwise unharmed. The teenagers followed, nursing various scrapes and bruises. Sionn crabbed at Rinn. "A little warning next time, lunatic." He cursed as he picked gravel from his wounded elbow. Molo and Marshal straggled out of the forest last, they had to chase down Marshal's spooked horse. They all stared in amazement at the destruction.

"If we are going, we should hurry." Calder remarked.

With trepidation, Rinn's army approached the V-shaped crevice in the Vallum. Rinn did not see any patrols, nor any bodies, so she assumed this remote part of the wall was relatively unguarded. She tentatively took a step into the fissure. Her journey had started months ago with her decision to return to Sevria, but this step was irrevocable. At any point in her travels she could have turned around, headed back to Hilltop, given up on her quest. Once she crossed this wall, she cast herself into the maelstrom of war and politics, no backing out. She steadied her shaking hands and took her first hesitant step, and then another. She walked into the wounded Vallum, down the narrow alleyway between towers of dirt and rockslide. The passage grew dark, and Molo risked lighting a torch to help them navigate the uneven path. The dwarf brothers walked undaunted across the broken terrain, as if they were taking a leisurely afternoon stroll. Marshal's horse Bayard had the most difficult time, horses do not fare well on loose, rocky soil.

Eventually, Rinn's army made it through. At the far end, Catherine was waiting. She waved hello. Rinn hurried over and hugged her sister warmly, not needing to exchange words. Everyone agreed to push on, to get some distance from the wounded Vallum before they risked stopping for the night. Rinn hiked in the center of the party, head hanging low. The magical assault on the wall had taxed her strength. She was still not sure if it was even her fault. The magic of the Vallum seemed to pull her in, as if it exploded itself. The situation baffled her, but she did not have the mental energy to fret about it. The party trekked for several hours. Rinn stared at the ground, trying not to nod off. Once or twice she had to climb over low stone walls. Eventually Marshal found a suitable place to stop under a rocky outcrop. Rinn fell asleep in minutes on the hard ground, never bothering to unpack her bedroll.

::

The next day, Rinn skipped hand in paw with Cat. A warm sun lazed in the sky and a light breeze tickled the tops of the wheat fields. Eastern Sevria stretched out before her, an endless patchwork of cultivated farmland, colorful fields blossoming in the late summer. Familiar smells welcomed Rinn back to her childhood home.

"It's beautiful." Cat squinted happily.

"Yes, it is." Rinn agreed. After spending almost two years in the wilderness, it was refreshing to be back in civilized lands. Rinn did not have to worry about giant moss spiders or tree wolves racing overhead or any of the other terrors that inhabited the Rustic Lands. "You're going to love it here, Cat. The people are nice, and the food is great." Rinn quickly amended. "But there hasn't been a Margot in the Empire for quite some time, so it might take a bit for them to warm up to you." Cat did not seem too concerned.

Rinn's army stopped at a low cobblestone wall and crawled over it. Marshal vaulted it on his horse. As they continued, Rinn questioned Molo. "When was the last Margot seen in Sevria?"

The giant stroked his bristly beard. "Not since the days of Vespertilio, two hundred years or more."

"Who's Vesper-what's-his-name?" Lutra joined the discussion.

Molo responded. "He was an emperor, the great-grandson of Ardea the Builder." Molo recounted history as they walked. "Ardea was a great leader, many of the grandest structures in Sevria were commissioned by him. He completed construction of the Vallum." Rinn gulped nervously, Molo continued. "Ardea had three sons he loved very much, and he divided the Empire between them. Petty family squabbles turned violent, and each son declared himself the rightful Emperor. In the decades of war that followed, all three sons would lose their lives and the conflict would be carried on by their children. It lasted until Ardea's great-grandson Verspertilio was able to reunite the Empire once again with the help of a Sigillum and her Margot companion." Rinn and Cat grinned at each other.

"So, this is not the first civil war in Sevria?" Lutra questioned.

"Hardly." Molo laughed. "There's been at least four that I know of."

Sionne grumbled. "Nice country. Is there any time it isn't at war?"

Molo countered. "War's a way of life in the Empire. Almost every family has a son or daughter who's served in the Legion."

"Tell me about the Legion." Feena did not want to be left out.

Molo behaved like a school teacher, surrounded by pupils. "A Legion is a standing army of 5000 men. There're twelve of them in total, spread out across the Empire. Each of the nine great cities hosts its own Legion. One's deployed to guard the borders. The two remaining Legions fall under the command of the Emperor, his own personal guard."

"And now those are controlled by the Curia." Rinn deduced.

Molo tensed up and Clive appeared in his hand. "I don't know much about that. I left the Empire years ago." The party stopped to cross another cobblestone wall.

"Why did you leave, Uncle Molo?" Rinn innocently asked.

Marshal rode up and rescued the fumbling giant. "We should hurry, I think we're near Agrilla and the lands of Praetor Serpio."

Molo frowned. "We're that far north?"

"Who's Praetor Serpio?" Lutra inquired.

"He's one of the Curia—the head of their military." Marshal replied solemnly. Rinn shuddered. Every problem in her life seemed to begin and end with the Curia. Their rise to power had plunged the Empire into civil war. The Curia imprisoned her mother and killed her grandmother, and, if they knew Rinn was alive, they would surely come for her. The Curia embodied the worst of humanity, a shadowy conclave of nine wicked men bent on domination.

"We need to leave." Rinn insisted, dragging Cat by the paw.

Marshal blocked her with his horse. "Slow down. Serpio may own these lands, but he doesn't reside here. He's probably at his lavish estates in Duriter or at the Imperial capital." Rinn did not feel any better, she wanted to be as far away from the Curia as possible. Her father reached into his saddle bag and pulled out a stout wooden baton about the length of a small sword. He handed it down to Rinn. She received it happily, cradling it to her chest. The baton was deceptively heavy with a round wooden knob at one end.

"What's that?" Lutra eyeballed the unusual object.

"A surprise." Rinn winked. Molo grinned approvingly at Felsic and Mafic.

Rinn's army headed south, avoiding roads and farm houses. Marshal led the way, periodically scanning the horizon from horseback. As they crossed another cobblestone hedge, Sionne whined. "Why does this country have so many damn walls?"

From his saddle, Marshal smirked. "There're millions of people in the Empire. Everything belongs to someone. These walls mark property lines. Most of them have been here for centuries."

"That's just stupid." Sionne scoffed.

The party moved briskly until Marshal was certain they were clear of Serpio's lands. They sheltered from a warm summer rainstorm in an abandoned barn that leaned precariously. Unloading their packs for the night, Rinn and her friends dined around a small indoor campfire. Lutra gnawed on a leathery piece of dried rabbit. "So, Rinn." He asked between bites. "Now that we're here, what do we do?"

The question caught Rinn off guard, she had not given it much thought.

"Yes, princess." Sionne jeered. "What's the plan?"

Seeing Rinn hesitate, her father answered for her. "We'll head to Viburna, and gather information. It's far from the capital where most of the fighting will be concentrated."

"We know our way around Viburna. It's where I was born." Rinn added with confidence.

"Actually." Marshal glanced to the side. "You weren't born in Viburna."

"What?" Rinn's childhood circled the drain. What little she knew of her mother was steeped in secrets, and now her own birthplace was in question. "Where?" Rinn demanded. "Where was I born?"

"Migalia." Marshal did not meet her gaze. "I brought you to Viburna when you were two years old." Rinn recognized the finality in his statement. Her mother was already gone by that time.

"Where's Migalia?" A childish tantrum boiled inside of Rinn.

Molo described it. "It's an uninhabited archipelago west of Sevria. The islands are savage and inhospitable. No one in their right mind would go there."

"Why?" Rinn yelled. "Why was I born on some god-forsaken island? What's wrong with me?" Her father had no response, he just stared at the fire. Rinn's heart fluttered like a cornered bird and her hands trembled. Her friends tried their best to calm her, but Rinn was inconsolable. She stormed out of the barn into the summer rain. Avoiding everyone she dashed into the night and cried openly. She raised her face to the dark downpour and let the drops mingle with her tears. A warm, wet arm wrapped around her waist. Rinn turned and hugged her sopping wet sister. "Why, Cat? Why don't we belong anywhere?"

"We have each other." Cat offered, ignoring the rain.

"I know." Rinn hugged her sister hard, fighting back sobs. "But we don't have a home. Hilltop doesn't want us, Sevria doesn't want us. It's like we're cursed to wander forever."

"I get bored staying in one place too long." Cat confessed.

Rinn sniffled and squeezed her sister's paws, cracking a smile. "You're the best sister ever."

"I know." Cat grinned.

Chapter 3

R inn's army trekked south, out of the rolling pastures and onto level farmland. Ever-present stone walls impeded their progress, but the weather was pleasant and the sky a gentle blue. Farmhouses dotted the countryside. Rinn spied the occasional worker feeding chickens or tending fields. Marshal steered the party away from locals until they were far from Serpio's lands.

"Why haven't we seen any patrols?" Rinn asked her father. Squads of soldiers in bright red livery were a common site in the Empire, even in rural areas.

"We didn't see any sentinels at the Vallum either." Marshal pondered. "If the patrols have been recalled, the fighting must be worse than we thought."

In the mid-afternoon, Lutra spotted tendrils of smoke to the south. Marshal headed that direction. In a damp hollow, a cluster of shanties huddled together like a mushroom ring. The homes were lumps of reused wood, tarp, and shod. Shifty people milled about, pushing broken-down carts and picking through feeble vegetable patches. Squalid children squealed as they wrestled in the mud. An unkempt mother nursed her infant in a doorway. Cat pinched her nose, the hollow smelled worse than a neglected pigsty.

"A squatter's village." Marshal observed. He cautioned everyone. "We are out of Serpio's lands, but be on your guard. Squatters aren't Imperial citizens, they live on the fringes of civilization, and they don't like outsiders."

"It stinks." Cat complained, her eyes watering.

"Why are we here?" Lutra asked covering his nose.

"We'll need Imperial clothing if we want to blend in, and these fine people will know how to steal it." Marshal dismounted and handed his horse's reins to Molo. He headed down the meager path to the village. "Anyone else coming?"

Sionne rolled his eyes and followed along.

"Wait for me." Rinn hurried to catch up.

As the three travelers entered the squatter's village, all eyes warily followed them. Marshal had no difficulty getting the squatters to trust him, with his road-weary clothes and noticeable limp he did not seem like much of a threat. He left his sword and bow back with his horse. Rinn carried her wooden baton, and no one trusted Sionne enough to give him a weapon. Rinn felt exposed and defenseless, though she imagined these people felt the same way.

"No misfortune." Marshal politely nodded to a gruff man who approached him. His age was impossible to tell, he wore no shirt and was covered in scars. He had very little hair except for bushy red eyebrows.

"No deceit." The man mechanically answered. He appraised the trio. "You're not kin." He reconsidered Sionne. "Well, maybe that one."

"We're family of circumstance." Marshal smirked playfully.

The scarred man guffawed. "I like you, skinny man."

"Know me as Marshal." He held out a wineskin in offering.

"Know me Cuan Otraich." He accepted the wineskin.

"Payment." Marshal assured him. Cuan opened the wineskin and sniffed its contents. He tasted the liquor and his eyes opened in delight. He took a second, longer draught, humming in contentment.

Curious men from the village stepped forward. Cuan shared the wineskin with them. Each man took a drink and passed it on. Rinn was amazed at how easily these people shared.

"You have our service. What is your need?" Cuan questioned.

"Imperial clothing." Marshal stated.

"Is that all?" Cuan laughed. He shouted to the people. "Fetch Milse. She has customers." The crowd murmured and a man in torn trousers ran off to get her. He returned with a black-eyed young woman who Rinn thought was too beautiful to be living in squalor. Milse was of the marrying age, thin like the other squatters; what little body fat she did have was in exactly the right places. She tossed her wavy mane of black hair as she approached.

"Who has need?" Her voice had a harsh foreign accent.

Marshal spoke. "Imperial clothing for three. More if you can spare them."

Milse strutted through the trio, measuring each one with her eyes. Rinn covered her chest and squeezed her knees as she was assessed, she was unaccustomed to people staring at her. Milse's gaze lingered on Sionne, and she lightly brushed a hand across his shoulders. "I can do three."

Marshal sighed in relief. He held up a bag of coins. Milse cupped her hands in expectation. He dumped thirty-odd silver coins out. Cuan whistled and the village tittered with excitement. Milse inclined her head politely and sauntered back to her shanty. Rinn watched her go, envious of her feminine grace. In Rinn's head, she believed she would never be as alluring and seductive as this squatter woman.

Marshal talked with the local village men. He questioned them about Imperial patrols and the civil war. Apparently, no major battles had been fought in this area and the soldiers stopped coming months ago. Eventually Milse returned with three outfits, loose flowing tunics colored Imperial red. She demurely handed Rinn a light blue stola and matronly shawl to be worn over it. Rinn frowned as she took the dress-like garment, she was not old enough to be married.

Marshal bowed to Milse gracefully and locked arms with Cuan before departing. On the way back, he examined his purchases with satisfaction. Sionne scoffed. "You were robbed. Thirty silver for a few outfits."

"I bought more than clothes." Marshal assured him. "I bought their silence."

"That's so much money for one person." Rinn fretted. "Won't the others try to steal it from her?"

"Squatters have no concept of ownership." Her father explained. "Living selfishly, they would surely perish. Squatters band together and share everything they have in order to survive. We could learn much from them." As she walked, Rinn re-evaluated her own beliefs. All the walls that divvied up the Empire somehow started to seem silly, almost petty. Maybe the squatters had tapped into some cosmic wisdom.

::

The trip to Viburna took three weeks. Rinn's army could have made better time had they traveled the Imperial Roads, but Marshal insisted on sticking to the smaller paths that weaved between farms. Finding food slowed them down considerably. Hunting was nonexistent in these neatly tilled fields and their supply of money had nearly reached its end. On several occasions, Rinn's army stopped at farmhouses offering to repair tools for food (farmers always had broken tools). Rinn hated feeling like an itinerant beggar, but it was better than being a thief.

Eventually the landscape started to become familiar, Rinn knew they were getting close. Her excitement began to build, she was returning home after more than two years away. She did not let the revelation that she was born on some far-flung island suppress her joy. Virburna was the backdrop of her childhood, the city she knew best: its lively marketplace and bustling streets, quiet alleyways and solemn shrines, even the austere Grove of Lucus. Marshal stopped the party late in the afternoon, when the city first became visible on the horizon.

"We'll camp here." He announced. "In the morning, Sionne, Rinn and I will make for the city."

"I'm coming, too!" Cat interjected.

"No, you stay here." Marshal ordered.

"Good luck with that." Lutra mused. Feena smacked his arm.

Marshal reminded his adoptive daughter. "I don't want you getting caught inside the city, like you did at the Vallum." She completely ignored him and began chasing crows in a nearby field.

"Cat knows how to stay out of sight." Rinn asserted. The issue was dropped for the moment and camp was pitched for the night. Marshal chanced a traditional campfire instead of one of the dwarves' underground fire pits. It was not unusual to see groups of people camped around cities, waiting for the gates to open the next morning. Everyone sat around the fire, dining on roasted crow-meat and wilted greens.

Feena took a seat next to Rinn. "What's Viburna like?"

"It's an average city." Rinn shrugged. "Marketplace, forum, temple, lots of people." Feena did not seem satisfied with Rinn's answer.

Molo suggested. "Rinn, why don't you tell your friends a little about Sevria."

Rinn collected her thoughts for a moment. She tried to trace an outline in the dirt with a stick, but the ground was crumbly and full of grass. She abandoned the idea and attempted to describe her home country. "Sevria is big—bigger than all the Rustic Lands put together. You all grew up surrounded by forests and rivers and mountains, but Sevria is different. It's mostly farmland like this, and it's warm all year long."

"You don't have winter?" Lutra boggled.

"Not really." Rinn admitted. "We have four seasons, tilling, planting, growing, and harvest, and all of them are warm. I really didn't understand what winter was until I came to Hilltop."

"It's horrible." Cat shivered.

Rinn continued with her lesson. "There are nine great cities in Sevria, each dedicated to a different god. My hometown, Viburna, was founded around the Sacred Grove of Lucus, the god of forests. Supposedly the city was once surrounded by trees, but they've been mostly cut down."

"Is there somewhere to buy food?" Lutra joked, chewing a mouthful of bitter crow meat.

"Absolutely." Rinn answered eagerly. "Viburna is known for its excellent food. The marketplace is loaded with merchants selling fresh-baked breads and smoked meats."

"Are there dwarves?" Felsic inquired.

Rinn shifted uneasily in her seat. "The truth is, there are a few dwarves and they aren't treated very well."

Molo fielded the difficult topic. "Technically slavery is illegal, but many dwarves work in slave-like conditions."

"I figured as much." Felsic admitted.

"It's one of the things I'm going to change." Rinn proclaimed.

Sionne inserted himself into the conversation. "About that. How do you plan on changing anything, princess? For that matter, what are we even doing here? Are we here to hunt down criminals? Or are we going to overthrow the government, maybe assassinate a few people? As fun as that sounds, I don't see why I should care."

Before Rinn could answer, Marshal intervened. "Sevria is teetering on the edge of all-out war. Millions could perish. We believe Rinn might be the key to stopping it."

"Why?" Sionne challenged.

"Because I'm the Sigillum. It's my job to protect the Empire, even from itself." Rinn admitted. In truth, she was not sure what a Sigillum actually was, only that they appeared when the Empire was in peril. But for Rinn, her magic and her adoptive sister had become a part of her everyday life. She could not imagine living without them.

Sionne would not let up. "So, what're you going to do? Kick the government around, make yourself queen? Beat up the Legions with a few freaks and a handful of teenagers? Sounds like a great plan." Rinn wanted to be angry. She wanted to put Sionne in his place, but she was not sure herself why she came, just that she needed to be here.

Her father stepped in. "We came to Viburna to gather information. It's a town Rinn and I know well, and it's far from the capital city of Peleon. We shouldn't run into too much trouble. Once we've found out what's happening in the Empire, we'll decide our next move."

For once, Sionne let it rest.

::

The next morning Rinn, Marshal, and Sionne donned their stolen outfits, flowing tunics dyed scarlet red, the favored color of the Empire. Feena had spent all night washing the squatter's smell out. Marshal's tunic fit him well enough, and Sionne's was an exact match. Rinn's stola, however, was too short, barely covering her knees. At first, she refused to wear it, but her father convinced her she would stand out more in her traveling pants and dragon-feather vest. Reluctantly, Rinn gave in and wore the stola and the matronly shawl. She strapped her heavy wooden baton on her back and buckled her boots. Her outfit seemed incomplete, she was missing her lunula. Unmarried girls in the Empire wore amulets to protect them from evil intentions. Marshal had sold Rinn's lunula when they fled Sevria years ago. Now, Rinn felt naked without it. She had the gold necklace that Duke Kapros had given her, but it was far too ornate to wear in public. She also had her mother's necklace, but it let off a faint green glow, a relic of her mother's magic. She tucked both necklaces into a leather pouch around her neck, and stuffed it inside her stola.

"Ready?" Her father asked. Rinn gave him a quick nod. She was nervous but eager to see her hometown again. Sionne adjusted his flowing tunic uncomfortably.

"We'll be back soon." Rinn reassured her friends.

Molo shook the trio's hands and wished them luck. Marshal mounted his horse and pulled Rinn up behind him. Cat followed along. Bayard refused to let her ride on him—not since the incident—so she walked with Sionne, making rude faces behind his back. Rinn jabbered as she rode, giddy with excitement.

"You're going to love Viburna, Cat." Rinn babbled on about the marketplace, the arena, the temples, and the bathhouses. As they crested a small rise outside of town, a light breeze blew through Rinn's curly blonde hair. Rinn's hometown came into view with its crumbling stone walls and rotting, faded banners. Disinterested guards picked their way across dilapidated battlements. The midday sun listed in a cloudless sky, simmering the odor of spoiled food, urine, and disease. The garbage of humanity was plastered against the city walls like lichen: scabbed beggars, rowdy urchins, and drunkards laying in their own filth. Rinn brought her hands to her mouth in shock.

Catherine winced as she pinched her nose. "And I thought where I grew up was bad."

Chapter 4

"It's not supposed to be like this." Rinn gasped. Her dearest childhood memories began to sour and fade. The grassy field where her father taught her to ride, once filled with fragrant wildflowers, was now a greasy, brown slick of mud. Viburna's proud entrance gates hung off their hinges, wrecked and ruined. The hardwood forests south of town had been largely levelled, leaving behind empty, barren hills.

Marshal brought Bayard to a halt. "This is my fault." Disbelief haunted his eyes.

Rinn chided him. "You didn't cause this. We don't know what happened here." She lied. For weeks she had been having dark dreams about Viburna and a strange creature infecting it. She had spoken to no one about it, not even her feline sister.

Marshal's voice cracked. "If I hadn't taken you out of Sevria, this would've never occurred."

"You don't know that." Rinn insisted. "When we left, you had no idea I had powers at all." Rinn and her father had agreed not to use the word Sigilla while they were in the Empire. Sigillum magic had been proclaimed illegal, an affront to the Church. Throughout history the Sigilla had fought to protect the Empire. But, they were loyal to the Sevrian royal bloodline, and when the last Emperor died forty years ago, their magic was deemed unnecessary and ultimately unlawful.

"I had my suspicions." Marshal flatly admitted. "That's why I whisked you away to the Rustic Lands, to hide you from the ones who wanted to harm you."

"And everything worked out." Rinn argued. "We're alive and the Rustic people are safe."

Marshal lowered his eyes. "At what cost? How many had to die?" Rinn had no answer. The terrible truth about her abilities in battle caused her constant anguish. Hundreds of people had died by her hands, not by some remote incantation, but by the very weapon she wielded. To add to her guilt, at the time Rinn had wanted to kill those clansmen, yearned to snuff out their lives. Now she had to live with that remorse and the very real possibility it could happen again.

"I'm bored." Catherine whined. "I'm going to take a look around."

Rinn held out her hand. "Cat, wait!" But it was too late. Once again, with a pop, the green-eyed feline girl vanished. Rinn dropped her outstretched hand and sighed. "I guess we don't have any choice now. We have to go in after her."

"She needs to be on a damn leash." Sionne rudely observed.

Rinn ignored him. Marshal clicked Bayard forward at a slow gait. As they approached the city entrance, Rinn saw three guards beating back beggars shoving to get inside. An officer stepped from a doorway behind the gate. Rinn noticed he wore the stripes of a decurion, a squad leader, but his cape was white, not Imperial red. The decurion spoke in an officious voice. "State your business."

Marshal straightened in his saddle. "Returning from a business trip."

"Identification." The decurion demanded.

"I own property in town, near market street." Marshal handed him five silver coins. The officer smoothly slipped the coins into a pouch at his waist.

"That area can be dangerous at night. Stick to the main roads, citizen." He waved them through. Marshal slowly guided his horse under the broken barbican and into the city. The once bustling thoroughfare was now a desolate lane of boarded up shops and burned out buildings. Roaming gangs of ruffians lingered in the alleyways, watching the newcomers pass. Marshal kept a hand close to his sword and Rinn cautiously unslung her wooden baton from her back. Sionne nervously kept pace with one hand on the horse.

Marshal whispered between gritted teeth. "We need to get somewhere safe."

Rinn nodded. "Our house is not far." She pointed north, burning with curiosity to learn the fate of her former home, despite the danger.

"We'll head there." Marshal turned Bayard down a residential sideroad, and stopped midstride. "What about Catherine?"

"She can find me." Rinn said cryptically. She was not ready to disclose the secret relationship she and her adoptive sister shared. Marshal pursed his lips but said nothing. He led the way down the winding side streets. Rinn spotted the ornate Temple of Aedis in the distance, just beyond the central marketplace. Its pristine white spires seemed out of place in the broken, decaying city. Rinn had always preferred the quiet solace of Lucus' Grove to the gaudy, white marble of the Aedian Temple. She looked south, trying to steal a glimpse of the sacred Grove. Instead, she spotted four untidy men casually following them. She discretely tugged at her father's tunic. "Daddy."

"I know." He replied, keeping his gaze locked on the street ahead. "We keep going and stay in plain sight. Those four aren't alone."

Rinn could not help peeking down every alley they passed. She nervously fidgeted with her baton, feeling comfort in its deceptive weight. Her father changed directions at each intersection, steadily angling toward their old home. They passed more boarded up shops and burned out houses. Rinn's breathing quickened as the four men trailing them drew closer. She whispered under her breath. "Cat, where are you?"

Less than a block away from her old house, their pursuers were joined by three others, carrying clubs. The ruffians fanned out like a pack of wolves corralling their victims. Rinn's palms sweated, she knew an attack was imminent. Sionne maneuvered around the horse, keeping it between him and the street thugs. Marshal leaned down to the boy, handing him a long knife. "Get her to safety." He slid Rinn out of the saddle and motioned to a nearby vacant home.

Without warning, Sionne grabbed Rinn's hand and bolted for the open doorway. He slammed the door shut behind them. Rinn looked out a boarded-up window to see the gang of thugs scatter as her father rode them down waving his sword. Sionne began barricading the door.

"Wait!" Rinn exclaimed. "My dad needs to get in."

"He's doing fine by himself." Sionn crabbed, piling debris against the doorway. Rinn recognized the home, it belonged to Pellis, the feltworker, or at least it used to. The house was a mess of broken furniture and smashed pottery. Tidy decorations that once brightened the room had been looted, and the walls had holes where brass sconces had been pried out. The senseless pillaging nauseated Rinn, this once a vibrant and happy home was in ruin. What had happened to Pellis and his family? The sound of pounding at the door brought Rinn to her senses.

"Upstairs." Sionne urged, bounding up the staircase. Rinn scurried after him as the noise grew louder. Out of the corner of her eye, Rinn saw a shape moving at the top of the stairs, green eyes glowing in the dim light.

"Cat!" Rinn arrived at the landing. "Where have you been? We were almost killed out there."

Cat planted her paws on her hips, her tail swishing in agitation. "I already took care of six of them. What's wrong with these people?"

Rinn could not believe it. Her hometown had been a happy, orderly place guarded by the Legion and guided by the Church. Now it was overrun with lawless packs of thieves and ruffians. Rinn, Sionne, and Cat struggled to get down the hallway, which was partially blocked by a collapsed ceiling. Cat wiggled through an opening and stuck out a paw to help Rinn through.

"We have to get out of here." Rinn squeezed through the space. "Can you take Sionne somewhere safe?"

Sionne was crawling through the narrow opening. "No one's taking me anywhere." He insisted. Cat's eyes widened with mischief and she nodded yes. Sionne started backing up into the hole, but Cat laid a paw on him with a devious grin. "No." Sionne yelled in absolute panic. "No. No. No!" With a wink and a pop, they were gone. The door downstairs flew open, and three savage men with clubs poured into the house. One spotted movement at the top of the stairs and gave chase. Rinn sprinted down the upstairs hallway to the far end of the building. She spied a boarded-up window in the back bedroom. Smashing through it with her baton she slipped outside. She carefully stepped onto a narrow ledge, clutching a nearby lead downspout for support. Desperately, she climbed for the roof. A thug reached a muscled arm out the window after her, but Rinn shimmied beyond his reach.

Rinn scaled the downspout to the terracotta roof. She scrambled over the eaves, unintentionally sending several tiles to the ground below. They shattered loudly, alerting the ruffians nearby. Brutish men circled the house like pack animals stalking their prey. As Rinn desperately scampered across the tiles, remembering a rooftop battle that took place more than a year ago, her father and the assassin Yallakh fighting on the ridge of her Hilltop home. She could hear shouts and commotion in the streets below.

Rinn scurried to the far end of the building, out of view from the ruffians. After several brave leaps, Rinn arrived at the rooftop of her former home. From this vantage, she could see the marketplace several blocks away. Dusty, colorless tents huddled together in the center of the vacant plaza like frightened sheep. Across the way, the facade of the city's amphitheater loomed, empty and unused.

Rinn leaned over the edge of the roof to see her old bedroom window, smashed and broken. She carefully swung down and slithered into the opening, avoiding the shards of broken glass. Her old bedroom fared no better than her neighbor's house, ransacked and ruined. Even the colorful murals she painted on her walls had been defaced. Rinn could feel a throbbing in her temples as her rage swelled. She was done running, the people who pillaged her home would pay. She hefted her wooden baton and resolutely headed down the stairs, kicking debris out of her way. She marched across the broken courtyard in the center of her home and threw open the front door. She walked defiantly into the street, ready to fight.

A hand reached out and grabbed her left arm. Rinn whirled around, and flicked the switch on her wooden baton. A long iron shaft sprang out of the handle, nearly impaling the person who held her. Her assailant faced a girl armed with a full-sized pilum, the javelin-like spear favored by the Legion. The frightened teenage boy released her arm and stared at her in shock.

"Skinny Rinn?" He asked in astonishment.

Chapter 5

R inn lowered the tip of her spear from the boy's throat.
"Grus?" She boggled. "What're you doing here?"

"What am I doing here? What are *you* doing here?" Grus
retreated a step. The teenage boy wore the armor and tunic
of the town guard, adorned with a white cape instead of the
traditional Imperial red. He carried a gladius, a short sword
used in close quarter fighting, but he held it at his side non-
threateningly.

"I'm here to see my home, but there are savages
everywhere." Rinn lamented. She remembered Grus as one
of the neighborhood boys a few years older than she was,
buck-toothed and knock-kneed, always playing with
wooden swords. He never singled out Rinn for torment nor
showed her any favor. Now, he had grown into a fit young
man, broad of shoulders but not of chest. His wiry arms
bulged with adolescent muscles and his tousled brown hair
hung in his eyes.

Grus surveyed the area. "My cohort is taking care of
these criminals, but this neighborhood is not safe." He
sheathed his sword and signaled for Rinn to follow him.
Rinn flipped over her spear and pressed the button in the
handle, the metal pole retracted back into the wooden
baton. Grus could not hide his curiosity. "That's some
gadget you have. Where'd you get it?"

"Some friends made it for me." Rinn replied sheepishly.

"Seems like you know how to use it, too." Grus paused to re-evaluate his childhood neighbor. He looked at her in ways that made Rinn uncomfortable. "You've gotten taller, but you're still skinny Rinn."

"No one called me that." She pouted.

"Everyone called you that." Grus laughed. "Let's go find my cohort."

Rinn hesitated, she needed to reunite with Cat and her father. "I really should be going."

"Nonsense." Grus argued. "I'm not leaving you out here alone. This part of the city isn't safe. I'll escort you somewhere less dangerous." Rinn wanted to argue, but Grus seemed resolute. If the soldiers were fighting the street gangs, her father should be safe, and Cat could take care of herself. Rinn resigned herself to go with Grus for the moment. She did not have much choice. She followed him to the empty marketplace, a dusty field surrounded on all sides by vacant buildings. A few wilted merchant stalls remained, stubbornly hanging on like brown leaves in the wintertime. A regimen of town guard assembled on the far side of the empty plaza, twenty armored men boasting white capes.

"That's my squad." Grus straightened his shoulders as he marched through the marketplace. He saluted a commanding officer. "Decurion, this citizen was caught in the fighting. I brought her to safety."

The commander was a lean, narrow-eyed man wearing a striped sash to denote his rank. Closely trimmed gray stubble covered his head and face. He squinted at Rinn suspiciously. "What was this citizen doing in the fallow parts of the city?"

Grus answered stiffly. "She was returning to her childhood home. She was not aware of the dangers in that area."

The decurion's one eyebrow raised. "She was traveling alone?"

"Of course not." Grus refuted. Even in times of relative peace proper young women did not venture outside unescorted.

Rinn defended herself. "I came with my father. He's on horseback, but we got separated." The decurion glared at her. Rinn immediately regretted saying anything, she knew better than to talk out of turn to a military officer.

The commander smugly answered. "We did find such a man on horseback—a cripple. He's been taken to the Temple for processing." He dismissed Grus. "Take this girl to her father. Make sure they both get registered." As they were leaving, he added. "Haril, go with them." A burly man joined Rinn and Grus. He was all soldier, tall and muscular with a professionally shaven face. He wore heavy armor, bands of metal strapped over his torso and shoulders. It clinked like an iron keyring when he walked.

"Let's go." Haril ordered. Rinn and Grus fell in behind him. Rinn's spirits sank as she was escorted through the city. The stores she loved as a child were boarded up or burned down. Green parks and public fountains had been fouled and misused. Decorative statues that once lined the streets had been defaced or stolen. Rinn felt hollow as she drifted through the shell of her former home. As they traveled west, the city became more civilized. White-caped soldiers patrolled in groups of four or five. Beyond the marketplace, the streets were well-maintained, and the buildings occupied and cheery. Townsfolk went about their daily routines, shopping, working, and socializing. Patrols of soldiers guarded every corner, scrutinizing the citizens, insuring their safety. Somehow, the patrols made Rinn feel less secure, she would not want to live under constant surveillance.

Ahead, the pristine, white towers of the Aedian Temple glistened in the midday sun. Rinn recalled visiting the Temple many times as a child, and it always intimidated her. Inside, the white marble dome was supported by tall, alabaster columns. Life-sized frescoes depicted the violent struggle of law over chaos. Rinn never liked the harsh sermons of the Aedean priests, she preferred the quiet serenity of the Lucan Grove.

As Rinn neared the Temple, it seemed larger than she remembered. Two grandiose wings had been erected on either side of the central dome. Rinn knew the additions must be wood painted to look like marble. It would take actual masons decades to complete stonework on that scale. The lawns around the Temple were perfectly manicured with raised flower beds and burbling fountains. Finely dressed citizens in colorful togas and flowing stolas idled about the grounds. Gold-caped sentries were stationed at every column.

Haril led Grus and Rinn up the wide marble steps to the main portico. Rinn knew coming to the Temple was a mistake, but with so many soldiers on patrol, she had little chance of escape. Her burly escort pointed to the ground just inside the entrance. "Wait here." He marched down a newly added side corridor. The angry frescoes and alabaster columns from Rinn's memory had not changed. Although daylight streamed through round windows in the marble dome, a luxurious array of candelabras burned anyway. It was not time for service, but the Temple was packed with people moving from office to office. Inside the worship space, citizens laughed and joked, ate and drank like revelers at some great festival.

"What's going on?" Rinn quietly asked Grus.

"They are commemorating the great victory in Peleon." Grus informed her. "When the Curia defeated the Legions from the west."

"The Curia?" Rinn squeaked.

Grus turned to her. "Yes, the Curia. The rightful rulers of the Sevrian Empire."

Rinn squirmed uncomfortably. Cat, where are you?

Haril returned. "Follow me." It was not a request.

Rinn trailed behind Grus, looking for any chance to get away. She was led down a wide hallway, full of people. The passage was lined with evenly spaced, numbered doors. Haril stopped outside of an office labelled "Registrar". He opened the door and ushered the pair inside. Rinn timidly followed Grus into the office. Several dozen people milled about the space, which was the size of a typical courtroom. Polished marble pillars lined the walls and between them the busts of famous civic leaders filled decorative alcoves. Four silver-caped sentries guarded the room, brandishing long polearms. Grus proceeded to a stout wooden desk dominating the office. A haughty, balding man looked up from his ledgers.

Grus straightened. "I have a citizen for registration."

The registrar squinted at Rinn. "And who is this citizen?"

Rinn felt ill at ease. She had been raised in Viburna, she dressed and behaved like a proper Sevrian, but the flowing Imperial outfit she wore offered her no comfort. She longed for her traveling clothes and the protection of her dragon feather vest.

Gus answered the official's question. "This is Rinn Amali, native of Viburna, returning to her hometown."

The registrar began leafing through several thick ledgers, absently repeating Rinn's name. He planted his finger on an entry. "Ah, here she is. Rinn Amali." Without lifting his eyes, he waved a dismissive hand. "Guards. Arrest this girl." Two soldiers in red uniforms stepped up and seized Rinn's arms. As she was being dragged away, Rinn shot Grus a venomous look and mouthed the word thanks.

::

Rinn sat on the cold stone bench carved into the wall of her prison cell, a dungeon-like alcove that reeked of mold and rust. Rinn wondered what a prison was doing under the Temple in the first place. Aedis was the god of ceremonies, his Temples were home to joyful weddings, tearful funerals, and festive holiday services. Throughout the history of the Empire, Aedian Priests served as arbitrators, the Temples chosen as neutral ground between political, military, and economic rivals. Aedis never took sides.

Cat suddenly appeared in the cell with Rinn.

"Cat?" Rinn caught her feline sister as she slumped over. "Are you okay?"

"Found you." Cat panted and collapsed on the bench.

Rinn laid Cat's feline head in her lap and stroked her fur. Cat purred appreciatively, kneading her paws and curling her tail. In the past year, Cat's tawny colored coat had mellowed to a soft cinnamon. Long tufts of black fur curled from the tips of her ears and her pink nose was now a deep red. Her eyes, ever since that fateful battle a year ago, remained a brilliant green. Somewhere along the way, Cat had lost the long brown robe Marshal had provided to cover her ears and tail. Rinn noticed that Cat's tight-fitting leather pants and vest were smeared with mud and grime, and her furry tail was limp and wet. Rinn brushed flecks of dirt away from her face. "Crazy, reckless girl." Abruptly, a thought struck Rinn. "Cat. What happened to Dad and Sionne?"

The weak feline sat up, not as exhausted as she first let on. "I took Sionne outside the city walls." She flattened her ears. "He doesn't travel well. He threw up several times. After that, we told everyone at camp what had happened." Cat slinked off the bench and stretched, shaking her fur. "Dad was captured by the guards. He's down here somewhere." She brought a paw to her chin. "I don't know where his horse is."

"Who are you talking to?" A voice asked.

"Hide." Rinn whispered to her sister. Cat vanished with a pop. Rinn answered innocently. "I wasn't talking to anyone." She was not very good at lying.

"I heard another girl's voice." The unseen person insisted.

"Just me." Rinn countered.

"I swear I heard someone else. Who are you?" The voice asked. It was a decidedly male voice, but Rinn could not tell how old.

"I'm no one important." Rinn dodged the question with one of her own. "What is this place?"

"This is the Curia's private prison." The answer smacked of resignation. Rinn wondered how long her fellow prisoner had been held here. Before she could ask another question, she heard the jangling of keys and unlocking of doors. Muffled voices issued from an unseen corridor. Lantern light illuminated the dim dungeon. Three officious churchmen drifted over, their feet hidden beneath their long billowing robes. Rinn recognized the balding registrar who had her arrested. He was accompanied by a tall, severe-looking priest and his tonsured assistant. The registrar bowed and motioned to Rinn. "This is the girl, your grace."

The tall priest peered into the cell, narrowing his eyes. Rinn felt naked under his gaze. She had no weapons nor armor; all her belongings had been confiscated by the guards. The priest finally turned his attention to the registrar. "You must be mistaken, Scaeva. This can't be her."

The registrar pleaded his case. "We already have her father in custody, Lord Caena. We've confirmed he is indeed Theodric Amali."

The priest studied Rinn again, and then waved his hand dismissively. "She's far too young. The so-called Amali girl would be at least eighteen." The tall priest glided out of view. "This must be some wretch who's assumed her identity falsely. Turn her over to the carcers, they will know what to do with her." With a click of lock and jangle of keys, the churchmen left the dungeon.

The voice called from down the corridor, broken with emotion. "Is it true? Are you Sabrinn Amali?" Rinn did not know how to answer. As the guards came to take her away, the voice continued to rant. "Are you Sabrinn Amali?" A soldier fastened manacles on Rinn's hands and pushed her down the corridor. Rinn passed the cell where the hysterical voice repeated her name. She saw a boy close to her own age, dressed in the brown robes of a scribe. His imprisonment had left him frail and thin and his robes tattered. He reached a defiant hand through the bars of his cell, Rinn could see the desperation in his stone-gray eyes. "Sabrinn Sevralis! Help me, Sabrinn Sevralis!" The guards beat him back with a club, but he would not be quiet, he kept repeating her name as they hauled her away.

Chapter 6

Rinn sat alone in the back of the armored transport wagon. She understood exactly how slaves felt, hopeless and trapped. Nothing was going right. Evil had permeated Viburna and turned her own town against her. Rinn was done waiting, watching, and being careful. People were suffering, and she would put a stop to it, right now. She whispered the word "onlithe" and her manacles opened and fell to the floor. She repeated the word and the barred door of the wagon swung open. Rinn stepped out into the air, breathing in freedom. Startled guards reached for their swords, confused by the young girl walking free.

"Cat!" Rinn called to the sky. In an instant, her sister appeared beside her. The guards stepped back, unsure of how to proceed. Gawkers in the streets outside the Temple murmured and pointed to Rinn and her feline companion. Rinn ignored them all. "Cat, take me to my necklace."

Cat bobbed in place. "Easy." She wrapped her paws around Rinn's hands. Rinn could hear the gasps from onlookers as she was sucked away into the ethereal realm her sister called the Mist. A familiar undertow pulled her through the purple void to a new destination. She reappeared in a shadowy basement room lined with shelves and chests. Cat navigated easily through the darkness. "Your stuff's over here." She pointed with a paw. Rinn fumbled through the dark to a locked chest. She opened it with a word and rifled through its contents. She found her baton and her personal belongings, including the leather pouch that held her mother's pendant and her own gold necklace. She withdrew her mother's medallion, it glowed with a pleasant green aura. Rinn hung it around her neck along with the necklace from Duke Kapros. She hefted her baton and headed for the door, using the faint green illumination to light her way. She pressed the button on her baton extending it into a full-sized spear.

"We're going to rescue Dad and get out of here." She told Cat. Kicking open the storeroom door, she stepped into the hallway outside. The musty odor told her she was in the dungeon tunnels beneath the Temple. "Which way, Cat?"

Cat sniffed at the air and pointed left. Rinn headed down the corridor ready to fight. Fortunately, the lowest levels were not heavily guarded. Cat did hear one patrol in the distance and recommended waiting. Rinn would have preferred going straight through them, but she did not want to kill unnecessarily, so she bided her time until the guards passed them by. Cat started down the corridor again, and after several turns, they arrived at the prison door that held their father, according to Cat's nose.

Rinn stepped through the doorway and was confronted by three startled guards. "Leave." She said with authority. The guards drew their swords, undaunted by a teenage girl with a spear. Rinn infused the metal point of her spear with Sigillum magic, it glowed a brilliant green. In one fluid motion she deftly sliced through the blades of the guard's swords. She took a threatening step forward. "Leave." She repeated. Cat hissed. The astounded guards backed away, unprepared to confront a magical adversary. They turned and ran.

"Daddy?" Rinn called out, her voice echoing off the dank prison walls. This chamber was more foreboding than the place Rinn had been imprisoned. Floor manacles and instruments of torture were scattered about the room, hardly appropriate for a prison beneath a church.

"Over here." Rinn's father answered. Rinn rushed to his cell. He was nursing a cut on his forehead and had a bloodied lower lip, but he otherwise seemed intact. Rinn concentrated until her spear tip glowed brightly and she slashed at the metal bars, carving through them with a hideous, grinding noise. Severed bars fell to the ground with a loud clang. Rinn and Cat dashed inside the cell and embraced their father tightly. He returned the gesture.

"Let's get you out of here." Rinn could not hold back the tears welling in her eyes.

Cat wore a pained expression. "There's something you need to see first."

"Wait, there's a boy down here. I want to get him before we go." Rinn blurted out. She could hear sounds of men in armor running down the corridor.

"We don't have much time." Cat rubbed her paws nervously. "This is really important."

"Okay." Rinn trusted her sister. She would come back for the boy, she would have to, she needed to know how he knew her true name. Cat wrapped her furry paws around Rinn and Marshal's hands, but nothing happened.

"What's wrong?" Rinn asked.

Cat scrunched her face up in frustration. "Something here is interfering with my ability to travel."

"Great." Rinn exhaled.

"We need to get outside." Marshal pointed down a corridor. "The guards brought me down that way."

Rinn hefted her glowing spear. "It's a start." Catherine shrugged. Together the three edged down the passageway. Marshal's limp slowed them down considerably. Rinn could hear shouting down distant corridors, apparently news of their jailbreak was spreading. They were nearing the end of the hallway, Rinn could see a staircase and a doorway ahead. If they could only make it in time.

"Stop!" Ten soldiers with swords thundered toward them. Marshal turned defensively, but he had no weapon. Rinn readied her spear, its metal tip already starting to corrode in her magical fire.

Cat's ears perked up. "Oh. It's fine now." She grabbed ahold of Rinn and Marshal and with a pop, they were gone. The purple void of the Mist was deep in color, filled with yellow lights that flitted by like fireflies. Rinn glimpsed an odd, shape in the distance, a glowing red box. She had never seen anything in the Mist before. Before she could get a better look, Cat deposited her and her father on a rooftop on the southern side of the city. Lucan's Grove was visible in the distance against the setting sun. The shrine was a circle of massive yew trees, their trunks so ancient they had fused together into a solid ring. Only a single, narrow path allowed access to the center of the grove. The once stately yews now appeared diseased, their healthy green leaves soured to a glossy black. A dread miasma hung over the blighted trees like dark rain clouds.

"What's wrong with Lucan's Grove?" Rinn feared for this beloved place from her childhood. The Grove was more than just a copse of trees, it was the holiest shrine to Lucus. Rinn had come with her father on many occasions to offer prayers to the forest god. Sometimes she came on her own, to find solace under the ancient trees and bask in the peace they exuded. Seeing them in ruin heated Rinn's blood. Her hand squeezed her spear tightly. "Cat, get me closer."

Cat shook her head. "I can't. Something's down there, blocking me."

"What?" Rinn demanded. "Is it some kind of barrier? Like the Vallum?"

"No." Cat brought a paw to her chin. "This is different. It's like there's something alive down there, pushing me away whenever I try to get close."

Rinn narrowed her eyes and concentrated on the Grove, past the black leaves and dark gray clouds. She faintly saw it, the milky blue taint of magic. The whole puzzle started to come into view, and Rinn believed she knew how to solve it. There was no mistake, Viburna needed her, begged her to come to its rescue. Rinn would not stop until this city was free. She brushed the blond hair away from her face and squeezed her pilum spear. "Cat, take us back to camp. We're going to war."

::

With furious determination, Rinn stormed through the campsite to her backpack. She ripped off her flimsy Imperial dress, inadvertently giving Lutra and Sionne an eyeful, and threw on her leather armor and traveling pants. She pulled her dragon feather vest over her clothes and tied her hair back into a ponytail. She grabbed her spear and stood in the center of camp, all eyes watching her warily.

"We attack at once." Rinn commanded.

"It's almost nightfall." Molo cautioned.

"They know we're here." Rinn explained. "The high priest will summon his troops to protect the Temple. This will be our best time to strike."

"Where are we going? Who're we fighting?" Lutra questioned.

"We make for Lucan's Grove, to the south." Rinn answered, her pilum spear planted firmly at her side. "Someone's set evil magic upon it, and it's corrupting the city. If we break the spell, it should free Viburna." One by one the members of her army rose and prepared themselves. Rinn noticed Sionne sitting alone. She walked over to him. "Glad to see you are safe."

Cat bounced over and patted him on the head. "He's fine." The redheaded boy glowered at Cat, but said nothing. He shoved his meager belongings into a bag and strapped on the knife Marshal had given him.

As everyone was making their preparations, Feena pulled Rinn aside. "How dangerous is this going to be?"

Rinn did not want to deceive her close friend. "I'm not sure. I don't want to fight unnecessarily, but we must get to the Grove."

Felsic came over and relieved Rinn of her weapon. He and his brother pulled out the glowing metal rod that was already half rust and replaced it with a fresh one. The design had been Felsic's idea, a spring-loaded reusable handle. This way they only had to carry a supply of metal rods and not an armload of premade spears. He retracted the spear tip and returned the weapon to Rinn. She thanked him and praised his ingenuity. Felsic's oversized nose blushed and he went off to don his own armor.

Rinn saw her father strapping on his sword belt. She laid a hand on his arm. "Daddy, please stay. You've been through enough today."

He argued. "You need me. I know the location of the southern sally port. It's a hidden door, and our best chance to get to the Grove without running into any patrols."

Rinn conceded. "I'll have Cat take you part of the way. But remember our promise."

"Stay safe. No heroics." He acknowledged.

::

Rinn's army assembled in the shadows of the southern city walls, twilight bathed everything in a wash of blues and grays. Marshal pulled overgrown ivy away from a small iron-banded door, the southern sally port. These hidden exits allowed defenders to mount sneak attacks on armies besieging the city. They were never meant to be opened from the outside. Marshal shook on the iron handle, without success. Molo pushed on the door with his giant strength, but it would not budge. Rinn considered cutting through the door with her spear, but the sound and light would give away their location. She could not see a locking mechanism, and she was not sure if her releasing magic would be effective. Unexpectedly the door opened. Everyone readied their weapons, bracing for an attack, but it was only Cat on the other side of the door. She waved silently, and everyone breathed out a sigh. Rinn's army filed through the sally port. Molo and the heavily armored dwarves led the way. Calder and Lutra followed flanking Feena, the least proficient fighter in the group. Marshal and Sionne brought up the rear.

"The Grove should be straight ahead." Marshal pointed down a narrow side street.

Molo led the way with a large hammer in one hand and Clive in the other. He lifted his rock companion over his head. Last winter, he had confided to Rinn that Clive was more than just a rock, it was a soul-stone. With it, he could sense the life energy of people around him. Molo made a pass with his purple-eyed rock. He whispered to the others. "There're four guards above us."

Marshal scrutinized their surroundings, a winding road that paralleled the outer wall and a rat's nest of narrow side streets and alleyways. He motioned across the way to a dark alley. "We head there first, and work our way to the Grove."

Sionne quietly seethed. "Are you an idiot? Guards always watch dark alleyways, that's where trouble comes from."

Lutra challenged the redhead. "Do you have a better idea?"

Sionne scowled. "Stick close to the wall, until we're out of sight. Then make for an alley." Rinn thought it was actually a good idea. She nodded approvingly. Molo shrugged, and Marshal grudgingly followed along. The party crept down the wall single file, staying to the shadows. Once Molo gave the all clear, they crossed one by one to an adjacent alley.

Lutra mussed Sionne's red hair. "Good job, sneak-thief."

"Don't touch me." Sionne batted his hand away. Calder silently adjusted his cloak and his long black ponytail. He was the only party member who did not have his weapon unsheathed. Rinn was not concerned, she had seen him rehearse draw-and-strike maneuvers during their sparring practices. He could handle anyone he confronted.

Marshal led the party down zig-zag alleyways, past clusters of loitering vagabonds and sprawling bodies of drunks. Rinn and her companions were largely ignored by the townsfolk, they were caught up in their own miseries. Rinn stopped several times to fish out food for groups of vagrant children as her party members watched impatiently. Cat eyed the food longingly.

Lucan's Grove was not far, Rinn could see the black tree tops over the next row of buildings. The dread miasma that hung over the Grove had blighted this entire part of the city. The buildings themselves were aged and cracked, leaning precariously. Some structures had toppled into the streets, blocking the most direct routes to the Grove. Their short walk became a maze of twists and turns through walls of debris. Rinn wondered why no city guards patrolled the area, but then who would be crazy enough to come here? Just us, Rinn thought to herself.

Marshal led the group around a corner and the Grove finally came into view. The ring of ancient yews waded in a pool of brackish water, its rotting roots exposed like mangroves. The tree bark was black and marred with rusty scabs, broken limbs floated in the still water. The Grove smelled like a cemetery after a heavy rain.

"The reek of death." Calder unsheathed his sword.

"I really don't like this." Cat whined, unwilling to get near the water. She sucked on her paw and shivered.

"Something's here." Molo concentrated on his rock. "I can't see exactly what it is."

"It's foul magic." Rinn said confidently. She could see the blue aura woven into the trees and perfusing the water. It breathed and moved like a sentient being. While Rinn was studying the Grove, an insect-like shape floated down from the tree limbs. If flew dangerously close to Rinn before she noticed. The gray, silent insect was nearly on Rinn's head when Calder's blade struck. Two empty halves of the thing fluttered through the air like ash.

Rinn jumped, startled. "What was that?"

Marshal prodded the hollow body of the insect with his sword. "It's a husk—an animated insect shell."

Lutra grimaced. "What kind of bug gets that big?"

"Grammites." Molo answered. "They mature into flying terrors as large as my head." He tapped himself on the skull. Lutra shuddered. The grove rustled, and more husks floated from the treetops, silently flapping their brittle wings. Their bodies were long and segmented, and their jaws ended in hideous pincers. Three dozen clear, gray insect shells hovered down to Rinn's army, each husk as large as a good-sized dog.

"Be ready." Marshal raised his sword. Rinn instinctively summoned her shield and lowered into a battle stance, exactly as Molo had taught her. The dwarves stepped forward to protect the teenagers. Calder and Lutra held their positions, swords out. Feena fell back and nocked an arrow in her short hunting bow. Sionne turned tail.

"I'm not fighting those things." He yelled as he ran. "You people are crazy." Lutra harassed him to come back, but Marshal held up a hand.

"Let him go." He said.

Feena shot a few preliminary arrows, horribly missing the slow-moving targets. She cursed to herself, but Rinn encouraged her with a hopeful smile. Feena resumed shooting, and the husks drifted within melee range. Several landed on Rinn's barrier, and she stabbed at them with her spear. A sharp piercing pain made her falter, the husks were biting her barrier, and it felt like a wasp sting. Molo batted away the insects gathering around Rinn while the dwarves crushed others flat with their hammers. Calder dispatched many enemies with efficient strokes of his blade. Lutra cleaved through a husk, but received a painful sting on his left arm. Feena took aim and shot the offending bug out of the sky.

"I hit one!" She jumped up and down in joy.

"Thanks." Lutra held his wounded arm fearfully. "But that was a bit close." Feena's arrow had only narrowly missed his head. Combat pressed on, and Rinn and her companions fought bravely. Eventually, the husks were defeated and Rinn's exhausted party rested.

Chapter 7

C atherine kicked the broken insect shells in disgust. Marshal began stacking the husks into a mound. "We need to burn them before they come back to life."

"Come back to life?" Lutra shuddered. "That's not right." He batted the remains with his sword, refusing to touch them. Rinn stabbed multiple shells, lining them up on her spear like beads on a string. She kicked them off into the growing pile. Molo and the dwarves helped deposit the remaining husks onto the heap. Marshal sprinkled fire salts over it and within minutes the pile erupted into an orange-yellow glow. Cat clapped her paws and danced around the fire.

Marshal asked Rinn. "Were these the things making the trees sick?"

She shook her head. "I don't think so. They're merely guardians." All eyes turned to her. Rinn could not shake her unease when she was the center of attention. She never liked being alone, but she also hated feeling self-conscious. Rinn chewed her bottom lip for a moment as she composed her thoughts. "I feel like there's something else inside the Grove, something alive. And it's poisoning the city."

Marshal stroked the wispy hairs on his chin. "If we could drive whatever is inside away, would the Grove go back to normal?" Other than Rinn, he was the only one who had lived in Viburna and knew what the Grove was supposed to look like.

"I think so." Rinn guessed.

Mafic hefted his weapon cheerfully. "Then what are we waiting for?" His brother nodded in agreement. Dwarves loved a good fight.

"Where're the druids?" Molossus asked, shouldering his giant hammer. He held Clive out with his off hand, scanning the area. "Shouldn't they be protecting the Grove?"

Marshal frowned. "You're right. They should be keeping vigil over the trees. It's their sacred responsibility."

Rinn felt a grim foreboding. In her memory, druids always kept watch over the shrine, tending to the trees and driving off pests. They were powerful men and women, gifted with woodland magic. Their strength was tempered by their compassion and kindness. Rinn did not see any bodies, but she feared for the druids—whatever force profaned this holy site must be powerful indeed.

"We have to get inside the Grove." Rinn insisted. "We'll find the druids there." The only entrance to the heart of Lucan's Grove was through a natural tunnel in the tree ring. The opening was a black wound half submerged in the brackish water. A dread feeling came over Rinn just looking at it, but there was no other option.

Lutra scowled at the ominous entryway. "Maybe Cat could get us inside."

"I can't." She whined, ears frowning. "There's too much magic in the trees, it's pushing me away."

"It's okay, Cat." Rinn patted her sister on the head. "We'll find a way."

Marshal stepped one foot into the pool of brackish water. "One thing's for certain, Rinn and Cat knew exactly where we needed to go. We should have faith in them. I don't like that tunnel any more than you do, but if that's the place they say we must go, then I'm going."

"Well said." Felsic shook his war hammer in agreement.

Lutra looked around curiously. "Anyone seen Sionne?"

Molo huffed. "We don't have time to hunt for that idiot. Whatever's in the Grove surely knows we're out here. It'll strengthen its defenses if we wait much longer."

"I agree." Rinn thumped the ground with the butt of her spear. "We'll do this like the canyon rescue. Everyone, gather close around me and I'll raise a barrier around us all." Cat immediately sided up to Rinn and grabbed her arm. Rinn loved the feel of her fuzzy sister.

"Are you sure this's a good idea?" Feena asked. "There's a lot of magic here, and your shield might react to it."

"Like what happened at the Vallum." Lutra reminded her.

"This's different." Rinn assured them. "The Vallum was drawing me in, pouring energy into my shield until it was overloaded. The magic here's repelling me, trying to keep me out." Cat nodded in agreement. Reluctantly, the party crowded around Rinn. It was difficult to stand close together with weapons drawn. Calder sheathed his sharp sword and stood in back. Rinn raised her shield, a barrier of transparent green triangles and swirls enveloped everyone. As a unit, Rinn's army waded into the pool and toward the menacing tunnel. Cat squealed miserably as she stepped into the water.

Normally, red candles flanked the entryway, reminding visitors to be respectful inside the sacred Grove. Their ornately-carved holders had been smashed and candle wax splattered against the trees like a bloodstain. As Rinn neared the entrance, she concentrated on shrinking her shield enough to fit through the opening. Everyone squeezed in close as they moved through the tunnel. Only the faint light from Rinn's magic illuminated the dark passage. Twisted tree trunks scraped against her barrier as they moved. Cat waded forward, easily able to navigate in the darkness. Lutra clung tightly to Cat, and Feena clung onto Lutra.

Halfway down the passage, a loud groaning of wood echoed out. The trees leaned inward, bearing their weight down on Rinn's shield. With a forceful grunt, Rinn pushed back, refusing to be overcome. She would not let her father and friends be crushed. Tree trunks constricted around her like a python. A squeezing pain shot through the back of Rinn's skull, her shield was faltering. She gritted her teeth and fought back tears. Her shield was stronger than this— she remembered the Vallum, when her barrier blew a hole through solid rock. Something was holding her back. The pain was getting worse, and Rinn cried out. Feena screamed in the darkness causing Cat to panic. Even the dwarves were rattled, their war hammers shaking in their hands. Everyone was going to die, fear was everywhere.

Fear, Rinn realized. She was scared. Not of dying, but she was afraid of damaging the Grove, a sacred and holy site. She was holding herself back. Her friends and family came first, she would risk Lucan's wrath. Rinn's shield glowed fiercely as it expanded out. Wood snapped and cracked as her barrier swelled. With a mournful groan, ancient tree trunks splintered as they were torn apart. A shaft of light poured through the gaping hole in the tree ring. Rinn could see the altar at the heart of Lucan's Grove. A thin man wearing druid robes was standing between it and a gruesome black creature.

The monstrous beast resembled an obese horse, with fat round legs and a belly that dragged on the ground. It had a great shaggy tail and a long thin face like an anteater. A tendril-like tongue protruded from its snout, and it used it like a whip. The druid dodged and blocked the tongue with his gnarled-wood staff. He landed a blow on the beast's head, but the creature only reared and stalked him from a different direction. The druid gave Rinn a wilted look as he blocked another attack.

Rinn let her shield fall. "That's the thing poisoning the Grove." She dashed forward, spear at the ready, but Molo grabbed her by the back of her dragon feather vest.

"Hold on." He cautioned. "We don't know what that thing is."

"It's a struma." Marshal hissed through clenched teeth. His knuckles were white as he gripped his sword.

The dwarves exchanged nervous looks. Felsic whispered. "Those things can't be killed."

Marshal gave details. "Struma are a walking disease, absolutely unstoppable. Their appetite's insatiable. They bring ruin and death wherever they go. The Legion once met a struma in Brigantum. A thousand men could not hold it back. The campaign was a total loss and we had to abandon the region."

As Rinn watched, the druid countered another attack, always remaining protectively between the altar and the beast. Rinn knew the man could not keep up his defense forever, she needed to take action. If the beast could not be killed, she would have to lure it away, far from Lucan's Grove and Viburna. The druid and the struma exchanged blows once more.

"Cat, what do you see when you look at the beast?" Rinn assumed command, wriggling out of Molo's grasp.

Cat cocked her head sideways. "It's sucking things into a weird blue hole."

"It's a magic eater." Rinn declared. "Molo, what does Clive see?"

Molo held up his round rock, pointing its eyeball at the beast who stalked the altar. "The kitten is right, it has no shape, it's just a vortex, pulling things inside."

"Okay." Rinn reasoned. "We can't kill it, because it's not a thing. It's trying to eat the altar because of its potent magic. There must be some way to distract it." Rinn curled her mouth into a wry grin aimed at her sister. "We just need to give it a different kind of bait." Cat rubbed her paws together excitedly. Rinn nodded her head yes. Cat nodded back with a fiendish gleam in her eyes. "Everyone. Cat and I are going to make some magic to draw the monster out, you keep it at bay with your weapons."

Rinn's companions split into two parties, flanking Rinn and Cat. Calder, Feena, Lutra, and Molo stood to her left and Marshal and the dwarves to her right. Rinn reached out to embrace her sister, Cat held on eagerly. Rinn breathed slowly, channeling her power into her sister. Cat began to purr loudly, her fur stood on end with static electricity. Her eyes sizzled with green light and sparks flickered around her. The struma disengaged from the druid and inclined its head toward Catherine, tasting the air with its menacing tongue. It reared up on its hind legs and crashed down, lumbering toward the glowing Margot. Rinn released her sister.

"Catch me if you can." Cat taunted, sticking out her feline tongue.

As the beast roared by, Rinn's soldiers hacked away at its sides, further infuriating it. Rinn held her spear steady, planting it against one foot as Molo had drilled into her. Cat blinked away to a nearby tree branch and launched jibes at the monster again, but the beast was unperturbed. It barreled ahead, straight for Rinn, the strongest source of magic. Instead of dodging, Rinn braced herself for impact, her spear tip brightly glowing. She did not know if she could kill this monster, but she had faith her enchanted spear would harm it, maybe enough to drive it off.

The struma impaled itself on Rinn's spear without concern. Its tendril-like tongue shot out and wrapped around Rinn's torso, pinning her arms. It began to feed, painfully sucking away her magic. Rinn screamed out in agony. Cat appeared beside her, biting and clawing at the tongue. Marshal, Molo, and the dwarves assaulted the beast's sides without effect. Even Calder's exceptionally sharp sword could not penetrate its thickened hide. Cat clawed and bit, howling in frustration.

"Cat." Rinn gurgled. "The Mist."

Cat's green eyes locked on the beast. "I'm going to tear you apart." The struma tilted its head toward the hostile feline, scanning her with its beady black eyes. Cat dug her claws into its black hide and phased out, taking Rinn and the monster with her.

Chapter 8

R inn drifted through the purple Mist, entangled in the struma's rope-like tongue. The monster's obese body hovered in the formless void, its fat legs futilely probing for ground. Rinn could no longer feel the powerful draining force from the beast, it was too disoriented to feed. Cat pushed away from the struma's body and floated comfortably in the Mist.

"We only have a few minutes." Cat insisted.

"Help get me free." Rinn pulled at the tendril-like tongue that wrapped around her body. Cat bit and clawed, but the tongue was tougher than steel. Rinn saw her spear, impaled in the bloated belly of the beast. She kicked at it with her feet, but it was out of her reach. "Cat, my spear."

Cat drifted over and jerked the pilum free from the struma's abdomen. She slid the weapon into Rinn's hands. Even though her arms were pinned to her side, she could maneuver the spear enough to reach the beast's tongue. Rinn compelled her magic to focus on the end of the spear causing it to burn greenish-white. The struma wheeled its head, its beady eyes reflecting the bright light from Rinn's spear. With a twist, Rinn cut into the coils that surrounded her, but it was not enough to sever the whip-like tongue.

"We're running out of time." Cat fought to pull Rinn free. The struma squealed like a pig, swiping violently with its powerful front legs. A claw raked through Rinn's spear, fracturing the wooden handle. Rinn quickly grabbed the metal tip before it floated away. The struma struck again, trying to rip through Rinn's dragon-feather vest, but it held fast.

"We have to end this." Rinn held her spear tip like a dagger. The struma pulled Rinn closer, tightening its grip on her. Like a wave, a forceful undertow began to expel the struggling trio from the Mist. Rinn yelled. "Cat. Take us up."

"Up?" Cat raised one ear.

"Up." Rinn pleaded. "As high as you can go!"

Cat grabbed Rinn and puckered her face. With a loud pop, all three were pushed out of the Mist into open sky, high above the clouds. They immediately began to plummet downward. Cat shrieked, arched her back, and twisted her tail until all four of her paws were pointing downward. Wind whipped past Rinn's face as she raced to the miniature landscape below. Ignoring her impending doom, she hacked away at the struma's tongue with the blade of her spear. She was making progress, slowly. The gray outline of the city came closer, Rinn could see individual buildings. She hacked and sawed furiously. To the west of the city, ant-like soldiers fought on the open plains with an unseen enemy. Rinn was almost through. She could see Lucan's Grove below her, its ancient tree ring partially demolished.

Rinn finally sliced through the foul tongue, the struma squealed in agony. She kicked away from the hideous beast. Rinn reached out. "Cat, grab hold." Her sister grabbed her tightly with both of her paws, she was mewing pitifully. Rinn took a breath and uttered the Sigillum word "ahebbe." Immediately, her descent slowed. Cat began to laugh as together they drifted like feathers, gently gliding downward. The struma was not so lucky, it streaked toward the ground like a missile. With the violent impact of a meteor, it smashed into a ruined building near the Grove.

Cat's eyes teared as she clutched her sister. "We're flying."

"Floating." Rinn corrected with a grin.

"This is amazing." Cat convulsed in laughter. "I'm actually flying."

Rinn firmly held her sister as they drifted. Below, she could hear the sounds of battle. To the west of the city, just beyond the crumbling city walls, soldiers with torches clashed with an unknown adversary. The invading army may have outnumbered the defending force, but they were disorganized and poorly equipped. The attackers were harassing the town guard more than they were trying to break through. The battle went out of view as Rinn and Cat drifted behind the city walls.

Rinn and Cat floated into the plaza, just outside Lucan's Grove. Rinn's friends rushed through the gaping hole in the trees to meet them. They cheered as Rinn and Cat gently touched down to the ground. Rinn felt the weight of her body return. She whispered a silent prayer of thanks.

Lutra and Calder reached the girls first. "We heard the explosion. We thought you were dead." Lutra sobbed as he reached out to hug Rinn and Cat, mostly Cat.

"We were flying." Cat smiled, rubbing Lutra's head.

Molo and the dwarves came second, followed by an out-of-breath Feena. "Thank the gods." Molo muttered when he saw the girls.

"What was that loud explosion?" Feena huffed.

Rinn answered. "The struma. It crashed into a building nearby."

Marshal limped into the scene, everyone parted as he approached. He put a hand over his chest. "You're safe." He doubled over, hands on his knees, sighing in relief. "What happened?"

Cat jumped up and down, trying to relate the tale, but in her excitement, her jumbled speech made no sense. Rinn laid a calming hand on her sister. Rinn recounted the events more succinctly. "Cat carried the beast through the Mist and deposited it high in the sky. The fall probably killed it, but we should find the body, just in case."

Rinn heard coughing coming from one of the ruined buildings. A thoroughly dusty Sionne stepped through an empty doorframe, spitting out dirt. He glared at Rinn. "You did that on purpose."

"No, I swear." Rinn held up her hands defensively. "It's a coincidence. I had no idea you were in there."

Mafic stifled a chuckle. He patted his brother on the back. "Come on, let's find that beast. Make sure it's truly defeated." Molo and Calder joined them as they fearlessly ventured into the broken building. Sionne dusted himself off, shaking rocks out of his shoes. He shot Rinn a nasty glance as he shuffled over to the Grove.

"What is it with you and blowing things up?" He complained, seeing the partially destroyed tree ring.

"I don't blow things up." Rinn cried plaintively. Feena and Lutra poked fun at her and Rinn pleaded her innocence. Cat played along. Even her father shrugged in deference, Rinn was a bit destructive.

From the rubble Molo hailed Rinn. "You'd best come see this." She cautiously entered the doorway of the ruined building. She held the rusting tip of her broken spear, the only remnant of her weapon. Inside, laying on a pile of fractured stone, was the struma, still alive. Its body was crushed, and the creature could only barely move its head. Beady black eyes tracked Rinn as she neared the beast. Rinn could see the blue magic-absorbing vortex inside the creature failing. The struma was dying.

Rinn knelt down beside the hideous monster. "I don't know where you came from or who brought you here, but you fought well. Now, it's over. I'll give you one last taste, to ease the pain of your passing." Rinn relaxed her breathing and brought up her shield, this time around the beast. The monster feebly attempted to lick the magic with the stump of its tongue. With a tear, Rinn collapsed the barrier, smaller and smaller until the beast was no more. She stood up and wiped her eyes.

Felsic whispered in astonishment. "She has killed a struma."

In grave tones, Molo added. "We've yet to see the extent of her power."

Rinn exited the building, crossing the plaza to Lucan's Grove. The trees were already shedding the effects of the poisonous beast, black wrinkled leaves fluttered from the branches and covered the brackish pool. The dark miasma that hung over the Grove dissipated, and streams of moonlight cut through the clouds. Rinn turned to her friends. "We should check on that druid, and make sure he's okay."

Together, Rinn's army picked their way through the pool and over fallen yew trees. Inside, the Grove was already showing signs of recovery. Green moss covered the rocks and clear water dribbled from a fountain. In the center of the Grove, the lone druid rested against his gnarled oak staff, exhausted. His amber eyes smiled as he watched Rinn approach.

"I knew you'd come." The druid spoke, his voice a pleasant tenor. He boasted a short curly beard and lively auburn hair. His age was impossible to guess, late twenties or early fifties, old and young at the same time. He wore a plain brown robe bound with a braided belt and simple sandals on his feet.

"Are you okay?" Rinn asked, though this young man seemed perfectly fit.

"I am." He breathed out a great sigh. "Thanks to you."

"Who are you?" Rinn questioned.

"I am Nemus." The druid bowed with a flourish.

"I'm Rinn." She curtseyed.

"I know." Nemus smiled. Rinn raised a curious eyebrow. The druid explained. "I have seen you visit this Grove many times as a child. You were always so respectful and quiet, unlike most children."

Rinn felt immediate pangs of guilt. She glanced at the damage she had caused—four ancient yew trees uprooted and destroyed. "I'm so sorry about the Grove."

"My child." The druid softly laughed. "You saved this holy place."

"But the yew trees." Rinn bit her bottom lip.

The druid walked forward leaning on his oaken staff. "The one thing nature does best is grow. The trees will return in time." Rinn's father and friends fanned out behind her. The druid addressed them all. "I owe you all a debt of gratitude, you each played a part in saving this Grove." He even eyed Sionne with a wink. The redheaded teen scoffed and turned away.

"Where're the other druids?" Marshal limped forward.

Nemus cast his eyes to the ground. "I am the last."

Rinn felt a pang of shock. She remembered hundreds of druids, men and women in their austere robes. Twice a year on the solstice, they bore white candles and garlands woven from fresh flowers. They chanted as they paraded across the countryside, filling it with song. Now they were gone. What could have happened? Rinn thought to herself. Who could have killed off such holy and innocent people? Tears started to well up in her eyes. Cat came up and held her hands in her paws.

Nemus waved a finger at Rinn. "Do not cry, little bird. The Grove is safe. The druids' duty has been fulfilled. In time, new druids will be called."

"How can you be sure?" Rinn sniffed.

"I have it on good authority." Nemus smirked. He reached out a hand to touch Cat's fur. She regarded him curiously. "You are an amazing creature. I never thought to see your kind again." Cat squinted her eyes at the druid and grinned. Her tail swished in pleasure.

Sionne interrupted the conversation. "Someone's coming."

Molo looked off in the distance and agreed.

"We should go." Rinn urged. Her friends were already heading out of the Grove.

"A moment, little bird." Nemus begged. "Before you go, I wish to give you a gift. A thank you for rescuing this Grove." Nemus stepped to an unbroken yew tree. The trees were already looking healthier, new buds sprouted where sickly, black leaves once hung. Rusty scabs sloughed away from the trees revealing healthy brown bark beneath. Nemus quietly chanted and reached deep into a tree trunk. He pulled out a long cylindrical staff of wood, rich in amber color. He reverently handed the staff to Rinn. "Heartwood. It will not break easily."

Rinn accepted the gift with uncertainty.

Nemus smiled in satisfaction. "The dverg will know what to do." His expression abruptly changed. He rested a hand on Rinn's shoulder, his touch felt incredibly warm. "Rinn, you must go to Peleon. Find the Emperors. It is the only way you can succeed." He withdrew his hand and leaned on his oaken staff. He glided back to his post near the edge of the altar and waited. Rinn was bewildered by his comment. She was not ready to go to the capital city. Who were the Emperors? How could she succeed? Rinn wanted to ask so many questions, but the druid was no longer paying attention, seemingly lost in his own thoughts. Cat returned to fetch Rinn, urging her to leave before the guards came. Rinn took one last fleeting look at the druid as she left, worried she would never see him again.

Chapter 9

Rinn and her companions hurried away from Lucan's Grove, secreting from one alley to the next, edging eastward, closer to Rinn's old neighborhood. Even though many of the buildings had been vandalized and burned, Rinn still felt at ease in the familiar surroundings.

"Where are we headed?" Lutra whispered to Marshal, who was at the head of the party. His limp slowed their progress, but it forced everyone to move with extra caution.

Marshal answered in hushed tones. "There's a safe place nearby. Old man Calamus kept a hidden workroom under his house. He fancied his privacy."

"I remember him." Rinn announced. Everyone in the party shushed her as they moved through another narrow alley.

Marshal peeked around a corner. "It should be an effective refuge, until we can better assess our situation." The party stealthily crossed another open street, just out of sight of a guard patrol. Ruffians and thugs still roamed the streets, but they did not harass Rinn and her companions. The sight of a well-armed giant kept them at bay. Rinn still felt vulnerable, her only weapon had been smashed in the battle with the struma. She had the wooden staff Nemus had given her, but without any metal to channel her powers, it was worthless to her.

"Almost there." Marshal assured everyone. He circled around to the rear of the building, avoiding the main streets. He attempted to push open the back door, but it was securely locked. "Sionne, can you open this?"

The redheaded teen took offense. "What do I look like, a thief?"

"Actually." Lutra started. Feena playfully smacked his shoulder.

Rinn stepped up to diffuse the situation. "Let me help." She touched the lock on the door and mouthed the word "onlithe". The mechanism clicked and fell open. She politely pushed the door open and motioned for everyone to enter.

Sionne whistled. "That's a handy trick. You could make a fair bit of money with a skill like that."

Rinn scowled. "I'm not here to make money, I'm here to help people." She shoved him inside the building. Everyone else followed in single file. Feena curtseyed playfully as she passed Rinn. The inside of the home was plain, even austere. It had not been heavily looted because it did not appear to have anything of value to steal. Wooden benches built into the walls were the only furniture, and plain cupboards held only chipped plates and mugs. With a click and a spark, the dwarves ignited some sort of collapsible lantern, providing light in the dim interior. Marshal led the party to a pantry behind the kitchen. He opened a hinged floorboard revealing a concealed stairwell leading down.

Cat scurried down the steps unphased by the darkness. The dwarves followed with their lantern. Rinn helped her father navigate the steep stairs. As she ran her hand along the wall, she could feel the impossibly smooth grain of the underground stone. Another example of dwarven construction, she thought to herself. Molo stooped as he traversed the low-ceilinged stairwell. The basement itself was deceptively roomy. Marshal lit several wall sconces from the dwarves' lantern. The floor was planked in hardwood, tables and workbenches lined the walls. A bookcase filled with leather-bound tomes proudly stood in one corner, a treasure worth more than the house itself. Feena and Lutra were immediately drawn to the bookshelf, and they began to leaf through the volumes it held. Cat sniffed around the room for mice.

Rinn settled her father into a dusty chair. The long walk across town had taken its toll on him. He thanked her as he relaxed his sore legs. Feena unpacked food and set out a meal for everyone. They ate in the privacy of the basement and talked about the recent battle at Lucan's Grove.

"So, Rinn, how did you manage to defeat that struma?" Mafic asked through a mouth full of bread and cheese.

Rinn sat on the floor, legs crossed. Her dragon-feather vest lay beside her. "When we couldn't defeat the beast in combat, I asked Cat to transport us high into the sky. I let the fall do most of the work."

Cat raced around the room, flapping her arms like wings. "We were flying like birds. The city looked so tiny, like a little toy."

Felsic winced, dwarves have no love of heights. "You fell from the sky? How did you survive?"

Rinn stared at the floor. "I know the word for 'drift'. We floated down."

Feena took her hand. "Rinn, that's amazing."

Rinn shook her head. "No, it's not. On the way down, I saw something. Fighting just west of town. An army of some sort was attacking the city." Rinn pounded her thighs in frustration. "I thought if we saved the Grove everything would be fine, but it's not. Viburna is still in trouble, and war is all around us."

Her father reached out a sympathetic hand. "There're some battles we aren't meant to fight. We can't stop every skirmish. We have to go where we're needed most. The Grove needed you, and you fulfilled your role admirably."

Rinn hung her shoulders, demoralized. "I wanted the city to be right, like it used to be. Just one city to be free of this stupid war. But the fighting is everywhere, nowhere is safe. I guess we'll have to go to the capital like that druid said."

Molo, who had been uncharacteristically quiet up until now, spoke. "That was no druid."

Rinn raised an eyebrow in askance.

Molo had a steely gaze as he related his tale. "That was no ordinary man. When I looked at him with Clive, it was like staring into the sun. The strength of his life energy was unfathomable. Clive still has a blind spot after one brief glimpse."

Everyone looked confused. Lutra blurted out. "Who was it then?"

"I think that was Lucus himself." Molo revealed.

Everyone turned to Rinn, who was completely aghast. She had talked to a god, he reached out and touched her. Marshal's hands trembled as he asked. "What exactly did he say to you?"

A cold chill spread across Rinn. "He told me I had to go to Peleon, to find the Emperors. He said it was the only way I could succeed." Rinn leaned over and picked up the strange wooden staff. "He gave me this."

Felsic examined it closely, running his hand along the wood grain. He backed up, startled by the revelation. "That's heartwood."

"He took it out of one of the yew trees." Rinn confessed.

Mafic drew closer to examine the staff, forgetting about the food in his mouth. "Thousand-year-old heartwood." He said in awe. He reached out to touch it, but he dared not.

"He said you would know what to do with it." Rinn handed the staff to Felsic. He received it reverently, as if he were handed a newborn infant.

"We do." Felsic admitted. "All Dverg know the legends of heartwood, but few ever see it in their lifetimes."

"What is it?" Lutra inquired, unimpressed.

"It's living wood, waiting for the sculptor." Mafic breathed. "If I crafted you a flute from heartwood, you could charm the snow off the very mountains with it."

"What?" Lutra boggled. He eyed the wood with renewed respect.

"What does it mean?" Feena asked.

Molo seemed as solemn as the grave. "Catastrophe is coming, something Rinn cannot defeat alone. The gods have only ever acted during the most dire of calamities."

Rinn tried not to be flustered. "I learned my lesson taking on Clanmorris by myself. No more going it alone. I need all of you." She squeezed Cat's paw. "We're in this together. If we need the gods' help, I humbly accept that, too. If Lucus says we need to go to Peleon, then that's where we're going."

:.

The next day was spent buying supplies and readying for the journey to the capital. Lutra and Feena proved exceptionally adept at blending in with the common folk, posing as simple townspeople. Sionne and Cat were sent on missions to acquire items that could not be purchased at the meager market. They hated each other, but the two functioned well as a team, Cat on lookout and Sionne doing the dirty work. The dwarves converted the kitchen oven into a makeshift forge and repaired the weapons of the party. A new spear was crafted for Rinn, simple in design and construction, but effective. Felsic reserved the heartwood until an appropriate metal could be found—regular iron was insufficient.

Rinn discussed strategy at length with Molo and her father. She had two priorities: rescuing the imprisoned boy and procuring a horse—her father could not make the long journey to Peleon on foot. They agreed to split up. Marshal deduced that Bayard would be held at the military stables. He believed he could bluff his way past the stable hands, they were typically not very smart. Somehow, Cat and Sionne managed to steal the white cape off a local guard. Once Marshal donned his military uniform and white cape, he could easily be mistaken for one of the local guards.

While Marshal, Calder, and Lutra were at the stables, Rinn and Cat planned to slip into the Temple prison and liberate the boy being held there. Rinn did not sleep well the previous night, unable to shake the memory of the scribe screaming her name. She regretted not taking a stand and rescuing the boy right then. She could have overpowered the guards and freed him. She would correct that error today.

"We're ready." Rinn told her father. She was wearing her dragon-feather vest and carrying a new spear. Cat was wearing her own dragon-feather accoutrements, shoulder pads and arm guards. She did not need any weapons other than her claws, but she sported a dagger belted to her waist.

Marshal gave his daughter a hug. "Be safe."

"No heroics." Rinn hugged back. Marshal wrapped an arm around Cat, drawing her in close. She added purring to the family hug. Rinn straightened, full of confidence. "We'll be back soon. And then, we'll set out for Peleon." She squeezed Cat's paw. Before anyone could depart, they heard footsteps on the floor above. Marshal motioned for everyone to be quiet. Rinn listened anxiously as the sound crossed the house to the staircase. The noisy hinge squeaked as the cellar door was opened. Molo moved to the bottom of the stairs, hammer held at the ready.

An elderly man carrying a lantern stepped into view. He paused when he saw the crowd of people in his basement. He waved an angry finger. "Which one of you polluted my kitchen?"

Marshal greeted the elderly man. "We're sorry about that, Calamus. We'll clean it up, we promise." He shot an expectant glance at the dwarves, who nodded sheepishly.

"Marshal, is that you?" The elderly man lifted the lantern higher, so he could see Marshal's face.

"How're you doing, old man?" Marshal limped over and offered a hug, the elderly man accepted it warmly.

"What happened to your leg?" Calamus questioned.

"Battle wound last year, still hasn't healed right." Marshal explained.

"You've been fighting with the Legions?" Calamus asked.

"Not this time." Marshal chuckled. "I've actually been living in the wilds for the last several years."

"That's no place to raise a daughter." Calamus chastised, surreptitiously casting a glance at Rinn.

"Way I see it, the Empire's not much better right now." Marshal replied.

Calamus had to laugh. "I guess you're right." He stepped in closer to Marshal speaking in almost a whisper. "There's talk about your daughter."

"What are they saying?" Marshal inquired. Rinn lingered close by, unable to restrain her curiosity.

"The guards are looking for her. Something about magic." Calamus spoke under his breath. Rinn heard him anyway. News of her escape travelled quickly. They needed to get out of Viburna as soon as possible, but the boy in the dungeon cell haunted her. She would not leave without him.

"I'm going to the Temple." Rinn announced.

Her father tried to dissuade her. "It's not safe. The town guard will attack you on sight."

"I'm going anyway." Rinn pursed her lips. "If I can handle an immortal monster, I can manage a few city guards."

"Do you want their deaths on your head?" Marshal objected.

Rinn was conflicted, trying to rationalize her decision in her head. How many guards could she justify killing to release one boy? Another variable entered the equation: the boy was alone. No one was coming to help him. Rinn might be his only chance for freedom. She made her choice. "I knew this would happen. It's inevitable. I was given fighting skills for a purpose. I believe I'm supposed to use them to help people, especially those no one else is willing to help. That boy needs me, and so I'm going."

Marshal hung his head, defeated. He let out a long sigh and then stretched. "Okay, general assault on the Temple. Everyone's coming along."

Calamus blanched. "Are you crazy? The Temple's crawling with soldiers."

Molo stood, as well as he could in the cramped basement. "Rinn knows what she's doing. If she says we're going to the Temple, we'll follow." As an afterthought he commented to Calamus. "I'd recommend staying hidden for a few days, this may get messy."

Chapter 10

C at pulled the straps on Rinn's feather vest and helped lace up her boots. Rinn was outfitted in her "battle dress". For some reason, she had an aversion to wearing pants. They always made her feel self-conscious, like everyone was staring at her behind. But long dresses were not well suited for combat, especially combat with a spear. On the trip through the Rustic Lands, Feena had fashioned a compromise—the back half of a skirt joined to a pair of leather pants. This discretely covered Rinn's posterior while leaving her legs open for combat footwork.

Molo and the dwarves donned their heaviest armor, thick bands of metal plates pounded together to form chest pieces. They wore matching helmets adorned with floefang teeth. When they brandished their war hammers, the trio was truly fearsome to behold. Marshal pulled on his riding armor, made of leather with an extra metal plate to protect his injured hip. He slid a quiver of arrows over his shoulder and belted on his sword. Calder wore almost no armor at all, but Rinn was certain that his skill with a blade would keep him safe. Only a fool would attack Calder outright. Lutra dressed in chain armor with a sword and a hefty shield. Feena begged him not to go, but he assured her he would be careful. Feena and Sionne were selected to carry the party's gear and provisions out of the city, neither one was proficient in battle. There was a hot spring just west of town, they agreed to wait there until the operation was complete.

"Let's review one last time." Marshal steadied himself against a table. The war party gathered around. He addressed Molo. "Your job is to attract the attention of the guard, to appear threatening, but not to engage them. Meanwhile, Rinn and Cat will slip into the Temple and Calder and I will head to the stables. We'll meet at the marketplace and make for the city exit. I've brewed up a batch of smoke salts to help mask our escape." Everyone nodded in satisfaction. Rinn was not sure what smoke salts were, but she could guess.

Rinn hugged Feena and gave a curt handshake to Sionne before they departed. She promised everyone they would be together before nightfall. With poise and resolution, Rinn lead her army down the residential streets to the Temple of Aedis. They paraded unnoticed until they reached the mostly abandoned marketplace. A patrol of city guard spotted them and hurried off.

"It has begun." Molo observed, holding out Clive.

Marshal pointed out the unused amphitheater to Molo. "Make your stand there. You can fall back inside if things aren't going well. The building's a maze of hallways with too many exits for the guards to cover." Molo acknowledged the plan. He led Lutra and the dwarves to the amphitheater entrance, metal armor clanking and weapons rattling as they jogged. Rinn could see the spires of the Temple jutting above the rooftops. Its perfectly polished pillars belied the ugliness hiding beneath it.

Rinn took Cat's paw. "Are you ready?"

Cat looked up from whatever distraction held her attention. "Huh?"

"We should go." Rinn insisted with a smile.

"Okay." Cat agreed. They stood hand in paw. With a pop, the familiar undertow pulled Rinn into the Mist. Somehow, it seemed different, still the same vast purple space but with streaks of red light along with the yellow sparks. Again, Rinn could only catch a glimpse before she was deposited on a stairway leading into the dungeons. Cat landed gracefully, but Rinn almost tumbled down the stairwell. She grabbed the wall for support, nearly losing her spear.

"Warn me before you land somewhere like this." Rinn barked.

"Like what?" Cat tilted her head. Rinn decided to let it go, they had work to do. She tiptoed down the stairs and peered around the corner into a long empty corridor. Somewhere, in the distance, she could hear the murmur of people. Rinn crept down the hallway until she came to an intersection. The noise of the crowd was all around her now, coming from every direction. All the passages looked the same, poorly lit narrow stone tunnels leading into the darkness. Rinn had no idea which way to go.

"There's a boy down here." Rinn whispered. "Can you find him?"

"What does he smell like?" Cat asked.

Rinn considered for a moment, she remembered the boy had been wearing a scribe's robe. "He'd probably smell like old books and ink."

"Books? " Cat twitched her whiskers. "Like the ones in that basement?"

"Exactly." Rinn nodded, proud of her sister. Cat squeezed her nose as she contemplated each corridor, sniffing at the air. The raucous noise around them was growing louder, making Rinn anxious. Finally, Cat chose the passage to the left, and they scurried down it. They encountered two soldiers heading their direction. Rinn summoned her barrier between the guards. Before they could draw their swords, she expanded the magic sphere, smashing the two into the walls. They crumpled to the ground, unconscious. Rinn and Cat dashed past them, deeper into the dungeons. Rinn could smell rust and decay, she knew the prison was getting close. The crowd noise was everywhere, and Rinn finally realized that it was coming from above her, inside the Temple sanctuary, some sort of grand celebration. She ignored it and focused on finding the boy.

Cat located the entrance to the prison wings. Rinn pushed the stout wooden door leading to the jailor's room open. Four guards reclined at a table throwing dice over a wooden game board. Rinn and Cat stormed into the room, but the guards were quick to react, drawing their swords and advancing on the girls. The lead guard bellowed. "Don't let them escape."

Without using magic, Rinn disarmed one guard and backed another into a wall. Swords had a difficult time fighting against spears, especially in tight quarters. A foolish guard swung at Cat, who dropped and rolled behind him. She wrapped her legs around him and, with a pop, they were gone. The other guards were shocked to see their companion vanish, but they would not back down. Rinn could easily defeat the guards, but she hesitated to kill people for just doing their job. She disarmed a second guard and grabbed his tunic. She breathed out the word "ahebbe", and lifted the guard to the ceiling. He floated there in terror, and his companions backed away. Cat reappeared with a smile.

Rinn motioned to a doorway leading to the cells. Cat danced through it as the guards tried to regain their composure. Rinn chased Cat. "Where did you take that guard?"

Cat just shrugged.

Rinn paced down the rows of empty cells, recoiling at the smell of decay. She could not fathom why this prison was built in the first place. Cat wandered down an adjacent hallway. She whistled, or made some kind of noise like a whistle.

"Hey sis." Cat called. "He's over here."

Rinn rushed over and found the boy huddled in the corner of his cell like a beaten dog in a kennel. His face was bruised, and his knuckles bloodied, but he was alive. Rinn sighed in relief and she squeezed her sister's paw. "Good work, Cat."

The boy opened his eyes and stared at Rinn. "I'm must be dreaming." He muttered to himself.

"No." Rinn corrected. "I'm real." The boy shot up, backing against the wall in a panic. "We came to rescue you." Rinn insisted. "Let's get you out of here before the guards return." Rinn readied her spear, but Cat raised a paw to stop her. She unsheathed a small knife strapped to her belt and handed it to Rinn. Good idea, thought Rinn. Save my spear for when I really need it. Holding the knife out, she imbued it with magic until it glowed silvery-green. Rinn used the knife to cut through the lock and the rusty bars of his prison cell. "There you go."

Like a timid puppy, the bewildered boy poked his head out of the cell. He stood even in height with Rinn, dressed in a tattered scribe's robe. His hair was straight and brown, cut close to his head and his skin was sickly pale, either from his time in the dungeon or too many hours spent copying manuscripts. He stammered. "You're Sabrinn Sevralis."

"Call me Rinn." She said. "Who are you?"

"I'm Tavin." The boy said meekly.

"How do you know my name?" Rinn asked.

"I've read about you." The boy explained. He wanted to say more but he was interrupted.

Cat tugged at Rinn's sleeve. "Soldiers are coming."

Rinn could hear shouting down the hallway. "We need to go." She gathered close to Cat and urged the scribe over. He was reluctant so Rinn reached out and took ahold of the boy's hand, he stiffened like a board. "Okay Cat, get us out of here." Rinn waited. The commotion drew closer. "Cat, anytime."

"It's not working." Cat whined, whiskers pouty.

"Of all the things!" Rinn dropped the scribe's hand and readied her spear. "Fine, we do this the hard way." Six guards burst into the prison area, wielding long polearms. Rinn smirked. "They're learning."

The head of the guard, a stocky man with a large goatee, barked a warning. "Drop your weapons and surrender. There is no way out."

Rinn grinned to Cat. "Time for a new lesson." With unexpected fury, Rinn ignited the tip of her spear and charged. Rinn's magic was definitely getting stronger, the metal of her spear did not glow green—it burned with green flames. Rinn carved through the guard's weapons and gave a solid kick to the leader, knocking him back. Cat ricocheted off a wall and knocked several others off-balance. Rinn grabbed the startled scribe, and pulled him down the hallway over the fallen soldiers. Rinn held the jailors off with her flaming spear, after a taste of her abilities earlier, they had lost the will to fight. Rinn, Cat, and Tavin rushed through the dungeon complex. Raucous sounds from the Temple upstairs echoed through the passageways.

Rinn wanted to exit the way she came in, but a large contingent of soldiers blocked her path. They advanced with spears and swords, Rinn even saw archers. She lifted her flaming spear and drew a line in the rock ceiling above her, crashing it to the floor. She turned and headed the opposite way down the corridor. "Come on, let's see where this goes."

Cat followed close behind, and Tavin struggled to keep up, his sandals flapping loudly against the stone floor. Rinn blindly angled down dark passageways until she found a staircase leading up. It was guarded by a single, teenage soldier: Grus. Seeing someone approach, he instinctively drew his sword, then recognition came over him. "Rinn? Is that you?"

"Hello, Grus." Rinn said stoically. "We need to get through."

Grus retreated a step, but he did not waver. "No one's allowed in the Temple." A thought seemed to occur to him. "Wait, didn't you escape from prison already?"

"I came back." Rinn snapped. She did not have time to deal with this idiot. "Now, stand aside." Rinn raised her spear. She would not actually harm her childhood friend, but she was not sure he knew that.

Grus' voice faltered. "You can't go up there. It's forbidden. The High Priest will kill anyone who sets foot in the Temple during a sacred ceremony."

"Sounds like odd behavior for a priest." Rinn challenged. Grus was clearly conflicted, caught between loyalty and reason. Shouting and clanking of metal echoed down the corridor, more soldiers making their approach. Rinn lowered her weapon and placed a hand on Grus' shoulder. She gently moved him aside and walked past. Cat and the frightened scribe followed, Grus did not stop them. Rinn climbed the narrow staircase toward the growing cacophony above her. The sound reminded her of the boisterous harvest fair, the din of crowd noise punctuated by shrill cries. The stout door at the top of the stairs was locked, but it proved no obstacle for Rinn. As she swung the door open, she stopped in horror—the ceremony inside the Temple was an abomination.

Chapter 11

S treams of afternoon light poured through the stained-glass windows, bathing the profane worshippers in a wash of blues, reds, and yellows. Hundreds of people, some half-clothed, some completely naked, danced to the sound of drums. Cups of wine spilled carelessly across the wooden parquet floor as the drunken revelers fondled and groped each other. Some were willing participants, but others were not, crying as they were restrained by strangers, friends, relatives. Even members of the town guard indulged themselves. Rinn recognized Grus' commanding officer, half out of his uniform, his arms wrapped around two bawdy harlots. Sitting in the middle of it all, draped across the altar as if it were his own private couch, was High Priest Caena. He was surrounded by scantily clad women of all ages, like a lion among his lionesses. In one hand he held a taught chain, the other end fastened to the collar of a sobbing young girl at his feet.

Rage boiled in Rinn's chest, her heart beat sped unnaturally. Her skin tightened as her entire spear was engulfed in green flames. Even her curly blond hair floated out, sizzling with sparks of green fury. Rinn finally understood—it was not the struma at Lucan's Grove poisoning this city, it was here, this Temple. The altar burned with the azure aura of magic, polluting this holy place. Rinn knew it had to be destroyed.

Rinn waded into the throng of profane worshippers, who parted at her approach. They were defenseless, drunk and mostly undressed. The High priest perceived the change in the atmosphere and noticed Rinn moving toward him. He ordered his guard to apprehend her. A force of twelve men assembled to confront Rinn. At first, she had reservations about fighting on holy ground, but there was nothing sacred about this place—she could not defile what was already defiled. The soldiers shouted for her to stand down, Rinn responded by cracking the lead soldier on the head with the butt of her spear. The others assaulted her with swords, but Rinn's reflexes were fueled by her fury, and she effortlessly dispatched eight of the men before moving on.

Cat nervously followed behind Rinn, tiptoeing over the bodies of the fallen. Grus and Tavin remained in the doorway, aghast at the proceedings. Rinn climbed the wide flat steps leading to the altar undeterred by the commotion around her. Some worshippers were gathering their things and heading for the doors. The party was clearly over. The tall High Priest rose, dropping the chain of his young plaything. He pointed accusingly at Rinn. "You don't belong here, vile pretender."

Rinn growled her reply. "No. You don't belong here, poisonous priest."

High Priest Caena curled his lip in scorn. "I am the hand of Aedis." As he spoke, he reached out and touched the altar. He was engulfed in a shell of red flames. He laughed out loud, drunk on power. The women around him fled in terror.

Rinn turned to Cat, who cowered behind her. "Help get everyone to safety."

Cat nodded her reply and dashed after the fleeing women. A general cry of alarm went up in the Temple, throngs of revelers stampeded for the doors, grabbing their clothes and hiding their faces. Rinn focused only on the High Priest and the altar behind him. She advanced a step forward. "You are no servant of Aedis, false priest."

"His powers are mine to command." The fiery priest gloated. "A gift for my years of faithful service." He grabbed the jewel-encrusted staff leaning against the altar, the symbol of his office. It burst into flames at his touch.

Rinn advanced another step, almost level with him. "You're being used."

"I am the hand of god." Caena sneered, burning with conceit.

Watch out! Rinn could hear Cat calling inside her head. Rinn spun and raised her barrier just in time to deflect a brutal blow from behind. In the green glow of her shield, Rinn recognized Haril, the professional soldier who had accompanied her earlier. He launched an assault against her barrier, probing it for weakness. The High Priest laughed as the two danced. He hurled a ball of fire at Rinn's back. It crackled and sizzled against the green triangles and swirls of her shield. Rinn could feel the heat of it on the back of her neck. She jabbed at Haril with her spear, but the warrior had hardened reflexes. He swatted her weapon away, careful to avoid her spear's flaming metal tip. The High Priest cast several more fireballs at Rinn's barrier, the heat growing steadily more intense.

Rinn rolled to one side, trying to get out from between the warrior and the priest. Haril tracked with her, continuously engaging her shield and keeping her spear at bay. The exchanged several more blows, their skills equally matched. In a desperate move, Rinn slid both her hands up her weapon just below the spear point. Her opponent had no way of deflecting her weapon without touching its burning metal tip. Rinn slashed with her spear head, aiming at Haril's sword. Instinctively, he attempted to parry the blow. Rinn reversed her grip and swung the long wooden handle of her spear around, catching him squarely on the temple with a powerful strike. He sank to one knee and his sword clattered to the ground. Rinn shoved him over with a kick and leveled her spear at his throat.

Undaunted, the High Priest continued his fiery onslaught. In his blind rage, he scorched the parquet floor and set rows of pews ablaze. The Temple had largely emptied, except for a few straggling guards and two boys standing transfixed in a doorway. The High Priest paced around the altar hurling balls of fire, as if he was delivering a grand sermon. "Your pitiful magic cannot defeat me. I am the will of Aedis. I am his chosen one. Your fake Sigillum tricks are nothing to me."

At the mention of the word Sigillum, Rinn could detect a glimmer of regret in the eyes of the man at her feet. The priest rained down hotter, larger fireballs. Her shield absorbed them, but the pain was intense. Rinn expanded her shield until it protected both her and Haril. Life and death hung in the balance. Rinn hated killing senselessly, so she decided to take a big risk. She raised her spear and reached out a hand to Haril. He accepted it and she hauled him off the floor. Their eyes met, his steel gaze locked with her ice blue stare. He lowered his head and hands. Cat appeared in the doorway near the two cowering boys. Rinn smiled as everything fell into place.

Rinn turned her attention to the High Priest. "I am no false magician, vile priest, and this is not the will of the gods." She moved protectively to the doorway, beckoning for the boys and Cat to join her. Cat urged the reluctant pair forward, through the fire to Rinn's barrier. She enclosed them inside her protective shield. Grus eyed Haril warily, but the big soldier remained passive, watching Rinn in expectation. The High Priest buffeted Rinn's barrier with jets of fire from his fingertips. Rinn sweated from pain, but she refused to back down. She focused her will on the priest, expanding her shield outward, pushing away the burning pews and smoldering debris. Roaring fire and smoke consumed the interior of the building, the High Priest laughing above it all.

Rinn pounded the floor with the butt of her spear. "I am Sabrinn Sevralis, and I am the Sigillum. You have been deceived, priest. Giving in to your selfish, petty desires is never the will of the gods." Caena's expression changed. Cracks of doubt could be seen behind his eyes. He hurled fire at Rinn with renewed fury. The Temple was a conflagration of red and yellow flames. Rinn's barrier held, shielding the others from the heat. Rinn felt like every nerve was aflame. She gritted her teeth and made her demand. "Tell me who you serve, sorcerer."

"I serve the gods of Sevria!" The High Priest professed with zeal.

"Then it is too late for you." Rinn closed her eyes and concentrated, forcing her shield outward. She pushed against the white alabaster pillars and stained-glass windows. Stones cracked and glass shattered as her shield strengthened and expanded. Rinn relived the sensation she felt at the Vallum, someone or something was adding power to her magic. This time, it was not reckless, it was gentle and persistent, like the touch of a friend. Rinn could control the energy. She raised her hands and pushed away, her shield solidifying into an impenetrable shell grinding away at the floor and crushing the walls. With a deafening sound, the dome ceiling split and massive stone blocks rained down into the Temple's interior. The High Priest screamed as he was buried under blue mosaic ceiling tiles. Dust clouds smothered his flames. Rinn did not stop, she stretched her shield until she toppled the glistening white spires and flattened the wooden additions built onto the structure. When the Temple of Aedis had been reduced to a pile of white rubble, Rinn stepped up to the only thing that remained: the altar. She wrapped her shield around it and spoke the Sigilllum word "onlithe". The pulsing blue magic that permeated the altar would not crack, it hissed back loudly with the ferocity of a deadly gale.

"Cat." Rinn reached out to her sister. "Give me your paw." Her sister hesitantly extended her paw and Rinn took ahold of it. "Say the word with me." Rinn called out. "Say 'onlithe'."

Together the two girls cried out in unison. The sound of roaring winds from the altar changed to high pitch cries. Rinn and Cat repeated the word and the altar trembled. A single crack appeared in it, bleeding an unnatural yellow liquid. Rinn surrounded the altar with her shield. She constricted her barrier, crushing the stone altar. The altar's magic thrashed and bucked against her like an unbroken stallion. Rinn firmly held onto the image of her hometown, how it used to be, in her head. She wanted her home back so much more fervently than this magic wanted to pollute it, and that was the tipping point. Rinn's power overwhelmed the defiled altar, pulverizing it into a mass of gravel. Just like with the struma, she compressed her barrier until the altar was only a speck, and then nothingness.

Rinn fell to her knees, exhausted. "It's over." Cat sat beside her, propping her up. Daylight streaked through the dusty clouds that hung over the remains of the Temple. Haril and the two teenage boys with mouths agape stared at the destruction all around them.

"What happened to the high priest?" Grus stuttered.

Rinn shook her head.

"What was that stuff inside the altar?" Tavin croaked.

"Unholy magic." Rinn wheezed, trying to regain her composure. Her spear was spent, its wooden handle charred and metal tip a smear of rust. Even the ends of Rinn's hair were singed with soot.

"How did it get there?" Tavin boggled.

"That's what I'm trying to find out." Rinn attempted to stand, but she was wobbly on her feet. Haril silently assisted her. Rinn heard a stirring in the rubble. The High Priest was still alive? She did not have time to investigate, a contingent of soldiers charged up the steps to the edge of the Temple remains.

"Citizens." An officer called out. "In the name of the law, stand down."

Rinn begged to Cat. "Get us out of here."

Cat gave her an agonizing reply. "I can't. We don't have any magic left."

Rinn knew, the destruction of the Temple had left her utterly drained. The soldiers advanced, picking their way through the debris, thirty or forty men armed with swords and spears. Rinn could not fight them all, she had no choice but to surrender. She did not worry about Grus and Haril, they were soldiers and would be treated fairly. Imprisoning Catherine would be as effective as trying to bottle sunlight. But Tavin, the poor boy from the dungeons, would be left to rot in another dark cell.

"Haril." The commanding officer shouted. "What's the meaning of this?"

The muscular mercenary stood with Rinn. His jaw tensed as he answered. "High Priest Caena has betrayed us. He's in league with sinister forces. I witnessed his dark magic myself."

"Liar!" A voice cried from the rubble. High Priest Caena had survived. "Arrest him. Arrest all of them for the destruction of the holy Temple of Aedis."

Chapter 12

W ary guards surrounded Rinn and her companions, weapons drawn. Rinn surrendered her worthless spear. The soldiers prodded everyone forward, out of the rubble and onto the grassy lawn surrounding the destroyed Temple. Iron shackles were slapped onto Rinn, Cat, and Tavin. Haril and Grus were hauled before their superior officer who conferred with the battered High Priest. Rinn looked over at Tavin cowering in his pitiful tattered robes and sandals. She could not let it end like this.

A sound like thunder rumbled in the distance, growing steadily closer. Like a prayer answered by the gods, a stampede of horses stormed into the line of soldiers. In the center of the pack, urging them on, rode Rinn's father on his trusty warhorse Bayard. Calder glided behind him on a sleek stallion the color of his hair. Lutra galloped with them on a dappled, chestnut roan. Soldiers scattered in every direction as the stampede broke through their ranks. With a deft hand, Marshal swept Rinn off the ground and deposited her on the saddle behind him. Calder snatched up the prisoner and Lutra gleefully grabbed onto Cat. She meowed happily and buried herself in his arms.

As they headed away, Rinn yelled to her father. "Turn around. We have to get Grus and Haril." Marshal veered his horse to the right and circled back.

85

"Which ones are they?" He asked, reaching out to grab a passing horse's halter. He guided the horse alongside his own.

Rinn pointed. "Those two, standing near the priest."

Marshal snapped his reins and the two horses accelerated. Calder and Lutra turned their steeds and followed. Marshal barreled at the captain and the High Priest. Caena retreated in fear, but the captain stood unflinching. Marshal skidded his horse to a stop a few paces from the commander.

"Stand down, Triari." Marshal ordered. "Equites rights."

The captain was tight lipped, but reasonable. He was a middle-aged man in stout metal armor with a hefty sword. "You're not part of the regular army, Equis."

"I am Marshal, from Brigantum." Marshal answered succinctly.

"I am Proculo." The captain replied in a terse but interested tone. "You're a long way from home, horseman."

"None of us need to die today." Marshal offered. "Allow us to take those two and we'll be on our way."

"Haril?" The captain appraised the muscular warrior warily. "What do you want with him?"

"He has business with my daughter." Marshal mouthed stoically.

Proculo smirked. "The so-called Sigillum." He eyed Rinn who was wearily clinging to her father. "She's not exactly what the old stories describe."

"History rarely paints an honest picture." Marshal said wryly.

"True." Proculo grinned. He surveyed the wreckage of the Temple. "Her talents certainly are undeniable."

"She has a tendency to overreact." Marshal conceded. "She is a teenager."

The commander laughed. Turning back to his troops he called out. "I release Haril and Grus from service. They will accompany the Equites."

"Thank you, Triari." Marshal dipped his head slightly.

The incensed High Priest surged forward. "I will not allow this. Arrest that girl and all these men at once. I am in charge here."

Proculo cast a long glance over the rubble. "You seem to have lost your church, priest, and with it your strangle hold on this city. I am displeased with the lewd display of patrons pouring out of your service earlier. The Legion will be taking control until this matter can be further investigated."

"Heresy!" Caena screamed as he was dragged away.

Proculo pointed a finger to Rinn. "You owe me one."

Rinn laughed to herself, nodding appreciatively. She would remember Proculo's name, an honest soldier in a world of deceit. Marshal handed the reins of the horse he was leading to Haril. The mercenary climbed onto the horse, riding bareback. He pulled Grus up behind him. The commander motioned for a guard to remove the shackles from Rinn and her friends. Marshal saluted to Proculo.

"Where are you headed?" The commander asked, returning the salute.

"West." Marshal replied.

"Be on your guard." Proculo advised. "There is an urchin army prowling the plains. They have been bold enough to attack the city from time to time."

"My daughter mentioned the same." Marshal nodded. He turned his horse to leave, but the commander added one more inquiry.

"We heard rumors of someone blasting a hole through the Vallum." The commander's stern eyes seemed amused as he asked Rinn. "That was you, wasn't it?"

Rinn's face flushed and her head shrank into her shoulders. "Maybe." Marshal grinned as he snapped the reins and the four horses galloped away. Rinn cast one long glance back at the wreckage of the Temple of Aedis. She was certain she did the right thing, just not the right way.

She would have to be more careful in the future, show more restraint. She hugged her father as the four horses rode on.

::

Marshal met up with Molo and the dwarves at the city walls. The sun was setting low in the western hills, and shadows stretched across the plains. The soldiers at the city gate had allowed the riders passage through without question. The dwarves greeted the remaining party members warmly, but Molo had a sterner expression.

"How did everything go?" The quarter giant asked, palming Clive in his left hand.

"We heard quite a ruckus." Mafic confessed.

Rinn did not know how to explain all the destruction she had caused.

"The Temple of Aedis needs remodeling." Marshal quipped.

"She levelled it, didn't she?" Molo said dryly.

"Pretty much." Marshal admitted.

"She can't keep destroying everything in her path." Molo fumed.

"I'm right here." Rinn pointed to herself in anger. She hated it when people talked about her in her presence.

"I'm sorry, m'lady." Molo apologized. "But we can't march into Peleon and blow things up. We'll have entire Legions after our heads."

"I didn't come here to blow things up." Rinn insisted, feeling flush.

Marshal intervened. "Now is not the time or place." He wheeled his horse around and headed in the direction of the hot springs. "We have to meet up with the others. I don't want Feena spending any more time alone with Sionne than she has to."

Calder and Lutra passed the giant solemnly on horseback. Haril and Molo exchanged uneasy glances. Molo sighed and eventually fell in line behind the dwarves and horses heading west, away from the city.

::

Rinn's army camped out in the rocky terrain just beyond the hot springs. The teenage boys pitched the tents while the girls prepared food. Marshal took Cat out hunting. Molo and Haril chopped firewood, and the dwarves scouted the area for threats.

"Sionne was a perfect gentleman." Feena told Rinn as they cooked together. "The hot springs were so inviting, that I wanted to take a dip. Sionne stood guard while I bathed. He made sure no one tried to spy in on me."

Sionne's ears turned red as he tried to ignore the conversation. Lutra smacked him on the head with a tent pole. "Watch it!" Sionne rebuked, but Lutra feigned innocence, until it happened a second time. Grus helped Tavin set up his tent, the young scribe had no idea what he was doing. Rinn idly stirred the contents of an iron cooking pot hanging over the campfire. She considered the two boys who recently joined her expedition. They could not be more dissimilar—one proud and fit with the promise of a powerful, muscular frame; the other thin, gaunt and hunched over. Tavin seemed so fragile to Rinn, like a new hatchling. His dark brown hair hung in his face as he fumbled with the tent poles, sweat beaded on his forehead. But his eyes, as gray as storm clouds, watched Grus intently with a keen intellect that piqued Rinn's curiosity.

Feena interrupted Rinn's thoughts. "So, how did everything go in town? I see you brought some new friends."

Before Rinn could answer, Grus asked. "Who are all these people? I thought you and your father traveled alone."

Rinn stood up and brushed off her skirts. "Let me make some introductions." She pointed to her three friends. "This is Feena, Lutra, and Sionne." The redheaded boy smiled mockingly. Rinn turned to the newcomers. "This is my childhood friend, Grus. And this is Tavin the scribe."

Lutra abandoned his tent pole. "You're a scribe? You write books?" He eagerly asked the intimidated boy.

"I read books." Tavin corrected. "And I copy them."

"But you can teach me to write." Lutra flourished with an invisible pen.

"I suppose." Tavin replied.

Grus' frustration finally burst free. "Would someone tell me what's going on here? Why are you traveling with dwarves and giants? And what in the name of the gods happened back at the Temple?"

Feena peered at Rinn innocently. "What happened?"

Grus would not be quelled. "She demolished an entire building. She was aglow with green flames." He pointed accusingly at Rinn. "You're not the Rinn I know. Who are you?"

"She's the Sigillum." Tavin blurted out.

Grus turned to him without comprehension. "What's a Sigillum?"

"Sit down." Rinn tried to ease the situation. "Calm down and I'll explain everything." The boys set down their tent poles and sat in a semi-circle around Rinn. Feena joined them. Rinn felt like a tutor lecturing a group of pupils. She sat down on the grass. "It's like this: for a long time the Sigilla have been the protectors of the Empire. They appeared whenever Sevria was in danger. They were great warriors who could use magic."

"And they were always women." Tavin pointed out.

"Yes." Rinn agreed. "My grandmother was a Sigilla who served the Emperor Tarandus. Her name was Virago."

Grus seemed puzzled. "But, she started the rebellion against the Emperor. She tried to rule in his place."

"Wrong." Tavin remarked. "Virago was trying to keep the Curia from taking over the Empire."

Grus argued. "But Tarandus had no heirs."

Rinn corrected him. "Tarandus had two children, both girls, and Virago was their mother." Grus seemed alarmed by this revelation.

"The Emperor was married to the heretic Virago?" Grus became agitated.

"She was not a heretic." Tavin refuted. "She was trying to put her daughters on the throne."

"And they killed her for it." Rinn admitted. Lutra listened impassionedly and Feena fought back tears.

"Virago died in battle as a traitor." Grus contended.

"She was a Sigillum." Rinn said soberly. "I doubt she died on the battlefield."

"Why not?" Grus demanded.

"Because Rinn's a Sigillum, too, idiot." Tavin rebuked Grus harshly. "Didn't you see what she did at the Temple? Can you imagine that kind of power unleashed in combat? The Legions would not stand a chance."

"Then how did she die?" Grus' question was laced with uncertainty.

"She was murdered." Rinn forced out the answer, fighting back bile. "The Curia somehow captured her and used dark magic to kill her."

"How do you know this?" Grus did not seem to want to know the answer.

"Because I'm her grand-daughter." Rinn confessed.

"I knew it!" Tavin sprang to his feet, pointing. "You're heir to the Empire."

"What?" Grus, Lutra, and Sionne gasped in unison. Feena cried giddy tears. Rinn tried to hide her embarrassment, and she wondered why. She should not be ashamed of her birth-right, she should be proud. But her Empire was a mess, racked by civil war, political intrigue, and dark magicks. Who would want to be the inheritor of that?

Molo and Haril walked in, carrying heavy armloads of chopped wood. They dutifully deposited them next to the campfire. Molo frowned at everyone sitting around while the tents remained half-constructed.

"Lazy teenagers." He grumbled.

Rinn exchanged hasty looks with her friends who stifled nervous laughter. Everyone went back to work. The rest of the story would have to wait.

Chapter 13

T he next morning Rinn's army broke camp and tracked west, following a well-used country road. Marshal still did not want to risk the Imperial Highways, for fear of running across large patrols. This lazy route to the capital would add an extra week to their travels, but Rinn did not mind. The countryside of Sevria was what she missed most during her exile in the Rustic Lands. The vibrant midmorning sun danced in the roadside blossoms, and a delicate breeze tickled her cheeks. Rinn breathed in the warm, fragrant air of home.

Cat entertained herself molesting wildflowers, especially the rows of foxglove growing in the ditches that flanked the road. Lutra and Grus struck up a lively conversation. Lutra explained that the people living in the Rustic Lands were not all barbarians, and Grus argued that all Sevrians were not tyrannical despots. Tavin trailed behind, listening intently to both opinions.

Feena asked Marshal a question. "How long is the journey to Peleon?"

Marshal rode on Bayard, leading the horse train carrying their supplies. He bent down to answer Feena. "Should take about three weeks, if the weather holds."

"Weather?" Feena puzzled.

Rinn explained. "In Sevria, summertime rain can be pretty fierce."

"I know." Feena agreed. "We had that heavy rain on our way to Viburna."

"That was nothing." Rinn smirked. "Summerstorms can flatten trees and drown valleys. Entire buildings have been reduced to rubble by the winds."

"That sounds awful." Feena grimaced.

"It's not as bad as it sounds." Marshal relaxed his reins. "Summerstorms don't happen very often and when they do, it's easy to see them coming."

Rinn held her hands over her head. "The sky turns a sick, green color and the temperature drops. If you see that, you need to take cover." Feena shivered at the thought. Rinn chuckled. The party traveled until past noon and then stopped for lunch. They spread out on the crest of a small hill not far from the road. Feena divvied out food from their stores while Cat hunted birds—her ability to teleport gave her an absolutely unfair advantage. Soon, the smell of roasting bird filled the air. Rinn reclined with her lunch, watching the clouds. She felt a sense of peace she thought she had long forgotten. Conversation was light as everyone ate. Rinn noticed that even Sionne participated. It was nice to see him included.

The only person sitting alone was Molo. Rinn decided to go over and find out what was vexing him. As she approached, the giant spoke. "Someone's coming." Clive rested on the ground nearby, pointing west. Rinn scanned the hillside and saw two boys in the distance heading toward them.

"Who are they?" Rinn squinted. The boys looked like farmhands, one carried a pitchfork and the other a hand sickle. Their clothes were dirty and in desperate need of patching.

"War orphans." Molo lamented. Rinn watched as the two boys circled the campfire like skittish mice. They eyed the food longingly. Everyone in the camp regarded the pair with suspicion, Marshal even had one hand on his sword. Rinn was not threatened in any way. She approached the newcomers, Cat followed at her side.

Rinn gestured a friendly greeting. "Would you boys like some food?"

The older of the two boys spoke, his vowels long and drawn out. "How much can you give us?"

"How much did you need?" Rinn asked, curiously.

"All of it." The boy responded. Rinn did not detect any hostility in his voice or expression. Surely, they would not try to steal food from a party this size. The boys were outnumbered six to one. Unconsciously, Rinn scanned the surroundings, anticipating an ambush—she had spent too many days being hunted by Clanmorris. But the boys seemed to be alone. Rinn wondered how desperate they could be.

Sionne broke the awkward silence. "Don't be greedy. Just take what you can eat right now."

"Oh. Okay." The older boy answered vacantly. He sat down near the campfire, the younger boy joined him. The others scooted around to make room for them. Sionne handed each boy a stick of roasted bird. Rinn was stunned by his generosity, but then she remembered how many months he had spent alone and hungry. The boys ate sloppily, but not greedily. Everyone sat in silence, watching them. Rinn offered them berries and mushrooms from Feena's pack. The older boy thanked her. The younger boy gobbled the berries but spit out the raw mushrooms. After they finished their food, they quietly stood and turned to leave.

The older boy paused. "Thanks." He said to no one in particular. They walked down the hillside, heading southwest.

"What's wrong with those two?" Grus asked.

"They're orphans." Marshal explained. "Their parents were probably killed in the fighting and now they have to look after themselves."

"Why don't they go to the city and get food?" Grus puzzled. "The Curia distributes grain to people in need every week."

"Technically, they're not citizens." Marshal replied. "They aren't old enough to qualify and they have no one to speak on their behalf." Grus was nonplused. He stared in astonishment at the boys walking down the hill.

Rinn rose and started off after them.

"Where're you going?" Her father asked, trying to rise.

"I'm going to follow them." Rinn admitted. "They can't live far."

"Then what?" Molo challenged. "What's going to happen when you get there?"

"I'll find out more about them." Rinn confessed with uncertainty. "They surely aren't alone. There might be others out there that need help."

"Rinn, think before you act." Marshal cautioned. "What's the best thing we can do for them? Isn't going to Peleon and stopping this useless war what we really need to be doing?"

Rinn felt herself getting flustered. "I can't just sit by while others starve. That boy wanted more food and I need to know why." She gathered her spear and travel pack. Cat bounced along after her. Calder and Lutra rose to accompany her, Sionne grudgingly went along. Rinn thanked them all with a smile. Molo hauled himself off the ground.

"I'll go, too." He grumbled. "Someone has to keep her out of trouble."

"Thank you, my friend." Marshal relaxed a bit. Haril attempted to rise, but Marshal laid a hand on his arm. With an almost imperceptible shake of his head, he mouthed the word no. Feena and the dwarves began to break camp.

Frustrated, Grus threw down the rest of his lunch and chased after Rinn and the others.

::

The orphan boys walked further than Rinn expected. She had to keep checking her surroundings to make sure she could find her way back to the others. After what seemed like more than an hour of walking, the boys headed into a hallow of overgrown brush and tangled vines. Molo placed a hand on Rinn's shoulder.

"We've come far enough. We should go back." His words did not sound like a request.

"What's down there?" Rinn tried to see past the dense overgrowth.

"Avius Arx, the lost citadel." Molo answered grimly.

"What do you mean lost?" Lutra questioned.

"It has changed hands many times." Molo seemed distracted.

"I've never heard of a fortress near Viburna." Grus said sourly.

"It's a relic from the first conquest of Sevria." Molo explained. "But it proved to be indefensible, built on low ground. When Lucan's Grove was discovered, the castle was abandoned." Rinn did not quite follow the ramifications of Molo's description. For her benefit he added. "Only fools would stay here, the fortress has fallen to every attacker that bothered to take it. It's no better than a swinging door."

"Why not tear it down completely?" Grus pondered.

"It has historical significance." Molo admitted. "It's one of the few remaining structures built by the Emperor Ichneumon."

"The son of Sevrius? The one who founded the Empire?" Tavin gasped. Rinn grappled with the realization that these ruins would be as old as the Empire itself.

"The boys are gone." Cat pointed out. Rinn hastily looked around, she did not see the orphans anywhere. Molo held up Clive and cursed.

"We're surrounded." He grumbled.

The teenagers immediately drew their weapons and Rinn readied her new spear. She turned to her sister. "Cat, go see how many of them are out there. But, be careful." Cat smiled with her whiskers. With a wink, she was gone. The rest of the party formed a tight circle with weapons pointing out on all sides. It did not take Tavin long to understand the tactic. Rinn heard rustling in the underbrush first, and then laughter and hooting. Children of all ages emerged from the bushes wielding every manner of weapon. Most held farm implements: hoes, rakes, sickles, and pitchforks. A choice few brandished actual swords and axes. The youngest, barely older than toddlers resorted to shaking pointed sticks or wooden spoons.

Rinn held out her spear defensively and faced off with a bright-eyed rogue caught somewhere between adolescence and manhood. He playfully pointed his sword at Rinn, a sword clearly stolen from the Legion.

"Welcome to our castle." His hazel-colored eyes twinkled. "Shall we dance?" He advanced a step toward Rinn, she slid her back foot out and sunk into a warrior's stance. However, Calder stepped protectively in front of her, his sword held low. The bright-eyed boy bounced eagerly, keenly studying Calder's calm but serious poise. The boy slid forward, slashing twice with his sword. On the third strike, his sword went flying from his hands, sticking into the ground nearby. Calder lowered his blade and remained motionless.

The children in the crowd gave a humiliating "ooh."

The boy frowned and picked up his sword. "That's a neat trick, mate." He sheathed his sword. "You'll have to teach it to me." The mood in the crowd relaxed, kids put away their weapons and murmured to each other. Molo stepped forward, confronting the lead boy.

"What are all these children doing here?" He demanded, holding Clive.

"Aren't you a big one?" The lead boy whistled.

"Who are you?" Rinn asked.

"I'm Reicio." The lead boy bowed with one hand out. "And this is the Urchin Army." He motioned to all the children, they returned the gesture with wild hoots and hollers and shaking of weapons. The littlest ones ran around wildly, barking like feral dogs.

"Leave at once." Molo fumed. "You don't belong here."

"We don't belong anywhere." Reicio replied. "We are the rejects of Sevria. Most of us lost our families in the war. When you don't have parents, it's hard to get by. Viburna became too dangerous for us, so we left. And we ended up here." He finished his speech with a flourish of his hand.

Cat materialized next to Rinn, she looked absolutely exhausted. "I can't count that high." She whined. Reicio and the children were startled by her sudden appearance, except one girl with coal-black eyes who studied her intently.

"What is that?" Reicio stammered, pointing at Catherine as he backed away. Rinn capitalized on the disruption. She thumped her spear on the ground.

"I am Rinn, and this is my sister, Cat." She called out. "We followed two boys who came to our camp asking for food. Have you seen them?"

One of the older girls in the crowd whispered in Reicio's ear. A broad grin broke across his face. "Why didn't you say you were friends of Hak and Gile? Anyone with food is welcome here." The crowd of children parted to allow him through. He gestured to a gap in the tangled hedges. "Come inside, and we'll talk." He ducked into the hole and was gone.

Chapter 14

R inn sat on the floor inside the ancient fortress. Barrel-vaulted ceilings of rough-cut stones loomed overhead. Thin streams of light slanted in from tiny windows high on the walls. A neglected firepit tried its best to hold back the shadowy darkness. Reicio sat on the stone floor, on some sort of animal pelt. The children, nearly two hundred of them, crowded behind him. Rinn's companions sat protectively in a circle around her, all except Molo, who was too large to fit through the hedge entranceway. He waited impatiently outside.

"Tell us about your unusual friend." Reicio inclined his head to Cat.

Rinn regarded her sister. Cat was tracking some unseen thing on the ceiling. Rinn lowered her voice, trying to sound confident. "Cat is a Margot from across the ocean."

"How can she?" Reicio waved his hand in the air.

"Disappear?" Rinn finished his thought.

"Yes." Reicio nodded.

"Margot can use magic." Rinn revealed.

"Can you?" Reicio's hazel eyes held a deep longing. "Do magic?"

Rinn did not answer with words. She held out her spear and whispered the word "ahebbe". Letting it go, the spear hung in the air, before it slowly floated to the ground. The older kids gasped, the younger kids pointed, laughed, and clapped. One pair of dark eyes in the crowd focused on Rinn with burning curiosity.

"Is that all you can do?" Reicio inquired.

Rinn shook her head no.

Reicio accepted her answer. He leaned forward with an expression of urgency. "Join us. Help us. Most of us haven't eaten in days. The littlest ones collapse after a few days without food." A somber shadow fell over him. "Sometimes they don't wake up." Fighting back emotion, he crawled toward Rinn. Calder placed a hand on his blade, but relaxed when he saw Reicio grab her hands in desperation. "Please, help us. We're dying and no one cares."

Rinn's composure cracked, tears welled in her eyes. These children were fighting for their lives, and the Empire was fighting back. All these kids wanted was a warm meal and a place to sleep, maybe someone to love them. Surprised at her own reaction, Rinn reach out and hugged the boy. Memories of Sionne flooded over her—the redheaded boy's shoulders hanging low as he walked alone into the snow, helpless, hungry, and dejected. She vowed to never let that happen again.

"I'll help you." Rinn promised through her sobs.

As if summoned by his memory, Sionne spoke. "How? Where are we going to get enough food for all these kids?"

A sandy-headed boy in the crowd broke the tension. "We could eat the giant." All the kids laughed. Rinn could not help chuckling herself. When she saw Cat with a pensive look on her face, she knew she had to say something.

"No one's eating Molo." She asserted. Some of the children actually moaned in disapproval.

"What can we do?" Sionne seemed prickly. "Food doesn't exactly grow on trees."

"Actually." Rinn smirked. "It does." A plan was swirling inside her head. Like colors applied to a canvas, the picture was becoming clear. Rinn rose and made her pronouncement. "You need food. And Viburna needs you."

"Viburna hates us." A restive shout came from the crowd.

"They hate your stealing and raiding." Rinn retaliated.

"We can't earn money." Reicio objected. "We don't have anything Viburna wants."

"Yes, you do." Rinn assured him. "Much has changed in the last week. The city needs rebuilding, and you are here, next to their greatest resource. Stop your attacks on the city, turn your axes and swords to the forest. Harvest the wood, we can teach you how. Trade it to the town in exchange for food."

"No one will buy wood from urchins." Reicio insisted.

Rinn reached out a hand and pulled him from the floor. "Not urchins. Druids."

"What?" Reicio seemed confused.

"The forest is yours. You are the new Druids." Rinn laid a hand on his shoulder. "Go to Viburna, ask for Proculo. He's in control of the city now. Tell him I sent you, he'll listen."

"But." Reicio seemed unconvinced. "We aren't Druids, I don't think Lucus is going to approve. No one cuts trees without performing his rites."

"Actually." Rinn smiled. "I think he'll be okay with it."

"How can you be so sure?" Reicio demanded.

"I've met him." Rinn rolled her spear in her fingers.

::

The next few days were a whirlwind of activity. Lutra and Marshal ventured into the forest with Reicio and the older children to teach them the art of logging. Feena, Sionne, and Molo delivered food from their larder to the smallest orphans. The delighted youngsters ate greedily and crawled all over Molo as if he were some great plaything. Rinn spent long hours spear-fishing in a nearby river to help collect food for the orphan settlement. A thoroughly exhausted Cat delivered piles of freshly caught rabbit and quail.

Rinn watched with pride as the first logs were hauled out of the forest. Mafic and Felsic built sturdy carts to bear the heavy load. Haril, Grus, Lutra, and Tavin joined the team of children tugging on long ropes. With so many hands, the work was possible. Rinn knew this would succeed, the forest would provide a livelihood for these orphans, and in return, the children would come to honor and respect the place they depended upon. Viburna would be well served and the forest cared for. These kids truly would become the next generation of Druids.

On the third day of harvesting, the first load of timber was ready to be sold. The oldest children carefully chopped slender logs and younger children dutifully stripped away the leaves and twigs. Rinn knew the time to move on had come, if she stayed much longer, she may become too attached to these orphans. Reicio already followed her with his eyes, his interest in her growing every day. One ten-year-old girl quietly trailed behind Rinn like a puppy. Her name was Dempsi, and she rarely spoke. But the girl's deep-set eyes burned with curiosity and intelligence, eyes as dark as the black mane of hair on her head. Rinn did not want to say good-bye to any of these children, but her mission must come first. Peleon awaited her arrival.

Rinn returned to the campsite where her friends remained, none of them wanted to sleep in an overgrown fortress packed with unruly children. The adults were away, prepping the logs for transport. Lutra, Feena, and Cat sat by the campfire, joking and laughing. Felsic and Mafic worked nearby, delicately decorating the heartwood staff with intricate carvings of leaves and vines. Rinn realized the gift Lucus had given her had been meant for someone else. Reicio was the next druid leader, and he needed a symbol of his office. Rinn would present the staff to him when she departed. As she drew closer, Rinn noticed a newcomer reclining against a tree stump. He was dressed in tattered black strips of cloth and sipped a strange, dark liquid from a leather mug. He looked up and smiled at Rinn with his tattooed teeth: Yallakh.

::

"How did you find us, assassin?" Marshal squeezed the hilt of the sword hanging at his side. Word of Yallakh's arrival had brought adults rushing to the campsite. Molo held Clive between himself and the tattooed man, and Haril studied the stranger warily.

Yallakh flung back his head in amusement. "How could I not? Your daughter left a swath of destruction as wide as the open sea." He winked to Rinn. She pushed down her own bitter feelings. Yallakh prattled on. "I followed your trail across the Rustic Lands to the breech in the Vallum. That was some glorious devastation, I haven't been so entertained in years." He fixed his eyes only on Rinn. "But when you razed the city's temple, my heart melted." He mockingly folded his hands across his chest. "You are the gift this ugly world deserves."

Marshal threatened. "We've had enough of you, villain. Leave us, before you find yourself in a pit so deep you'll never escape."

"Temper." Yallakh tsked. "Such animosity when I've come all this way to help."

"We don't want your help." Molo seethed, Clive's eye wavered with magic.

Yallakh stared him down. "I'm not afraid of you. Any of you." He whirled around passing his bony finger over everyone until it stopped at Rinn. "Except her." The corners of his mouth twisted into a smile. "You could kill me with a thought, and it's intoxicating. I didn't even know I could die. But now I am certain I can, and it fills me with the urge to live. I'm drawn to you like a moth to the flame. I can't let you out of my sight—my doom, my dear, my leige." He knelt down low before Rinn, his hands held out wide in supplication.

Rinn choked back nausea, she hated his theatrics. "Get up." She demanded. Yallakh rose, politely bowing his head. "What is it you want?"

"Only to help, my queen." Yallakh's words were the sweetest hemlock. "You do not know the enemy you fight, but I do."

Once again, Rinn was seized by this vile man's insight. The polite smile on his lips was as repulsive as the blood-ink tattoos that covered his body, but if he had knowledge that would help Rinn save Sevria, she would listen. "Speak your piece."

The corners of Yallakh's mouth curled impossibly high. He straightened and addressed the entire camp, like some grotesque troubadour. "Following my heart's desire, I journeyed into the nearby city. I visited the broken grove where the sacred trees bowed to my queen. I walked among the exalted remains of the temple she laid low. And I discovered the connection. I knew my queen was righteous and her enemy most foul."

"Who?" Rinn insisted. "Who is it?"

"Elves." Yallakh drew out the word, his eyes consumed with madness.

Marshal distracted the assassin away from his daughter, who was clearly unsettled. "We know you have a personal history with the Elves, but I do not see any signs of their involvement in this. This is a Sevrian affair."

"Then you are a fool." Yallakh slinked close to Marshal, who remained taut, but unflinching. "I know elfcraft when I sense it. My skin burns with longing when I am near their vile magic. And it was there, in the temple, in the grove, the profane magic of the Elves."

Rinn tried to process Yallakh's information, but it made no sense. Elves were not creatures of evil, they were mystical, holy beings from a faraway land. They had no quarrel with Sevria. Elves were almost immortal, and did not mingle in the affairs of the lesser races. Rinn brushed the curly blond hair out of her face, trying to clear her mind. "What do the Elves want with Sevria?"

"Only its destruction." Yallakh pulled his lips tight in seriousness.

"We've heard enough of your propaganda, assassin." Molo planted himself squarely in front of Rinn like a palisade wall. "We will not be pulled into your personal vendetta."

"Yet you walk willingly into it." Yallakh mocked. A great hush fell over the camp. Rinn had no idea how to respond to Yallakh's accusations. What if the Elves were somehow involved? What did it mean? The teenagers glanced at each other nervously, while the adults maintained their rigid, defensive positions. Eventually, Yallakh broke away, and strutted toward the forest. "Heed my words, my queen. The Elves lay traps for you even as we speak." He cautioned before evaporating into the trees.

Chapter 15

A misty rain fell as Rinn and her companions prepared to leave. Yallakh's words hung over the party like the dark storm clouds gathering overhead. Felsic and Mafic had the foresight to construct two carriages to hasten the journey to the capital. With four horses at their disposal, they could make good speed. And, as Marshal pointed out, a caravan on the Imperial roads would draw less suspicion than a heavily armed group of travelers on foot. Rinn loaded her belongings into the wagon, including her heartwood staff—the one she had intended to give Reicio. Apparently, she did not understand the whims of the gods as well as she thought. Earlier in the day, the leader of the Urchin Army had been met in the forest by an unusual man in white robes. The curly-haired stranger gifted him a laurel wood staff and then vanished.

Heavy drops began to fall, evolving into a steady downpour. Confused thoughts plagued Rinn as she climbed aboard the wagon, dipping under the tarp that served as a rain shield. Marshal sat in the driver's seat, along with Lutra, who was learning how to handle a team of horses. A thoroughly soaked and miserable Cat huddled in the back of the wagon with the rest of the teens: Feena, Calder, Sionne, Tavin, and Grus. Haril piloted the other wagon which was occupied by Molo's oversized frame, two dwarves, and the bulk of their supplies.

A group of orphans came out to send them off. The oldest children braved the storm which was gradually growing stronger. Reicio stood alongside Rinn's carriage, as somber as a statue. "We're sorry to see you go." The braided laurel wood staff rested comfortably in his hand. He corrected himself. "I"m sorry to see you go."

Rinn mustered her courage. "I don't have a choice. I need to stop this senseless war."

"I believe you can do it. I just wish you didn't have to, that's all." For a moment, it looked as if he was going to reach his hand out, but he took a step backwards instead. Sadness settled into his hazel eyes. "Thank you, Rinn, for everything you've done for us. As you predicted, Proculo bought our first shipment of timber. The children have an abundance of food, for now. You showed us the way, and we're forever in your debt."

"Promise me one thing." Rinn choked on the words.

"Anything." A hopeful look crossed those hazel eyes.

"Visit the Grove at Viburna. Check on the trees to make sure they are doing okay, as a favor to me." Water from Rinn's wet hair trickled down her face, or maybe it was tears.

"As you wish." Reicio bowed deeply. While Marshal and Haril readied the horses for departure, a ten-year-old girl sprinted to the wagons. Dempsi climbed over the sideboards and wrapped her arms around Rinn's neck, her black hair hanging limply in the rain.

"Take me with you." She whispered to Rinn, her voice a half sob.

Rinn tried to wriggle out of the girl's grasp. "Dempsi. You don't know what you're asking. We're heading into war, people may get hurt or killed."

"I don't care." The dark-haired girl pursed her lips stubbornly.

"You belong here, with the other children." Rinn said in her most matronly voice.

"No, I don't." Dempsi cried defiantly. "I'm not like the other kids." She released her grasp around Rinn and stood in the torrential rain. Raising her fists to her head she pushed back her hair, contorting her face in concentration. When she finished, her black hair was perfectly dry, even in the downpour. In her hands she held a ball of water, hovering above her palms. Her black eyes pleaded with Rinn.

Cat reached a paw out of the wagon excitedly. "Oh! Do me next!"

::

The wagons rumbled down the sloppy, muddy trail. The rain had paused for the moment, but ominous skies threatened future storms. Rinn huddled under the tarp with her friends. Catherine cozied next to the new girl, her fur coat perfectly dry. The other teens regarded Dempsi with trepidation.

Sionne opened his loud mouth. "So, you're some kind of witch?"

"No." Dempsi rebutted. She shifted uneasily in her seat. "Maybe."

Sionne relaxed against a sideboard. "Well, hello, little witch. Welcome to the family of freaks."

"I'm not a freak." Lutra responded harshly.

"Shut up, flute-boy." Sionne snapped. Lutra took a swipe at him, but Sionne dodged.

Feena scooted closer to the girl. "Don't mind him. Sionne's always like that. He can be nice if he wants to, but usually he prefers the attention." Sionne looked stung. Feena put her hands in her lap. "So, I'm Feena. Tell me your name."

"Dempsi." The girl answered, her eyes downcast.

"Nice to meet you, Dempsi." Feena introduced everyone in the cart. "This is my brother Calder. This is our bard, Lutra. Tavin is a scribe, and Grus is a soldier from Viburna. Rinn's father, Marshal, is driving our carriage."

"I'm Cat." Cat said. She smiled at the little girl.

"Who's the big one?" Dempsi asked.

"Molo." Feena answered. "He's a quarter giant. His dwarven friends are brothers. Mafic has the black beard and Felsic's is brown. Haril is driving the other carriage, he's a soldier from Viburna, like Grus."

"Who's the rock?" Dempsi asked.

"Clive?" Feena replied. "He's not really a who, he's just a rock."

"Oh." The little girl seemed disappointed.

Rinn leaned closer. "Dempsi. How did you end up in the forest?"

The girl sat on her hands to keep them from fidgeting. "My Pa." Everyone listened. She haltingly told her tale. "I was in the market, playing in the fountain, when a guard saw me. . ." A slight pause. ". . . do things. The next day church soldiers came to my home and took me away." Dempsi drew her legs up and wrapped her arms around them. "Ma and Pa visited me in prison every day, telling me everything would be okay. When the church decided to send me away, Pa broke in and helped me escape. He lowered me over the city walls with a rope." She paused again. "But he was caught. The guards chased after me, so I ran. I never saw Pa again."

Grus stammered. "I never heard anything about this."

Rinn countered. "But you've seen the prison under the Temple. You know what they did there." Shock registered across Grus' face.

"I lost a year of my life down there." Tavin seethed. When Grus did not respond, a hush fell over the wagon. It occurred to Rinn how much animosity must exist between Tavin and Grus. It reminded her of the situation with Lutra and Sionne—they each had reasons to hate one another. Still, they had managed to work it out somehow, they even grudgingly shared a tent. Rinn needed to believe there was a way to bridge the gulf between Grus and Tavin. She would pay careful attention to them in the future.

Dempsi muttered under breath. "I won't go back to that prison. I'll destroy it first."

Cat mussed the little girl's hair. "Sweetie, Rinn already took care of it. The prison is gone."

"The Temple, too." Lutra grumbled.

Dempsi jerked her head up, wide eyes staring at Rinn. "You destroyed the entire Temple?"

Rinn nodded.

"With magic?" Dempsi's dark eyes flickered with admiration.

Rinn nodded again, biting her bottom lip. For the sake of everyone, she recounted the events of the last few days. They listened as she described her return to the city, the attack by street gangs, her imprisonment, and ultimate escape. Cat pointed out a few corrections. Rinn vividly detailed what occurred at Lucus' Grove—the slaying of the struma and the meeting with Nemus. She finished with her return to liberate Tavin. She made an account of her battle with the High Priest (omitting her combat with Haril) and the destruction of the Temple of Aedis. As she recounted these stories, she became aware that only one person had been with her the whole time: Cat. Her sister repeatedly threw herself in harm's way whenever Rinn needed her. Her heart swelled with love for her feline sister. She promised to give Cat an extra-thorough brushing that night.

::

The clouds broke the next morning, and the fields were a riot of colorful wildflowers and bright green grasses. The smell of growth filled the air. As the muddy ruts dried out, the dwarves' wagons made good time. The roads and the landscape gently sloped downward, gradually descending to the coast. Rinn had visited the sea several times as a child. She remembered frolicking in the sand and tasting the salty tang of seawater. She had stayed with friends of her father's, but she could not picture their names nor their faces. Around midday, the caravan stopped on a grassy knoll for lunch. Calder prepared a fire while Feena prepped a meal. Marshal gathered the other teen-agers and adults together.

"We're heading to Peleon, straight into the heart of the war." He had the poise of a commander. "If we're going to work together, we have to know each other's capabilities. Every day, we're going to stop at noon for sparring practice. No one's excused." He levelled a gaze at Cat, who was chasing some insect through the grass. "These daily training sessions will condition us during the long journey and may help keep us alive in a fight."

Marshal distributed wooden weapons to everyone, even Feena. Rinn wondered where he had gotten all this practice equipment, but then she remembered Felsic and Mafic— they could fashion just about anything. The session began with an exhibition match between Marshal and Haril. Both men used slender wooden swords and small buckler shields. The muscular mercenary clearly had the advantage of size, but Rinn was confident in her father's prowess with a blade. Everyone watched as the bout began.

Haril struck first, battering at Marshal's shield several times before reversing direction. Marshal was not fooled, and he easily blocked and countered each blow. Seeing an opening, Marshal slid his sword forward at Haril's unprotected midsection. The mercenary dodged to one side, avoiding the lunge. The two traded exchanges many more times, their skills closely matched. Rinn noticed that Haril kept circling right, around Marshal's injured hip. Her father's graceful swordplay was hindered by his awkward limp. She could see sweat on his brow and discomfort in his eyes. Haril was relentless, repeatedly attacking Marshal's weak side. He winced as he blocked the onslaught, his leg painfully giving way. She could not bear to see her father humiliated. Without thinking, she dashed forward spear in hand to intercept a savage strike aimed at his bad hip. The blow had not been as severe as Rinn anticipated, Haril had been pulling his shots.

Marshal leaned on his knees, huffing. "Rinn, I'm okay."

Haril studied Rinn for a moment before withdrawing his sword. The fight was over, and Rinn was troubled by her own actions. Her father did not need saving, she probably caused him unnecessary embarrassment in doing so. Marshal regained his composure and set about pairing up combat partners. Haril sparred with Calder, who kept pace with the mercenary. Lutra and Grus traded blows nearby. They were entertaining to watch, they bantered as much as they fought, each trying to out-jibe the other. Feena struggled with a mock short-sword, trying to land a blow on Cat. Their combat looked more like a rowdy game of tag, but Cat seemed to be enjoying herself. Sionne was doing his best to keep two dwarves at bay with a pair of short swords. Molo sat in the grass with Clive, quietly talking to Dempsi.

Rinn saw Tavin standing by himself, and she immediately understood. What did a scribe know about fighting? He was just like Rinn two years ago, before she picked up a weapon for the first time. He was frightened, confused, and alone. Rinn pulled an item from the practice stash and tossed it to the boy. Tavin fumbled trying to catch it.

"What's this?" He said, picking up the dropped weapon from the ground.

"It's a spear." Rinn replied. "You're going to practice with me."

Tavin backed up three large steps. "I can't fight you."

"You're not going to fight me." Rinn laughed. "We're going to run through some drills." Tavin seemed unconvinced, but he let her show him how to hold the spear and where to plant his feet. Rinn started slow—a thrust, a parry, a slash. Tavin did his best to follow along. He was clumsy, but he tried. Rinn showed him more. Together, they stabbed, blocked, and twirled. Tavin did not exactly grasp the concept of twirling, he spun with the grace of an injured albatross. His bungling efforts amused Rinn, but she refused to laugh. His ability to quickly learn the drills impressed her, even though he could not adequately execute them. After an hour of practice, Marshal called time. Weary teens and adults descended on the lunch Feena had laid out, quenching their thirst with jugs of water and filling their bellies with dried fruits and cheese. Each person was allotted a small amount of meat, spiced with peppercorns. After the meal, the passengers loaded into the wagons and set off down the road once more.

Chapter 16

T he next few weeks were a blur. Rinn rose early each morning to fish at nearby ponds and streams. Feena and her father hunted with bows, Cat sniffed out prey. If there was a farmhouse nearby, Molo and the dwarves would offer their services hauling and mending. Haril sometimes accompanied them. Lutra and Sionne slept in, they were responsible for night watches. Calder cared for the horses and Grus helped him.

One morning, Dempsi followed Rinn to a burbling stream not far from their campsite. Rinn enjoyed the companionship. "Want me to teach you how to spear fish?" Rinn asked. The little girl made no reply, but watched intently. Rinn rolled her skirts to her knees and tied them off with a cord. She tiptoed across several wobbly stones to the center of the stream. She studied the waterflow and the skittish swimming of the little fishes. With the speed of a snake, she jabbed her spear into the water, one, two, three times. She proudly held up the end of her spear with three flapping fingerling fish impaled on it.

Dempsi grinned and crawled to the edge of the water. She touched the surface of the stream with one finger. The water began to sparkle and shimmer like quartz. Curious fish nosed over to investigate. Dempsi calmly reached into the water and selected a fish. She pulled it out and set it on the ground next to her with a smile.

Rinn put her hand on a hip. "Well, that's handy." She hopped over to quickly spear the other fish teaming around Dempsi's lure. The subtle shades of magic glistened on the water, the azure glow Rinn had come to recognize as magic. She wondered why magic seemed to glow blue, but her own powers emanated a green color. She had wanted an excuse to talk to Dempsi about her abilities, and now seemed as good of a time as any. "How long have you been able to do that?"

"Catch fish?" Dempsi inquired.

"No." Rinn sat down next to her by the bank of the stream. "How long have you been doing magic?"

"Since my last birthday." Dempsi admitted. She was clearly uncomfortable talking about it, but Rinn suspected she needed to.

"It's been almost three years for me." Rinn wondered if sharing some of her own experiences would help. "Growing up, I never knew I could do magic. I thought I was a boring, ordinary girl, not very smart, or athletic, or pretty."

"You're pretty." Dempsi protested.

"Not really." Rinn demurred. In her mind, Rinn saw herself as that skinny awkward girl from Viburna. The only reason the residents of Hilltop treated her with respect was because of the power she wielded. Internally, Rinn never believed she had much to offer, it was the reason she worked so hard to be helpful. "But I can do this." Rinn stood and shook out her skirts. She raised her hand and chanted the word to summon her shield. A brilliant sphere of green triangles and swirls surrounded both Rinn and Dempsi. The young girl was dazzled by the display.

"Beautiful." She whispered.

Rinn picked up a rock and threw it, the stone bounced off the inside of the barrier. "And it's strong. Nothing gets through." Rinn grinned. "Supposedly, I can do many other things, too, but I don't know the right words. It's frustrating having magic and not knowing how to use it. I'm sure it's the same with you."

"Can you teach me?" Dempsi pleaded.

"I don't know." Rinn confessed. "But I'll try. Maybe together we can learn more about each other's abilities." Dempsi seemed satisfied with that. Rinn collected the pile of fish in the hems of her skirt, she wished she had thought to bring a basket. The two girls headed back to the caravan holding hands.

::

Over the next few days, Dempsi really opened up. She talked more and participated in the midday practice sessions. The dwarves fashioned her a small bow, so she could learn archery from Feena, who was developing into a reliable shooter. Rinn continued to drill with Tavin, who was gradually gleaning the art of spear fighting. He was still clumsy, frequently dropping his weapon, but he was improving.

"Your feet are too close together." Rinn corrected, bumping his calves with the butt of her spear.

"My feet are just like yours." Tavin objected.

"Yes." Rinn replied. "But you're a boy, you're top heavy." She tapped him on the shoulders. "You carry your weight up here. You need to spread your feet wider. Girls carry their weight down here." Rinn patted her own hips. She found Tavin staring at her hips, and her face was suddenly aflush. "Keep your eyes on your spear." She barked. Rinn mercilessly marched him through repeated drills until Marshal called time. She swiped his practice weapon and sent him off to eat in a huff. Rinn could not explain her harsh reaction, she liked sparring with Tavin, but something uncomfortable was stirring inside her.

Confused thoughts filled her mind for the rest of the afternoon. That night, in the girl's tent, she lay awake thinking about it. Feena and Dempsi slept in their bedrolls, and Rinn shared hers with Catherine. Her sister's furry chest rose and fell as she slept.

"Cat." Rinn whispered.

"Mm?" Cat's feline eyes glimmered in the darkness.

"What do you know about boys?" Rinn asked softly.

"They're fun to chase." Cat answered drowsily.

"What do you do when one of them is chasing you?" Rinn asked.

"Run." Cat nodded back off to sleep.

The next day was worse, Rinn noticed everything Tavin did. He spent very little time with the other boys. He ate breakfast with Rinn and Dempsi. Cat never ate dried fruit or porridge, instead she foraged for field mice, leaving Rinn alone with Tavin. Rinn chatted with Dempsi, doing her best to ignore the boy. At noon, he readied himself for spear drills with Rinn. Flustered, she fostered him off on Molo, with the excuse that he needed help with his technique.

That night, Tavin sat with Rinn at dinner, joking about Molo's brutal teaching methods. Rinn felt smothered. She recognized Tavin had very little in common with the other boys. He was a scribe and not accustomed to male camaraderie, he knew nothing of hunting, camping, and fighting. Rinn also realized that this boy had spent the last year in prison, and she felt partially responsible for his predicament. But, in a similar way, she had rescued Sionne, and he never paid her any attention, not that she wanted him to. Rinn was struck by the realization that she was the only available female in the party. Feena was clearly smitten with Lutra. Catherine could not grasp the idea of a relationship. And Dempsi was only ten years old. Rinn did not like her precarious situation. She refused to believe she was leading Tavin on. What did she know about flirting?

Fortunately, a distraction came along to occupy everyone's free time—the discovery of Sionne's book. Apparently, the redhead had pilfered the volume from Calamus' basement book collection. Lutra found it one morning while packing up their tent. Marshal and Molo gave the thief a serious scolding and thoroughly searched his belongings, but found no other contraband. Rinn found it curious that Sionne would steal a book when he could not read. Lutra ribbed him about the pictures inside the work, but Sionne vehemently denied any interest in them. The book ended up with Tavin, who spent many hours poring over the tome.

"What's it about?" Rinn asked one afternoon, as they rode in the back of the wagon. The bright sunny afternoon was warm, and for the first time in days, all of their belongings were dry.

"It's a ballad." Tavin confessed, somewhat embarrassed.

"Like a bard's song?" Rinn wondered.

"A little, but this story is too long to be sung out loud." Tavin admitted.

"What's it called?" Rinn peeked at the thick calligraphy written on the pages, embellished with pink and red ornaments.

"'The Dragonslayers' Wives'." Tavin reluctantly said.

"What's it about?" Rinn asked, her curiosity piqued.

"You can read it for yourself." Tavin handed her the book.

Rinn shied away. "It would take me a hundred years to read that."

"It's easy." Tavin assured her. And thus began long afternoons of story-telling as the caravan plodded down the gently sloping countryside. What started with just Rinn and Tavin eventually spread to all the teens, each taking turns reading passages aloud before handing the book on. Tavin helped with difficult words and phrases. Most everyone had a fairly easy time except Sionne, who

119

stumbled over every word. But he was not as bad as Catherine. Even with patient instruction from Tavin, she could barely read anything. She lost her place frequently and tore the pages with her claws. Eventually, it was agreed to skip over Cat when it was her turn. She seemed just as happy to sit and listen instead.

Over the next few days, the story unfolded, a tale of the wives of the great dragon slayers Martell and Owen. The story opened with the women begging their husbands not to go on such a dangerous quest, but the men's valor demanded it. The two wives roomed together while their husbands were away and faced a series of arduous trials themselves. When they were not reading, the teens discussed the characters at length. The stories were light-hearted and sometimes a bit risque. Sionne usually got stuck reading the racy passages, and his ears would turn bright red. Cat always begged him to read those parts again, which he never did. Rinn and the others would laugh, including little Dempsi, who probably should not be listening to such a ribald story. Having a close group of friends seemed like a dream fulfilled to Rinn, she always considered herself a loner. Even Tavin seemed to be thoroughly enjoying himself. Seeing the boy smile helped Rinn drown the memories of him as a desperate, screaming prisoner locked in a cell.

The caravan left the soft agricultural plains and journeyed into the barren rocky moors closer to the coastline. The wagon jostled and jerked uncomfortably across the rocky road. Several times, progress stopped to repair broken wheels and axels. Molo would lift the wagon while the dwarves worked. Hunting was scarce in this landscape of exposed stone and tangled, weedy heather. Cat could catch a few birds, but not enough to feed anyone other than herself. The party made do with hard tack and rainwater.

Seabirds cawed in the cloudy skies overhead. Rinn could almost taste the salt in the air. The caravan slowed as it made its final descent to the coast. A great arm of the ocean swept inland as the Aspero Sea, a giant body of water reaching halfway across the Empire. At its eastern end, lay the harbors of Ostreum, one of the nine great Imperial cities. Rinn had visited Ostreum in her childhood, and she remembered the city as being crowded, smelly, and expensive. The route to the capital traveled along the northern coast of the Aspero Sea, away from the fabled port city.

"We're almost at the coast." Marshal called down from his driver's seat. "We'll need to stop in one of the larger fishing towns. We need money to enter Peleon. We may have to stay a few days to work."

Rinn did not seem too concerned, they stopped occasionally at farmhouses along the way, sometimes staying a few days as itinerant laborers. If food remained scarce and hunting non-existent in this barren rocky land, they would have to work to eat. Lutra spotted a patrol, eight men on horseback waiting in the road ahead of them. They wore red livery adorned with white sashes and carried long lances. Light glinted off their highly polished helmets. As the carts neared the patrol, Rinn felt a nervous apprehension in the pit of her stomach. She reached for her spear and signaled for the other teens to ready their weapons. Marshal held the reins of the horses tightly as he approached the impending encounter.

Chapter 17

"Turn this caravan around." The patrol commander ordered. He rode high in his saddle, straight-backed and expressionless. The medallions on his white sash jingled in the salty breeze.

"We've ridden all the way from Viburna, decurion." Marshal objected.

"The road to the capital is closed." The commander replied in slow intent words.

"You can't just turn us away." Marshal insisted. "Surely the ports of Ostreum are still open to traders."

"These lands are now under the jurisdiction of Duriter, and Praetor Serpio has ordered all civilian traffic to be cleared." The formal officer offered the tiniest hint of concern. "It's for your own good. We're trying to keep you citizens away from danger."

Rinn recalled that Duriter lay far to the north, nowhere near the Aspero Sea. It was home to the Castrum, a giant military fortress and holy site to Parma, the god of protection. The clerics of Parma were more warrior than priest, their holy symbols were mighty shields blessed by the god they served. War clerics trained the most skilled soldiers in the Legion, sometimes indoctrinating them into their order. The paladins of Parma were thought to be unstoppable, their divinely-enchanted shields unbreakable.

Rinn also remembered the name Serpio, he was one of the Curia and leader of the military in Sevria. Rinn knew their paths would cross eventually, but she had hoped it would not be so soon. His Legions terrified her. Rinn could stand against any single warrior, but fighting against ten or twenty thousand men seemed utterly hopeless.

Rinn shook her head to clear her thoughts. A simple problem presented itself, one that needed an immediate solution. They must get past these eight stubborn guards, hopefully without killing them. Rinn understood that they were just doing their job, trying to help the people of Sevria. Rinn focused on the situation, trying to mimic her father's tactics. The first step was to divide the warriors. Next, overwhelm them and force them to stand down.

"Cat." Rinn whispered. Feline ears perked. "I need you to run, as fast as you can away from the caravan. Get some of the guards to chase you. Once they have nearly caught up with you, jump back here." Cat nodded in understanding. Rinn slowly reached for her spear.

Lutra leaned in. "What do we do?"

"I'll disarm the soldiers. You get control of their horses." Rinn kept her voice low. "Without their mounts, they lose their advantage. The others will pick up on our plan." Lutra nodded in agreement. Rinn winked at Cat, and the Margot leaped out of the wagon and dashed across the rocky moors.

"Hey! Stop!" The commander yelled. Three of the guards peeled off after her. Only five left, Rinn thought to herself. The other guards backed up defensively and leveled their lances at the caravan. Perfect, Rinn thought as she rolled off the back of the wagon. With her spear in hand, she charged the five men on horseback. Servian infantry were trained to battle enemies on foot, on horse, and even behind thick stone walls. But a skinny, blond-headed teenage girl was not something they were prepared for. Rinn intercepted the startled soldiers and severed their lances with her glowing spear. The commander and two of his men drew swords, but Rinn carved through those as well. A flurry of teens poured from the wagon and within moments the combat was over. The patrol was defenseless and surrounded. The teen boys firmly held the reins of the soldier's mounts.

Rinn kept her spear squarely levelled at the commanding officer. Molo climbed out of the other wagon and sauntered over to the patrol. He stood eye to eye with the commander on horseback. "You seem to be in a tight spot, decurion." He relieved the men of their swords and hunting knives. The dwarves ferreted them into their wagon.

Cat reappeared. "Did we win?" She asked, tail waving madly.

"Yes, Cat." Marshal smiled. "What happened to the others?"

"Oh, don't worry about them." Cat waved a paw.

"Cat." Marshal said sternly. "We talked about this."

"What?" Cat planted a paw on her hip, just like Rinn.

The commander maintained a facade of control. "You have no right to do this. Stand down immediately."

Marshal replied. "We're just ordinary citizens seeking passage to the capital city."

"I will see you in chains for assaulting an Imperial patrol." The officer promised in ire.

Molo edged dangerously close. "Consider yourself lucky, decurion. Not many fight a Sigillum and live to tell about it."

"Sigillum?" The fear in the officer's voice was palpable.

"That's right." Molo continued. "That little girl outwitted your patrol and single-handedly disarmed you. But she's chosen to spare your lives, don't waste the chance she's giving you."

"But the last Sigillum died a hundred years ago." The commander's breathing was uneasy and rapid.

"If the Sigilla were dead, the Curia wouldn't need to outlaw them, now would they?" Marshal quizzed the bewildered officer. The ghost of recognition haunted the commander's stoic face. "We don't want trouble." Marshal stated. "We'll just take your horses and be on our way."

"Take the horses?" Molo questioned.

"Oh, yes." Marshal bantered with his friend. "We have to take the horses. That way we can ride hard for the capital. These poor sods will have to walk all the way back to Duriter. Even if they send reinforcements, there's no way they could catch up with us."

"Good plan." Molo stroked his beard. "Okay, you heard the man. Off your horses." Reluctantly, the guards dismounted. Molo ushered them away. "Hurry home."

The captain regarded the giant coolly. "What about my three other men?"

Molo looked to Cat. She shrugged her feline shoulders.

"Either they'll turn up, or they won't. Hard to tell." Molo admitted. "Now, go, before any more of you end up missing." Two of the disgraced guards actually took off running, but the commander turned and strutted away with his head held high, desperate to maintain the illusion of dignity. Once the remains of the patrol disappeared over the rise of a hill, Rinn climbed onto one of the guard's horses.

"What are you doing?" Molo demanded.

"Riding." Rinn was startled by his reaction.

"Get down." He admonished. "We're letting the horses go."

"We are?" Lutra asked in confusion.

"Of course." Molo seemed to think it was obvious.

"Why?" Rinn slid out of the saddle.

Her father offered the explanation. "It won't take long for those guards to reach a town, and then word will spread fast. They will be looking for a team of armed riders speeding for the capital. We, however, will be a simple trade caravan."

"Clever." Haril admitted.

"Why don't we sell the horses?" Sionne whined. "If we stripped off the soldier's gear, no one would know."

Molo pointed to the horses' hooves. "Everyone would know. Imperial horses have the royal crest emblazoned on their shoes. It's best to let them run free, after we remove their gear."

Haril and Grus stripped the horses of their saddles and bags. As Rinn helped load the cargo into the wagons, she reflected on her impulsiveness. She quickly devised a plan to divide and overtake the patrol, but she had given no thought as to what would happen next. Her father's quick thinking had spared unnecessary bloodshed. Rinn recognized she had charged headlong into Sevria with no thought of the consequences. What would happen if she successfully ended the war? She assumed her father would tidy up the loose ends and life would return to normal. But the events at Hilltop taught her that real endings were never so simple. The Rustic people had gained a new fortified refuge, but they had lost homes and lives in the process. Rinn needed a plan, some way for the Empire to thrive once the Curia were ousted. The forest god Lucus had told her to go to Peleon, it was the only way she could succeed. Hopefully, she would find a solution there.

::

The caravan rumbled down the steep, rocky trail to the sea. In the distance, glints of light could be seen, reflections of the afternoon sun on the choppy waters of the Aspero Sea. The teenagers who grew up in the Rustic Lands tittered with excitement. Up till now, the largest body of water they had ever seen was a forest lake. The vastness of the sea was beyond their imaginations.

"You're being awfully quiet." Tavin sat next to Rinn in the wagon bed. He leaned against one of the confiscated saddles for comfort.

"She's thinking." Cat replied for her sister.

"About what?" Tavin inquired.

"How to get rid of nosy people." Cat's nose twitched as she spoke. Tavin took the hint and retreated. His interest was soon distracted by the stunning coastal panorama— an endless expanse of blue-green water flocked with white choppy waves. The Aspero Sea pounded warm, sandy beaches with mighty rollers. Flocks of herons glided in the breezes blowing in from the sea. Moist salt air filled Rinn's nose, and the wind mussed her hair. The road led down a low cliff that bordered the seacoast and joined with a beachside path. Wooden signposts pointed south to Ostreum, but Marshal ignored them and turned the caravan north.

The giddy teenagers could not help themselves, the warm sand and rolling waves were too inviting. They jumped out of the moving wagon in droves and scampered across the beach hooting and hollering. Rinn reluctantly joined them. She worried about how well her sister and the ocean would mix, but she found Catherine blissfully kneading the warm sand with her paws. She had lost most of her clothes and wiggled her fur into the sand.

"Cat, are you okay?" Rinn asked, perplexed by her strange behavior.

"I haven't done this in years." Cat purred. "I love sand."

Rinn helped her crazy feline sister up, every inch of her fur was covered in sand. Cat shook violently, like a wet dog, sprinkling grit everywhere. Rinn brushed some out of her hair. She took ahold of Cat's paw. "Let's go see the waves."

Cat pulled away. "I'm fine right here." She slunk down and wriggled in the warm sand once again. Rinn left her contented sister and joined the others at the shoreline. Lutra and Feena had kicked off their shoes and were stomping in the ocean. Even the taciturn Calder waded through the waves.

Sionne reached down and dipped his hand into the water and took a drink. Spitting it out he yelled. "This tastes awful, like salt."

"Of course, it does, idiot." Grus chastised. "It's seawater."

"What good is water you can't drink?" Sionne complained.

"I don't know." Grus replied. "Sailing, fishing, swimming, diving. Oceans are good for lots of things."

"I thought you said this was a sea, not an ocean." Sionne argued.

"What's the difference?" Grus challenged. Neither boy knew.

The teenagers thoroughly enjoyed the beach, but none more than little Dempsi. She laughed as she plowed through the waves, her linen dress completely soaked. Rinn had to haul her out of the water before the undertow carried her away. The little girl seemed unconcerned.

"I've never seen so much water." Dempsi beamed.

"The Aspero is the biggest sea in Sevria." Rinn acknowledged, settling her down on the sand.

"It's talking to me." Dempsi stared out at the water with the longing of a sea captain too long ashore.

"What's it saying?" Rinn listened to the girl with keen interest.

"Death is coming." The girl was detached from the cryptic words she spoke. "By this time next week, this beach will be littered with the dead."

"You can see the future?" Terror seized Rinn.

"Not the future." Dempsi corrected. "The battle is already over, all that's left is the work of the tides."

Chapter 18

R inn sat uneasily in a seaside tavern. The wooden
building was gray and weathered, like the hull of a
ship. The wall facing the sea was entirely made of shutters,
left open to let cool ocean breezes blow through. Nautical
implements lined the remaining walls: nets, buoys, and
curved hooks on long poles. Rinn paid these things no
mind, she was haunted by her conversation with Dempsi.
She told Molo and her father about the exchange, and they
were equally disturbed by the little girl's dark prediction.
They decided to stop at a fishing village for fresh food and
information. After their encounter with the patrol, they
were flush with funds.

Teenage boys crowded around a thick table, ravaging a
large platter of chopped seafood cooked with grains. Boiled
muscles lined the edges of the platter, popped open and
ready to eat. The boys joked and laughed loudly, mouths
full of food. Their energy was spurred on by weak ale—the
only beverage the tavern served. Marshal, Haril, and Molo
conferred at a separate table, while the dwarves labored
furiously at a third. They were dissecting the confiscated
saddles and fashioning the scraps into armor for the party.
Cat sat on her haunches at the shoreline with Dempsi. The
little girl lured fresh fish out of the ocean, and the happy
feline promptly ate them.

Feena set a bowl of seafood stew before Rinn and sat down next to her. "You seem to have a lot on your mind."

"Yeah." Rinn accepted the food and began mechanically eating.

"Want to talk about it?" Feena lifted a spoonful of the steaming stew.

Rinn's pent-up emotions spilled out. "What am I going to do, Feena?"

"About what?" Feena asked, trying not to look overly curious.

"About everything." Rinn emptied her bag of problems. "Sevria, the war, the gods, the Legions, magic, Dempsi, boys, and this lost Emperor I'm supposed to find?"

Feena let it all absorb for a moment. "Well, what needs to be done first? Let's make a plan."

Rinn thought about it. "Finding the lost Emperor. If I did that, it could solve many problems at once."

"Okay." Feena smirked. "We'll start there."

Tavin slipped away from the rowdy boys and joined Feena and Rinn. "What's this about a lost Emperor?" He set his half-finished mug on their table.

Rinn whispered the next words. "Molo thinks that if I'm a Sigillum, there must be an Emperor somewhere."

"There isn't." Tavin declared.

"How do you know?" Rinn pouted.

"I was apprenticed under Brother Oriar." Tavin's grey eyes seemed distant as he spoke. "He was obsessed with genealogy, especially the royal bloodline. Over the years, I copied hundreds of documents for him. It's impossible to write something down without reading it first. I've copied the Imperial lineage so many times, I could probably recite it from memory."

A glimmer of hope seized Rinn. "So, you would know who the next heir to the throne is."

"I already told you, there isn't one." Tavin countered. "The only surviving member of the royal family is you. And you're not supposed to exist."

"Huh?" Feena lifted a curious brow.

Tavin sipped at his ale before he spoke, just like Rinn's father did. "Your mother is recorded as dying of a fever in Peleon in 508. But Brother Oriar discovered documents from a remote Temple in Amne Dua, the initiation of a two-year-old girl into the Sevrian Church, one Sabrinn Sevralis. That's you. You were born nine years after your mother supposedly died."

"You're wrong." Rinn argued, voice growing louder. "My mother didn't die in Peleon, she was killed by the Curia." She added with contempt. "And another thing, Molo told me I have an aunt, so I can't be the last Sevrian."

"Yes." Tavin drew the word out slowly. "But she's a special case. She renounced all her ties to the royal family."

"But she's my blood relative." Rinn insisted angrily. "If she has a son, he could be the one we're looking for."

Marshal came over and ushered out his flustered daughter. "We need to go." He laid money on the table and urged everyone outside to the wagons. The dwarves scrambled to gather up their workshop and rushed out.

::

The next few days were tense, and Rinn's mood foul. The caravan plodded down the broken path that paralleled the shoreline. To make the wagons less conspicuous, Molo and the dwarves fashioned sideboards and draped the tops with fishing nets. Riding inside the wagons was miserable, excessively hot and reeking of rotting fish. Sionne complained incessantly. Calder and Grus opted to ride in the other wagon with the dwarves to avoid his litany of bellyaching. Rinn ignored everyone, consumed by her own dark thoughts about the Empire, about her mission, about her mother.

At noon, the caravan stopped on a remote beach for their daily sparring session. Everyone enjoyed the excuse to be away from the smelly caravan. Rinn had barely spoken a word to Tavin since their argument at the seaside tavern. She pulled out her practice spear and began her drills. Without saying a word, he dutifully lined up alongside her and followed her through the motions. He was still clumsy, and in the shifting sand his footwork was atrocious.

Molo noticed them struggling and came over. "Fighting in the sand is different than fighting on hard ground." He politely relieved Tavin of his weapon, and faced Rinn. "Without solid footing, your strikes will lose power, but so will your opponent's." He thrust a spear at Rinn, who blocked it effortlessly. She stabbed back at him, and he jerked her weapon away with his hand. Caught off balance, she pitched forward into the sand.

"No fair." Rinn griped, brushing sand off her face.

"No, not really." Molo admitted. "But realize that you and your adversary suffer the same limitations. When you fight in sand, work to unbalance your opponent first. You can overpower him once he's down." Molo handed the practice spear back to Tavin and walked away. Rinn detested Molo's teaching methods, but she understood his message.

Lunch was a subdued affair. The novelty of ocean fish was wearing off, even for Cat. Lutra had encountered several fishermen playing music on small flutes of rolled metal. He keenly listened to their songs and tried to emulate their technique. His new tunes were upbeat and lively, but the teen bard had not exactly mastered their style. Rinn sat alone, pushing her lunch around with her spoon. Her father sat down beside her.

"You've been awfully quiet these last few days." He observed.

"I know." Rinn muttered.

"Anything you want to talk about?" He asked, gentle concern in his voice.

"Mom." Rinn stared into her bowl

Marshal breathed in and sighed. "Okay."

Rinn tried not to get her hopes up. "Really?"

"You deserve to hear what happened to your mother, all of it." Her father confessed. He settled down in the sand, making himself comfortable. Cat appeared next to him, reclining on one arm. Marshal laughed. "Can't really tell one of you, can I?"

Cat shook her head vigorously, her feline ears flapping.

Marshal took a cleansing breath. "The decade following the death of Emperor Tarandus was chaos. I spent six years in the cavalry fighting border wars and skirmishes. Many pretenders came forward, claiming to be heirs to the Empire. The Curia suppressed their uprisings with brutal efficiency. Eventually, I was offered a position in the Imperial Palace." Rinn raised her eyebrows in surprise. "It was nothing special. I was one of hundreds of soldiers stationed there. We were tasked with guarding Virago and her two daughters who were small children at the time." Marshal uncorked his wineskin and took a drink. "I befriended a young monk at the palace named Cassinius. He was irreverent for a monk." He laughed. "I'd never met anyone like him. He spoke his mind, never worrying about the consequences. He was always in trouble, but he could not change his nature."

Rinn had never heard her father speak so candidly about his past. After another sip, he continued. "I watched Virago's daughters grow up. For some reason, the younger princess took a liking to me. I taught her how to ride and how to shoot a bow. She was a fireball, full of energy and curiosity, the complete opposite of her older sister, Cecilia, who was quiet and reserved."

Marshal downed another swig. "As the girls matured, Virago pressured the Curia to put one of them on the throne. No one knows who struck first, but the Curia called for your grandmother's arrest and sent soldiers to apprehend her. Virago somehow escaped, at the cost of leaving her daughter's behind. She was a cunning warrior, and I now recognize that she was probably a Sigillum. Virago fled west, to raise an army and march on the capital. Her goal was the rescue of her daughters. The Curia mobilized the Emperor's Legions to stop her. Forty-thousand men clashed on the plains outside Gadiom."

Marshal was so engrossed in his storytelling he hardly realized others were starting to wander over to hear the tale. Molo, Haril, the dwarves, and all the teenagers gathered around. Marshal cleared his throat, and drank deeply from his wineskin. He continued. "The Imperial princesses were kept under constant guard, for their protection. At the time it felt wrong, and I regret my careless treatment of them. But I was an officer, more worried about my career than doing the right thing." He downed another long swig. Rinn was not sure her father would be able to go on. His voice trembled and cracked, but he persisted. "The older sister Cecilia fell ill a week later. A fever, we were told. She could barely eat or speak. She was kept locked in the dungeon—for her safety. That night, Tabitha pleaded with me to help her escape, to run away with her. She was seventeen, skinny as a stilt, and the most beautiful thing in the world. I wanted to break every oath I swore that day, to abandon my life with the Legion and run away with this girl. But I didn't."

Rinn could hear the lump forming in her father's throat as he delivered the next line. "She died the next day. And a part of me died with her. When Cass found me, I was so drunk I could barely stand. He hauled me out of whatever pub I was in and dragged me to the Great Temple of Aedis." Marshal shuddered slightly. "The Temple was as quiet and dark as the grave. I saw your mother, laid out on a bier, hands folded across her chest. Cassinius forced me to stand beside her. Even in death Tabitha was beautiful. I couldn't bear to look at her, guilt consumed me. I tried to leave, but Cass forbade it."

Marshal became more animated, like an actor. "I yelled at him. 'Why? Why would you bring me here?'" Marshal drained whatever was in his wineskin. "His reply froze my soul."

"'She needs a reason to live.' Cass replied. His eyes were filled with mystery. He made me take hold of her cold hands. Then, he touched her pale lips and uttered a word, one single word. It sounded like no language I had ever heard. The power of that word shook the very walls of the Temple. Tabitha's cold hands thawed, and she drew a deep breath. Her eyes opened and there I was, like a fool, holding her hands." Marshal stopped. Everyone stared at him expectantly.

Rinn demanded. "What happened next?"

"We ran." Marshal admitted. "We were fugitives. The Curia carried on with the funeral the next day. I'm not sure whose body they buried, but it wasn't your mother's."

"Where'd you go?" Rinn needed to hear everything.

"We fled west." Marshal said. "The Curia hunted us to the very edges of Sevria. We boarded a ship bound for Brigantum. I thought my childhood home would be a safe haven, but the Curia's assassins found us there. We were forced to seek refuge in the one place no one would ever dare go: the cursed islands of Migalia."

Chapter 19

R inn sat in the back of the wagon with her thoughts. The seaside road rose higher as the sandy beach gave way to lofty cliffs. White-capped waves hammered the rocky shores with a sound like distant thunder. The caravan had entered the Isthmus of Desper, the last leg on the long journey to Peleon. To the north, maybe a few day's travel away, stretched the coast of the Lenis Sea, the great inland lake that was the heart of the Sevrian Empire. Marshal opted for the southern route, hugging the ragged shoreline of the Aspero Sea. The road was treacherous and veered dangerously close to the cliff's edge, but it avoided the crowded Imperial highway to the north. The ground here was barren and inhospitable. The caravan was forced to stop at waystations to buy hay for the horses to eat.

At one such stop, Lutra walked to the edge of the promontory. The strong ocean wind made his wavy brown hair dance around his head. He stared out to the sea with a deep longing in his eyes.

"Don't get too close." Rinn cautioned. To her, the view of the ocean was breathtaking, but the height was nauseating. Cat bounced over to Lutra.

"What do you see?" Cat asked, trying to match Lutra's gaze.

"Inspiration." Lutra murmured. He said no more and headed back to the wagon. Cat shrugged. She picked up a small rock and tossed it off the cliff. After an excessively long time, the stone struck the shore with a hollow clack. Cat giggled in glee and hurled down a battalion of stones. Rinn eventually dragged her back to the caravan.

Lutra played his flute the rest of the afternoon, a haunting tune somewhere between the bawdy melodies of the Rustic People and the lilting sounds of the fishermen's metal whistles. Over the next few days, he redoubled his efforts to learn to write from Tavin. He repeatedly traced letters on a broken slate stone with a chalky rock. He wiped it clean and started over. Even Grus and Calder were impressed by his efforts.

On the fourth day, the caravan passed The Gib, the highest point on the isthmus. The wagons stopped at midday for sparring drills and lunch. Rinn and Tavin drew their spears from the pile of weapons. They were talking amicably again. In the weeks they had practiced, Tavin had gained some degree of skill with a spear. He no longer wore his scribe's robe, but favored a pair of workman's breeches and a tunic that hung to his midthighs. As they rehearsed their drills, Rinn was struck with how handsome Tavin seemed. His coffee colored hair was growing out and it framed his round face pleasantly. But the intensity of his grey eyes was still what captured Rinn. They studied everything as he rehearsed his drills. He was no natural warrior, but he clearly grasped the concepts of defense and foot movement. Sometimes, when he faced off against Lutra or Sionne, he would land a successful blow.

"Lucky shot." Sionne would whine. But Rinn knew better. Tavin could eventually be a more formidable fighter than any of the teens except Calder, who already fought with the ferocity of a seasoned adult. Or Cat, but she was a special case. Rinn ran through her drills with renewed vigor, sweat pouring from her brow. Molo watched and nodded in approval.

::

While the adults were mending an axel damaged by a rock in the road, the teens decided to climb The Gib. The rise was a single massive rock jutting out of the ground like the top of a skull. It was devoid of plant life, swept smooth by the constant ocean winds. Rinn and her friends clambered up the curved rock face. Before long, the group was high above the road and the caravan. From the summit, the horizon stretched out for miles. To the north, Rinn spied the placid blue waters of the Lenis Sea, to the west, a smattering of farmhouses and villages. She knew that beyond them lay the Laetus Straight and the city of Peleon.

"It's great up here." Cat beamed, her fur buffeted by the strong winds.

"It's nice." Rinn masked her fear of heights.

Grus shouted out. "You can see the whole Empire from here."

"Probably not the whole Empire." Tavin panted. The climb had been arduous, and he was winded. He sat on the rocky crest catching his breath. Rinn came and sat next to him.

"The view is pretty spectacular." She offered the exhausted boy a sip of water from her waterskin. He gratefully accepted it. Rinn pointed to the north. "You can see the Lenis Sea from here."

"And Farann Fada." Tavin said with all seriousness. Rinn had heard stories of the fabled land of sorcery. Technically part of the Empire, the peninsula of Farann Fada lay on the far side of the Aspero Sea. It existed as a nearly autonomous state, governed by the worshippers of

Sidus, the goddess of magic. According to legend, the high city of Hyalos was made entirely of glass. In the Astrarium, the Temple to Sidus, sorcerers practiced all manner of magecraft. The hills and forests south of Hyalos were teaming with their magical mishaps, twisted creatures with unnatural abilities. Rinn turned her gaze south and found the hazy green coast far across the sea, the shores of Farann Fada. This was the closest Rinn ever wanted to be to that accursed land. Magic reacted unpredictably with her Sigillum abilities.

Molo waved his arms over his head, signaling for the teens to return. The group slowly trickled down the rocky hillside. Cat was kind enough to transport the exhausted Tavin down instantly—an experience which left him shaken.

"You let her do that to you willingly?" The mortified scribe asked Rinn when she reached the bottom.

"It's not so bad once you get used to it." Rinn countered. "I think the Mist is quite charming."

"The Mist?" Tavin coughed weakly.

"That purple place Cat goes through." Rinn explained.

"It was purple?" Tavin groaned, holding his head.

::

That evening, as the caravan camped for the night, Rinn watched the western skies. She was sitting on the back of the wagon, reorganizing her rucksack. The sun set long ago, but the orange glow on the horizon refused to fade, even in the darkness of night.

"Those are the lights of Peleon." Molo chased her distant gaze. Rinn was amazed, the capital city was so vast it could defy nightfall. That evening as she laid in bed, she recalled her visit to Peleon as a small child. The only memory that stuck out was getting lost in the Great Temple. Her father brought her there to see the sights, but he disappeared for a short while. Little Rinn became turned around in the forest of polished marble pillars. She felt terrified, abandoned, all she could do was cry. Her father came and rescued her, but the experience had left her with a lifelong distrust of large buildings, churches in particular. She instead gravitated to the quiet closeness of small shrines. Memories of Viburna flooded over her: the battle with the awful struma, the sacrilege in the Temple, her conversation with Lucus. With regret, she recalled all the destruction she had unleashed. She had enjoyed it, and that thought disgusted her. She was more than a weapon. Rinn's dark thoughts turned to Yallakh. Where was he now?

::

Rinn woke groggily in the morning. Most everyone had packed and were finishing up their breakfast. Marshal coaxed Rinn out of bed. "Today's the day." He helped her up. "We'll reach Peleon by nightfall." Rinn pulled on her Imperial outfit, the demure dress-like stola her father had purchased from the squatters' camp. Marshal, Haril, and Grus donned their military uniforms. Molo and the teen boys wore simple workman's clothes. Cat reluctantly wrapped herself in a long, hooded robe and Feena squeezed into a maid's dress. Her figure spilled distractingly out of the snug outfit.

Felsic offered Rinn a heavily embellished walking stick. "We have a present for you." She gratefully accepted it, somewhat confused.

Mafic handed her the metal spear tip. "It clicks into the top." He demonstrated the action to her, and the concealed button that would release it.

Rinn gave both dwarves a hug. "I don't know what I'd do without you. Thank you so much."

"Wouldn't want you walking around defenseless." Felsic blushed. Rinn loved her dwarven companions. She reminded herself to do something nice for them once they reached the city.

Marshal assembled the party like a squad of soldiers and outlined his plan. "We'll reach the port city of Coram by midday. From there we will secure passage on a ferry across the Laetus Strait to the capital. Peleon is a city of a thousand harbors, so it will be easy to slip in unnoticed." He walked up to Rinn and handed her the pouch with her mother's and grandmother's necklaces. "I've given this a good deal of thought. I want you to wear these."

"Why?" Rinn hesitantly received the pouch.

"Molo or I could lead the way through the city." He confessed. "But only you know where we need to go." Rinn accepted the pouch with uncertainty. Marshal addressed the group. "Rinn will be playing the part of a wealthy merchant's daughter. Haril, Grus, and I will be her paid escort. Everyone else will be part of her entourage." He signaled to the dwarves. They rolled back a tarp from the second caravan wagon, revealing a wealth of carved figurines. "As we traveled, Mafic and Felsic have been busy crafting these." Rinn and her friends rushed to examine the exquisite figures. Each one was unique, soldiers, sailors, cooks, priests. Rinn selected a weary shepherd boy leaning on his crook. Lutra marveled at a detailed fisherman. Sionne thumbed a bawdy barmaid.

Once everyone finished ogling the merchandise, Marshal continued outlining his plan. "We will pose as a trading caravan, seeking to sell our wares at the city markets. At the port, the guards will extract a heavy toll, which we will grudgingly pay. Convinced they have gotten the better of us, they will admit us into the city."

Rinn voiced her objections. "But I don't know the first thing about trading or paying tolls."

Marshal dismissed her. "Don't worry. The daughter of a wealthy merchant wouldn't deign to talk to lowly guards. Haril and I will do all the negotiating." Rinn was uncertain. She had spared Haril's life back at Viburna, but she had not spent any time getting to know him. Entrusting him with such an important task seemed risky. But her father seemed to have confidence in the warrior, so Rinn let it go.

Once everyone understood their assigned duties and the caravans were loaded, they set out for the port city of Coram. Rinn rode on the driver's bench next to her father, her walking stick resting in her lap. She fingered the metal spear tip in a pouch at her side. She turned to Cat, who sat behind her in the wagon bed. "Stay close, I'm going to need you."

"I know." Cat said.

Rinn felt guilty for always relying on her sister. She offered some consolation. "We'll be passing through a huge fish market."

"Sounds stinky." Cat winced.

"Maybe we could find you something nice in Peleon." Rinn noticed that Cat looked unconvinced. "There's an herb market, they might sell catmint." That possibility made Cat's eyes twinkle.

::

After a few hours of travel, the winding southern road joined the crowded Imperial Highway. Marshal merged into the traffic, a line of lumbering wagons, couriers on horseback, and clusters of pedestrians. The teens gawked at the vast number of people. The highway was a parade of humanity, a mixture of all colors and stations. Proud merchants filed in behind humble farmer's carts. Squadrons of soldiers patrolled the masses, keeping the peace. They paid Rinn and her caravan no mind, she was just another face in a sea of faces.

Ahead, Rinn could see the Gates of Coram. The fortified port city lay behind stout stone walls studded with crenulations. At the corners, tower-like bartizans reached out from the walls, offering archers exceptional line of sight and shooting angles. The vaulted entranceway was protected by massive iron gates that could be lowered in times of attack. The line of traffic poured through the portcullis into the city proper. The bustling city of Coram was smaller than Viburna, but more densely populated. The unending stream of wagons headed for the harbor where a flotilla of ferries awaited them. Rinn's caravan passed gilded storefronts promising the hottest, freshest food or the finest quality clothing. Jewelers, locksmiths, and cobblers all hawked their wares. Wafts of freshly baked bread mingled with the distant harbor stink.

The noise, the crowds, and the smells were too much for Rinn. They assaulted her senses and left her feeling disoriented and afraid. She scooted close to her father and clutched her walking stick for comfort. As a kid she loved to visit the crowded marketplace, but now it seemed like a thing of terror. With a start, Rinn realized it was not her. It was Cat. She was feeling her sister's emotions. Cat hated crowded places, the commotion overwhelmed her heightened senses and left her feeling vulnerable.

"Cat, come sit with me." Rinn reached back to her shivering sister.

"Is that a good idea?" Marshal asked.

Rinn answered with a silent nod of her head. She pulled her sister forward and sat her on the driver's bench. She held her sister's paws in her hands. The feeling of terror abated, a little. "We're almost at the harbor." Rinn reassured her.

The parade of traffic ended at a large, open promenade that bordered the waterfront. Marshal directed his wagon to an available stopping place, and Haril pulled beside him. The two climbed down from their driver's benches. Marshal bowed to Rinn. "Wait here, m'lady. We'll arrange passage for the caravan." In an afterthought, he handed Rinn several silver coins and whispered. "Have some of the boys go find food for lunch. There are plenty of merchants on the waterfront. Just make sure they don't stray too far." Rinn understood and accepted the coins. Marshal and Haril marched off to the port authority.

Chapter 20

T he journey across the Laetus Strait lasted several hours. Marshal secured passage on a ferry bound for Peleon. Rinn felt pangs of mistrust as she boarded the wooden barge, but she suspected that was also her sister's apprehensions boiling over. Rinn took Cat by the paw and led her to a safe place in the center of the vessel. One by one the wagons were loaded on, making the barge sway and dip precariously. With each lurch Cat looked like she was going to have a hairball. Rinn did her best to comfort her sister. Sailors queued the boat up for a turn on The Chain, a massive cable of braided metal stretching halfway across the strait. When their turn came, the crew used a giant windlass to crank the barge out to sea.

Rinn leaned against a side rail squinting at the choppy water of the Laetus Strait. Fishing vessels, delivery boats, and pleasure craft darted in every direction, and clouds of seabirds squawked overhead. Rinn felt an unusual sense of peace watching the waves rise and fall. At the far end of the barge, Rinn spotted her father doing the same, staring wistfully out to the sea. She wondered what he was thinking about.

The far end of The Chain was anchored to a small, weathered island halfway across the strait. The captain piped orders and the crew uncoupled the windlass. Long wooden oars were hauled out, and the sailors rowed the vessel the remaining distance. Peleon grew steadily closer. The sprawling city became the horizon, an endless landscape of buildings. The majestic towers of the Imperial Palace lorded above the skyline like a mountain, and lofty spires of the city's temples rose like greedy pines.

A nervous tension knotted in Rinn's stomach. At long last, she had come to Peleon. With any luck, she would find the lost Emperor and restore peace. Rinn could endure the upcoming conflict, so long as an end was in sight. But one thing terrified her—the Curia. As the barge neared Peleon's harbors, Rinn spotted the Curia's warships, floating fortresses that dominated the waterline. These hulking timber monstrosities eclipsed every other boat at sea. Rinn recalled Dempsi's ominous prediction. "The beach will be littered with the dead." Had these warships been involved in the battle that cost so many lives? Rinn scanned the ferry and found Dempsi contentedly kicking her feet off the prow. She was conversing with the water. Rinn should have been concerned for the little girl's safety, but it was unlikely she would drown.

The barge eventually docked at Peleon's bustling port. Rinn felt a wave of relief as Cat's paws touched solid ground. Rinn disembarked with the dwarves and the other teens. Marshal, Molo, and Haril stayed with the caravan. It would take quite a bit of time to unload the ferry and pass through inspections. Rinn and her friends wended their way through the crowded wharf to a lane of seaside shops. Lutra and Sionne purchased hot pastries from a local vendor—teenage boys were always hungry. Cat devoured a meat-filled pie with feline satisfaction. Rinn and Feena opted for sweet rolls topped with fruit and creme. The air was warm, and a salty ocean breeze skipped across the wharf. The teenagers settled onto a pair of stone benches facing the sea. The dwarves went back to check on the wagons.

Feena pointed out a cylindrical building to the north. "What's that?" She asked Rinn.

"A Haven." Rinn squinted against the sunlight. "A temple to Onrigo, the ocean goddess."

"Tell me about the Sevrian gods." Feena seemed so innocent, so full of wonder. Rinn was embarrassed to discuss religion with her. The modern churches of Sevria were a disgrace, petty and bureaucratic. They frequently squabbled with each other and amongst themselves. Rinn found it challenging to find anything nice to say. She instead recounted their history. "The ancient Sevrians immigrated from far away. Their voyage across the Pernic Sea was treacherous, and many were lost on the way. When those that survived did make landfall, it was on a broken, desolate coast teaming with hostile monsters."

"Sounds like the Inimic Coast." Feena wondered. "The one north of the Roinn Mountains."

"It was." Rinn agreed, and Feena shuddered. "The ancient Sevrians could find no food or shelter, and they were hounded by carnivorous beasts. All hope seemed lost until nine heroes appeared. They guided the tribes of Sevrians across the Roinn Mountains and through the Rustic Lands to the Lenis Sea. Those heroes turned out to be the gods of Sevria. Each god led a portion of the people to a different, ideal place to build a settlement. These became the nine great cities. You can find a shrine to the founding god at the heart of each city."

"The Grove was the shrine at your hometown?" Feena asked.

"Yes." Rinn agreed. "Viburna was founded by Lucus. It's a land rich in forests and wildlife. Its people grew to be great hunters and loggers."

"Who founded this city?" Feena wondered as she finished off her pastry.

Rinn choked back her reply. "Aedis."

"What's he the god of?" Feena's curiosity was unquenchable.

Rinn struggled to explain. "He's supposed to be the god of ceremonies. According to legend, he brought Sevrius himself to this site and dictated that he build a city here. But Sevrius was killed in a tribal conflict. It was his son, Ichneumon, who founded Peleon and built the first Temple."

Feena frowned. "Sevria's history seems pretty bloody."

"It is." Rinn took the last bite of her pastry. It tasted dry and flavorless in her mouth, ruined by the memory of her destruction of the Temple at Viburna.

::

"We're all finished." Molo escorted the dwarves and teens back to the caravan. Everyone assumed their positions quietly. Rinn boarded the driver's bench with Cat and her father. She tried to act haughty, like a merchant's daughter. In her head she imitated Tristy, the snobbish girl from Hilltop.

"Driver." She snapped. "Let's get moving." She winked at her father. He rolled his eyes. With a flick of the reins, the caravan lurched forward, down a flagstone road leading to the city proper. The entrance to Peleon was modest compared to the grandiose arches of Coram, just a simple guard checkpoint and a tunnel leading through the thick city walls. Rinn guessed this was one of hundreds of entrances into the sprawling metropolis, they could not all be ornate. The caravan stopped to have its documentation inspected. Rinn breathed nervously, trying to avoid eye-contact with the guards. After Marshal surrendered a few more coins, the wagons were allowed to pass.

The caravan rumbled down the narrow tunnel into the city proper. The size and grandeur of Peleon was beyond comprehension. Rinn and her companions gawked at the wide, statue lined boulevards and lavishly decorated storefronts. Chariots zipped by on their way to some urgent destination. Thousands of people coursed along the walkways bordering the main road. Marshal followed the lines of traffic into the heart of the city. From the driver's bench, Rinn could see the manicured gardens of the Imperial Palace. The center of the palace complex rose like a cloudburst of marble above the neatly trimmed rows of hedges.

Just when Rinn thought she had seen the finest parts of the city, the harbor road intersected with the ostentatious Grand Concourse. The thoroughfare was as wide as the marketplace in Viburna and more crowded than the bustling harbors of Coram. The concourse was lined with elaborate guild-houses six stories tall, a pageantry of stonework and color. A boulevard of gaudy marble fountains and statuary ran down the center of the thoroughfare. Rinn could only gape at the opulence displayed along the way: sculptures of silver and gold, frescoes covering entire buildings, banners and flags woven from the finest silks.

"This place ain't real." Sionne summed up exactly what Rinn felt.

Feena leaned close to Rinn. "Is this some sort of festival?"

Marshal shook his head. "No. This is an average afternoon in Peleon."

"Amazing." Feena awed. Even Cat gaped at the pompous splendor all around her. Doubt and fear crept into Rinn. Rescuing a sacred grove and unseating an evil priest was one thing, but this was something altogether different. This was Peleon, the capital of Sevria. Even with all her abilities, she was nothing compared to a city of this size—a tiny insect in an immense forest. Her dreams of conquering the Curia and restoring the Empire fizzled.

"There you are!" A baritone voice hailed from afar. A rotund man flocked in richly embroidered robes called to Rinn's caravan. He rode in a gilded chariot pulled by four white horses. His driver was a decorated military officer. Rows of soldiers on foot escorted them. The baritone man motioned for his driver to pull alongside Rinn's wagon. The fat man wiped sweat from his brow with a lace handkerchief. He addressed Rinn with a flourish. "I wish you'd let us know you were coming. We would've arranged a proper escort."

"Who are you?" Rinn squeaked, overwhelmed by crowds, guards, and this boisterous man in his gilded chariot.

"Me?" The man laughed, the gold and purple chain around his neck jingled as he shook. With the slightest tilt of his head, he introduced himself. "I am Aculeus, the Grand Merchant." He leaned in close to Rinn, she could smell his sweat. "We need to get off the road. Not everyone is as excited about your arrival as I am, your Highness."

With a wave of his hand, the Grand Merchant urged his driver to pull in front of the caravan. Gold-caped guards formed columns on either side of Rinn's wagons. The commanding officer ordered the drivers forward. Marshal and Haril had no choice but to comply.

Rinn whispered to her father. "Who is that man?"

"He's one of the Curia." Marshal hissed between tight lips. Shock and revulsion carried Rinn's breath away. She had been captured by the Curia. She clutched her walking stick and withdrew the metal spear point from her pouch. As she attempted to fit it into the handle, her father motioned for her to stop. "It's best if we play along, for now."

"Where's he taking us?" Rinn asked in a muffled voice.

"We're moving south." Marshal observed. "Probably to the Imperial Palace."

"Why would he do that?" Rinn pondered. She swiveled her head back to check on her sister, but Cat was gone. Rinn mouthed a question to Lutra. "Where's Cat?"

Lutra mouthed back. "I don't know. She vanished."

Cat was the smart one, Rinn decided, she sensed something was amiss. Rinn scanned the rooftops, trying to catch a glimpse of her sister, but she saw no sign of her. Rinn trusted that Cat could find her, help her get out of this predicament. The caravan was escorted through the high-walled gardens to the very gates of the Imperial Palace. With a word from the Grand Merchant, the elaborate iron doors swung open and the guards admitted Rinn and her entourage of shabby wagons. The grandeur of the royal residence was on a scale Rinn had never witnessed. The splendor of Peleon paled compared to the opulence of the Imperial Palace, a miniature city built atop a daunting fortress. The lowest levels appeared ancient, a mighty rampart of rough stone walls with ominous, narrow arrow-slits for windows. Above the fortress walls, lines of battlements wrapped around the palace. An army of stone sentries kept watch: statues of archers, lancers, swordsmen, and more. Above the battlements, perched quaint rows of villas, three and four stories tall. Arcades of arches fronted the buildings, adorned with frescoes and more statuary. A wide-open terrace surrounded by white marble towers occupied the next level. Fountains the size of public bathhouses graced the area, boasting elaborate figures cast in bronze and gold. Sitting high above it all, like a crown, was the Royal Pavilion.

Aculeus brought his white chariot to rest at the foot of the grand staircase leading up to the royal residence. Rinn's humble caravan pulled behind him, like a beggar following a lord. Their soldier escort politely insisted everyone disembark. Rinn stood in awe at the foot of the tremendous stairway. Everyone gawked at the ostentatious display of wealth and power, except Marshal, Molo, and Haril, who stood behind Rinn, battle-ready. A detachment of soldiers marched down the staircase and fanned out before Rinn.

The Grand Merchant smiled widely. "Your personal guard will escort you inside. You must excuse me, but I find the grand staircase overly burdensome. I'll enter my usual way and meet you at the Pavillion." With a flourish of his handkerchief, he signaled for his driver to pull away. Rinn and her party were left alone with the detachment of palace guards.

Their commander, an iron-jawed man in a plumed helmet, beckoned Rinn and her companions forward. "This way, your Highness." Her escort was twenty serious soldiers in banded armor with green sashes, bearing shields and gladius swords. Rinn hesitated to take the first step. Her friends anxiously packed in behind her. Molo and Calder flanked her left, Marshal and Haril her right.

"You don't have to go." Marshal whispered to her.

"I think I do." Rinn whispered back. Swallowing the lump of fear in her throat she addressed the commander. "Where are you taking us?"

"To the Royal Pavilion, your Highness." The commander brought his hand to his chest in salute.

"What does the Grand Merchant want with me?" Rinn asked, not as a challenge, but as an honest question.

"I am not certain." The commander stood at attention, unflinching. "You are a Sevralis, and it is our sworn duty to protect you." Rinn was reminded of her father's story. This soldier was a good man, doing his job. He probably knew nothing of the Curia or the things they had done to her family.

"What is your name, commander?" Rinn inquired.

The officer answered without hesitation. "Onager, your Highness."

"I'm Rinn." She replied with a smile. "Thank you for looking after us." With a bounce in her step, Rinn started up the grand staircase, walking stick in hand.

Chapter 21

R inn was winded before she reached the first landing. She lingered at the terrace with the burbling fountains to rest. Intricately sculpted dolphins and giant bronze seahorses spouted water into an azure pool. The blue tile basin of the pool was adorned with marble starfish and sand dollars. Rinn's friends refreshed themselves by the cool, flowing waters. Sionne lingered by a fountain where lithe marble mermaids chased each other through an artificial coral reef.

Rinn mopped her head with her sleeve. Onager motioned to one of the guards and she produced a small red towel and offered it to Rinn. Accepting it graciously, Rinn noticed that nearly half of her escort were female. The Legion had always accepted capable female warriors, but they were uncommon. Seeing nine or ten in one place was quite a feat. Someone had gone out of their way to make Rinn feel comfortable. She handed the towel back to the female guard who saluted and returned to her position.

Rinn gathered up her strength for the next ascent. She steadied herself with her walking stick and headed up the wide staircase. Her companions followed. Molo carried the exhausted Dempsi in his arms. At the apex of the climb loomed the Royal Pavilion. It reminded Rinn of a temple built in the classic style, rows of thick marble columns

153

supporting a massive overhanging roof. Above the columns carved figures paraded around the roofline in a pantomime of Sevria's history. The entire town of Hilltop could easily fit inside this one building. Rinn looked back to her companions, and she saw the urban fabric of Peleon unfolding before her, an endless tapestry of roads and metropolitan buildings filling the entire peninsula. Rinn's gaze swept from the calm waters of the Lenis Sea to her right to the rough, oceanic waters of the Aspero to her left. She felt like the world was at her feet, an uncomfortable and unnatural sensation. She urged her friends on and climbed the rest of the way to the Pavilion.

"What do we do?" She asked her father before they reached the top.

"The Curia are not to be trusted." Molo reminded Rinn in his best giant whisper.

"I'm aware." Rinn was annoyed, she thought her hatred of the Curia was understood. "But we need a plan."

"We should find your aunt first." Marshal recommended.

"My aunt?" Rinn questioned quietly.

"If Cecilia is alive, she'd be here." Marshal reasoned. "She's certainly no friend of the Curia. She could be a valuable ally."

Rinn nodded in agreement. She gave her friends a hopeful smile as they climbed the final steps. She looked around one last time, hoping to catch a glimpse of her feline sister, but she was nowhere to be seen. With a calming breath, Rinn braved the arched doorway into the Royal Pavilion. The entrance was so large Molo did not have to duck. Rinn and her companions stepped into a huge, open foyer perfectly decorated with delicate statues and polished travertine floors. Palm trees and fern forests sheltered private fountains and sitting areas. Gold-caped sentries guarded every exit.

Grand Merchant Aculeus strolled across the Foyer, his shoes clicking on the marble floor. "Good to see you've made it. Quite a climb, hmm?" He directed everyone to a side portico. "But the view is worth every step." The robust merchant introduced a second man, shorter in stature and thinner in build. He wore his dark hair slicked back and tied up in an elaborate topknot. He beheld Rinn with narrow, intelligent eyes. "This is Praetext Serica, head of the Artist's Guild." He wore a heavy chain of orange and gold around his neck. Another member of the Curia, Rinn thought to herself.

"Call me Serica." The thin man reached out and took ahold of Rinn's right hand. She feared he was going to kiss it for a moment, but instead he bent a knee only slightly and released it. "Your unexpected arrival caught us off guard. Had you given us notice, we would have prepared something more elaborate." He drew out the last word unnecessarily.

"Nonsense." Aculeus argued. "Her ladyship is here now, and that is what matters." The two exchanged a furtive glance.

Before these men could control the situation any further, Rinn blurted out. "I want to see my aunt."

Their answer was not immediately forthcoming. Serica gave a small shrug and Aculeus turned to Rinn. "Of course, my dear. We can visit her villa after you are settled in."

"She doesn't live here at the Pavilion?" Rinn questioned.

Serica answered delicately. "She's chosen a more modest residence. Her apartments are below us, not far from the Flurian Fountains." Rinn assumed those were the ones she passed on her way up the grand stairway.

"All in due time." Aculeus assured her. He snapped his fingers and Onager, the head of Rinn's escort, appeared at his side. "Please show our guests to their rooms." Rinn clearly understood the unintended meaning in the Grand Merchant's command. She was a guest, temporary, and she was trespassing on what was rightfully his. Even Serica winced at his partner's choice of words, but he made no addendum.

Onager led Rinn and her entourage across the foyer and down an elaborate hallway with richly woven wall-hangings and mirrors in gold-gilt frames. They passed through several antechambers before reaching the royal apartments. Members of Rinn's personal guard opened the doors to the rooms, revealing spacious living quarters with astounding views of the city. Sionne voiced his approval. Lutra moved to smack him, but restrained himself. Little Dempsi immediately ran to the terrace and wowed at the view. Onager led Rinn to a further set of doors.

"These are your private chambers, your Highness." He pulled open the doors.

"Please, call me Rinn." She reminded him. Rinn entered the apartment with her father close behind. Onager followed them in and closed the doors behind him.

"Never thought I'd see you again, Theodric." The commander smirked.

Marshal returned a wily grin. "Good to see you, too, crazy man." The two men embraced like long-lost friends.

"You know each other?" Rinn felt stupid even asking.

Onager confessed proudly. "We were the best archers in the seventh cavalry."

"When you shot straight." Marshal pointed out.

"You've developed a limp." Onager observed.

"Got in a tussle in the Rustic Lands." Marshal rubbed his right hip. "Lucky archer caught me off guard."

"That's not like you." Onager laughed. He quieted down and took a long look at Rinn. "She's the spitting image of her mother."

"I know." Marshal agreed.

"You knew my mother?" Rinn's heart skipped a beat.

"Of course." Onager replied. "Your father and I were part of her personal guard here at the palace."

"I never thought you'd stay on." Marshal admitted.

"I wasn't sure myself." Onager said. "But it beats getting killed on the front lines."

"Where's the fighting the worst?" Marshal asked.

"Mostly around Messis." Onager reported. "Also, to the north, Tritica, Campis, even as far as Saxitum." He abruptly changed subjects. "Can she actually do the magic?" He waved his hands mystically.

"Hey." Rinn protested. "I'm right here. And yes, I can do the magic."

Marshal hushed everyone. "Now's not the time or place. We should regroup with the others."

"Agreed." Onager said. He led Rinn and her father to the outer chambers where everyone except the dwarves and Molo were lounging. The demi-humans huddled anxiously in one corner, talking among themselves. Onager recommended the group freshen up before dinner. He promised to send new clothing for everyone, except Molo, he'd need to have something custom tailored for him. The commander departed, leaving half of his detachment behind to secure the royal apartments.

Sionne settled into a luxurious couch. "I could get used to this."

Marshal chastised him. "Well, don't." In hushed tones he cautioned everyone. "We're in real danger here. The men we met acted like they're our friends, but nothing could be further from the truth. They're members of the Curia, and they'll happily kill us if we give them the chance."

Everyone seemed to be shaken by the realization that the pair they had met were part of the Curia. Rinn always described them as inhuman monsters capable of any crime. Molo came forward and added another piece of disturbing evidence.

"Some of you may be aware, but I am older than I appear." He began. "I served Lord Tarandus and his wife Virago personally. I fought by her side during her rebellion against the Curia. I've seen Praetext Serica and the Grand Merchant before. And they haven't aged a day in the last forty years. There's magic at work here."

Marshal acknowledged what Molo said. "They didn't seem to recognize who Molo is, so we should avoid using his name. For the time being, he shall be known as Catulus."

"Seriously?" Molo frowned. Rinn stifled a snicker, Catulus was a name kids gave to small dogs. Even Dempsi laughed at Marshal's joke.

"So, what is your plan?" Haril asked Marshal.

"We really don't have one." Marshal admitted. The mercenary seemed displeased.

"First, we need to find Catherine and then meet my Aunt Cecilia." Rinn recommended. She really wanted to find her sister.

"I mean, why are we here in Peleon?" Haril asserted.

"To find the Emperors." Rinn answered honestly.

"The who?" Haril puzzled.

"The Emperors." She repeated. "The ones Lucus mentioned."

"Lucus? The god of forests?" Haril looked at Rinn like she was a crazy person. Rinn wanted to explain, to justify herself, but she could not find the words to accurately describe her encounter with the amber-eyed god.

Her father intervened. "We believe there might be an unknown Emperor somewhere in Sevria."

"That would explain your daughter's Sigillum abilities." Haril surmised. Rinn frowned inwardly. Why does everyone know how this works but me?

"Exactly." Molo said. "Logically, Peleon would be the best place to start our search."

"Sounds reasonable." The mercenary seemed satisfied. Servants came to offer refreshments, a sweetened lemon beverage and silver platters of sliced fruit. Two dwarven girls carried in the food. Rinn did not like the idea of dwarves as servants, but she did not see any signs of shackles or collars on these girls. Felsic and Mafic followed the pair with their eyes. Rinn wondered how old the dwarven girls were, she had difficulty guessing dwarves' ages. She could not hazard a guess at how many years Felsic or Mafic had seen. The servants departed and Onager returned with fresh clothing for (almost) everyone.

"Dinner will be in one hour." Onager announced. "You all are invited to attend." Rinn did not want to go to a fancy dinner, she wanted to find her sister. But maids conducted Feena and Rinn into a spa-like chamber off the main living area. They were stripped and scrubbed down. The maids made small talk as they worked, complementing the girls on their fine skin and hair. Feena accepted the praise politely, but Rinn was absolutely mortified. She abhorred the shape of her body. Her bony frame stuck out awkwardly and she had a large scar on her left shoulder, a remnant from the vicious duel she fought last year. She dressed quickly, before she had a chance to completely dry off. Her delicate silk gown clung to her damp frame. She sat, miserable and wet, as the maids detangled her mat of curly blond hair. They braided her curls up, fastening everything in place with gold and silver pins.

After more than an hour of preparation, the maids finally decided Rinn was ready. She was escorted from her dressing chamber to the main room where the boys waited, lounging in fine, full-length togas. Marshal and Haril had been given fresh military uniforms, and even little Dempsi had a new dress. The dwarves were clothed in palace outfits. Molo still wore his oversized tunic, tattered and stained from months of hard travel. Rinn stepped into the room wearing a clinging blue dress of silk embellished with silver thread and rows of pearls.

Sionne could not take his eyes off Rinn. "You're beautiful."

"Have you been drinking?" Rinn protested, pulling her arms across her chest. With her hair pulled up, her neck and upper back felt bare and exposed.

"He's right." Tavin concurred. "You look amazing."

Rinn sized up the scribe, freshly bathed and wearing a new toga. He looked quite handsome himself, but Rinn did not know how to express it. Instead she muttered. "Thanks." Marshal appraised his daughter and oozed fatherly compliments. Rinn was skeptical of his judgement. She did notice Feena and Lutra exchanging private words, each wearing a broad smile. Marshal walked his daughter to dinner, holding her arm in his.

"I'm worried about Cat." Rinn commented quietly.

"I am, too." Her father whispered back. "We'll have to wait for her to return. She'll come back when she thinks it's safe."

"I hope you're right." Rinn fretted.

Chapter 22

D inner at the palace was nothing less than miraculous. The feast hall was wide and inviting with burbling fountains and alcoves boasting statues of the nine gods. Large, arched windows opened onto broad terraces brimming with exotic flowers. Even the sunset seemed to be part of the show, the sky perfectly dappled in deep shades of orange and red.

Rinn and her companions reclined on soft couches while servants paraded by an endless stream of delicacies. Warmed and chilled wines were offered from ornate silver urns. Rinn always opted for juice, she still had reservations about mixing her Sigillum abilities with alcohol. Everyone dined on exotic fruits and spiced cheeses, decadent pastries and tender meats. Rinn even sampled roast fowl that Aculeus promised was peacock. Lutra and Feena fed each other delicacies from the sumptuous feast. Sionne and Dempsi ate like children. Marshal, Haril, and Calder ate sparingly. Rinn noticed her father did not partake of the wine. Molo and the dwarves were served, but they were relegated to a remote corner of the room.

Aculeus and Serica were joined by a third member of the Curia, a thick-necked man they introduced as Furticus. He held the office of Aedile, keeper of public buildings and provisioner of agriculture. His chain of office was yellow and gold. Furticus spoke very little, but his appetite was astonishing. He sampled every dish that passed him. Dinner conversation was light, no one spoke of politics or war. Rinn was amazed at how Aculeus and Serica could talk so much without actually saying anything. During the feast, Rinn spied Aculeus speaking into a small brass funnel.

Rinn whispered to her father. "What's that thing he's talking into?"

"A palaver." Marshal quietly replied. "A magical device for communicating over long distances." Rinn squinted and she could see the faint tint of blue magic emanating from the device. As she surveyed the room, she found subtle hints of magic everywhere—from the bronze oil lamps to the burbling fountains. Rinn excused herself from the feast and strolled around the room. Gold-caped guards were posted at every exit. Rinn realized that no one in her party wore weapons. With the offer of new clothes, the Curia had stripped Rinn and her companions of their ability to defend themselves. It did not matter, Rinn concluded. She was not defenseless. In her hands, every serving spoon and fork, anything with metal in it, could be a potential weapon.

Rinn lingered by the alcoves adorned with figures of the gods. She chuckled to herself, the statue of Lucus did not look a thing like him. Rinn found little Dempsi at her side.

"Do you see the magic?" She whispered to the little girl.

Dempsi nodded. She pointed to the fountains.

"That's right." Rinn smiled. "But that doesn't mean you can do magic here." She touched the girl on the nose, just like her father used to do to her. "Everything here is expensive, and we don't want anything to get broken."

Dempsi nodded in agreement. Rinn brought her back to her seat, where the little girl laid down to rest. The dinner had lasted several hours already. Sionne had passed out, snoring loudly. The others were doing their best to ignore him. In the corner, the dwarves ate heartily of roast fowl and fruit pies, but Molo only glowered, his food untouched. Lutra produced his flute and played a series of original tunes, much to the delight of their hosts.

Preatext Serica leaned over to Rinn. "You have talented associates. See that he finds his way to my offices at the Lautus Ampitheater."

Spurred on by Lutra's performance, Aculeus called for entertainers. A choir of quality performed traditional hymns in four and five voice polyphony. Serica summoned his own musicians, virtuoso instrumentalists who stunned the audience. After several more competing acts, Rinn felt the need to end this charade. She already knew the Curia were rich and powerful, she did not need opulent displays to convince her.

"I'm getting sleepy." She stated, rising. "I'd like to return to my quarters."

"But the chef has yet to bring out the creamed herring." Aculeus objected with grandiosity. "It is one of his finest dishes."

"Another time." Rinn deflected. Her friends rose one by one. Lutra held Fccna's hand as she stood. Marshal lifted the drowsy Dempsi from her seat. Calder shook the sleeping Sionne awake. The three members of the Curia quit their feasting and moved to the doorway.

"We regret seeing you leave so soon." Serica touched the silk scarves at his throat. "We were so enjoying your company." The gruff Furticus grunted in agreement, he was still wiping food from his face with a linen napkin.

"Another time." Rinn assured them, and took her leave. To her surprise, they let her go. Outside the dining chamber, Onager waited with Rinn's personal guard.

"Everything alright?" He asked, a question directed more at Marshal than Rinn.

"Seems to be." Marshal admitted. Rinn's guard led them through the twilight halls of the palace. In the evening, the Pavilion became a maze of dim corridors. It would take an ocean of candles to keep every corner of the palace alight. Rinn sleepily filed down dim hallways with her friends. As they rounded a corner, a hand reached out and covered Rinn's mouth. She kicked and fought as she was pulled into a dark alcove.

"Quiet." A fiendish voice wheezed. "Your pet is in danger." Rinn recognized the speaker and the bandaged hand over her mouth. Yallakh.

"Cat?" Rinn asked, her voice muffled by the assassin's hand.

"Yes." He hissed. He slowly released her. Even in the shadows, Rinn could see that Yallakh was a mess. His bandages were filthy and torn, and his left arm moved awkwardly, but his red and brown eyes sizzled with life.

"What are you doing here?" Rinn demanded.

"I came to warn you." Yallakh's gravelly voice showed his urgency. "This palace is not safe. You are surrounded by magic wards that dampen your power."

"What?" Rinn stifled a gasp.

"Come. We don't have much time." Yallakh insisted. He peered down the hallway, to see if anyone was watching. Unexpectedly, he yanked Rinn into the darkness. She could tell they were doubling back, heading toward the feasting hall.

"Where are you taking me?" Rinn whispered.

"To the kitchens." Yallakh hissed. It seemed completely irrational, to trust a known assassin, a villainous scoundrel who tried to kill Rinn on several occasions, but Rinn allowed herself to be led down dark hallways. In her head she had tried repeatedly to contact Cat, with no answer. If Yallakh knew her whereabouts, Rinn would have to trust him. The clandestine pair crept down twisting corridors to the food preparation rooms. A few servant girls were chatting as they washed large bronze pots. Yallakh crouched low and passed through the room unseen. Rinn summoned her courage and squatted down, crawling across the slick tile floor. Her hand slipped and she knocked her chin on the floor. She clapped her hand over her mouth in shock and pain. The servant girls did not seem to notice, they were too engrossed in their work. Yallakh waved Rinn forward. She crept cautiously to him, blinking away tears. The dark assassin led Rinn to a dead-end corridor.

"We're here." He opened a large wooden hatch in the wall. It smelled like a disaster.

"What is that?" Rinn covered her mouth and nose.

"The kitchen waste chute." Yallakh explained. "It leads to the very lowest levels of the palace."

"I'm not going in there." Rinn was feeling squeamish just smelling the passageway. She absolutely did not want to climb inside.

"Your feline does not have much time." Yallakh warned. "This is the fastest way." Without further discussion he slithered into the chute and disappeared. Rinn was not left with any choice. I'm doing this for Cat, she reminded herself. She afforded herself one luxury, she pulled her mother's triangular pendant out from the pouch around her neck. It glowed softly in the darkness. She held her breath and entered the slimy disposal chute. Rinn immediately lost her grip and tumbled downward, sliding through greasy, rotten refuse. As she fell, Rinn instinctively called out her Sigillum word "ahebbe". The effect stuttered, but eventually took hold, and Rinn's fall slowed to a gentle descent. She floated down the narrow chute bathed in the dim green glow of her mother's pendant. The acrid smell of rotting food burned her eyes and assaulted her nose. Rinn forced herself not to get sick. She reminded herself that she was doing this for her sister.

At the bottom of the chute Yallakh waited in a pile of refuse the size of a house. He looked ready to catch Rinn as she fell, but she delicately floated by and touched down on her tiptoes. He scowled at her. "Show off."

"Was that a joke?" Rinn asked, momentarily pleased.

"Let's go." He turned away and waded through the garbage. Rinn followed him as best as she could. Her fine silk dress was utterly ruined, shredded and smeared in putrid grime. Yallakh led Rinn out of the refuse and to a stout door in a thick stone wall. This was the most ancient part of the palace, once a bastion of defense long before it became an object of luxury. Yallakh produced a set of lock picks and went to work on the door. Rinn reached over and whispered "onlithe", and the lock fell open. Yallakh peered up at her, moderately impressed. Rinn shrugged and smiled. He pushed open the squeaky door just a crack and slinked inside. Rinn followed.

As she crept through the low-ceilinged corridors, Rinn wished she had a spear or at least a knife. Yallakh led her deep into the structure, pausing several times at the sound of people passing by. He navigated the dimly lit hallways until he came to a room with an armored steel door at its far end. Four soldiers, two on each side, guarded the doorway with polearms. They had the muscles and scars of seasoned warriors.

"I need a weapon." Rinn whispered to Yallakh. He quietly slid a curved knife from a sheath strapped to his leg and handed it to her. The black blade glinted in the darkness, it felt unnecessarily heavy. Rinn touched the knife and realized it was glass, or something very much like it. She handed the weapon back to Yallakh. "I need metal."

The assassin let out a hiss of frustration as he returned the knife to its sheath. He backtracked away from the room and settled Rinn into a dark alcove. "Wait here. Do not make a sound. You'll know when the time is right to move."

"Yallakh." Rinn reached out for his bandaged hand. "Thank you."

His red and brown eyes were unreadable in the darkness. The corners of his mouth curled as he produced a small clay jar. "I borrowed this from your father. He's quite clever." The assassin turned away and charged the room with the four sentries. He smashed the jar on the floor and the room filled with billows of thick, gray smoke. Rinn could hear the ensuing struggle, but she could see nothing. Eventually, several shapes rushed past her, one after another. Rinn waited before she risked moving. The smoke settled, and the room was empty except for the armored door and one polearm laying near it. Rinn offered a quiet word of thanks to Yallakh and quit her hiding place. She grabbed the abandoned polearm, it did not have the same balance as a spear, but it was close enough.

Rinn could faintly feel her sister close by. The only thing standing in her way was the stout, armored door. Rinn squinted and it glowed deeply with the rich, blue aura of magic. She spoke the Sigillum word "onlithe", but door remained stubbornly locked. Rinn imbued the head of the polearm with magic, its axe-like tip burned green in response. She slashed at the armored door, but it effectively resisted, sending showers of sparks across the stone floor. Rinn raked the weapon across the door several more times without success. She cursed in frustration. She knew Cat was in there, barely clinging to life.

Damn the door! Rinn poured her energy into the weapon and mercilessly carved a hole into the rock wall beside it, the stones crumbled at her approach. She burst into the chamber, weapon ready. Cat hung limply in midair, arms and legs pulled taut by magical bonds secured to crystals embedded in the floor and ceiling. She had been stripped of her clothes and her fur was badly burned in several places. Two of her claws were broken, and blood trickled from her mouth.

"Cat!" Rinn cried out and ran to her sister, but a magical force stood in her way. She gritted her teeth angrily. "Fine. You want to see a barrier—I'll show you a barrier." Rinn concentrated and summoned a blazing sphere of triangles and swirls in rage. It glowed fiercely, five layers of magic spinning like a saw. Rinn pushed forward, grinding her shield into the magical barrier around her sister. The two forces screamed out as they clashed. Cat's bruised eyes fluttered, and her head twitched. Rinn pushed to her sister with unbridled ferocity, the noise was deafening and the heat intense.

A hand touched Rinn's shoulder. She turned around with a start—somehow Yallakh had gotten inside her shield. "This is elfcraft. You can't force your way through." She stared at him in amazement. He peeled the bandages from his right hand, exposing his intricate blood tattoos. He traced a symbol on one of the crystals with his finger and the magical restraint released. Cat's right leg fell free, dangling in the air. Rinn rushed up to collect her sister. Yallakh unlocked the remaining bonds. Rinn noticed that he did not need to touch the crystals, just trace the strange symbol in the air. As the last bond released, Cat fell into Rinn's arms. She was so light.

Cat opened her bleary eyes. "Rinn." Her left front fang was broken.

Rinn held her sister tightly and cried tears of rage. The Curia would pay for this.

Chapter 23

Rinn kicked open the door to the royal apartments, cradling Cat in her arms. The teenagers and dwarves were pacing the room and Marshal and Molo were in a heated discussion with Onager. They all turned to see Rinn's violent entrance.

Marshal rushed forward. "Oh gods, Catherine." He lifted the injured feline from Rinn's arms. "What happened?"

"Take her to my bedroom." Rinn commanded. He did as she asked without question. Rinn's worried friends gathered around her. Onager pushed himself forward and fell to a knee.

"Your Highness. I failed you." He bowed low to the ground.

Rinn was beyond anger, but she knew better than to vent it on this man. Instead, she made a pronouncement. "I need time with my sister. You will secure my chamber." She strode across the room and gathered her walking stick. The bag with the spear point rested on a nearby table. Rinn clicked the metal tip into place. "Anyone who disturbs us will be killed. Is that clear?"

"Yes, m'Lady." Onager vowed. "It will be as you say."

"See that my friends are protected." Rinn demanded. "I will return in the morning." She spun on her heel and pushed her way to the bedroom chamber. She closed the doors and barred them with her spear. She shuttered and locked the windows. The room was dark and quiet, the only sound was Cat's labored breathing. She was sprawled out on the wide, soft bed, burned and naked. Rinn stripped off her own filthy clothing and briefly wiped the grease from her face, arms, and legs. She brought a clean cloth and a pitcher of water to the bedside. Climbing onto the fine linen sheets, she tended to Cat's wounds, gently wiping the blood from her mouth and delicately sponging the blackened fur and burn marks on her sides. Her sister made small grimaces.

"Oh, Cat." Rinn shuddered, wiping her face. She toweled her sister dry and crawled in bed beside her. She lifted the thin silk sheet over them both and pulled her sister close. Rinn knew that the best cure for Cat was magic, her magic. Rinn closed her eyes and wrapped her arms around her fuzzy sister, she cried herself to sleep with Cat in her arms.

::

Rinn woke the next day groggy and aching. She rolled over in bed, reaching out her hand, but Catherine was not there. Rinn shot up, desperate to find her. She found her sister standing by a terrace window, wearing a thin robe. Her fur had bald patches where it had been burned away, but she seemed healthy and strong. Cat stared out the window, lost in thought.

"What do you see?" Rinn asked, reclining back in bed.

Cat did not answer immediately. She never took her eyes off the city. "Are we wrong?"

"What do you mean?" Rinn leaned on one elbow.

"Should we be helping these people?" Cat questioned. "This city is a sham. It sparkles and shines on the surface, but underneath it's filth."

"Why would you say that?" Rinn rose.

Cat turned from the window, the hurt in her eyes was fathomless. "You didn't see the men who captured me. They laughed as they taunted me, tortured me." Cat's tail swished angrily. "I want them to die."

"You don't mean that." Rinn insisted.

Cat flexed her broken claws, resolute. "I do."

"People do bad things, but that doesn't mean they are beyond all hope." Rinn argued.

"I don't care." Cat spat.

"Cat." Rinn softened her tone. "Do you know who helped me find you? It was Yallakh. You and I both know he's done terrible things, but he helped me save your life. People deserve a chance. This city deserves a chance."

"No, it doesn't!" Cat yelled. "Burn it down." Rinn embraced her sister. Cat resisted at first, but then melted into Rinn's arms and burst into tears. "Burn this damn city down. I know you can do it, Rinn. Wipe it off the map." Cat cried. Rinn stroked her sister's head, letting the emotion pour out. Eventually, Cat's fit of anger subsided.

"We're going to do things differently." Rinn assured her. "I'm tired of playing games. We're going to meet this Curia on our own terms."

::

Rinn stood toe to toe with the Grand Merchant, Cat by her side. She was dressed in her battle outfit complete with dragon-feather vest and a spear. Cat wore her own armor over her burns, daggers strapped to her legs. "Explain yourself." Rinn demanded, thumping her spear on the ground.

Aculeus mopped his fat head with a lace handkerchief. "We had no idea she was a member of your company. We caught her sneaking around the palace. We thought she was an unnatural assassin." He shuddered as he said the last two words.

171

Cat snarled and raised a claw but Rinn restrained her. Rinn faced down the Grand Merchant. "Don't play me for a fool. You know who I am, and you know what I am. Therefore, you know who she is. Catherine is a member of my family, your maltreatment of her is a direct attack on me. Do you really want me as your enemy?"

Aculeus, red-faced and flustered, rebuked her. "This is not the time or place for threats. We are a civilized people trying to uphold the law."

"Does your law require torture?" Rinn challenged.

"We maintain order." Aculeus answered smugly.

"You're tyrants." Rinn accused. "And your bloody reign is tearing this nation apart."

"Sevria would have perished long ago had we not intervened." Aculeus jutted out his bottom lip. "You should be thanking us."

"For what, decades of civil war?" Rinn thumped the butt of her spear on the marble floor. "You'll answer for that and more. I demand a meeting with the Curia two days from now. Exactly at noon."

"Such a thing is not easy to accommodate." Aculeus stammered, breaking out in a new rash of sweat. "The members have many duties to attend."

"You have two days." Rinn repeated her ultimatum.

"It can't be done." Aculeus insisted.

Rinn leaned forward. "Do you know what I find most amusing? My assassin is the one person you never found. He's still sneaking around the palace unseen." Arculeus' eyes bulged wide. With pursed lips and a wave of his handkerchief he summoned his guards and left.

::

"Are you crazy?" Marshal asked in disbelief. Rinn's companions huddled in the shared living area of their apartments. Onager and five of Rinn's personal guard accompanied them.

"No." Rinn replied. "I demanded a meeting with the Curia."

"You can't just walk into a room with those men." Marshal insisted.

"It's madness." Molo reiterated, Clive in his hand. "They have dark powers you don't understand. You saw what they did to Cat."

"And they will answer for their crimes." Rinn promised.

"Rinn." Her father put a hand on her shoulder. "You're walking straight into the fire. Don't do this. There has to be another way."

"If the Curia are here, dealing with me, then they aren't out abusing and killing my people." A subtle change was taking ahold of Rinn. She did not hear herself refer to Sevrians as her people, but her father did. Rinn continued. "We now have two days to search for the Emperors. We can't do that here under the thumb of idiots like the Grand Merchant."

"What're you suggesting?" Her father asked.

"We leave the palace, split up." Rinn advised. "Explore the city, find any leads we can. I'll call on Aunt Cecilia before I leave."

"Where'll we stay?" Molo asked.

"We don't have many allies." Rinn conceded. "Is there a shrine to Lucus in Peleon?"

"He's the only god who doesn't have a presence in the city." Marshal sighed. A thought struck him. "I may have a few contacts still around. I'll seek them out. Let's meet at the Natatorium."

"The shrine to Imber?" Rinn questioned.

Molo nodded in agreement. "It's a complex of public pools, crowded and difficult to watch."

Marshal added. "And it's far from the palace, on the western edge of town. We'll split up and meet there at sundown."

"I can sneak you out of the palace two at a time." Onager offered.

Rinn charged him with a task. "Provide escorts for my companions, keep them safe. But your guards need to lose their green sashes, they are too conspicuous." An idea struck her, she moved to the dwarves. "Felsic, do you think you and your brother can fashion medallions? Something small but recognizable?"

"Certainly." Felsic brushed his brown beard, it was growing in nicely.

"What style shall we make them?" Mafic asked.

"Use this." Rinn fished out her mother's pendant from the pouch around her neck. She lovingly handed it to Felsic, the metallic triangle glowed softly in his hands. He studied it reverently. "Morton thrane, the rarest of all metals."

"Onager will get you any supplies you need." Rinn asserted. She gathered her friends together and addressed them. "It's too dangerous to stay in the palace. We're heading out into the city today, leave nothing behind."

"Including the food?" Sionne eyed the scrumptious breakfast left out for them.

"Take as much as you want, but leave something for Yallakh. He's around here somewhere." Rinn instructed. "Everyone divide into small groups. No one should travel alone. Haril: go with Grus and Tavin. Search the public archives. See if you can find any clues. Feena: take Lutra and Sionne and explore the markets and taverns. Listen to what the common people have to say. Molo: infiltrate the demi-human quarters with Felsic and Mafic. Take Calder for backup." Rinn gently squeezed the dwarves' arms, they nodded in response. "Onager: go with my father and ready our horses. Make sure he gets to the Natatorium."

"I should stay with you." The head guard objected.

"No." Rinn's voice was stern. "Protect my father. The Curia will likely make a move against him. Be swift, get away from the palace before they can act. Cat and I will leave immediately after we visit my aunt."

"I'll send an attachment to go with you." Onager insisted.

"That would slow us down." Rinn softened. "Don't worry. Together we'll be safe, even from the likes of the Curia and their cronies. Make certain my friends and family get out of the palace. We'll meet tonight at the Natatorium. Speed of the gods to you all."

Chapter 24

R inn wasted more time than she wanted readying herself for her meeting with her aunt. Even though she donned her scruffy travel clothes and dragon feather vest, she combed and styled her hair, fastening it up with silver and gold pins from last night's feast. She washed her face and scrubbed her teeth. She even tied a bit of ribbon around her collar, to soften her militant outfit. Cat wore a matching bow on the end of her tail. Together, the two girls exited the royal apartments. Her father and all her friends had quietly departed earlier, each group bound for a different destination. In the hallway outside, two of Rinn's personal guards waited for her. They wore their green sashes over their armor, but both women sported small triangular medallions with swirls etched into them. Rinn winked at the guards as she passed, they smiled back.

Rinn and Cat made their way down the grand staircase, hand in paw. A warm sun lazed in the late morning sky. Wispy clouds drifted in from the ocean. Below, the city of Peleon was alive with movement. Trickles of citizens merged into great pedestrian rivers flowing down the Grand Concourse. Fleets of wagons and carriages waded through the sea of people. Rinn and Cat descended until they arrived at the fountain-filled terrace. Rinn had wanted to spend time with Dempsi at the fountains, but that would not happen now. She would make it up to her at the Natatorium later.

Rinn surveyed the villas facing the terrace, they all looked alike. Rinn turned to her escort. "What are your names?" She asked kindly.

Taken aback, the female guards answered. "Lepas, ma'am."

"Velle, m'lady."

Rinn touched the calloused hands of her two guards. "Thank you, Velle and Lepas, for accompanying me. I need to visit my aunt, Princess Cecilia. I think she lives in one of these buildings."

"That one, m'lady." Velle answered, pointing out a villa in the distance. Velle was a muscular woman with a short brown ponytail. She led the way to a modest building south of the fountains. Before they arrived, Rinn gave her escort strict instructions.

"The two of us are going inside. Do not wait for us." The women began to object, but Rinn reassured them. "We'll be leaving another way. After we're inside, depart the palace discretely and rendezvous with everyone at the Natatorium before nightfall." They saluted in acknowledgement. Rinn added with a nod. "Be safe. No heroics."

Rinn led her sister to her aunt's villa. She tingled in anticipation, eager to meet her mother's only living relative. Rinn knew very little about her mother, her father rarely spoke of her. A wide, stupid smile settled on Rinn's face as she approached the villa. Who would know more about her mother than her own sister? Two gold-caped sentries posted outside the doorway did not bother Rinn. She and Cat strolled right past them. Rinn gently pushed the door open and entered shyly into a small foyer. Aunt Cecilia's apartments were bathed in shadow, every door shut, and every window shrouded with heavy drapery. Rinn tiptoed through the room, Cat close at her side.

"Hello?" Rinn called meekly. "Aunt Cecilia?"

No answer came. Rinn ventured deeper into the crypt-like house. Signs of occupation could be seen in a dim hallway—a table with a pitcher of water beading sweat and a platter of half-eaten food. Rinn skulked deeper into the shadows. Cat pointed to a secluded room at the far side of the villa. There, in the light of a single oil lamp, a frail woman reclined on a sofa, gauzy bedsheets pulled around her. Rinn dared not take another step forward.

The woman lifted her head to her visitors. "Tabitha?" She murmured, her voice was soft and musical, but at the same time breathy and hoarse.

"Aunt Cecilia?" Rinn braved a step into the room. "I'm Rinn. I'm Tabitha's daughter."

"Oh, little Rinn. My, you look just like your mother." Cecilia raised her hands, bony and shriveled. "Come closer, my dear." As Rinn neared, she could see the deep creases around her aunt's eyes and mouth. Her hair was thinning, gray, and limp. Her lips were parched and cracked. Rinn's aunt should be younger than her father, but she appeared ancient. Cecilia coughed into her bedsheets. In the dim lamplight, Rinn could see that her aunt must have been beautiful in her youth, before it was ruined by her premature aging. Cecilia rested a cool hand on Rinn's arm. Rinn wanted to recoil at her touch, but she restrained herself. "It's nice of you to come. I do not get many visitors."

"Aunt Cecilia, can you tell me about my mom?" Rinn asked.

"Is Tabitha here?" Cecilia glanced around the room, expecting to see her sister. She squeezed Rinn's arm softly.

"No, Aunt Cecilia." Rinn replaced her aunt's hand on the bedsheets. "She died a long time ago."

"Oh." Cecilia replied. "Every morning, I look out at the fountains and expect to see her playing in them, just like when we were kids. She was such an unusual girl. Did you know she could talk to fire? I once saw her put out an entire blaze with just a word. It was in the kitchens, a cook spilled oil over the stove and set the whole place aflame. And there was Tabitha, standing in the middle of it all. She spoke and suddenly, the fire was out. Just like that." Cecilia laughed weakly and coughed into her bedsheets again.

Rinn knelt down at her aunt's side. "Auntie Cecilia, did my mother ever talk to you about magic?"

"Auntie." Her elderly-appearing aunt cackled. "That's nice."

Rinn was becoming impatient. "Her magic. Did my mother talk about it?"

"Oh, no." Cecilia moaned. "She was always hanging around with that soldier boy."

"Marshal." Rinn stated. "That's my father."

"No." Cecilia corrected. "His name was Theodrus. A handsome young man, but far too serious for her. My Tabitha was so happy and carefree. One time she found a bird on the terrace, too weak to fly. She nursed the poor creature back to health. She never kept it in a cage, she let it hop around her bedchamber. Finally, one day the bird flew off, and Tabitha was so full of joy. Sad, but also happy. Such a funny girl."

Frustration filled Rinn. Her mother must have left behind some clue, some secret to unlocking her powers. Rinn was desperate to find it. "Auntie Cecilia, I need to know about my mom's abilities. How did she learn how to use them?"

"Abilities?" The elderly woman quizzed.

"Her magic." Rinn insisted. "Where did she learn to use her magic?"

"Oh, dearie, Tabitha was no magician." Cecilia seemed cross. "Those priests of Sidus came and examined her. They declared that she had no gift for magic, but the Curia was not fooled. Especially not Gentris, he was always suspicious of her."

Rinn whispered softly. "Did the Curia do anything to her?"

"To her?" Cecilia sat up on her sofa agitated, her mouth a sneer. She leaned dangerously close to Rinn. "They did *this* to me. Those bastards made me drink harbane. A curse on every one of them." She slumped back into her pillows, caught in a rack of coughing. Rinn did not know what harbane was, but the way her aunt said it made it sound like poison. Rinn was trying to formulate another question when her aunt asked. "Who do you have with you?"

"Oh." Rinn turned and remembered Cat behind her. She had not touched anything in the room, she waited silently. Rinn drew her close. "This is my sister, Catherine."

"She's so lovely." Cecilia weakly smiled. "Are you a Margot?"

"I am." Catherine answered, her tail swishing softly.

"Nice to meet you, Catherine." Cecilia held out her hand to shake, Cat accepted it in her paws. Cecilia giggled. "Your fur is so soft."

"Call me Cat." She let the elderly woman touch her arms and tail.

Cecilia sat back, satisfied. "That was my mother's one regret, that she was never blessed with a Margot of her own. It's so nice to meet you, Catherine." She whispered in her feline ear. "Don't let the Curia find you. They don't understand the bond between the Sigilla and the Margot. They'd do anything to find out." Cat gave the elderly woman a small hug. The old woman smiled and settled peacefully into her pillows, closing her eyes.

Rinn curtseyed to her aunt. "Thank you, Auntie Cecilia. We'll call again another time."

"Please do." Creases wrinkled around her aunt's closed eyes. Rinn waved a brief farewell and took her leave. Cat led her down dark hallways to the front foyer. Rinn could see an entire cohort of gold-caped guards assembled outside waiting for them.

"We should be going." Rinn reached for her sister's paw.

"Where are we headed?" Cat asked.

"You decide." Rinn smiled. "We don't have to be at the Natatorium until nightfall. Is there anything in Peleon you'd like to see?" Cat thought about it for a moment and they disappeared.

::

Catherine dragged Rinn on a whirlwind tour across the rooftops of Peleon. Skipping over heights of the city was exhilarating, a private landscape of peaked stone roofs and terracotta tile. Ornately carved obelisks poked above the rooflines bearing bronze statues of soldiers, heroes, and famous politicians. The steeples of the seven churches pierced the skyline and the mountainous palace complex sat high above everything like a watchful mother. Rinn wandered through a landscape of vibrant color, immense frescoes of wealth, power, and influence. She could not believe such artistry was wasted in a location where few would ever appreciate it.

Somewhere along the way, Rinn lost her fear of heights. It was possible she was feeding off Cat's excitement or maybe her experience hurtling through the sky over Viburna had changed her. Either way, Rinn became emboldened, even reckless. She raced down precarious ledges and scaled precipitous peaks, buoyed by the knowledge she could float with a word. A giddy energy bubbled up inside her as she traipsed across the rooftop landscape of Peleon with her sister. Cat reverted to her usual, playful self and her energy and enthusiasm were contagious. Rinn worried that her sister would be permanently scarred by her cruel treatment at the palace, but Cat seemed to have recovered nicely.

The pair arrived at the Natatorium winded and content. The evening sun was setting in the western sky, and long shadows stretched across the streets. The light from elaborate outdoor lamps danced on the surface of the vast public pools of the Natatorium. A dwindling number of evening visitors lingered around the waters. Rinn found Dempsi sitting poolside, her shoes off and her feet dangling in the water. Marshal watched over her from a nearby bench. Rinn saw a new cane leaning beside him.

"Hi, Daddy." Rinn plopped down beside her father.

"Hi, Rinn." He smiled with relief. "How was your day?"

"Great." Rinn answered, squeezing her sister's paw. Cat climbed onto Marshal's lap and lifted up her chin. He patted her head and scratched her under the chin. Cat purred with feline bliss.

"How was your meeting with your aunt?" He asked Rinn.

Before Rinn had a chance to answer, a guard patrol rounded the corner in the distance. Marshal rose, grabbing his cane. "We should get inside before we're seen." He stretched out his hand to the little girl. "Come on, Dempsi, we're headed inside."

"Okay." She called back, plucking her feet out of the water. She reached for Marshal's hand and let him lead her inside. In her other hand, Rinn could see the little girl was palming a ball of water. Rinn laughed to herself. She grabbed her sister's paw and followed them into the Natatorium.

Chapter 25

The humidity inside the Natatorium was oppressive, making it momentarily hard for Rinn to breathe. Cat winced and stuck out her tongue in protest. Imber was the goddess of rain, and her temples were huge enclosed pools. A life-sized porcelain figure of the goddess graced a western alcove, a demure woman clothed in clouds bearing a large urn. Mosaics in blue and white tile covered the walls, depicting all the blessings rain can give. But the ceiling was a work of genius, a vaulted dome studded with thousands of stone projections, like stalactites in a cave. Moisture dripped from the stony points into the pool evoking the sounds of constant light rain.

When Dempsi saw the giant pool, she could not restrain herself. She dashed into the water, laughing and splashing. She held her hands over her head as she twirled in the indoor rain. A blue-robed parson tending oil lamps rushed over to scold the girl. He intercepted Marshal and Rinn. Cat had disappeared.

"These are sacred waters." The parson's brow twisted in disapproval. "Remove your daughter at once." Rinn could understand the parson's assumption, her father's dark hair color matched Dempsi's black mane almost exactly.

Obediently Marshal called out. "Dempsi, come here."

The little girl splashed to the edge of the pool, all smiles. "The rain is singing to me." She stretched her hands out wide and the drops fell more fervently, like a torrent in a summertime storm. Even though Rinn was not standing in the pool, she covered her head against the downpour. Dempsi reveled in it. The parson trembled, tracing a sign over his chest.

"A rain-bringer." The parson's voice cracked as he fell to his knees. The temple filled with the deafening sounds of rain as it began to fall with the ferocity of a waterfall. Curiously, Rinn saw that the sacred pool was not overflowing, the mystical rain was exactly contained within its boundaries.

Unsure what to do, Marshal called out over the din of the storm. "Dempsi!" As he caught the little girl's attention, the downpour abruptly ended. The Natatorium became unnaturally quiet, the only sound an occasional drip from the ceiling. Marshal reached out his hands. "Come here, dear." He lifted her from the pool and set her on the dry walkway. Neither her hair nor her clothing appeared to be wet.

The parson, a middle-aged man with short ash-colored hair whispered. "Miraculous." He reached out to the little girl with reverence. He beseeched Marshal. "You must take your daughter to the holy temple at Messis. She has been blessed by Imber. Such a thing has not happened in hundreds of years."

Oblivious to the conversation around her, Dempsi tugged at Marshal's sleeve. "I want to talk to the rain some more."

Marshal looked to the parson, who fumbled his hands nervously. He never made an answer, so Marshal decided for him. "Okay. But just for a bit."

"Yay!" Dempsi happily waded back into the pool. Water poured from the ceiling in a symphony of drizzles. Dempsi danced and laughed.

::

Marshal crept through the nighttime alleyways with Cat, Rinn, and Dempsi. They made for an old warehouse a few blocks from the Natatorium. They slinked through the shadows to the building. Marshal rapped gently on the door. It was opened by a dark-skinned woman at the peak of middle age. Her body was lean and muscular, and her sharp, angular face was both proud and beautiful. Marshal introduced her as Niveus, an acquaintance from his soldiering days. Marshal placed his hands on Rinn's shoulders as he introduced her. "Niveus, this is my daughter Rinn."

"By the sky." The woman had a foreign accent. "She looks just like her mother. You must keep her far from the Curia, they will wish her ill."

Marshal brought forth his adopted daughter. "And this is her sister, Catherine." Niveus was momentarily shocked by Cat's appearance.

"Someone you liberated from Migalia?" Niveus eyed Marshal suspiciously.

"She is not from Migalia." Marshal corrected. "Catherine's a Margot."

"Good gods." Niveus hurried them inside. "Quickly, get out of the streets before anyone sees you."

Inside, the warehouse was cluttered but clean. Rinn's friends reclined on wooden crates scattered about the room. They were joined by Onager and several members of the palace guard, Rinn recognized Velle and her partner Lepas. Brass braziers provided light for the assembled company. Feena rose when she saw Rinn enter. She came over and gave her friend a warm hug. "You're late." She chastised Rinn.

"Sorry. I didn't mean to make you worry." Rinn apologized. "I promised Dempsi I'd let her play at the Natatorium."

"How did it go?" Feena asked.

"Um." Rinn did not know exactly how to explain what happened inside the Temple to Imber. "Better than expected."

"Come get some dinner." Feena pulled her along by the hand.

"Food?" Cat raised her ears in interest. Rinn sat between the dwarves and her personal guard. Felsic cut her a thick slice of bread from a barley loaf, it was soft and fresh. Mafic handed her a plate with cubes of cheese, dates, and olives. While Rinn ate, Niveus interrogated Marshal.

"Who are all these people you travel with?" She assessed the odd group. Marshal eased down onto a crate, and leaned his cane against the wall. "And what happened to your leg?"

"Battle wound." Marshal smirked. "We've seen our share of conflict."

"I could tell." Niveus folded her arms. "You dress like traders but are armed like soldiers. What are you doing in Peleon?"

"Rinn needed to see her aunt." Marshal explained.

"At the palace?" Niveus pursed her lips. "Out of the question. You are not going anywhere near that den of wolves." Onager frowned.

"Too late." Marshal confessed. "We left there this morning."

"With your heads intact?" Niveus inhaled. "You are a reckless fool, horseboy."

"I go by Marshal now." He glowered.

"Not to me." Niveus declared. "You will always be horseboy." Rinn bit her lips to hold back her laughter. Others in the party were not as kind.

Molo stood up for his friend. "Leave him be. We've had a long journey from Viburna."

"Viburna?" Niveus snapped. "Why would you go to that grashel nest? The city is haunted, some even say cursed."

"Not anymore." Cat smiled, kicking her feet off the edge of a box. She resumed nibbling away at a side of salted fish.

Niveus squinted crossly at Marshal. "Explain yourself."

Lutra stood and cleared his throat. He bowed and played a few notes on his flute. Then, he delivered a detailed account of the events that occurred at Viburna, much of his story was told in rhyming couplets. Lutra's voice was pleasant and lyrical, he held the room in his hand. Rinn wondered where he came by this newfound talent. Onager and the palace guards were completely awed by his performance. Feena proudly smiled. "Nightsong strikes again." When Lutra's tale ended, everyone applauded his performance.

Onager turned to Marshal. "Is this all true?"

"More or less." Marshal assured him.

"Amazing." He stared at Rinn with renewed reverence, it made her rather uncomfortable. She hated feeling self-conscious.

Niveus seemed impressed with the presentation, but her sharp nature quickly returned. She chastised the group of adventurers. "You cannot go gallivanting all across Sevria. War is brewing."

"Don't blame us." Sionne mumbled, mouth full of food. He pointed accusingly to Rinn. "She's the one dragging us everywhere."

Niveus studied the skinny blond teenager dressed in her dirty travel clothes and strange dragon-feather vest. "Little girl, if you truly are a Sigillum, you should get as far from Sevria as you can. Flee to Brigantum or Corta or Murstein, anywhere but here. This country is doomed."

"I know." Rinn's nerve was steel. "I'm here to save it."

Deep concern gripped Niveus. "Child, do you know what the Curia did to your grandmother? They killed her with dark magic."

"And they made my aunt drink harbane." Rinn added.

Marshal inhaled sharply and Molo let out a gasp, far too girlish for someone his size. Even Felsic and Mafic were taken aback.

Onager was beyond irate. "Harbane? That is witch-work. One sip will sterilize you for life. Only the most desperate prostitutes resort to that venom."

"I think they tried to make my mother drink it." Rinn confessed. "She refused and that's when they had her killed."

Marshal was haunted by a memory. "Cass never told me." Rinn moved to her father and enveloped him in her arms. Cat tried awkwardly to imitate Rinn, but her clumsy hug sent all three of them to the ground. Rinn and Marshal laughed in spite of the discomfort.

"He's here." Niveus announced.

"What?" Marshal mouthed, from the ground.

"Cassinius." Niveus clarified. "He's here, serving at the Great Temple." Niveus collected her inner thoughts. "But he's changed. He's not the carefree man you once knew. He's obedient and keeps to himself. He rarely speaks."

Marshal extricated himself from beneath his daughters. "I must go to him."

"You cannot!" Niveus rebuked. The two bickered at length until they were interrupted by Molo's gruff voice.

"Remember why we're here." He huffed. "We need to find the Emperors."

A timid voice in the dark replied. "I already did." All eyes turned to Tavin, who sat quietly on the floor.

"Well." Felsic insisted. "Spit it out boy. Where are they?"

"You're not going to like it." Tavin cast his eyes downward.

Rinn crawled across the floor to him. She grabbed ahold of his hands. "Please, if you know something, tell me."

Even with Rinn's insistence, Tavin seemed hesitant. "It's not what you think. I saw some kind of monument."

"A what?" Rinn questioned.

Tavin shifted uncomfortably. "A stone column with the names of the Emperors written on it. I only saw it for a moment before an Imperial patrol came by. The area was heavily guarded."

Molo knelt down to the scribe. "Where was it, boy?"

"Near the Forge of Caminus." Tavin replied.

Marshal lowered his eyebrows. "That's right next to the Curia's headquarters."

"Perfect." Rinn stated. "I can visit it when I meet with the Curia the day after tomorrow."

"You can't be serious." Molo bellowed. "You aren't walking into a room with the nine most dangerous men in Sevria."

"Rinn." Marshal held Rinn in his fatherly gaze. "None of us thought you'd be crazy enough to meet with the Curia. They're bound to lay a trap for you, it'd be suicide going there."

"I have to." Stubbornness welled up inside Rinn. "Aculeus and Serica are bureaucratic buffoons. They don't have the power to harness the dark magics we've been fighting. I think Yallakh might be right. It feels like someone or something is behind the Curia, controlling them. And if my hunch is correct, he'll be the one person who doesn't show up to that meeting."

Onager addressed Rinn formally. "M'lady, I feel it is unwise to proceed." He produced a folded parchment, stamped with a seal. "The Curia have ordered your father's arrest, and any who are caught aiding him."

"Further proof they are scared." Rinn countered. "They can't attack me directly, so they're trying to get to me through my family and friends. These aren't the tactics of people who're confident of victory."

"No." Molo gruffed. "These are the tactics of men who'll stop at nothing to win. The Curia have no scruples. There's no limit to their greed and lust for power. They cannot be reasoned with."

"Who said I was going to be reasonable?" Rinn smiled wickedly.

Chapter 26

R inn woke sore and cramped, she had not slept well in days. She camped out on the flagstone floor of Niveus' warehouse with her companions. Haril and the palace guard kept watch. Rinn squirmed out of her bedroll and stretched. Today would be a day of preparations. No doubt the Curia were making plans of their own, but Rinn had one factor in her favor: she was an unpredictable teenager. As long as she did nothing the Curia expected, she would stand a fair chance.

Over breakfast, she devised a strategy with her friends and family. Warrants for her father's arrest had been published all over Peleon, he could not afford to stay in the city any longer. Cat agreed to transport him beyond the city walls. Feena and Sionne would depart by the west gate and meet up with him at a waystation outside of town. Lutra was not happy about Feena traveling alone with Sionne, but there was nothing he could do about it.

After preparations were complete, Rinn addressed her companions. She used a wooden crate as a podium and unfurled a crude map of the city before her. "What I'm about to suggest may seem like madness, but I believe it's the quickest way to end this war. I'm meeting with the Curia tomorrow at their headquarters." Disgruntled murmurs spread through the room. Rinn tried to calm them. "Yes, I know it's a bad idea. Yes, I know they'll have a trap laid for me. But I'm still going, and I need all of your help."

Haril solemnly asked. "Do you mean to fight the Curia?"

"No." Rinn answered succinctly. "We're too greatly outnumbered, and we don't know what magics they possess. And that's our problem, we don't know what our enemy can do." Rinn motioned for everyone to join her at the map. Her army gathered around. "I want it to appear to the Curia that we're planning an attack. That way we'll see what methods they use to defend themselves."

Onager advised. "The Curia have two legions inside the city." He counted heads. "We number around twenty."

"That's more than enough to create confusion." Rinn pointed to a building on the map. "The Curia's seat of power is here, south of the Forum. We'll gather in the Remo Marketplace, to the north. We march in an orderly fashion, like an army, but only Cat and I will proceed into the Curia's headquarters, the rest of you disperse into the city and create havoc."

Molo protested. "I am going with you."

"No, Uncle Molo." Rinn shook her head. "I need you to keep the troops distracted. Draw them away from the headquarters."

Onager's eyes widened in wonder. "You're Molossus? Molossus the giant?"

Molo crossed his massive arms. "What of it?"

"What are you doing here?" Onager boggled. "You're supposed to be leading the rebellion. The Curia has been combing western Sevria hunting for you."

"You're mistaken." Marshal defended his friend. "Molo has been living in the Rustic Lands for years."

Molo remained silent, stoic. Onager questioned him further. "Have you really been in the Rustic Lands? Aren't you the giant of Messis, Virago's general? Didn't you lead the assault on Gadiom?"

"I did." Molo confessed, head held low. "Twenty thousand men and a Sigillum, and it was not enough. The Curia still managed to defeat us." He sat down heavily on a crate, nearly crushing it. Rinn was stunned by his words. She knew Molo was acquainted with her grandmother, but to think that he fought by her side at Gadiom—the largest, bloodiest conflict in all of Sevria's history. It was unbelievable. Molo had been there when Virago was defeated and killed. Rinn could not fathom what degree of power it would take to overcome a Sigillum on the battlefield.

Marshal comforted his friend. "Molo. I'm so sorry. I was blind not to make the connection. That was you at Gadiom. It must've been terrible." He rested his head on the giant's shoulder. "But we need to know what happened, if we're going to have any chance of stopping this war."

"A war I started." Molo growled, shrugging him off.

"A war the Curia started." Rinn corrected. "None of this is your fault. You were trying to save my aunt and my mother."

"Tell that to the families of the tens of thousands that died." Molo glowered.

"Stop feeling sorry for yourself!" Rinn stomped her foot. "We need you. I need you. I can't do this alone. I learned that in the Rustic Lands, we all have parts to play. I'd love to run away from my past, but I can't. I've killed hundreds of clansmen, and I have to live with that every day. But it doesn't stop me from moving forward." Rinn laid a hand on the giant's knee. "Don't let it stop you."

"Please." Marshal pleaded. "We need to know what happened after Gadiom."

Molo rubbed his eyes and cleared his throat. Lutra produced a small wax tablet and stylus. Molo began. "After our defeat at Gadiom, all hope seemed lost. The Curia marched unopposed across the countryside, purging all who defied them. I retreated west with the remains of my army to Messis. Knowing an attack was imminent, we fortified the town, made it unassailable."

"How?" Onager questioned. "Messis is an agricultural city, surrounded on all sides by farmland. It has no natural defenses."

"True." Molo agreed. "We built walls around the city. Three of them."

"That must have taken years." Marshal pondered.

"I had help." Molo nodded kindly to Felsic and Mafic. "Hundreds of dwarven refugees, many of them Dvalinn, had fled to Messis. In their greed, the Curia raided the mines of Saxitum, desperate to finance their conquest of Sevria. The dwarves ended up turning the tides of the war. The walls they built were horrific obstacles, designed to topple when soldiers scaled them. A great number of the Curia's men were crushed. Beyond that first line of defense lay a ring of pitch and hay waiting to be set ablaze, and a second layer of walls built to collapse just like the first. Serpio never made it to the third layer of walls, he had lost half his army. The siege of Messis was lifted and the city became a refuge for all who fled the Curia's oppression."

Rinn could see despair in Molo's eyes. He did not want to say more. Marshal attempted to piece the rest of the story together. "Messis was spared, and for a while all was quiet. Onager, when did the fighting start back up?"

The guard captain thought for a moment. "There'd always been small scale skirmishes in the vicinity of Messis, but organized conflict did not resume until about three years ago. It boiled into open rebellion, the armies of Messis, Campis, and Saxitum have banded together to resist the Curia."

"And the Giant Molossus is leading this uprising?" Marshal asked.

"Yes." Onager asserted. "Everyone knows Virago's General leads the rebel Legions. But the situation is a stand-off. He does not have the numbers to threaten Peleon itself, and the Curia are reluctant to meet him on the open plains." Marshal looked at his friend, but Molo remained silent, stoic.

Rinn begged a question. "Was there a naval battle recently?"

"Yes." He admitted. "But very few people know about it. Molossus attempted to sneak troops past Peleon to capture Ostreum. The flotilla was caught in the Aspero Sea by the Imperial Fleet and utterly destroyed. How did you come to find out about it?"

Rinn hesitated, glancing uneasily at Dempsi. "We heard stories of bodies washing up on the beaches on our way to Coram."

"Ah." Onager accepted her explanation.

Marshal summarized. "So, someone posing as Molossus is prowling the western plains with three Legions of soldiers." He sat on a crate near his giant friend. "Do you have any idea who it could be?"

"No." Molo answered, Rinn could tell he was lying. She could not let whatever regrets he had in the past impact the success of her current mission. She had to meet with the Curia tomorrow, she needed to know if her worst fears were realized. The hours in the day were growing short and Rinn had much to do. She needed to meet the Emperors, and for that she needed Tavin. But first, she had to get ahold of Yallakh, he would be her secret weapon at tomorrow's meeting. She tasked Felsic and Mafic with creating round, iron medallions. On them she engraved a message to the assassin: "There is an elf in the Curia. Forum, noon, tomorrow."

When the medallions were complete, six in total, she asked her sister to deliver them. "Cat, I know that Yallakh can sense our magic. I'm going to instill some power into these medallions. Hang them on the highest places you can find around town. Steeples, towers. Start near the palace. Hopefully Yallakh will find one before the magic burns the metal up." Cat nodded in understanding. Rinn gathered up the iron discs and concentrated, imbuing each with just enough magic to make them glow. Felsic and Mafic slipped twine through holes in the medallions and handed them to Cat. With a swish of her tail and an awkward salute, she vanished.

Rinn zeroed in on Tavin, sitting alone in a corner. She reached out a hand to lift him from the floor. "It's just you and me. I need you to take me to the Emperors."

"Alright." Tavin reluctantly took Rinn's hand and rose. His skin was soft and warm to touch. Rinn's cheeks flushed until she released him. Standing, Tavin dusted off his pants. "If we're going, we'd better hurry. It's quite a trek across town." Onager insisted Rinn's guard accompany her, but Rinn declined. She wanted to move quickly and quietly. Niveus pointed out a merchant nearby that specialized in second-hand clothing. Rinn promised to visit his shop en route. Rinn gave her father a firm hug and departed, Tavin straggling along behind.

::

"Are we almost there?" Rinn asked the scribe. She held the hood of her new dappled grey cloak close to her face. In her off-hand she clutched her walking stick, the pouch with its spear head dangled at her side.

"Nearly." Tavin assured her. The trip across the city had taken most of the afternoon and the sun sagged low in the sky, heavy and orange. The midday crowds were thinning out as citizens retired to their homes for dinner. Evening meals in Sevria could last for hours, consuming most of the twilight time before nightfall. Rinn was reminded of the sumptuous feast held for her at the Palace, her stomach began to rumble. She ignored it. Finding the Emperors must be her first priority.

Rinn and Tavin arrived at the Forum, a vast public plaza bounded by civic offices on one side and the massive Remo Market on the other. The market glowed with golden lamplight as merchants tried to squeeze in one last sale for the day. Rinn pulled her hood tighter around her face as she approached the Curia's main offices—a tall, windowless, building behind an edifice of red, marble columns. Statues of the nine gods graced the roofline, each bearing their sacred symbol: star, shield, and staff, scales, feather, and net, hammer, urn, and axe. Compared to the other buildings in Peleon, the Curia's headquarters was strikingly austere: plain, whitewashed walls boasting no frescoes nor mosaics. The entrance was modest, two solid brass doors devoid of ornamentation except a fine green patina. Gold-caped sentries had been stationed every twenty paces in a tight perimeter around the complex. Rinn and Tavin blended into the thinning crowds and hurried past.

Just east of the civic buildings stood Caminus' Forge. Like all sanctuaries to the god of fire, the Forge was a massive, open furnace burning brightly. Black obsidian columns supported a metal roof pocked with chimneys. The musical ringing of hammers on anvils emanated like heat from the shrine. The smell of soot and smoke permeated the square. Sweat beaded on Rinn's forehead, the heat was nearly unbearable. Tavin touched her arm and pointed south.

"This way." He urged. Rinn nodded and followed along. He led her to a small, round plaza graced by quaint burbling fountains. It was a refreshing break from the heat of Caminus' Forge. In the center of the plaza stood a stocky, square obelisk made of pink granite. Ancient writing covered four sides of the monument, chiseled into the stone. A weathered inscription on the circular base read: "For the grace and preservation of Sevria, her history is recorded here." Compared to the grandeur and artistry on display in Peleon, this chunk of rock was an eyesore, an ugly heap that listed slightly to one side. Even the writing on the stone was unkempt and messy, as if the symbols had been carved in a hurry.

Tavin raised his hand to the obelisk. "This is it. These are the Emperors." Rinn scowled at the solitary monument. This was not at all what she had envisioned.

"You're kidding, right?" Rinn frowned.

Chapter 27

T he granite obelisk stared back at Rinn. It possessed neither grace nor beauty, it was dirty, brown and sagging with time. But it intimated the qualities of advanced age like a venerable stone grandmother.

"This can't be right." Rinn quarreled disparagingly.

Tavin pointed to the top of the monument. "It's a record of all the Emperors of Sevria, starting with Sevrius himself." Rinn squinted to see the name inscribed at the pinnacle of the monument, but it was written in letters she did not understand. Tavin circled around the obelisk, scanning the inscriptions. "Your grandfather should be somewhere near the bottom." He exclaimed triumphantly from the far side of the ugly stone. "Found him."

Rinn rounded the obelisk to see her grandfather's name, but she could not decipher the strange script. "Where?" She asked.

"Right here." Tavin pointed out. "Tarandus Sevrialis, Emperor."

Rinn squinted at the unfamiliar words. "What kind of writing is this?"

"It's Cibean." Tavin answered. "Many of the original documents in Sevria are written in it."

"Where's it from?" Rinn questioned.

"It's an ancient language from the ancestral home of the Sevrian people, somewhere across the Pernic Sea." Tavin explained.

"Who does it say Tarandus is married to?" Rinn inquired, studying the strange writing.

Tavin consulted the obelisk and answered. "Acwin."

"What?" Rinn gasped. "That's a mistake. My grandfather was married to Virago."

Tavin recited the entry. "Tarandus Sevralis, Emperor, Last Sevrian. Espoused of Acwin." He added. "It makes no mention of offspring."

Rinn's temper flared. "This is a lie. Clearly the work of the Curia. My grandfather was married to Virago and he had two children. I've never heard of this Acwin." As Rinn spoke the name, the entire plaza was plunged into darkness.

Tavin squealed in the pitch black. "What's happening?"

"I don't know." Rinn fumbled in the dark. She reached out and found Tavin's hand, warm, soft, and reassuring. Very slowly, faint light returned. Rinn could see the distant glow of Caminus' Forge. She headed toward it, pulling Tavin behind her. She stumbled on the shallow steps leading up from the plaza. Tavin did the same. Rinn felt safer as she neared the light and noise of the Forge. Behind her, the obelisk was obscured by darkness, a murky blotch against the cityscape.

Tavin rummaged through his pouch and produced a small oil lamp. He uncorked the opening and slid a dry wick inside. Rinn looked at him quizzically. Tavin responded. "What? Scribes always carry lamps. We need light to read." Rinn shrugged. Tavin lit the wick from the coals of Caminus' Forge. Together Rinn and Tavin crept back to the shadowy plaza, the feeble light of his lamp leading the way. When they arrived, Tavin examined the lampposts in the area. Their flames had been extinguished, as if snuffed out by a great breath. Tavin looked at Rinn accusingly. "What did you do?"

"I didn't do anything." Rinn pleaded her innocence. "We were arguing about the errors on the obelisk."

"And?" Tavin questioned dubiously.

"I said that woman's name." Rinn admitted.

"Which woman?" Tavin asked.

"Acwin." Rinn replied. And the light of Tavin's lamp went out.

::

Rinn burst into the warehouse long after midnight, panting and giggly. Tavin trailed after her, exhausted and exasperated. Marshal crossed the room to scold his daughter. "Where've you been?" He demanded. Her friends were all awake, awaiting her return, all except one snoring redhead.

"We found the Emperors." Rinn could barely speak through her giddiness.

Her father was beyond cross. "Rinn, you had us worried sick. We thought you'd been captured. I sent Cat out to hunt you down."

Rinn ignored his sour mood. "We found them, Daddy. It's just like Lucus said. " She danced around the warehouse floor, laughing.

Marshal turned to Tavin. "Is she drunk?"

"No, sir." Tavin exclaimed. "We found something important."

Rinn stopped her twirling and called out. "Hey, everyone. Watch this."

Tavin waved his hands frantically. "Wait! Rinn, don't do it."

"Acwin." She breathed and the warehouse was plunged into darkness. Everyone panicked. Feena screamed. Someone stepped on Sionne, who woke up cursing. Somewhere a clay urn shattered on the floor.

"Rinn Amali." Marshal bellowed. "Stop this right now."

In the darkness, Rinn meekly replied. "It goes away by itself after a few minutes."

Sparks flew in the pitch black as the dwarves lit one of their metal lanterns. Illumination returned to the warehouse interior. Lutra was tangled on the floor with Sionne, and Grus stood by the remains of a broken urn. Liveus frowned at the mayhem. Marshal grabbed his daughter by the arm. "Explain yourself."

Rinn seemed hurt by his severity. "We found the Sigillum words, hidden in plain sight." She lightly pulled herself away, and her father relinquished his hold. "We recorded as many as we could."

Tavin inserted himself into the tense situation. "I showed Rinn an obelisk with the names of the Sevrian Emperors. I've studied the royal lineage, and the list contained many errors. We suspect those errors were bits of the Sigillum vocabulary recorded in secret. You've just witnessed the result of one of those words."

"It's exactly like Lucus said, we needed to find the Emperors to succeed." Rinn pleaded. "He meant for me to find those words. We recorded as many as we could in the darkness, but there may be more." Her deep blue eyes sank into her father. "Daddy, with these new powers, who knows what I can do." With a sigh Marshal's anger fizzled out.

"It's getting late." He said aloud. "Everyone get some sleep." Rinn's weary companions headed to their bedrolls spread out across the warehouse floor. With a small popping sound, Cat appeared in the center of the room. She pointed to Rinn in excitement.

"I found her." Cat exclaimed. A quiet chuckle circulated through the warehouse. Rinn waved her feline sister over.

"Hey, Cat. Watch this." Rinn said with a mischievous gleam in her eye. "Acwin."

Once again, the room was plunged into darkness. Cat shrieked in astonishment, followed by feline laughter. "That's awesome."

Marshal yelled out. "Rinn!"

::

Rinn woke quiet and calm, sobered by the reality that today she would confront the Curia. She ate a brief breakfast and dressed for the day, heavy leather armor under her dragon feather vest. She pulled back her mop of blond hair and tied it into a ponytail high on her head. Cat donned her own armor after she finished her morning bath. She strapped four knives to her thighs and pulled a robe over her head.

Marshal reviewed everyone's assignments. Cat was tasked with transporting him out of Peleon. Feena and Sionne would ride horses through the Emmer Gate and meet him outside the city walls. Meanwhile, Rinn and her army would march through Peleon, keeping the attention of the Curia firmly on them. Onager and Haril offered to lead the procession. Grus lined up with the palace guards, Velle and Lepas made room for him. Lutra and the dwarves fell in next, ready to make mischief. Rinn would trail behind the procession and wait on her sister. That left only Molo and Dempsi. Rinn knelt down to the little girl. "We're counting on you." She brushed a lock of black hair from her face.

"I'll do my best." Dempsi beamed.

"I know you will." Rinn smiled. She reached under her shirt and fished out her mother's pendant. "Cat, come touch this." Her sister obeyed, pawing the softly glowing object.

"Wow." She said in astonishment. "It tastes just like you."

"Do you think you can locate this in the city?" Rinn asked.

"Certainly." Cat blinked her eyes.

Rinn hung the pendant around Dempsi's neck. "You hold onto this. It'll help us find you." Dempsi's lively eyes danced as she rubbed the glowing medallion. Rinn lifted the girl to Molo, she looked like a doll in his arms. Clive rested on a nearby table. Rinn unnecessarily handed him to Molo, Clive weighed more than she expected. "Clive, take good care of them both. Keep them safe." Rinn joked.

"He will." Molo chuckled.

"We'll see you soon." Rinn affirmed. "My audience with the Curia should not take long." Rinn hefted her spear, it's fresh metal point firmly attached. She embraced her father. "I'm ready."

"Be safe." Her father urged.

"No heroics." Rinn responded. She embraced her father warmly. "I love you, Daddy."

"I love you, too, Rinn." He held her tightly. After a close moment they separated, and Marshal straightened his daughter's armor. Rinn's army assembled at the doorway, and Niveus joined the party, two short swords strapped to her waist.

Marshal objected. "You are not coming."

The tall, dark women stood proudly in line. "After everything I have heard, how could I not accompany you? Your daughter is the breath of life this city needs."

"Rinn is walking into the lion's den." Marshal argued. "People may die. You won't be coming with us. It's too dangerous. You aren't a seasoned warrior."

Niveus rebuked him. "Every caravan I drive across this accursed country is attacked by bandits or soldiers or something worse. In the past twenty years, I have probably seen as much combat as you."

"I seriously doubt that." Marshal crossed his arms.

Niveus ignored his comment. "I know what the Curia are doing to the people, to our livelihoods. They tax us into starvation and imprison any who speak out against them. I once owned seven storehouses, and employed hundreds. Now, this is all I have left." She waved her hand around the meager warehouse. "The Curia are a plague on Sevria, a disease no one is willing to fight." Niveus walked over and laid a hand on Rinn's shoulder. "If this girl will stand up to these tyrants, then I will stand with her."

"Thank you." Rinn touched Niveus' hand. The woman smiled back.

Marshal conceded defeat. "Have it your way."

Lutra remarked to Tavin. "She has that effect on people." Tavin nodded in agreement. Marshal saluted Rinn's army. Haril, Grus, and Molo saluted back. Catherine took Marshal's hands in her paws and in a blink, they were gone. Feena gave Rinn a hug, fighting back her worries.

"You take care of yourself, m'lady." Feena said.

"See you soon." Rinn replied. Their hands lingered together for a moment, then Feena took her leave, but not without giving Lutra a kiss. She left to join Sionne outside with the horses. Grus knuckled the blushing Lutra's arm. Rinn assessed her remaining friends as they prepared for battle. She approached Tavin. "After you copy the remaining Sigillum words, you could go with them, out of the city. It'd be safer for you."

"And waste all that sparring practice?" Tavin winked at her. "Never."

Rinn's heart skipped a beat. The support and care she received from her friends astonished her. Rinn hardly felt worthy. She was an ordinary girl with ordinary fears—she did not want to be lonely, she did not want to die. But special gifts had been given to her, abilities that appeared when Sevria was in peril. To Rinn, this nation was not the institutions or trappings of the Empire, but the people itself. She was fighting for the people's sake, to make their world better.

A menacing thought crept over Rinn—what if she won? Would her powers fade? Rinn could barely remember what it was like before she could use magic. Even in her dreams she summoned her barrier and fought with glowing weapons. In the past two years, Rinn had completely embraced her role as a Sigillum, a transformation that could not be undone. What terrified her the most about losing her magic was the fate of her bond with Catherine. She could feel her sister outside the city talking to their father. Even from miles away she could sense Cat's concern and love for him. Rinn did not know what she would do if she ever lost her.

Rinn did not have time for uncertainty. She needed to confront the Curia. There was valuable information she must know. Hopefully, Yallakh had received her message, and he would meet her. Rinn would need every trick she had. As her father had said, she was walking into the lion's den, and getting back out again would not be easy.

Chapter 28

R inn marched to the edge of the Forum, spear in hand.
Her entourage paraded before her in two orderly
columns. Their journey across Peleon had attracted
significant attention. Gawkers of all ages tagged along, like
spectators drawn to a mummer's parade. As they marched
through the crowded Remo Market, throngs of curiosity-
seekers followed, expecting to see a show, a motley
collection of men, women, children, dwarves, minotaur,
and more. It reminded Rinn of the crowds of clansmen that
assembled before she underwent The Trial—a one-on-one
combat to the death. Rinn was also aware that the city
guard took note of their passing. Gold-caped soldiers
flanked her procession at regular intervals. Rinn ignored
them for now, her focus was the Curia.

Rinn stepped forward and gathered her friends around
her. "Thank you all for believing in me. Now is the time."
She whispered, hugging as many as she could. "Cat and I
will approach the building. You all know what to do."

Rinn slid her hand into Cat's paw and together they
strolled across the Forum, like two dancers on display.
Behind them, Rinn's army melted into the crowds. Lutra's
head appeared above the others, he must have been
standing on a table or someone's shoulders. He called out
in a loud voice, like a bell ringing through the plaza.

"Down with the Curia and their damnable taxes!" Lutra raised a fist to the sky. Grumbles of discontent rumbled through the crowd. Lutra riled the masses further, denouncing the war, crime, and deplorable condition of the Empire. City guard moved in to disperse the unruly crowd. Mafic and Felsic joined the fray from a different location, demanding dwarven freedom. The crowd turned near riot. Pockets of fighting broke out in various places, led by Calder, Haril, and Niveus.

Molo appeared before the Forum, rising above the crowd. In a thunderous voice he bellowed. "I am Molossus, the Giant of Messis. I have come for your city." He pointed to the gold-caped guards surrounding the Curia's headquarters. His challenge could not be ignored, the chance to capture such a notorious enemy lured more than half of the gold-caped soldiers away from their posts. Molo ducked back into the fracas. In a separate part of the Forum, another fight broke out. Rinn could not tell for sure, but it looked as if Onager had started a bar brawl.

As Rinn climbed the steps to the Curia's offices, the Forum was in complete pandemonium. Step one, divide your enemy, Rinn thought to herself with a smile. She pulled her sister to the building, Cat was distracted watching the chaos outside. Giant bronze doors swung open at Rinn's touch, unusually light for their size. Inside, the Curia's headquarters were as plain and austere as they were outside. The marble floor was a muted checkerboard of white and gray. No frescoes or embellishment graced the stark, polished marble walls. A gold-caped officer appeared from a side passageway with an escort.

"This way." He motioned down the central corridor. Rinn was taken aback by his lack of courtesy. She started down the hallway. "Your companion must remain here." The officer commanded.

Rinn stopped in place. The officer confronted her with ten soldiers. Rinn's piercing gaze was unwavering. "It would be easier to separate the sky from the ground than to keep me and my sister apart." Rinn walked through them down the hallway. Cat stuck her tongue out at the soldiers and skipped along happily after her sister. Rinn descended deeper into the Curia's headquarters, passing innumerable pairs of gold-cloaks guarding every aspect of the building. The roof had skylights illuminating the interior, tiny shafts in the thick stone roof, too small for even Cat to climb through. Eventually, Rinn found herself at a pair of bronze doors, exact copies of the ones at the entrance.

"We're here." Rinn said, a nervous flutter in her stomach. Cat did not reply, but Rinn could feel the pent-up energy in her sister. She was ready. The doors opened, and six soldiers processed out, led by an armored chamberlain with a plumed helmet.

"Weapons are not allowed in the council chamber." He relieved Rinn of her staff and spearhead. Soldiers stripped Cat of her knives. Rinn had expected this, she was prepared. The chamberlain opened the door and directed Rinn inside. "They are expecting you."

Rinn steeled her nerves and stepped into the lion's den. The meeting room of the Curia was a high-ceilinged chamber with featureless quartz walls. The floor was an intricate mosaic of geometric tiles, the only source of color in the bone-white room. Rinn liked the design on the floor, she almost felt sorry for it. The members of the Curia sat at a long marble table on a raised dais. A stone balustrade divided the room in half, separating the Curia from its petitioners. Soldiers filled the room, shoulder to shoulder along the walls. Rinn smirked to herself, the Curia were scared.

Rinn assessed the men who had killed her mother and ruined her life. She recognized Aculeus, the fat one mopping his head with a handkerchief, and Serica, the weaselly master artist sitting next to him. At one end of the table was the stocky Furticus, always eating. Rinn did not recognize any of the others, but she could guess at least one of them. Sitting in the center of the table was a dangerous-looking man in a military uniform. His nose was crooked, clearly having been broken in the past. A single hairy brow crossed over his eyes, thick, bushy, and black. Under his moustache, his mouth was a scowl. That would be Praetor Serpio, the leader of the military, Rinn thought to herself. He wore a heavy chain of gold and black around his neck.

An ornately dressed man sitting behind a collection of scrolls addressed the chamber. "Let us call this meeting to order."

An older man with drooping jowls read from a parchment. "Rinn Amali, we summoned you here to answer for your crimes against the Empire." He wore the robes of a cleric, the holy symbol of Aedis hung below his gold and white chain. Typical, thought Rinn. Law is their best weapon and they'll use it against me. The graying cleric listed the offenses. "You are charged with a treasonous attack on the Vallum Wall, profaning the Sacred Grove of Lucus, destruction of the Holy Temple of Aedis in Viburna, harboring known fugitives, assaulting Imperial patrols, and the murder of palace soldiers."

Rinn was not sure about that last charge, but the rest were spot on. "I've been busy." She responded nonchalantly.

The gaudily-dressed man behind the scrolls stated. "How do you plea to these charges."

Rinn studied the eight pairs of eyes that stared her down. Like she thought, one member did not show up to the meeting. She knew the Grand Merchant and the head of the Artists Guild, the Aedile Furticus and the head of the military Serpio. Her accuser was clearly the High Cleric, and the one running the meeting was likely the

Guildmaster. That left three members of the Curia unaccounted for. Seated next to Serpio was a weathered man wearing knee-high oiled boots. Rinn guessed he would be the Harbormaster. Other than the missing person, the only one unidentified was a man seated at the far left of the table. His face was partially concealed by the cowls of his gray robe. A staff leaned against the wall behind him. As Rinn held him in her gaze, her palms began to sweat, and her heart race. She felt an overwhelming hatred and rage against this man. He was cruel and evil. He had done unspeakable things, all while laughing, and he needed to die.

Oh, gods. Rinn thought. Cat. She turned to her sister, but it was too late. Cat launched herself across the room, flying unexpectedly at the man. Instinctively he reached for his staff, but Cat was too quick. She landed on his chest, and before the guards could draw their swords, she raked her broken claws across his throat.

"Cat, no!" Rinn cried out. The members of the Curia backed away from the feral animal in their midst. Cat jerked her paw away from the hooded man's chest, yanking a crystal and gold pendant from his neck. The man looked at her with terror in his eyes.

"Justice." Cat sneered as she bit into the medallion, breaking it in two. With an inhuman wail, the mage crumpled to the ground, dead. Scores of soldiers descended upon Cat.

"Acwin." Rinn yelled. But nothing happened. As she suspected, the room was sealed against her magic. She reached inside the folds of her vest and pulled out one of her father's small pottery bombs. She smashed it on the floor, and the chamber filled with thick gray smoke. Havoc reigned over the room. Rinn could hear faint laughter echoing from somewhere nearby, her assassin.

Serpio shouted for order. "Guards, bar the doors! Don't let that witch escape." Rinn moved to the center of the room. She could feel Cat nearby. She willed her to come close, and Cat's furry body appeared next to hers.

Rinn called out to the smoke. "Yallakh, the wards."

"Yes, my queen." His voice reverberated through the chamber. Rinn squinted her eyes, and through the smoke she could see blue light emanating from crystals cleverly hidden in the corners of the room. One by one, the lights extinguished. The smoke in the room thinned and Rinn found herself surrounded by thirty or forty armed guards.

An incensed Serpio, his face red with anger, berated Rinn. "I should kill you myself, you villainous witch. But I'd rather see you publicly executed."

As the last blue light blinked out, Rinn replied. "I have a message for your master. Tell him I am coming." She whispered the word "acwin", and the room was plunged into darkness. By the time the light returned, Rinn and Cat were gone, a giant hole in the floor mosaic where they once stood.

::

Rinn splashed through the sewer tunnels with one hand gliding across the mossy walls and another on her sister. Cat's feline vision navigated the pitch-black passage with ease. Rinn waded in ankle deep water that reeked of refuse. It reminded her of the palace garbage chute.

Rinn called out to the darkness. "Cat, what happened up there?"

Her sister bristled. "I had no choice."

Rinn tugged on her sister's vest, stopping her. "Cat, you killed one of the Curia. They'll hunt us to the ends of Sevria now." Rinn could feel her sister's intermingling fury and regret. Rinn summoned her shield in the darkness. The vaulted stone tunnel was washed in soft green light. "There's something you're not telling me."

Cat's ears folded flat and her whiskers poked out in every direction. "He's the one who tortured me. The vile, horrid man who laughed as he burned me with magic. He was evil. I couldn't stand there and do nothing." Rinn could see the misery in her sister's eyes. She still had pink balding patches in her fur and her left front fang was broken.

Rinn squeezed her sister's shoulder. "Then it was justice." Cat meekly nodded her head. Rinn held her sister's paws fondly. They would deal with whatever happens together.

"I thought it was hilarious." A gravelly voice commented. Yallakh emerged from the shadows into the pale green light. He walked through Rinn's magical barrier as if it did not exist.

Rinn backed against a slimy stone wall. "Yallakh. How did you? What just?" She was too stunned to make sense. The tattooed fiend tilted his head to one side, lifting a curious eyebrow.

"I thought you would've figured it out by now." Yallakh shrugged. He reached one of his bandaged arms through her barrier, wiggling his fingers on the other side. "Your powers are built on emotion, fueled by them. Your shield protects you from hatred and evil intent. But those who love you can pass right through it."

"Yallakh." Rinn clutched her shirt over her chest. This hideous assassin stood before her draped in rotting bandages like a walking corpse. His red and brown eyes regarded her like a beloved daughter, or maybe something else. Rinn shuddered at the thought.

Yallakh laughed. "I would never do anything to hurt you. I'd give my life for you, if I could. Whatever these people did to deserve your ire, I'd personally kill them a hundred times over."

With downcast eyes Rinn confessed. "They murdered my mother and grandmother. They tortured my sister, and now they are hunting me and my father."

"Fine." Yallakh snapped. "Let's go back and finish this." He slid a black knife from the sheath at his side.

"It's not that simple." Rinn exclaimed, shocked by his directness.

"Isn't it?" Yallakh raised an eyebrow. "If these men are causing all the problems, eliminate them. Problem solved."

"No." Rinn rebuked. "Killing the Curia won't solve anything. They aren't the ones behind this. Someone or something else is out there, pulling their strings."

Yallakh resheathed his knife with a wry grin. "So, you do understand."

"Yes." Rinn admitted. "I'm beginning to believe that Elves are behind this war, and maybe much, much more."

Cat had been listening the whole time, saying nothing. Finally, she interrupted. "We need to find the others."

"Agreed." Rinn replied. "Can you take us to Dempsi? She should be carrying my mother's pendant." Cat sniffed at the foul air and nodded yes. She led the way down the sewer tunnels illuminated by the soft green glow of Rinn's shield. Yallakh followed in the distance, half-shrouded in darkness.

Chapter 29

M olo and Dempsi were waiting for Rinn in a large underground chamber, a confluence of many sewers before they emptied into the sea. Molo let out a sigh of relief when he saw Rinn, but when Yallakh exited the tunnel behind her, he stiffened. "What's he doing here?" Molo growled, Clive suddenly in his hand.

Rinn stepped protectively in front of the assassin. "He's with me. Yallakh helped us escape the Curia's stronghold." Cat nodded her head in agreement.

Molo huffed in frustration, and Clive vanished. The giant stretched as well as he could in the cramped space. "How did it go?"

Rinn bit her lip. "We'll talk about it later."

Molo eyed her with suspicion. "That bad?"

"Cat may have killed someone." Rinn spilled. Cat innocently whistled and stared off into space.

"She did what?" Molo ranted, face turning red. "Surely not one of the Curia."

Rinn declined to answer.

"Of all the knuckleheaded things you could do, you murdered one of the Curia in their own headquarters." Molo's fury echoed down the tunnel. "Rinn, you're smarter than this. Now they will stop at nothing until you are dead."

"What's done is done." Rinn declared. "Let's find the others and leave Peleon before the Curia have a chance to respond."

Dempsi sat on a stone ledge peering down into the brackish water. She had been doing her best to ignore Molo's angry outburst. Rinn came and sat down next to her. "Hi."

"Hi." Dempsi replied timidly.

Rinn touched the necklace around the little girl's neck. "Thanks for keeping this safe." Dempsi lifted the necklace from her neck and handed it back to Rinn. Rinn asked. "Are you okay?"

Dempsi turned to Rinn, her black eyes wide with disbelief. "Did you really kill someone?"

"Yes." Rinn admitted, staring down at her mother's necklace. "I've had to kill people. But I'm trying to stop all this fighting. I only kill to keep people from dying." As the words left her mouth, they made no sense.

Dempsi seemed dejected. "If you kill people, aren't you making the war worse?" Rinn wanted to explain, needed to justify herself to this little girl, but there was no simple way to do it. The world was messy and broken, and solutions were sometimes worse than the problems.

"I guess in some ways I am." Rinn wallowed self-loathing.

Dempsi looked at Rinn with lamblike eyes. "Will I have to kill people too?"

"No, sweetie." Rinn grabbed the girl in her arms and held her close. "I'd never ask that of you. You're a rain-bringer. We're taking you to Messis, where there's a humongous pool of water waiting to talk to you." The little girl cracked a half-smile. Rinn brushed the dark hair from her face. "But we need to find our friends first. Can you help with that?"

Dempsi nodded wordlessly. Rinn helped her up and gathered with Molo and Cat. The giant was still cross with the misbehaving feline, but he cooperated for the benefit of others. Rinn explained their next step. "Our friends are out there trying to distract the soldiers. I told them to find pools of water or fountains and stand in them. I'm counting on you, Dempsi, to find them, Clive will help. Cat can transport them here. Once we're all together, we'll make our escape."

Molo understood and held out his round rock. Dempsi rested her little hands on its purple eye, which turned an aqua-blue color. After a few moments she exclaimed. "I found one! No, two!"

"Where are they?" Cat asked curiously.

"Come take a look." Dempsi pulled her paw over to Clive.

Cat raised an ear and nodded. "Oh, okay." In a blink she was gone. The brackish water in the chamber rippled as she departed.

Yallakh tittered to himself. "A water mage, a soul-stone, and a liminal feline working together. The Curia could never have predicted this."

"What's liminal?" Rinn wondered.

"Half in, half out." Yallakh answered. "Someone sitting on the threshold between two places." Rinn guessed that pretty much summed up her sister. A few moments later, Cat returned with two slightly damp dwarves. Mafic doubled over, holding his stomach.

"What was that place you took us through?" He lurched forward, trying to steady himself against the damp tunnel walls. His face was green and his eyes glazed.

Felsic brought a hand to his oversized nose. "What is this place you brought us to?" Both dwarves looked sick as school children.

Rinn bounced with excitement. "Great job. Let's find everyone else." It took the better part of an hour to reassemble Rinn's army. Some members handled Cat's teleportation better than others. Calder was cool and collected, but Haril sat in the sewer water wide-eyed, staring at the walls. Onager was more than a little freaked out. Lutra was the only one who seemed to thoroughly enjoy the experience.

"That was amazing." He held Cat's paws tightly. "You do that all the time? Outstanding. We've got to do that again." Cat pulled herself away. Clearly the effort of transporting so many people was taxing her strength. Her tail sagged and her ears flopped over. Rinn helped support her sister.

"Do we have everyone?" Rinn asked.

Molo counted heads. Dempsi was able to find most everyone. Apart from Onager, she could only locate two of Rinn's palace guards, Velle and Lepas. She had heard them say their names, and apparently that was an important part of location magic. Molo completed his count and frowned. "We're missing someone."

"Who?" Rinn asked.

The giant furrowed his great brow. "The scribe."

::

Rinn raced through the streets of Peleon, desperate to find Tavin. She held the hood of her cloak over her face as she ran. Cat was too exhausted to teleport and Dempsi could not locate the boy. Either he could not find water, or something had happened to him. Tavin was already known to the Curia, he was the one who first revealed Rinn's existence. They imprisoned him once, they would not give him a second chance to escape. Rinn needed to find him before the Curia did.

Rinn darted through the crowds, dodging Imperial patrols. She brought no weapons, everything she and Cat carried into the Curia's complex had been confiscated. Sionn and Feena had taken the rest of their supplies outside the city. Rinn did not care, if she required a weapon, she'd find one. She sprinted to the last place she wanted to go, back to the Forum and the Curia.

When she arrived, the plaza was a sea of soldiers, their metal armor glistening in the afternoon sun. Almost an entire Legion assembled on the steps of the Curia's headquarters. They displaced the townspeople and shuttered the shops in the vicinity. Carriages and wagons were ruthlessly searched, and pedestrians manhandled in a reckless manhunt for Rinn. She waded into the crowds fleeing the chaotic scene. She needed a plan, some way to get through without being noticed. She wished she had brought Yallakh with her, but she feared he would be too conspicuous in the open daylight. There had to be another way.

Rinn watched as the broad-shouldered Serpio exited the Curia's compound. He was decked in heavy plate armor with as many swords as he had medals, he looked like a porcupine made of steel. He assumed control of the troops and in a thunderous voice ordered every man and woman to hunt down and kill the murderer Rinn Amali and her accomplices. Rinn panicked. She slipped behind the pedestal of a stone statue. She was weaponless and surrounded by soldiers. It was only a matter of time before she was discovered. She would have to fight her way through an entire Legion to escape, and she would lose her chance to find Tavin.

Rinn held her head in frustration. There must be a solution, but if she cast darkness or summoned her shield, she would alert everyone to her presence. Rinn wished she could teleport like her sister, but she never learned how. Only Tavin knew the new Sigillum words they had discovered. She suspected he was at the Emperors' obelisk right now, trying to record the remaining names. Rinn wondered why she had risked everything to come, did she really care that strongly about Tavin or did she just want the words he possessed?

219

A glint of light distracted her, sunlight reflecting off a metallic object. Rinn realized it was a triangular pendant around the neck of one of the soldiers. She spotted two of her female palace guards mixed in with the rest of the troops. Rinn inhaled deeply and braved her way into the plaza. She approached the two guards and held out her hands. "Arrest me."

"Excuse me." One of the women replied.

Rinn pulled her hood back just enough to let the woman see her. "Arrest me." She pleaded. The two guards looked around nervously. The younger guard, a short woman with steel-gray hair, took charge.

"You there." She ordered a passing soldier. "Give me those manacles." He reluctantly complied. The woman slapped the irons on Rinn's wrists and snapped off the securing pin, locking them firmly in place.

"Thank you." Rinn silently replied.

"Where to?" The woman whispered.

"The Forge." Rinn mouthed.

The gray-haired guard tugged on Rinn's shackles. "Come on you scum, you're not going anywhere." She shoved Rinn across the plaza, her partner skittishly keeping watch. The soldiers mostly ignored what seemed to be a mundane arrest. Rinn was escorted through throngs of the Curia's warriors. She became aware of how improbable the situation seemed. Just when she needed it, two of her guard appeared. They helped her without hesitation, putting their own lives in peril. Rinn never accepted the convenient concepts of fate and destiny, but an uncanny series of events was falling into place. Rinn was starting to feel like a pawn in some cosmic game.

"You there." A stern voice called. It belonged to a Legate, a senior officer. "Where are you taking that prisoner?"

Rinn's escort stopped suddenly. Her partner blurted out a cover story. "To a carcer barge about to depart. We're hoping they could squeeze on one more criminal."

The Legate smirked. He walked up to Rinn and pulled back her hood. Rinn's curly blond hair hung limply in her face and she smelled of sewers. The Legate gripped her jaw and jerked her face upward. "By the gods, she stinks. The carcers know what to do with vermin like this." He pushed her away. "Carry on."

Breathlessly, the two guards urged Rinn on with feigned hostility. They hastily exited the Forum headed for the heat and noise of the Forge. Rinn's escort argued quietly among themselves.

"Why the barge?" The steel-haired woman demanded.

"It's the only thing I could think of this direction." Her partner snapped. "The prisons are to the south. I was trying not to raise suspicion." The guards stopped at the outskirts of Caminus' Forge. Heat from its furnaces rippled the air, and sweat trickled down Rinn's face.

"Where to now?" The younger guard asked, mopping her brow on her sleeve.

"Just around the other side." Rinn explained. "There's a small courtyard with an obelisk." The guards marched Rinn around the Forge, the pounding of hammers ringing out loudly as they walked. The courtyard with the ugly stone obelisk came into view, and climbing awkwardly up one side of it was Tavin. Rinn rushed over to him. "What are you doing?"

Tavin attempted to shimmy up higher. "There's one name near the top I can't quite read."

"Get down here, right now." Rinn commanded.

"Just a moment." Tavin defied her. "I can almost make it out." He struggled to pull himself a bit higher, but he lost his grip and tumbled down. Rinn instinctively called out her Sigilllum word for float, and the boy drifted down like a feather. He touched down harmlessly on the ground. "That's handy." He smirked at Rinn. She spoke the word for release, and her shackles fell to the ground. Her personal escorts seemed in awe of her abilities.

Rinn stretched out a hand to help Tavin up. "We need to get out of here. There are soldiers everywhere." She pulled.

Tavin dusted off his pants. "You brought a couple with you."

"They are members of my palace guard." Rinn replied.

"Can we trust them?" Tavin countered.

Rinn looked at the two women who accompanied her. Over their armor, they wore the triangular pendants that Felsic and Mafic had made. Rinn smiled at them warmly. "Yes, I trust them." The women returned her smile. Rinn tugged Tavin by the hand. "Now, let's get out of here before the Legions find us."

"A bit too late for that." A haughty voice called. The Legate led a detachment of troops into the secluded plaza encircling Rinn and her friends. "That carcer barge left hours ago." The Legate stared down the palace guards in disgust. The steel-haired woman drew her sword and flanked Rinn protectively. The Legate's soldiers fenced everyone inside a circular shield wall. Tavin cowered behind Rinn. When things seemed like they could get no worse, the shield wall parted and Praetor Serpio himself stepped into the courtyard, drawing one of his many longswords. His face contorted in an angry scowl as he walked forward.

Chapter 30

Praetor Serpio, commander of the armies of Sevria, brandished a heavy steel blade aimed directly at Rinn. "Your reign of carnage ends here." Rinn had tried her best to avoid conflict, but somehow it came down to this. Serpio was out for blood. "Surrender and your deaths will be swift."

Rinn's first thought was protecting Tavin and her palace guards. She needed a distraction, and a weapon. She whispered to Tavin. "The Forge." He nodded in understanding. Rinn faced Serpio and his battalion of soldiers. She let the hood of her robe slip back, revealing her mop of curly blond hair. "You'd draw your weapon on an unarmed girl?" She challenged.

The assembled soldiers seemed to hesitate, but Serpio's response was unwavering. "I fight every enemy of Sevria, no matter what size or shape." Below his massive, singular brow, Rinn could see icy resolve in the Praetor's eyes. He would stop at nothing to protect the country he loved. How could he not see that the Curia were the ones tearing it apart?

"Hold on tightly." Rinn breathed. She grabbed her two palace escorts by the wrists. She invoked her magic barrier, it glowed bright green in the midday sun. Rinn expanded it outward, knocking the soldiers closest to her off their feet.

Serpio braced himself and resisted Rinn's magic. Unfazed, he advanced on her sword in hand. "Acwin." Rinn shouted. The sunny courtyard was plunged into absolute darkness. Rinn plowed through the pitch black and past the disoriented bodies all around her. She headed for the distant Forge of Caminus, the only source of light that could not be extinguished by her enchantment. She could not see Tavin in the dark, but she trusted that he knew what to do. Soldiers cursed and stumbled as she rushed past them dragging her two guards behind her. As Rinn dashed out of the courtyard, she could hear Serpio bellowing out commands.

"Seal off the area." He shouted. "Don't let her escape." He was close, closer than Rinn expected. She charged directly to the Forge. Hopefully, she could find a weapon there. The darkness was thinning out and Rinn saw anvils ahead. Most of the craftsmen had stopped hammering, distracted by the commotion in the courtyard. Rinn was almost at the Forge when something struck her from behind, sending her sprawling to the ground. She lost ahold of her escorts and knocked her head against the pavement. She rolled onto her side, fuzzy-headed and ears ringing, just in time to see Praetor Serpio swipe at her with a massive, blue shield. Rinn ducked, narrowly dodging the impact against a nearby anvil, which shattered like glass. Rinn looked up to see Serpio standing over her, in one hand he held a formidable longsword, in the other, a body-length shield made entirely of magic.

My gods, Rinn inhaled sharply, he's a paladin. Rinn scampered behind another anvil as the Praetor smashed his way into the workshop. Craftsmen scattered at his approach. The Legate and other soldiers fanned out behind him. Rinn crawled in terror to the central furnace, the heat was intense, making it impossible to breathe. Serpio was undaunted, he closed in on Rinn with his sword and indestructible blue shield.

"Rinn." Tavin's voice cried from afar. "Scieppan. Say the word 'scieppan'!"

Rinn did not have time to wonder what he meant, she just obeyed. She let the unfamiliar word fall from her lips. Immediately she could sense all the metal in the Forge, the great anvils, the hammers and tools, the pools of slag at the bottom of the furnace. For some reason, she knew fire could not burn her. She reached one hand into the scorching coals and touched the liquid iron beneath it. She drew out the metal like pulling yarn from a skein. It obeyed her will, lengthening, solidifying until Rinn held a full-length iron pilum.

Serpio's advance halted when he saw Rinn pull molten metal from the furnace of Caminus' Forge. She faced him in a ready battle-stance, a steaming spear in her hands. "Let me and my friends go." She demanded.

The Praetor moved into a defensive posture. "You are a criminal." He sneered from behind his magic shield. "You will answer for your sins against the Empire."

Rinn advanced slowly. "You're a priest now? It's your job to decide what's good and what's evil?"

Serpio issued a resounding response. "I am justice. I uphold the law."

Rinn ranted like a furious teenager. "Laws that are being abused. The citizens of Sevria suffer, and you don't care. They are starving and homeless, and you don't care. You Curia only care about yourselves."

"I don't have to listen to the tirades of insolent little girls." Serpio advanced, emboldened.

"I'm no little girl." Rinn lit the spear in her hands, it burst into green flames. "I am Sabrinn Sevralis. And I am a Sigillum."

Serpio suffered Rinn's defiance no longer. He bowled into her with his glowing blue shield. Their magic barriers collided with a crack like a whip. Rinn's shield withstood the impact, but she was flung backward. She landed unflatteringly on her rump, her legs akimbo. Serpio laughed. He reminded Rinn of Deel, Clanmorris' brutal warlord—brawny, arrogant, and self-righteous. Rinn wanted nothing more than to stand up and teach this bastard a lesson; however, out of the corner of her eye, she spotted Tavin cowering behind a workbench. Rinn calmed her inner ire, Tavin and the safety of her friends from the palace must come first.

Serpio attacked again, using his shield like a bull uses his horns. Instead of taking the blow head on, Rinn dissolved her barrier and rolled to the right. Serpio charged unexpectedly past her. Rinn saw an opening—the Praetor's shield only protected him from the front. She extended her spear and slashed from behind, severing the blade of his sword from its hilt. Serpio growled as he spun, reacquiring his target, setting his shield squarely between them.

"You are full of tricks." He growled, throwing down the worthless handle of his weapon. He slid a long dagger from a sheath across the small of his back. The blade shimmered an unnatural color. "I have a few tricks of my own."

Before he had a chance to strike, Rinn summoned her shield around the Praetor. Serpio found himself trapped inside her green, glowing barrier. He battered against it with his own shield to no avail. Rinn backed up a step and took three bounding leaps toward the Praetor. He braced in expectation. With all her weight, Rinn kicked her shield like a giant ball. It bounced backward, tossing Serpio around inside like a ragdoll. He rolled into a line of troops, scattering them like pins. Rinn's barrier evaporated, depositing the Praetor inelegantly on the ground. Rinn did not have time to gloat, she dashed to Tavin and grabbed his hand.

"Stay close to me." She beckoned as she ran. Rinn looked around for her palace guards. They were together, surrounded by a detachment of the Legate's soldiers. Rinn sped to them, using her barrier to plow through anyone blocking her way. Swords and spears slashed at her and Tavin, but simple weapons could not penetrate her shield. Rinn reached her guards. If what Yallakh said was true, they should be able to pass through without her lowering her shield. Rinn deflected two attacks with her spear and delivered two sharp strikes with the butt of her weapon to their captors.

Rinn reached out her hand. "Hurry. Come on through." The steel-haired guard winced as she stepped into Rinn's barrier, she phased easily through it. Once inside, she looked around at the magic sphere in amazement. Rinn held out her hand to the other guard urgently. "We must go." The second woman hesitated, but she stepped to the glowing barrier. It held firm—she could not pass.

"What's happening?" The first guard panicked.

Rinn stared hard at the woman. "She betrayed us."

"Allex, why?" The younger guard begged her partner. The older guard's expression was stone. She retreated from Rinn and her companions. "Why?" The young guard screamed in frustration.

"We don't have time for this." Rinn jerked the younger woman away. "More soldiers are coming." Rinn fled down a wide avenue with Tavin and the steel-haired guard at her side. The soldiers started firing arrows at the trio, a reckless tactic in a crowded city. "Which way?" Rinn panted as she ran.

"South." The young guard advised. "Into the slums. We can hide there."

"North." Tavin countered. "There's a public bathhouse."

"Perfect." Rinn smiled as she huffed.

"A bathhouse?" The female guard protested. Rinn ignored her and turned north. Tavin pointed to a wide stone building with arched marble entrances. Water drizzled into two small fountains near the arches.

"We'll have to go inside." Rinn yelled. Tavin nodded as he ran, too winded to speak. Rinn lowered her shield as they rushed through the marble arches. They dashed past the reception area, where an attendant shouted at them. Rinn looked bewildered, she had never been in a public bathhouse this size, doors and hallways extended in every direction. Tavin urged her through a passage leading to a dirt courtyard where people were exercising. Everyone stopped and stared as the trio rushed past.

"In here." Tavin directed them through another doorway. Rinn and the palace guard followed him into a humid room with pink plaster walls. A steamy pool dominated the room where a few casual bathers lounged. Tavin splashed into the pool without a thought. Rinn held her breath and jumped in after him, spear and all. The water was hot! Rinn let out a little squeak. The palace guard threw up her hands and jumped into the pool after them. Disgruntled bathers gathered their things and exited in a huff.

"It won't be long." Rinn promised. The water was not deep, only up to her waist. "Hold onto my hands." Tavin timidly wrapped his hand around Rinn's. The young palace guard did the same. A commotion could be heard outside in the vestibule, men barking orders and the clamor of armor. Come on, Cat, Rinn thought to herself. Tavin cast Rinn an apprehensive look. "She'll be here." Rinn insisted. The shouting of men came closer, echoing down the hallways. Rinn bit her bottom lip.

Cat appeared at the side of the pool, tongue out, breathing hard. The woman accompanying Rinn was startled by her sudden appearance. Rinn tried to calm her with words. "It's okay. She's on our side."

Rinn sloshed through the water. She wanted to give Cat a huge hug, but she knew how her sister felt about getting wet. In broken speech, Cat panted. "I can only take one." Rinn could see that her sister was thoroughly exhausted.

Rinn pushed Tavin forward. "Take him." The scribe started to protest, but Rinn would not have it. "Go." She demanded. Cat touched the boy's shoulder and the two of them vanished, the water eddying where Tavin once stood. Heavily-armored soldiers stormed into the room, weapons drawn.

"She's in here." The first soldier beckoned to the others. The warriors fanned out, surrounding the pool. Rinn held her spear defensively. Standing in waist-deep water was not an ideal way to fight a battle. An officer entered the room, joining the twenty soldiers at the pool's edge.

"The game is over. Throw down your weapon and come out." The officer demanded. A curious idea struck Rinn, spurred by the officer's choice of words.

"These pools are heated from below, right?" She asked the woman accompanying her. The silver-haired guard cocked one eyebrow in response. "Hold on." Rinn said, raising her spear. She stabbed downward, into the mosaic floor of the pool, slicing through tile and stone. The pool cracked and the bottom fell out. Water flooded into the heated chamber below, filling the room with steam. Rinn and her friend were sucked down with the draining water.

"You're crazy." The young woman cried.

"I know." Rinn laughed. The scene was chaotic, soldiers disoriented by the sudden rush of steam. The bathwater tide spread out into the crawlspace under the floor, carrying Rinn and her escort with it. Rinn pointed to a glimmer of light in the distance. "There's our exit." She kicked at some of the fallen stones around her and slithered between them. Her partner followed without hesitating. The heating system ran the length of the building, supported by endless rows of square, tile columns. The crawlspace was not tall enough for Rinn to fully stand, so she crouched over and squeezed her way between the columns, trying to follow the draining water. Rinn's spear was the only source of light in this subterranean place. Yelling and heavy footsteps could be heard overhead. Voices entered the underground chamber.

Rinn glanced backward making sure her companion was following. The steel-haired guard was having no trouble keeping up. The woman's short, stocky legs and wide feet navigated the underground space easily. Astounded, Rinn noticed there was something very dwarfish about her friend. She let it go for the moment. "I can see the exit up ahead." Rinn squeezed between another stack of tile columns.

They came to a vaulted stone archway clogged with damp firewood. Rinn kicked the debris away from her exit and crawled through to daylight. She was momentarily blinded by its brightness. When her vision returned, she found herself in an enclosure behind the bathhouse. A crew of workers were chopping wood for the fire. Work stopped when Rinn and her companion emerged from the furnace. She shook her wet mop of hair and helped her drenched friend up.

"Hurry." Rinn urged. "It won't take long for them to figure out where we've gone." Rinn stared blankly at the maze of alleyways behind the public buildings. "Which way to the Natatorium?"

Rinn's companion grabbed her by the hand. "This way."

"What's your name?" Rinn panted.

"Sora." The gray-haired woman replied as they both ran.

Chapter 31

Rinn arrived at the Natatorium full of doubts. She was
not sure how she would find her friends, or if her
escape plan would work. Sora's help had proven
invaluable, together they skirted the backstreets of Peleon,
avoiding many Imperial patrols along the way. They had
passed uncomfortably close to the Great Temple of Aedis, a
colossal complex of ivory white towers. The manhunt
became more intense as night closed in. Soldiers lined
every major intersection, and military chariots streaked by
in flashes of red and gold. The sun had set, and the visible
moon dangled in the eastern sky like an opal pendant. Rinn
had no idea where the invisible moon might be.

Sora peeked out from a narrow alleyway. "Once these
soldiers pass, we should be clear." The more Rinn watched
her companion, the more dwarfish she appeared. Sora was
not quite as tall as Rinn, short for a full-grown woman, but
tall for a dwarf. Her stocky frame and her wide jaw belied
her heritage. Rinn wondered which tribe she belonged to.
She would have to worry about it later, finding her friends
and escaping Peleon came first.

Rinn reached out in her mind to contact Cat. She could
feel her sister passed out asleep. She was being carried by
someone, Lutra, and she liked it. Rinn shuddered. Her
connection to her sister was getting dangerously intimate.

Rinn wondered how long it would be before their souls were actually inseparable.

"Are you okay?" Sora whispered voice full of concern.

"Yes." Rinn shook her head, trying to clear her mind. "I know where my friends are, the sewers south of the city. They're going to sneak out through the main drain."

"That's a terrible idea." Sora exclaimed in a hush.

"Why?" Rinn asked in alarm.

"That sewer empties into the Aspero Sea." Sora grabbed Rinn's shoulder. "The fleet will be scouring the coast. Your friends are sure to be caught."

"We need to get to them first." Rinn's volume was raising in anxiety. Sora shushed her.

"We'll have to cross the slums." Sora hushed Rinn, as a patrol came into view in an alleyway opposite their hiding place. An officer pointed to the other alleyways, directing his troops to search every last one. Sora motioned back the way they had come. "We need to move." She mouthed. Rinn nodded and started backing up, careful to keep her metal spear from touching the ground. Its magic flames died long ago, and what remained was mostly a hunk of crumbling rust. Rinn and Sora crept quietly down the alley, until they met a surprised soldier with a torch coming the other way.

"Over here!" He announced.

Rinn blurted out "acwin" in self-defense. The soldier's torch sputtered out and the alley was draped in darkness. Rinn floundered in the pitch black, but she managed to reach out and find Sora's hand. Rinn attempted to trace the wall to her left, but she was still holding onto her spear. She ran into something or someone, it may have been the guard, Rinn was not sure.

A soft, feminine voice called to her. "Rinn, come this way." At first, she thought that it might be her sister, but the timbre was different. This voice was delicate, eloquent, musical. Completely blind, Rinn followed the voice that spoke her name. With her back to the wall, she felt her way down a murky side passage, hauling Sora behind her. In the darkness Rinn could see a young woman with a veiled face beckoning her to follow. Rinn obeyed reluctantly, firmly holding her wasted spear. "Hurry." The woman insisted, leading Rinn through twisted passages in the dark. She carried no torch or lantern, but somehow Rinn could see this strange woman. "Here." She pushed open a door and led Rinn and Sora inside.

After she had closed and barred the door, the woman let the black veil fall from her head and face. She was beautiful, with long silver hair and eyes like ice. Her round face seemed youthful for a woman, and her lips pale as snow. She politely sat down on a shipping crate, folding her dress behind her.

"Who are you?" Rinn asked, trying her best not to be defensive.

"I am Tenebra." The woman's voice was soft as song, and just as mesmerizing.

Sora retreated in horror. "The goddess of Darkness." She clutched her chest protectively and backed away. The idea of being in a room with Tenebra was insanity. She was the embodiment of darkness, lies, and primal passions, the very evil the Aedian priests preached against. But she was also the unseen moon, an invisible celestial body that pulled at the tides and maddened herds of cattle. Every farmer knew about Tenebra's curse, the one night of the month when cows would bray and stamp instead of sleep. Tenebra was counted with the Forsaken Gods, a pantheon that included Fear, Burden, Guilt, and Destruction. Together, they opposed the Sevrian deities in every possible way. Rinn held her spear defensively against the goddess, realizing how utterly preposterous she must seem: a drop of water railing against an ocean. Tenebra waited patiently on her perch, watching Rinn with a curious smile.

"Why would you help us?" Rinn's quivering voice was barely a squeak.

"You called to me." Tenebra responded, every syllable a melody. Rinn was seized by remorse. Every foul thing she had done in her life swirled in her thoughts: the destruction of Lucus' Grove, the levelling of the Temple of Aedis, the bloody massacre of Clanmorris, her awful treatment of Sionne. A dread fear took ahold of her, a certainty that she was going to die, pay the ultimate price for her lifetime of atrocities.

"You're here to kill me." Rinn breathed out.

Tenebra delicately shook her hair and mused. "Sweet child, I would never do anything like that. You spoke my name. Right here, in fact. " She waved a glowing hand around the room. Rinn became aware she was inside Niveus' warehouse. She had summoned darkness here, several times for no good reason at all. Rinn sank to the ground, letting her rusty spear fall from her hand. Regret tapped her strength.

"I'm so sorry." Rinn pleaded.

Tenebra rose from her seat. "Don't be. I should be thanking you." She drifted close to Rinn. It did not make any sense, but Tenebra's silvery light illuminated the entire room. The goddess reached out a hand to help Rinn up, but Rinn was too terrified to take hold of it. Instead, Tenebra joined her on the ground, long black skirts billowing out as she sat. The goddess laid her hands in her lap. "You have nothing to fear from me. I'm here to help you." Rinn sensed an ulterior motive.

"Don't listen to her." Sora pleaded.

Rinn should have known better than to pick a fight with a goddess, but she could not shake the feeling she was being tested. "What do you really want?"

"Clever girl." The goddess half-smirked. "You see right through Darkness. In truth, I came to ask you a favor."

"A favor?" The skin on the back of Rinn's neck prickled.

"In just over two hours, I will eclipse my sister, the moon. I will be at the height of my powers, and my darkness will spread over the city. You should make your escape at that time." Tenebra reached into the folds of her dress and tore off a portion of the cloth. Somehow, her skirts did not seem diminished in any way. She offered Rinn a pitch-black riding cloak. Reluctantly, very reluctantly, Rinn reached out a hand to touch the delicate fabric. It was softer than the finest velvet, and neither warm nor cold.

"What is this for?" Rinn accepted the gift warily. Sora shied away from it.

"My faithful servant will know what to do." Tenebra answered.

A dread anticipation welled up inside Rinn. "Why are you helping me? Aren't you one of the Forsaken?" She regretted saying the words even as they came out.

If Tenebra was perturbed, she did not show it. "Child, we have been helping you since the beginning. Who do you think laid the Vallum low for you? That was my brother Onero. Who taught your soul-sister to roar? My brother Timor. And Reneo, I think he may be in love with you."

Rinn's heartbeat pounded in her ears. Reneo the Unraveller was the embodiment of chaos itself, the demolisher of worlds. How could she have attracted the attention of such a monster? The answer terrified her, but Rinn asked anyway. "Did he destroy the Temple at Viburna?"

Tenebra rose from the floor, adjusting her skirts. "No, my dear. You called his name, but it was Aedis himself who sundered his own house."

"I called his name?" Rinn gulped.

"Yes." Tenebra assured her. "Usually, my brother's name is invoked in rage with the self-control of a summerstorm. But you whisper it softly, deftly painting his power with the skill of an artist's brush, and he adores it."

"What's his name?" Rinn whimpered.

"Onlithe." Tenebra replied, as if it were obvious.

Rinn remembered her father telling her that her abilities were not magic, but divine gifts. Rinn had never thought about the source of her powers. She rose to her feet, on wobbly knees. This was worse than death, she had allied herself with the forces of evil. "My soul is damned." And if she was damned, her sister was too.

Tenebra graciously stepped back, giving Rinn room. "Innocent child. That could not be further from the truth. The gods have set aside their petty differences for you. For the first time in many millennia we are working together. We have not been a proper family in such a long time."

"Why?" Rinn pleaded to the point of tears. "I'm just a girl. I'm nothing special."

There was no melody or unworldly echo in Tenebra's voice as she answered. "You are special, dear girl. You alone walk the path of salvation. So much is happening that you do not yet understand." She caressed Rinn's cheek. "We need you Rinn. I need you. Please. Rescue my sister."

::

Rinn and Sora dashed down the evening streets of Peleon, keeping to the shadows. They sprinted through the city slums, running short on time. Tenebra's shadow would fall over the city in less than an hour. Rinn needed to find her friends before they exited the sewers—the Curia's fleet was waiting in ambush. Rinn could sense that Cat was still sleeping off her magical hangover, but she was not far away.

"Straight ahead." Rinn panted, pointing down the next street.

"We shouldn't listen to that woman." Sora huffed. "She's evil."

Rinn was too winded to craft an effective rebuttal. "We don't have much choice." As she rounded a corner, she careened right into a patrol of soldiers. The startled men lowered their polearms.

"Stop right there." The head soldier called. Rinn had no intention of stopping. She surrounded the four men with her barrier and cast them into a nearby wall like she was swatting a fly. The men crumpled to the ground in a pile. Rinn momentarily bent down to retrieve one of their polearms. She balanced it in her hand and nodded to herself. Sora stared in astonishment.

"Let's go." Rinn rushed to the southern docks, Sora following behind wordlessly. They encountered two more patrols, which Rinn dispatched in a similar way. The streets grew narrower and the homes shabbier as they headed south. They were angling through the narrow dockyard streets when Rinn heard the first explosion. Several blocks away, a pillar of flame erupted in the night sky. She spotted a second fireball hurtling through the air to the same destination. Rinn sprinted, trying to outrun the missile, but she arrived too late. A second blast shook the area, dousing everything in flames. Sora covered her head and face against the smoke and flying debris. Rinn enshrouded them both in her barrier. They arrived at Poorman's Wharf, a rickety wooden walkway along the southern banks of Peleon's slums. In the distance, seven warships were anchored offshore, prickles of orange torchlight dancing on their decks. Ahead, splintered sections of the wharf burned furiously. Rinn ran into the heart of the conflagration, desperate to find her friends.

At the center of the inferno she found the exit to the sewers, a round brick opening that emptied into the sea. And clogging it like a cork, was an immense round rock with a purple eyeball painted on it. Rinn ran up to Clive, laughing hysterically in relief. "Molo! Open Up! It's Rinn!" She shouted as she waved her arms at the giant stone. Sora grimaced and watched the harbor warily. A third fireball was launched from the ships at sea. "Molo! Let us in!" Rinn yelled, bracing for impact. Clive's purple eye looked down, noticing Rinn for the first time. The eye blinked and in an instant, Rinn and Sora were standing inside the sewer tunnel. Outside a violent impact rattled the ground.

Tavin jumped forward, embracing Rinn. "You're okay." He squeezed her tighter than was comfortable, but Rinn did not mind. She hugged him back. Rinn could see all her friends gathered in the sewer. Dempsi huddled near the dwarves, their metal lamps providing the only illumination. The little girl was talking to herself or maybe the water at her feet. The two palace guards Velle and Lepas welcomed their friend Sora warmly. Lutra leaned against a wall, holding Catherine in his arms, she slept like a cat in a beam of sunlight. Molo braced himself against Clive, beads of sweat trickled off his brow. Another explosion rocked the wharf outside.

Haril and Grus stepped forward, bruised and bloodied. "What's the plan?" The mercenary asked, all business. Rinn pried herself away from Tavin, who seemed embarrassed at his own reaction.

Rinn addressed everyone. "In a short while, darkness will descend over the city of Peleon. We'll make our escape then."

Grus marveled. "You can do that?"

"No. I'm getting help." Rinn winked. "We have to hold out just a bit longer." She sided up to Molo who was struggling to keep Clive in place. She laid a hand on his shoulder. "We should retreat back into the sewers." She noticed that the giant man seemed different, she could touch him without standing on her tiptoes. "Uncle Molo, are you smaller?"

Molo gritted his teeth, but did not deign to answer.

Onager counseled Rinn. "The nearest sewer drain is miles to the east. If we go back, we'd have to cross half of Peleon to get to it."

Rinn replied. "I don't intend to go far, just out of range of those fireballs."

Onager cautioned. "And if they storm the sewers? We could be trapped."

"They won't get past me." Rinn assured him, clutching her polearm tightly. "When the time comes, I'll clear the exit."

Sora shuddered. "I've seen her fight. She's scary." Lutra said nothing, but nodded in agreement. He shifted Catherine's weight in his arms, she snuggled in closely. Rinn suspected her sister was no longer asleep, but she did not make a fuss. Another explosion shook the ground outside. Molo clenched his jaw in an effort to hold the enlarged Clive in place.

"We should go." Rinn advised. She pointed down the sewer tunnel. "Everyone, give us room." Onager and Haril ushered the party members deeper into the tunnel. Little Dempsi kept talking to herself as she followed along.

"What's the plan?" Molo said through gritted teeth.

"You let go, I take over. I want to send a message to those boats." Rinn readied her weapon. "On the count of three. One. Two. Three." With a snapping sound, Clive shrunk back to his original size and Molo grew, bashing his head against the ceiling. He doubled over in pain. "Down the tunnel, quickly." Rinn commanded as she raised her barrier. Another fireball streaked toward her. Rinn drew in a deep breath and forced out the word "acwin". The fireball sputtered and snuffed out. A slag of porous rock smashed against the side of the sewer entrance, leaving behind an oily stain of volatile liquid. Rinn grimaced at the pungent vapors.

Rinn hefted her polearm and lit the tip with green, glowing magic. "I hope this works." She chanted the word "ahebbe" and felt the weight of the spear lift from her hand. She chucked the weapon as hard as she could at the lead warship. It sailed through the air like a green missile. The fleet was quite a distance away, but the ships were huge targets, easy to strike if her spear flew far enough. Rinn could not see if her aim was true, but a commotion broke out on the deck of one of the warships, a scrambling of distant torchlights. She did not wait around to watch, she retreated into the sewers using the soft glow of her barrier to light the way.

Chapter 32

Rinn's army gathered at the intersection of four tunnels, a spacious chamber with vaulted ceilings tall enough for full-sized Molo to stand. Rinn counted off all her companions in her head. One was missing. "Where's Yallakh?" Rinn questioned.

A lanky figure in tattered black ribbons stepped from the shadows. "Right here, my queen." He curled the corners of his mouth unflatteringly. The other party members shied away from his ominous presence. Cat's sleepy eyes roused, watching the dread assassin emerge. Lutra set her down ruefully.

"I think I have a present for you." Rinn fished under the panels of her dragon feather vest and pulled out a pitch-black cloak. Its fabric was so thin and weightless, Rinn nearly forgot she was carrying it. She shook out the cloak and offered it to Yallakh. "A gift from a friend of yours."

When his long, bony fingers touched the fabric, his red and brown eyes shot open in surprise. He snatched the cloak greedily, but then, as if feeling remiss, he knelt before Rinn in the brackish sewer water. "You honor me." A question hesitated on his tattooed lips. "Did you meet with her?"

"Yes." Rinn admitted. "She was quite charming. She called you her most faithful servant." Yallakh looked as if he were actually capable of shedding tears. Rinn waved her hand. "Go ahead. Try it on." Yallakh stood his full height and drew the cloak over his shoulders. The dark fabric enveloped his body, spreading down his torso to his arms and legs. Tattered bandages unwound and faded away, allowing the new fabric to take hold. The cloak became a black tailored suit, boots and gloves, and waist-length cape. A long, pointed riding cap with a rounded back and black plume formed on his head completing the outfit. Standing tall, Yallakh looked regal in his new velvety outfit the color of night. All that was left of his old bandages was a single scrap of cloth floating in the sewage water.

"Wow." Rinn popped. "You look stunning." The others agreed.

Yallakh bent down and plucked the faded scrap of cloth from the water and held it tightly in his fist. He touched it to his chest like a precious treasure. The scene was broken by the distant sounds of men shouting and footsteps splashing through the shallow water.

"They're coming." Onager unsheathed his sword. Haril and Grus did the same.

Rinn held out her hands to stop them. "Wait. There's an easier way." She sloshed over to Catherine who was yawning and rubbing her eyes. Rinn scratched her drowsy sister's chin. "Cat, would you mind helping us?"

"No more teleportation." She whined in her feline voice.

"That's not what I had in mind." Rinn grinned mischievously. She motioned down the corridor with her eyes and covered her ears. A spark of recognition flashed across Cat's face.

"Really?" She asked. Rinn nodded yes. Cat smiled wickedly with her one-and-a-half fangs. The clamor of soldiers grew steadily louder, accompanied by the staccato clank of armor.

Rinn threw her hands over her head. "Everyone. Cover your ears and turn away. Cat's going to roar."

"Samria, save us." Lutra cried. He pressed his palms to his ears and clenched his teeth. The others did the same, except Molo, who held his giant hands over Dempsi's dainty ears. Catherine crouched in the tunnel leading out, arching her back to its full height. She sucked in a great breath and opened her mouth wide like a lion. Her roar rippled down the tunnel like an earthquake, the reverberations shook loose stones and splattered sewer water against the walls. It lasted an entire minute, and Rinn's ears were pounding by the time it was over. Slowly, like trampled grass, Rinn's friends recovered, addled by the experience. Dempsi had big tears in her eyes, and Molo held her close. Even Lutra seemed shaken and a bit terrified.

Rinn patted her sister on the head. "Thank you." Her voice was unnecessarily loud. Catherine licked her mouth and face with a self-satisfied expression. Rinn led the way down the wide drainage tunnel to the exit. The shouts of men and the clank of armor was gone, or maybe Rinn could not hear them—her ears were still ringing. As the party neared the exit, they found it engulfed in an unnatural darkness, so thick it was almost liquid. Without hesitation, Yallakh plunged into the pitch black, in one step he was gone, utterly consumed by the night.

"We're going into that?" Lutra's teeth chattered.

Cat sniffed at the wall of darkness. Rinn asked her. "Can you see anything?"

Cat considered for a moment, twitching her ears. "Sort of." She replied with a screwed up look on her face.

Mafic and Felsic produced a length of twine. "Fashion this to your belt, m'lady." The always practical and inventive dwarves secured everyone to the line, like beads on a string. Rinn and Cat took the lead positions and Molo the far end. Felsic looped the twine around Cat's waist and tightened it snugly, he then took his place in line.

"Okay, Cat." Rinn directed. "Lead on."

"Head west to the Emmer Gate." Onager advised. "If we can figure out which way west is."

"Cat can do it." Rinn brimmed with confidence, even though she regarded the inky darkness with apprehension. Cat bounced twice on her haunches and dipped herself into the liquid night, tugging her reluctant companions along behind her. Rinn submerged herself in the blackness, utterly lost. Her sightless eyes cried out in explosions of blues and yellows, ghosts of shapes she had recently seen. The twine attached to Rinn's waist became her lifeline. She reached out blindly for her sister, but could not find her. The darkness seemed to swallow sound, Rinn could not even hear her own footfalls. She was so disoriented she felt like she was falling, floating in some magical space, something akin to the Mist she drifts through with Cat.

"Keep ahold of yourself." A sinewy voice whispered from the dark. "The way is not far."

"Yallakh? Is that you?" Rinn tried to call out, but no sound came.

"Your feline knows the way." The voice promised her, and then left. Rinn made several more attempts to speak, but her words were lost in the void. The twine continued its constant tug forward, Rinn's only reassurance that her sister was still there. In the syrup of night, minutes stretched into hours. Rinn's legs ached like she had walked clear across Peleon. A sudden panic shook her, what if they were going the wrong way? They could be heading straight into the Legion and never know it. Rinn had been walking for what seemed like a very long time, never encountering any people or walls or anything. Something was wrong, that should not be possible in a city of this size. They were lost! Rinn fought back the urge to summon her shield and lash out at the darkness. The twine at her waist tugged at her like a gentle friend. Rinn gripped it with both hands, thinking of her sister.

We're almost there, Cat's voice echoed in Rinn's head. The darkness will end soon. She promised. Then, abruptly, Rinn collided with something solid, metal. She reached out blindly, her fingers curling around cold metal bars. For a moment, Rinn thought she might be in a prison, but she slowly became aware of the stone gate around her. The darkness was withdrawing, hints of gray light returning. Rinn rested her hands on the metal portcullis, drawn closed for the night. Behind her, Rinn's companions emerged from the shadows dazed and spent, exhausted by the darkness. Molo carried little Dempsi in his arms, her eyes squeezed shut in fear. Felsic and Mafic came and untangled everyone from the towline. Tavin shook his head, attempting to clear away the aftereffects of the darkness.

Molo grumbled at Rinn, cradling the terrified girl in his arms. "We will never do that again. Understand?" His creased brow punctuated his ire.

"It was the only way." Rinn insisted, shrinking away like a mouse. The dark blues of evening were returning, and city guards stirred on the battlements above them. In the distance, a single torch broke the veil of night, soon joined by another and another. Soon, the streets and buildings came alive as light slowly returned to the city. Citizens poured out into the streets, bewildered attendees at some great nighttime festival.

Haril attempted to budge the heavy bars of the portcullis. "We must get through before we're seen." Grus and Calder joined him, straining at the effort. Molo was about to set down Dempsi when Rinn stopped him.

"This is my obstacle." Rinn focused on the metal bars. The guards above called down a warning, but she ignored them. She enunciated the Sigillum word "scieppan" and took ahold of the portcullis. The metal turned molten in her hands. She pulled two of the bars away like sticky taffy, twisting them into a new shape—iron spears with spiral handles. The steaming weapons cooled in her hands. She tossed one to Tavin, who caught it reluctantly, as if it would burn him. A soldier on the battlements fired a warning shot over Rinn, it clattered off the stone street.

"Hurry." Haril urged, nudging Grus and Calder through the gap. More followed, squirming through the portcullis. Haril held his shield over the exit protectively. Soldiers above continued their shouting. Rinn was tempted to summon her barrier, but she feared it would be too easily recognized. She did not want a Legion of troops hounding her halfway across Sevria. Molo handed Dempsi through the gate to Lutra, and somehow managed to squeeze through the gap himself. Tavin ducked through last, beckoning Rinn to follow.

Beyond the gate, Rinn's companions slinked along the city walls, out of range of the archers above them. Onager motioned south and the party followed in the shadows. A few watchmen let arrows fly, but the angle was difficult, and the lighting was terrible. A hundred paces down the wall, Rinn and her companions regrouped.

"What now?" Lutra asked holding Dempsi by the hand. Soldiers on the walls above continued to hound them, barking out instructions.

"I could summon darkness." Rinn offered.

"No." Molo fumed. "No more darkness." Everyone seemed to be in agreement. Rinn shrank back, a dejected teenager surrounded by adults. Together the adults made a strategy to distract the guards while the rest slipped away. Rinn quietly obeyed, running when she was told. She sprinted across the open field, dodging the occasional arrow that whizzed by. Once she crested a small rise, she was in the clear. Her party mustered at the bottom of the ridge, seemingly unscathed, though Onager did find a fresh arrow stuck in the shield slung over his back.

Molo held up Clive and pointed west. "Let's go find Marshal and the others." Rinn followed wordlessly behind. A silvery moon drifted through a cloudless sky offering unsatisfying illumination, enough to see shapes but not detail. Rinn fixed her gaze on the heavens, searching futilely for the invisible moon. She knew Tenebra was up there, somewhere close. Rinn could still picture the glowing woman draped in a thick black mantle. In her musical voice she begged Rinn. "Please. Rescue my sister." Rinn had no reason to believe or trust her, but she wanted to. The Queen of Darkness seemed reasonable, polite, even caring—qualities she should not possess. Rinn wondered if this was some elaborate trap or if the goddess legitimately needed her help.

"Hello." Tavin waved his hand in front of Rinn's face. "Rinn, we need to catch up, before we get lost out here." Rinn let him take her by the hand and lead her into the night.

Chapter 33

R inn's army reached the waystation well past midnight. It was a beehive of activity. On the busiest Imperial roads, waystations never slept. Travelers checked in and out at all times of the day, needing nourishment, rest, and supplies. Rinn and her companions stayed behind while Haril and Grus ventured inside to locate Marshal, Sionne, and Feena. Little Dempsi snored softly in Molo's arms. Catherine curled up at the foot of a scrubby tree, Lutra reclined against its trunk. The landscape west of Peleon was a bland continuum of grass and rocks, this tree was a novelty. Rinn laid down next to her sister on the hard, rooty ground. She was so exhausted she did not let discomfort keep her from sleep.

In her dreams, Rinn floated over a city, not Viburna, but an alien-appearing assemblage of crystalline buildings. Perched on the roofs were bizarre, metal contraptions— oversized versions of navigational instruments a sailor might use. As Rinn glided closer, she could see the blue aura of magic everywhere, the city stank of it. Enchantments permeated every door, window, and stone in the street. Tides of magic ebbed and flowed around the strange instruments on the buildings. But the brightest, hottest source of magic was inside a triangular tower at the city center. Rinn drifted closer, caught in the pull of its power, but it felt wrong, polluted. Rinn struggled to get away, clawing at the air. She could feel hands gripping her, shaking her.

"Rinn. Wake up." Her father's voice cried.

Rinn jerked awake in a panic. She was being held by the ugliest woman she had ever seen: beady eyes, long beak-like nose, single black hair hanging down from her chin. Yet, somehow, she seemed vaguely familiar.

"Daddy?" Rinn stammered in disbelief. Her father straightened his wig, an awful ash-brown mop that clashed with his olive skin color. He was dressed in a hideous smock of homespun burlap that bulged in all the wrong places. "What're you wearing?" Rinn sat up, trying to clear her head.

Sionne came into view with a haughty expression. "That's some of my finest work." Rinn became aware of her friends gathered around her, all eighteen of them, enough to man a military squadron. Half of them were trained soldiers, armed for battle. Rinn's army was beginning to take shape. So why did she feel a sense of foreboding? A dread certainty that things were moving beyond her control. The battle lines for Sevria were being drawn and Rinn did not know where to stand. She felt like an outsider, sitting alone in the cold while everyone else partied inside the house. A paw reached down to help her up. Rinn remembered her one constant in all this mayhem, her sister. Cat smiled, squinting her feline eyes.

Rinn rose and straightened out the crumples in her skirts. "That's the ugliest disguise I've ever seen." She informed Sionne.

The redhead looked taken aback. "Of course, it is. That's the point. If I made him beautiful, everyone'd want a second look. If he's repulsive, they'll pay him no mind."

Marshal seemed ambivalent to his new disguise. "It's worked so far." He admitted. Rinn wondered where they came by the hideous ash-brown wig. Then she saw Feena.

Her friend's long hair was cut short above her ears. Her round cheeks and forehead poked out playfully. Somehow, her cropped hair made her look older, like a new mother. Lutra spoke with her, pretending to enjoy her new look, but casting sidelong glances at Sionne.

Molo suppressed a grin as he spoke to Marshal. "I hear you've arranged passage for us."

Marshal gestured to Sionne. "We have that one to thank for it. Turns out, he's quite useful." Niveus, Onager, and the palace guards eyed the red-headed teen suspiciously.

"I know how to strike a deal." Sionne strutted, chest held high.

"He secured transportation to Gadiom." Marshal related the story. A disgruntled farmer, called Segnis, came to sell wheat in Peleon, but the Legion impounded it and paid him half the market price. Segnis had to forfeit an opportunity to buy trade goods bound for Gadiom. He was forced to return home with an empty wagon train. One mention of the rebellion at Messis, and Segnis was more than happy to provide passage for Sionne and his friends for a small fee.

Under the cloak of night, Rinn's army loaded into the backs of three hay wagons bound for Gadiom. They laid down in the wagon beds to avoid being seen, at least until they were clear of the waystation traffic. Molo recommended everyone stash their weapons and armor to keep up the appearance of hired laborers heading to a farm. As the horses plodded down the darkened highway, Rinn lay awake staring at the stars. Little worries eddied in her mind. Nearby, her father spread out in his itchy burlap dress.

"Daddy?" Rinn asked, unsure if he was asleep.

"Yes." He answered, no drowsiness in his voice.

"Where's Bayard?" Rinn questioned.

"We had to leave him behind." Marshal sighed. "The Legion was confiscating any war-worthy horse entering or leaving the city. I boarded him with a reliable friend on the west end." Rinn could hear how difficult it must have been to leave his best friend behind. Since his injury, her father had spent nearly every day in the saddle, and now that was over. Rinn had many more questions she wanted to ask, but she really needed sleep. Eventually, the stars lulled her to bed.

::

The next day, Dempsi sat on the back of the wagon, kicking her feet off the end. "How long are we going to be traveling?"

Feena sat beside her. "Just two more days. It's not so bad. There's a nice breeze, and this beats walking."

"I like this wagon. It doesn't smell like fish." Dempsi pinched her nose. Feena laughed in agreement. Rinn sat in one corner, stewing in her thoughts. She tried to recall what happened to the wagons Felsic and Mafic had built. The last place she remembered having them was at the Imperial Palace. Even though only a few days had passed, the Imperial Palace seemed a lifetime away: beautiful clothing, ostentatious rooms, gourmet food. She spotted the palace guards who accompanied her in an adjacent wagon. In their own way, Onager, Velle, Lepas, and Sora had all demonstrated their loyalty to Rinn and her cause, but she did not think they understood the magnitude of the problem she faced. The only one who seemed to have any inkling was Yallakh. He was another one of those worries that swirled in the back of Rinn's head. She had not seen any sign of him since the tunnels. He donned Tenebra's gift and melted into the night.

"Gotcha." Two furry paws tickled Rinn's sides, breaking her concentration. "Go away dark thoughts." Cat chanted the words like a spell.

"I'm not having dark thoughts." Rinn refuted. Cat cocked her head dubiously, her tail twitching. Rinn confessed. "Okay. Maybe a little."

"We made it out of Peleon." Cat plopped down next to her sister and laid her head in her lap, clearly wanting it to be scratched. Rinn obliged. "We're heading to Messis. That should be fun, right?"

"Not really." Rinn huffed. Cat lifted her chin, hoping for more scratching. "The city's mobilized for war. I just want to get Dempsi to the Water Temple and leave."

Cat looked up at her sister curiously. "How can you stop a war without getting involved in it?" She sat up, paws in her lap. "Well, I'm curious to find out who this mysterious Molossus person is."

Rinn stole a glance at the giant, sitting in the last wagon. His somber expression made Felsic look cheerful. Rinn stretched her legs. "We should talk with Molo before we arrive. There is something he's not telling us."

"We all have things we hide." Cat declared.

Rinn locked eyes with her sister, contemplating revenge tickles. "What are you hiding, Catherine?"

"What do you want to know?" She answered honestly.

Rinn forestalled her attack. Sitting back, she asked. "Where did you come from? I mean originally."

Cat put a paw to her chin in thought. "I was just a kitten, but I remember cages. I know I'm not the only one like me, because there were others in cages, too. Slavers were there with their whips and chains."

"How did you escape?" Rinn wondered.

"I didn't stay a kitten." Cat replied, as if that answered everything. Rinn was starting to understand that everyone had trials in life to overcome. Cat endured years of slavery. Her father and mother survived the accursed isle of Migalia.

Rinn was certain that Molo had been through some terrible experience that he would not share. She could not get the vision of his bone-filled cave out of her mind. What had happened to him?

::

The hay wagons stopped at another waystation that evening. Rinn and her companions stayed some distance away, taking shelter in a grove of trees. As they traveled westward, the barren grasslands evolved into undulating hills blanketed by forests of birch and beech trees. These woods were sparse compared to the dense, ancient forests of the Rustic Lands, but they offered some shelter and sense of security for Rinn.

Resources were running low. Onager bartered one of Rinn's silver hairpins for food and supplies. Feeding twenty people was becoming difficult, exhausting their reserves. The farmer Segnis shared what little he had, especially with Dempsi. Rinn wanted to thank him for his generosity, but the less he knew about her the better, so she stayed away. A few miles outside of Gadiom, Marshal recommended parting ways with the wagon train. Everyone unloaded their things and strapped on their armor and weapons. Marshal fervently thanked Segnis for his assistance and offered to pay him what he could.

"You don't owe me anything." The farmer waved his hand dismissively. "Just stick it to those Curia bastards." That was exactly what they had in mind, Marshal answered him.

Little Dempsi climbed up the side of the wagon. "Do you have a farm?"

Segnis beamed. "Yes, I do, missy. The finest acres north of Gadiom."

"Okay." Dempsi returned his smile.

Marshal leaned close to his daughter. "That is one lucky farmer."

"What do you mean?" Rinn whispered.

"I have a feeling his fields are going to be blessed with favorable rains for years to come." He observed.

Rinn's army trekked west around the city, across the rolling hills. A lazy, muddy river picked its way between the hills as it flowed to Gadiom and the Lenis Sea. They skirted the southern banks of the river, but travel was slow, Marshal could only move so quickly. The dwarves offered to build a litter for him, but he refused to be carried. He persisted, limping along painfully.

Rinn took Molo aside. "He won't make it all the way to Messis like this."

"I know." The giant replied. "But your father's a proud and stubborn man. If only we could find a horse for him. He needs to be in the saddle." Rinn asked around, trying to formulate a solution. The river seemed the obvious answer, but they did not have their own boat, nor the funds to afford passage on one. The party stopped on a river bank for lunch. The midday sun was baking the ground, making it almost too hot to sit upon. Meager shares of food were brought out for everyone. Felsic and Mafic attempted to fish in the muddy river without much success.

"We need a boat." Onager stated over lunch. The other's nodded in agreement.

"We could fashion a raft." Mafic offered.

"For twenty persons?" Haril argued. "That might take weeks."

Dempsi pointed her finger at the river. "There's a boat down there."

Rinn reclined next to her. She peered out to the muddy water. "I don't see anything."

"It's at the bottom of the river." Dempsi explained.

Felsic grumbled. "How are we going to get a boat from the bottom of the river?"

"I can help." A female voice answered. Sora raised from her seat and stepped to the water's edge.

"You're Náin, aren't you." Felsic asked in awe.

Sora answered without turning back. "My mother was Náin." She slowly began stripping off her clothes until she was dressed only in her undergarments. She was undeniably dwarven, bulging muscles in her calves and thighs and tufts of steel-colored hair across her back and shoulders.

"You never told us." Velle gathered her clothes and folded them neatly.

Sora inclined her head to the side. "Did you really want to know?"

"It's nothing to be ashamed of." Velle insisted.

"My mother was a slave." Sora replied with distant regret in her voice. "She died at Gadiom fighting for her freedom." Molo balled his hands into fists, tortured by emotion. Sora stood at the river bank, her dwarven figure plain for all to see. "I don't blame you, General Molo. My mother spoke fondly of you. But she never mentioned anything about a beard."

Molo choked back his words. "You're Orine's daughter."

"Yes." Sora admitted. "My father raised me, taught me to blend into society. But I am what I am." With that she dove into the muddy river. Rinn gasped, and moved to dive in after her. Mafic took ahold of her arm.

"She's Náin." He stated. "She's in no danger."

"What's a Náin?" Rinn asked, staring at the water.

Felsic answered her. "A water dwarf. Very rare. I should've recognized her heritage." Rinn gave him a puzzled look. "Her hair. Water dwarves always have metal-colored hair."

Rinn stared at the water. Sora had been down there a long time. "She's not coming up. We need to do something."

"Be patient." Molo clarified. "Náin can stay under water for hours at a time. She'll resurface when she's ready." Sora remained underwater for almost half an hour before she finally emerged. Water and mud rolled off her body as if she were a duck, but strands of stonewort clung to her underclothes. Felsic offered her a cloth to dry herself off. She thanked him and wiped her face and hair. Felsic followed her with his eyes as she pulled her clothes back on.

"There is a boat down there." Sora explained. "A big one in fairly good condition, except for a breech in the side hull." She lowered her head. "There are Imperial soldiers among the wreckage, drowned by their armor."

Marshal surmised. "They must've been mounting an attack on Messis." Molo looked away. An uncomfortable silence fell over everyone, a somber expression of remorse for the lives lost. No one wanted to speak, Rinn's own words stuck in her throat.

"So." Finally, Sora broke the quiet. "How're we going to get it out?"

Chapter 34

M arshal, Molo, and the dwarves devised a plan to haul the sunken boat from the riverbed, but they needed rope, lots of rope. The remainder of the day evolved into a rope braiding party. The teenage boys harvested wispy strands of grass and the men pulled rushes from the riverbanks. The dwarves divided them into fibers and the women braided them. The work had a satisfying rhythm and Rinn found herself enjoying it. She sat with Feena and Dempsi. The little girl did not quite understand the steps to braiding, but she was learning. Cat was given the task of tying knots every few feet, a job she excelled at. Velle, Lepas, and Sora laughed and talked while they worked. Niveus had no talent for braiding, so she accompanied the men harvesting rushes.

By nightfall, ten lengths of green and yellow rope were drying on the riverbank. Rinn flexed her sore fingers, stiff from the day's work. A campfire was built, and a modest dinner served. Someone brought out a flask of spirits and passed it around. The mood was lively and conversation light. Rinn felt the tension of her days in Peleon slipping away. She missed country life. There had been difficulties at Hilltop, but most of her days spent there were good ones. Part of her longed to go back, but Rinn knew she was not the same naive girl picking flowers in the wilderness. The world was a bigger place, and she had a role she needed to play. "Please. Rescue my sister." She could almost hear Tenebra's voice calling to her.

Rinn summoned her courage and stood up. "I have an announcement." Her companions around the campfire turned their heads to her. "After we finish our business at Messis, Cat and I are leaving."

Questions and murmurs rippled through her friends. Like a parent, Marshal inquired. "And where do you think you're going?"

"Farann Fada." Rinn informed everyone. Astonishment spread through the group. Even Cat raised one ear in surprise.

"What's the meaning of this?" Marshal demanded.

"Don't listen to her." Sora blurted out. "She can't be trusted."

"Who?" Marshal turned her attention to Sora.

"Tenebra." Sora answered in a whisper.

Marshal's volume began to rise. "Rinn Amali, what have you done?"

"I didn't do anything." Rinn denied.

Molo gruffed. "I knew that darkness was tainted. That was her work wasn't it."

"Yes." Rinn admitted. "But she was helping us."

Marshal's face was beet-red as he yelled. "The Queen of Darkness doesn't help anyone. She's the embodiment of evil."

Like a teenager, Rinn hollered back. "You don't know anything. She's not like that at all."

"You met with her?" Marshal exploded. "You made a deal with the Queen of the Night? Rinn, are you insane? Nothing good can come of this."

Yallakh emerged from the shadows. "Heed your daughter's words."

Once the initial shock of is appearance died down, Marshal thrust an accusing finger at him. "I don't have to listen to you, assassin. I'm her father. I won't have my daughter cavorting with demons."

"She's not a demon. She's a goddess." Rinn objected.

"You're taking her side?" Marshal ranted. "Rinn, what's gotten into you?"

Rinn inhaled deeply, trying to reason with her father. "You said that my abilities weren't magic, they were divine gifts. You were right, but all the gods have been aiding us, not just the nine."

"What?" Marshal croaked in disbelief.

"Sigillum words can invoke any of the gods." Rinn's voice softened.

"This is not what your mother intended." Marshal clenched his jaw.

"She used their powers, too." Rinn confessed. "When I spoke with Aunt Cecilia, she mentioned Mom once put out a kitchen fire with a word. Extinguishing flames is Tenebra's power. Mom surely knew that." Her father had no response, he just stared at her wordlessly. Yallakh stood by Rinn, still as the grave.

"What does this mean?" Molo rotated Clive in his hand.

Rinn tried her best to explain. "The gods have put aside their differences and they are working together. After thousands of years, they are cooperating with each other."

Molo boggled. "What kind of catastrophe would unite the gods?"

The answer oozed from Yallakh's lips like a disease. "Elves."

::

The next morning, the party assembled on the river bank. The revelations of the previous night were not forgotten, but salvaging the sunken ship came first. Sora stripped down to her swimming clothes and waded into the river. Mafic and Felsic tossed her ropes which she hauled underwater and secured to the wreck. Groups of two or three gathered on each line, except Molo, he took two ropes himself. At first, it looked as if the ship was not going to budge, but Dempsi spoke to the water, and the vessel broke free. Using their combined strength, they hauled the ship to shore.

The wreck was covered in river mud, but other than the hull breech, it was in reasonable condition. Molo and the dwarves went to work mending the hull. The teenage boys, Haril, and Niveus ventured out to chop timber for the repairs. Feena, Velle, and Lepas started the arduous process of demucking the boat. Rinn rolled up her sleeves and joined in. The river slime was disgusting and smelled of sulfur. Cat would have no part of it, she frolicked on the river banks with Dempsi, chasing dragonflies and tormenting crayfish in their mud holes.

"Try catching some of those." Molo called. "They're good eating." That became the game for the rest of the day, see who could trap the most crayfish. Dempsi had a decided advantage, being able to manipulate water. Even with the dwarves' crafting skills, repairs consumed most of the day. By dinnertime, everyone was exhausted. Feena somehow managed to cook up the bountiful harvest of crayfish. Marshal cracked one open and passed it to Rinn. She braved a tiny bite. It tasted okay, as long as she did not look at it. Catherine devoured about twenty of them.

Grease dribbled down Onager's chin as he ate. "Could use some butter." He joked. Someone threw an empty crayfish shell at him. A flask of spirits was passed around. When Rinn sniffed the pungent liquor, she was happy not to partake. She spotted Yallakh in the shadows reclining against a tree. She brought two cooked crayfish to him. He raised an eyebrow. She held out her offering, which he accepted dubiously. She cracked the shell for him, and he sampled the strange meal. He took a second bite, then a third. Satisfied, Rinn returned to the campfire.

::

The next morning, Rinn woke eager to get underway. Her energy deflated when the dwarves told her that it would be another day before the craft was seaworthy, the tree sap they used in the repairs needed time to dry. Rinn fretted that she was going to have a boring day with nothing to do, but her father lined everyone up for sparring practice. This time, it felt different. With the addition of new people, mostly trained soldiers, practice looked more like authentic military drills. Everyone mustered in orderly lines and moved with precision. The teenagers struggled to keep up with the adult soldiers. But when it came time to pair off for sparing, the teenagers showed their mettle. They surprised Onager and the others with their competence.

Rinn ran through her usual drills with Tavin. It felt good being able to do something familiar. As she watched Tavin work through his routines, Rinn decided that she needed to sit the boy down for a talk. She wanted to discuss the gods, the Sigillum words, and a few other things. Before she had a chance, Niveus singled Rinn out. "I would spar with this one." The tall, dark woman sported a mock combat spear, its tip smeared with dark berry juice. Niveus applied the same substance to the end of Rinn's weapon. "This is custom in my homeland. First to receive three stripes loses."

When the two faced off, a crowd of spectators gathered. Rinn realized that this was just like the combat with Haril and her father. Niveus wanted to see the strength of her allies. She would attack fiercely, but with restraint. Rinn would have to do her best, showing both power and mercy. This would be an extremely challenging combat. Rinn and Niveus stomped their spear butts on the ground and the contest began. Cat bounced excitedly and chanted Rinn's name.

Niveus made the first move, a snake-like thrust to Rinn's right thigh. Rinn spun and deflected the blow, just barely. Niveus nodded in approval. Now, it was Rinn's turn. She delivered a feint to the head and swung at her opponent's midsection. Niveus countered both shots and returned with a chop down the middle. Rinn sidestepped and aimed at Niveus exposed abdomen, but it was too late. With a flick, the first stripe was drawn—a bright red streak across Rinn's left leg. The crowd oohed in surprise. Rinn backed up defensively. Clearly, winning this would be harder than she anticipated.

Rinn reversed her spear, pointing the blunt end at her opponent. Niveus raised an eyebrow momentarily, then attacked. Rinn blocked three aggressive strikes and then stepped and spun, catching Niveus with the painted tip of her spear in the center of her back. The crowd made more appreciative noises. Niveus wiped her back with her hand, when she saw the paint, her lip curled in admiration. She twirled the spear in her hands and laid into Rinn with fervor. Rinn could barely keep up, she had to dodge and roll to safety several times. In the flurry of attacks, both she and Niveus received another stripe.

The endgame was near. Rinn needed an opening, but Niveus was relentless. Her attacks came from every direction without rhythm. It took all of Rinn's concentration just to keep up. In the pit of her stomach, her magic began to well up. Rinn knew she was losing, and her instincts fought against that. The last thing Rinn wanted was to unleash her powers on this woman. She'd rather lose first. Inhaling deeply, Rinn made one last desperate attack, aiming straight for Niveus' neckline. To her surprise, her shot connected. But when she looked down, she saw Niveus' spear touching her own throat.

"Who hit who first?" Lutra questioned out loud. There was significant grumbling in the audience, no one could tell who won. Niveus lowered her spear and extended her hand to Rinn. Her heartbeat still fluttering like a bird, Rinn accepted her hand.

"I acknowledge you." Niveus shook firmly. "You are warrior."

"You should see her fight with magic." Sora called out.

Niveus raised an eyebrow. Rinn leaned on her spear, trying to catch her breath. "Another time, maybe." She huffed.

Niveus laughed. "You have proved yourself a woman, you drink with us tonight."

Rinn vehemently declined, but Niveus draped an arm over her shoulders and insisted. The other's laughed as Rinn was dragged away.

::

"Help me." Rinn begged Tavin. "That woman is crazy." Night had fallen and the party gathered around the evening bonfire. The orange light danced on the gleaming hull of their newly repaired ship. They dined on roasted fish, slimy green bottom-feeders that Sora managed to collect. Uncooked they looked hideous with ugly grey whiskers, but after a short time on the fire, they began to smell wonderful. Everyone ate voraciously, except Cat, who satisfied herself with field mice. After dinner, the usual bottle of spirits broke out, and now Rinn knew who was to blame: Niveus. She chased Rinn around with the bottle, declaring that she would be victorious.

"It's just alcohol." Tavin seemed unconcerned. "It won't hurt you."

Rinn was aghast. "Would you let Cat drink?"

"No." Tavin winced. "That would be a terrible idea."

"It would be even worse with me." Rinn exclaimed. "Who knows what I would do."

Tavin sighed, a bit crestfallen. "That's a shame. I was looking forward to seeing you a bit tipsy." Rinn slugged him in the shoulder, probably harder than she should have.

"Now is not the time." Rinn added.

"There will be a time?" Tavin raised a hopeful eyebrow. Rinn slugged him again.

Chapter 35

T he barge was floated into the water the next morning. It took everyone's strength to heave it off the shore, but it was a river boat with a flat bottom and no keel, so it was manageable. The craft had not been in the water for more than ten minutes before a passing merchant captain offered to purchase it. Marshal declined, even at the buyer's insistence. Traffic on the river had been scarce, an occasional grain barge or cattle boat. Rinn had not seen any military patrols or signs of immigration in either direction. The lands west of Gadiom seemed oddly desolate.

Rinn's army squeezed onto the river boat, weighing it down in the water. The craft was clean and dry, but it still had a lingering odor of sulfur. Once everyone had situated themselves on the bench seats, Molo and Haril pushed off from the shore with two long trunks cut from thin birch trees. River boats did not employ sails or rudders, they were steered by poles pushing off the bottom of the channel. Almost immediately, Rinn knew they were in trouble. Even though the river appeared lazy and slow-moving on the surface, strong undercurrents grabbed ahold of the boat and began to pull it downstream toward Gadiom. Molo and Haril poled furiously, trying to fight the river, but the boat just spun in circles. Finally, Dempsi plopped down on the bow of the ship and had a talk with the river. Like magic, the boat righted itself and began to glide gracefully upstream.

Marshal leaned over to Rinn. He motioned to Dempsi with his eyes. "Is she going to be okay?" Dempsi wandered from the bow to the stern to watch the water eddy as they passed.

"I don't think she's the one moving the boat." Rinn admitted. She could see no blue aura around the craft. This unnatural movement was somehow natural. "I think the river is doing this all on its own." The passengers all seemed to have a newfound respect for the little girl, but they also gave her a wide berth. Catherine seemed genuinely amused, which is quite a feat considering how she felt about boats in general.

Rinn watched the landscape slide by, the boat was moving the same speed as the river current, just in reverse. Their progress was not swift, but it was steady, and no one had to steer or navigate, the boat wound effortlessly through riverbends as if it was water itself. Tavin came and sat next to Rinn.

"Can you see anything?" He asked.

"No." Rinn stared out at the rolling hills and grasslands. "It's weird. There are no houses, no roads, no people. There's nothing here."

"That's because no one lives here." Tavin responded.

"Why not?" Rinn asked, finally looking him in the face. His gray eyes seemed distant, melancholy.

"No one will ever live here." Tavin lifted his hand to the horizon. "This is where it happened, on those hills, the Battle of Gadiom."

Rinn scanned the countryside in disbelief. Innocent hills covered in brown, late-summer grassland was all she could see. No bodies. No monuments or grave markers. Nothing to tell the story of how 40,000 men and women died on this very spot. Rinn let her gaze fall on Molo, the giant sat at the back of the vessel holding his head in his hands. Even Clive seemed distraught, listing from side to side on the floorboards. A hush had fallen over the entire craft, as if everyone but Rinn knew where they were. Somber faces looked like mourners at a funeral. Rinn remembered her grandmother Virago had died here, too. Rinn wondered if she left behind some hint of her magic, some clue as to how she was overcome. Rinn squinted her eyes and the blue aura of magic came alight, a corruption spreading across the hills for miles.

"Stop this boat!" Rinn jumped up, rocking the craft.

::

Rinn forged her way through the grasslands, into the heart of the battleground. Cat picked her way through the weedy hills, clearly aware that something was amiss. Her pupils were dilated, and her ears twitched this way and that. The countryside was eerily quiet, no birds flew overhead, and no insects chirped in the fields. Only Lutra and Marshal dared to venture into the battlefield-graveyard on Rinn's foolish errand.

"It's everywhere." Rinn proclaimed. "The ground is saturated with magic. I've never seen anything like this." But she had. In her dreams she had seen a city of glass bathed in magic: Hyalos, the capital of Faran Fada. Tenebra had told her to go there, to free her sister. This battleground and that city were obviously connected. Molo was not to blame for the deaths of thousands, this was the working of foul magic.

Rinn stopped at the crest of a hill and stretched out her arms in caution. "Everyone, stand back." They obeyed without question. Marshal limped heavily on his cane, Lutra helped him as best as he could. Rinn explained. "You are not going to like what I'm about to do, but you have to trust me."

Rinn turned her back to her companions and breathed out the word "acwin". The hilltop before her was immersed in blackness. Rinn knew her father disapproved, but this was important. Rinn called out to the darkness. "Yallakh, I need you." A few long minutes passed, and then the assassin emerged from the void, resplendent in his pitch-black suit. His brimmed hat was pulled low and a velvety mask shielded his face from the sun.

"Yes, my queen." He bowed before Rinn.

"Yallakh, this's elfcraft, isn't it?" She gestured to the entire battlefield.

Even behind his mask, Rinn could see the grin spread across his face. "You are most wise, my queen."

Rinn paced around the hill top. "What does it do?"

"It kills." Yallakh's voice was like a viper's.

"Is it poisonous?" Rinn asked.

"No. It is death." Yallakh placed a hand on the ground. "In its presence, any injury is lethal. The smallest scratch bleeds like a goring. Even the worms do not dare enter here. Take great caution, my queen, and leave this place as quickly as you can."

"Thank you, Yallakh." Rinn gave him a warm smile. "I'm sorry I had to call you here, but I needed to know the truth." The assassin's skeletal features seemed to soften. He bowed to Rinn and vanished into the darkness, as it faded from view. Rinn turned to Lutra and her father. "Find me a wineskin, I'm taking a sample of this dirt with me."

::

Rinn boarded the riverboat with her bag of tainted soil. Lutra told the tale of everything that transpired at the battlefield. Rinn found Molossus, who was still moping on the aft benches. She confronted him with her evidence.

"It wasn't your fault." She proclaimed loudly.

Clive looked up, but Molo did not.

"You aren't to blame for the deaths at Gadiom." Rinn protested. "I have proof. Both you and the Curia were betrayed by the Elves. They laid an elaborate trap and drew both of you into it." Molo lifted his head, eyes red and bleary. Rinn held out her bag of dirt. "The soil on these hills is tainted with Elf magic. Any small injury will lead to death. You were all duped."

Molo examined the bag in Rinn's hand, but he dared not touch it. The sting of remorse did not fade from his eyes. "It does not matter."

Frustration welled up inside Rinn. She shook her fist at him. "What do you mean 'it doesn't matter', you giant buffoon? You're not guilty, not for the death of Virago, not for the deaths of 40,000 men, not for any of it."

Molossus lamented in a soft voice, like a little boy. "But I am guilty. Guilty of something far worse." Rinn wondered, what could be worse than the deaths of 40,000 men? Molossus slumped back onto the aft bench, jostling the entire boat. Clive rolled to his foot, as if to comfort him.

::

Rinn sat alone with her bag of cursed dirt. No one dared sit near her. Catherine was curled up in a ball in the center of the boat fast asleep. Their vessel glided silently upriver without sails or poles, like a ghost ship. The battlefield of Gadiom was far behind her, but Rinn still felt haunted. The specters of the past would not let go. Rinn started this journey hoping to stop the Curia and end the civil war. Now she had a new enemy: the Elves. Sevria was embroiled in war with no end in sight, and the Curia were certainly making things worse, but Rinn now realized that if she killed them all off, nothing would change. This situation was so complicated, it was Hilltop all over again, but so much worse. When she unleashed her power and saved that village from attack, she alienated herself. The townsfolk had needed her help, but afterwards they did not want her back.

Rinn let the hours slip by, wallowing in misery. Tavin eventually joined her. He held out a page with writing on it. "We should work on these." Rinn glanced at the page, fifteen entries in a forgotten language.

"The words of warfare." She muttered.

"I wrote them down in order." Tavin pointed to the beginning of the list. 'Beorgan' was written at the top of the column. "I think you understand what some of these words do, and maybe together we can decipher the rest."

Rinn was torn. Did she really want to know the words to summon the powers of the gods? All the gods, good and evil. No one should be burdened with that kind of responsibility, especially not a scared teenage girl. She wanted to help people, to ease suffering. The happiest moments of her life had been when she freed the dwarves and reunited Felsic with his brother. These words would pull her deeper into a world of carnage and bloodshed. She trembled as she recalled the battlements of Hilltop soaked in the blood of clansmen she had killed.

"Are you okay?" Tavin asked. "Rinn?"

Rinn glanced at the strange words on the page. Even though she did not know the language, some of them seemed familiar: ahebbe, beogran, gifan, onlithe. They were old friends. These were her words, her chance to save her friends, her family, and all the suffering people in Sevria. "Okay. Where do we start?" Rinn steeled her nerves.

Tavin outlined his approach. "I can read some Cibean, and I think you understand what these words do. We'll start by eliminating the ones you already know, and then we'll try to decipher the rest together."

Rinn indicated which words she had used and which god they were associated with: beorgan, Parma the god of protection; ahebbe, Divum the goddess of skies; acwin, Tenebra the Darkness; onlithe, Reneo the Unraveller. Tavin shuddered at that last one. That left one word unclaimed: gifan. The unconscious thought Rinn released to summon her enchanted weapon. She did not know who to assign that power to.

Tavin revealed one more word's origin: scieppan. Back in Peleon, when Rinn was battling Serpio, Tavin saw the word written on the side of the Forge. He deduced that they were somehow connected. Scieppan summoned the power of Caminus: smithing. That left five members of the Sevrian pantheon unclaimed. Rinn listed them in her head, Sidus the Star, Lucus the Wood, Imber the Rain, Iugo the Mountain, and Inrigo the Ocean.

"I think we should start with Lucus." Rinn decided. "His word should be fairly straightforward."

"You spoke with him." Tavin recalled. "Did he give you any clues?"

"Yes." Rinn replied proudly. "He told me, 'The one thing nature does best is grow.'" Tavin studied the list straining in concentration.

"Here." He selected a word. "Weaxan, I think it means grow. Like, 'aweaxe!', which means 'grow-up'. My mentor used to yell that at us scribes all the time."

Rinn found comfort in the word, a connection to Lucus, the god of gentleness and growth. She did not dare utter the word, not while she was on a ship. But at the first opportunity, she was going to find a plant and test her new discovery.

Chapter 36

R inn's friends gathered around her on the grassy knoll. "Don't stand too close." She advised. "I'm not sure what will happen." Collectively, they retreated a few steps. Rinn selected a delicate blue flower for her experiment. The plant was small, not ostentatious: plain, flat leaves and tiny blossoms the color of the sky. Her father called the plant 'mouse-ears'. Rinn concentrated, summoning the warm, tranquil image of Lucus. She whispered the word 'weaxan' to the plant. It responded to her voice, longing for direction: up or down. Of course, Rinn understood, plants grew both directions. Rinn said. "Up."

Immediately, the plant erupted skyward. The ground rumbled as the tiny plant expanded and climbed until it was the size of a tree. It grew until its green stem could not bear any more weight. The towering flower teetered in place, Rinn's friends scattered as it swayed overhead. "Down!" Rinn commanded, and the plant's roots dug deep into the ground, spreading out to provide support and nourishment. The simple flower was now immense, its dainty petals larger than palm branches.

"Well." Tavin admitted. "I'd say that was a success."

Rinn staggered away from the gargantuan flower, feeling drained. Feena came and offered her a steadying arm. "Rinn, that was amazing."

"This is Lucus' gift." She explained. "It makes things grow."

"Can it make anything grow?" Sionne asked peevishly. "Cause I'm hungry." Lutra was not the only one who bopped him on the head.

Rinn shrugged. "Well, if you find a berry bush or something, let me know." The experiment was over, and everyone piled back into the boat. Dempsi coaxed the river to continue to carry them upstream. Curiosity overwhelmed Rinn, she had to know. "Dempsi, how are you making this boat move?"

Dempsi smiled with dimples. "Rivers are proud of their sources, how clean and pure they are. I simply asked this river to show us."

The craft steadily progressed westward, and the river grew narrower and shallower. Soon they would have to abandon their boat altogether. Along the way they had passed a few tiny villages, nothing more than a few farmhouses huddled around a fishing pier. Rinn gazed out at the countryside, and her father came and sat beside her.

"We'll be coming upon Macellum soon." He said. "That's the last navigable stop on the river."

"What'll we do then?" Rinn asked.

"We sell the boat and see if we can find passage to Messis." He replied. "It's about a week's journey, across the Great Western Plains."

"What's Macellum like?" Rinn pondered.

"It's a market town." He answered. "A place where farmers sell their grain to shippers who transport it to Gadiom."

Rinn stared out at the horizon, puzzled. "We haven't seen any signs of fighting. Where is this war I keep hearing about?"

"Well, we haven't seen many people either." Her father remarked. "Normally, this river is teaming with barges. During the harvest season locals joke that you can walk from Gadiom to Macellum on nothing but boats."

"It's sad." Rinn saw herself reflected in the muddy water. "Where has everyone gone?"

::

The waterfront of Macellum looked artificial, neat timber and plaster buildings arranged in tidy rows, like children's toys. Picturesque docks jutted into the river, complete with stacked barrels and coiled ropes. A waterwheel rolled lazily in the river current. However, the town was devoid of people, and its central fountain flowed green. The streets were weed-strewn, and ivy crept up the sides of the buildings, threatening to overtake them. The town's crane hung idle and limp over the docks. Window shutters clacked ominously in the afternoon breeze.

Dempsi crawled onto Marshal's lap and clung onto him for security. Molo and Haril poled the boat to the docks. The river wanted to continue carrying it upstream, the ship bucked like a reluctant colt. Molo finally managed to moor the vessel, and its erratic behavior abated. Wary passengers disembarked and wandered into the desolate town with weapons drawn. Feena clung onto Lutra, Tavin trailed behind Rinn. Cat sniffed at the air. Molo led the party with Clive in his hand, Haril and Onager flanking him on the right and left. They entered the town square and found themselves confronted by a row of rag-tag warriors with crude polearms. Their uniforms were rotten, and their weapons weathered. They looked to Rinn like a battalion of toy soldiers that had been left outside and forgotten about. Onager and Haril threatened the men with their swords. Rinn readied her spear and could feel her magic welling up inside her, but her father limped forward, holding his hands outstretched.

"No misfortune." He stated. The soldiers murmured to each other. Marshal repeated the phrase louder. "No misfortune."

"No deceit." One of the soldiers finally answered. Rinn recognized the red hair, the short stocky stature, the questionable hygiene. Squatters.

"You are not kin." One of the squatters challenged, a square man in his thirties.

"We have traded with Cuan Otraich." Marshal professed.

Another round of murmuring. "How do we know you speak the truth?"

Sionne blurted out. "His daughter is hot."

The square man guffawed. "Truly, you do know Cuan." The soldiers lowered their weapons. Curious faces of women and children, all with familiar red hair, poked out from windows and doorways. Marshal turned to Sionne, who winked at him. He went over to talk with the head-man for the squatters. Rinn pulled Sionne aside.

"How'd you know Milse was Cuan's daughter?" Rinn asked under her breath.

Sionne gave her a puzzled look. "You couldn't tell?" He shrugged and joined Marshal's negotiations with the squatters. Apparently, less than a year ago, Imperial soldiers stormed the town and depopulated it. The squatters moved into the abandoned buildings several months ago, drawn by the unharvested wheat fields. Western Sevria served as the breadbasket for the Empire, endless swaths of grain and beans. Small Imperial detachments have tried to retake the village, but the squatters drove them away. Now they live every day expecting a large Imperial force to arrive.

During the negotiations, Niveus questioned Rinn. "Who are these people and why does one travel with you?"

"These are the natives of Edera, before the Sevrians arrived." Rinn explained. "We encountered Sionne in the Rustic Lands. He seems to understand these people's ways."

Niveus nodded in comprehension. "Your father also seems to know much about them."

Rinn contemplated. "He's traveled a lot in his life. I suspect he stayed with a squatter community at one time or another."

Negotiations took more than an hour. By the time they were complete, the squatter families had largely come out from their hiding places. A pack of boisterous children chased Cat around the town square, and Dempsi played in the fountain cleansing away the moss and grime. Marshal returned to appraise everyone of the situation. Messis and the surrounding territories were held by revolutionaries, seeking to separate from the Sevrian Empire. In exchange for the riverboat, the squatters agreed to provide food and transport to the nearest revolutionary outpost.

Once the deal was agreed upon, a feast was held in the town square. Long tables were hauled out of the houses, and cheery fires lit. Women prepared the meal while men played music and passed around drink. Lutra brought out his flute and exchanged several melodies with the town's musicians. Someone passed a canteen to Rinn, a short redheaded teen with buckteeth and a scrawny beard. Rinn took a sniff of the spirits, it reeked like one of her father's military concoctions. She politely declined much to Tavin's dismay. The scribe sampled the liquor, and immediately regretted it. Squatter men guffawed heartily as he coughed and tried to catch his breath. Rinn rubbed his back to make sure he was okay. Some foolish redhead offered alcohol to Catherine who responded with her disappearing act. Rinn and her friends laughed while the squatter men looked around, perplexed.

The celebration lasted until late in the night. Rinn and her party were led to a row of empty houses on the town's east side. All the furniture and the decorations had been left behind. Rinn curled up on a soft goose-feather mattress and Catherine snuggled in bed with her. The room was musty, and the sheets smelled stale, but this was the best night of sleep Rinn had had in weeks.

::

Rinn woke early the next morning to freshen up before her long journey. As she walked to the town's main fountain, she spied Sora exiting the house that Felsic and Mafic shared. Rinn stayed out of sight, Sora's own private life was her business. Rinn returned to her cottage with a pitcher of extremely fresh water—Dempsi really knew how to clean a fountain. She found Cat sifting through their belongings.

"Do we need armor today?" She asked as Rinn entered.

"I don't think so." Rinn replied. "But you might keep it handy." She amended.

Rinn washed up and Cat completed her morning bathing routine. The bald patches in Cat's coat were fading as new growths of cinnamon colored fur returned. The girls dressed in their travel outfits. Rinn pulled her hair back with a green ribbon and Cat tied a small bow around her tail. They met their friends outside. Feena, Lutra, and Tavin all looked refreshed. The squatters, along with Calder, were already loading the wagons. The only one who looked bleary-eyed was Sionne. Apparently, he had been drinking well into the night.

"Ready to go?" Marshal asked Rinn and Cat.

Rinn held up her neatly packed satchel. "All ready." Cat did the same.

"We'll be heading out soon." He assured them. The squatters had prepared three farm wagons for travel pulled by a trio of shaggy mules. The teenagers largely loaded into the back of one wagon. The adults, along with Calder, filled the second. Molo and the dwarves rode in the third. Sora accompanied them. The road to Messis was a weedy trail cutting through the wheat fields. While they traveled, the teens joked boisterously. Tavin sat next to Rinn and unfurled his list of words.

"We should pick another word to work on today." He suggested. Rinn agreed, reluctantly. The novelty of new powers had been replaced with apprehension. She knew seven of the fifteen commands, but the remaining eight were a mystery. Half of them summoned powers of the Sevrian gods, the other half, unknown dark abilities.

"We know there are four Sevrian gods left: Imber, Inrigo, Sidus, and Iugo." Rinn twirled her hair nervously. "Any clues that might connect with them?"

Tavin studied the list. He pointed out a word near the middle. "I think this one means truth. 'Soth.' I remember reading about the 'soth-cyning', the true kings of Sevria. I'm not sure which god it corresponds to, but it seems like a safe choice."

"Doesn't sound too dangerous." Rinn conceded. Truth would not likely invoke the powers of the malicious gods, if they were malicious at all. Rinn decided to risk it. She closed her eyes and took a cleansing breath. She spoke the word "soth". She opened her eyes to a violent eruption of color. Everything looked wrong: the skies were every shade a sky could be, the wagons were brilliant green, and the fields of wheat blue. Even more disturbing was how people appeared. Looking at Lutra, Rinn could see his father and mother's faces reflected in his own, she could even see his little brother, now four years older. She could see Feena's parents, she could see Sionne's gaggle of siblings, eleven in all. The experience was jarring, Rinn had to look away.

Then she saw it—the monstrous beast riding in the first wagon. The creature was larger than the wagon itself, with hideous gnashing teeth, spiny back, and hunched-over neck. Its head seemed too small for its body and its shoulders too broad. The monster acted enraged, sick, snarling and snapping. No one else seemed to notice or care. Then Rinn saw a man standing beside the beast, holding it by the hand. He was an average-sized human with a neatly trimmed beard and soft features. He looked right at Rinn with eyes of deepest purple.

"Stop it!" Rinn slapped her own face. "Make it go away. Quit it. Stop."

Tavin shook Rinn, calling her name in dismay. The wagon train came to a halt. Rinn's fit lasted several minutes. Lutra helped Tavin lower her out of the wagon. When Rinn recovered herself, she was laying between Catherine and her father. Her sister cradled her head in her lap.

"Shh." Catherine whispered. "It's okay. Everything's okay."

"I saw a hideous monster." Rinn breathed rapidly. "What was that thing?"

"He won't hurt you. It was just a vision." Catherine brushed the hair from Rinn's face. "You're safe now."

"What did she see?" Marshal asked.

Catherine answered. "Molo's true form."

Chapter 37

T he wagon train to Messis stopped in the late afternoon to rest and water their mules. Progress was slow, but there had been no more incidents since Rinn's outburst. She huddled in the back of the wagon, knees pulled to her chest, refusing to look at anyone or anything. The effects of the magic wore off long ago, but Rinn could not get the image of the grotesque beast out of her head. Nauseating memories of Molo's cave returned to her: a hideous chamber of bones—bone tables, bone chairs, bone chandeliers, and a bed made of bone. She had not believed Molo was capable of that, but after seeing the monster inside him, she knew the truth.

"Come." Tavin tugged at her hand. "Get some food." Rinn brushed him away. He left, dejected. Rinn hated making him feel that way, but she could not bear to see any one right now. Furry paws slid across her shoulders.

"Let's go." Catherine coaxed Rinn out of the wagon. She led her into a field, away from the others. Rinn resisted every step. "Wait here." Catherine commanded. Rinn did so, unsure of what was about to happen. Her sister returned with their father.

"What's this all about?" Marshal questioned.

"She has to see the truth." Cat set him in front of Rinn. "Now, take a look at your father." She ordered.

"No." Rinn clamped her eyes shut like a stubborn child.

"Do it." Cat challenged. "It's the only way. Look at him for real."

"I'll never use that power again." Rinn refused.

"Rinn, you need me like I need you." Cat swished her tail in agitation. "And you need these powers, all of them. There's something you need to see, a longing that's been haunting you all your life. Now, open your eyes and look."

"I'm afraid." Rinn cried.

"I'm know." Cat hugged her. "But it's the only way you can see her."

Rinn's eyes opened. Her? She examined her father, quietly standing before her, not sure what to do. She saw his olive skin, his pointed nose, the wispy hairs on his chin. He had a scar through his left eyebrow and lower lip, and he leaned his weight on his left side. But he was her father, every inch of him. She knew him and loved him. He was a soldier, he had killed, just like Rinn had, and that knowledge did nothing to detract from her love of him. The truth about him could not hurt her.

"Do it." Cat insisted.

Rinn let the word "soth" escape from her mouth and her world turned upside down. She saw her loving father, carrying her in his arms, but she also saw the savage warrior battling the nightmare jungles of Migalia. The terrors on that island made the beasts of the Rustic Lands seem tame. Then, deep inside him, Rinn saw her. At first Rinn thought she was looking at herself, a little girl dancing around a garden, but she never owned a dress like that. The girl grew into an indomitable teenager, and then a young woman in wildling furs and leather. She charged headlong at a giant hairy lizard five times her own size. She cried out a word of power, and the beast shrank back, crashing through the trees in a panic. The young woman brushed blond hair away from her face and turned back to Marshal as if to say: hah, who's the helpless one now?

Tears welled up in Rinn's eyes. She could see her mother, fierce, headstrong, and beautiful. She fought to save her father's life as many times as he saved hers. Their love was one of equals, a perfect balance without heed of age or rank. When she was taken from him, it tore his soul in half. He had not been there when she died, but the chasm of sorrow remained. The only thing that kept him from teetering into that abyss was Rinn herself. She finally understood the truth.

"Mom." Rinn sobbed. She turned to Catherine. She could faintly see a loving Margot woman with soft, brown fur, but she was very small and far away. When Rinn looked at her sister, she saw herself. She was not daring, she was not brave, she did not have unshakable resolve. Cat had given her all these things. In return, Rinn had filled her sister with gentleness and compassion. And love. Apart, she and Cat were inferior versions of themselves. Only together could they do what needed to be done.

"Now you understand." Cat said. Rinn reached forward and hugged her sister, warm tears spilling down her cheeks.

"You knew all along?" Rinn sobbed.

"Of course." Cat sniffed. "Why do you think I chose you?"

Marshal found himself caught between two teenage girls who sandwiched him in an embrace. "What's going on here?" He asked, flustered.

Rinn looked up with soggy eyes. "I saw her. I saw Mom."

Now, it was Marshal's turn to fight back emotions. "How? Is she?"

Rinn shook her head no. She squeezed her father tighter, as if she was physically keeping him from plunging over into the abyss. "I love you, Daddy." Together they cried until the tears were no more.

::

The revolutionary guard came around midnight. The squatters made no effort to hide their campfire, it could be seen for miles over the level farmland. Twenty men in grey uniforms and Legion issue swords walked out of the night. They made no pretense of authority, they filed into two neat lines and their commanding officer stepped forward. Rinn spotted a minotaur in their midst.

"What are you doing here?" The commander demanded. "This area is under control of the Revolutionary Guard."

Marshal parlayed with the commander. "We mean no harm. We are on a pilgrimage to the Shrine of Imber."

"Are you asylum seekers?" The commander regarded the dwarves in the party.

"No." Marshal replied. "Just simple travelers."

The commander seemed unconvinced. "And where are you traveling from?"

Before the conversation could digress, Molo rose and hailed the revolutionaries. "Take me to see General Molossus." The troops noticed the giant for the first time, and they began to waver, shifting in place, exchanging nervous glances. Even the minotaur was wary of Molo and his oversized hammer.

"What business do you have with the General?" The commander alone did not falter in the presence of the giant man.

"It's personal." Molo replied slowly, coming toe-to-toe with the commander. The smaller man backed away and ordered his troops to get the caravan moving. The campfire was efficiently extinguished, and everyone loaded into the wagons. Much to their dismay, the mules where harnessed and forced to march late into the night. The revolutionary guard flanked the wagons, ten on each side with the minotaur in the lead. Rinn and her friends slept fitfully as they traveled. By morning they arrived at an orderly military camp. Rows of tents spread out across former bean fields with sentry towers stationed at the four corners. Rinn and her companions were transferred to another set of wagons pulled by fresh horses. The squatters were sent on their way, Marshal thanked them for their service.

"Where're we going?" Rinn asked her father as she climbed into the revolutionary wagon. Everything felt out of control, Rinn wanted to draw her spear and make a run for it. Oddly, the guards had allowed Rinn and her companions to keep their weapons. Either they did not consider them much of a threat, or they did not want to offend the giant.

"We're headed north." Her father confided. "Probably to their main camp."

"What will happen to us?" Rinn questioned. Against a force of twenty men, Rinn did not feel particularly threatened, but the thought of battling hundreds or thousands of soldiers was more intimidating.

"I'm not sure." Marshal admitted. "I have a feeling our giant knows who this General Molossus really is. I just hope he's friendly."

The caravan meandered down rambling dirt trails through endless wheat fields. With the sun high in the sky, it was easy to lose all sense of direction. Rinn assumed that was the point. Their caravan turned left and right, seeming to double back, and then forward again. Finally, Lutra spotted a city of white tents in the distance. Feena and Grus chattered anxiously. Sionne complained. Onager and the other soldiers appeared resigned, as if they were already prisoners of war. Rinn would have to trust Uncle Molo to see this through.

The wagons stopped at a barren field outside the military encampment. The trampled dirt suggested that this was a practice yard. Between the field and the tent city, two cohorts of soldiers, more than 500 men, lined up in expectation. They were dressed in clean grey uniforms and carried military issue swords and shields. Their numbers included humans, dwarves, and a handful of minotaur.

Mounted archers flanked the army providing extra protection and flexibility. Four senior officers stood at attention before the assembly. Standing with them was a colossal warrior in heavy plate armor. He wore a full-face helmet shaped like a gnarling hound. Slung across his back was a beam of steel pounded into the shape of a sword.

The escort ordered Rinn and her companions out of the wagons. Soldiers relieved them of their weapons, all except Molo. He was singled out and directed to the center of the field. The armored giant strode forward, Rinn assumed he must be General Molossus. He was nearly as tall as Molo, only inches separated them, but his build was different, stockier in the legs and narrower in the shoulders. The two giants faced off, saying nothing. The escort fell back, as if they were waiting for something.

Without warning, General Molossus drew his sword and attacked. "Murderer!" He cried. Molo barely had a chance to deflect the blow with his own hammer, but he did. General Molossus circled and launched two more savage strikes. His sword was the size of a wagon's axel and he used it with speed and precision. Molo countered both blows and staggered backwards. The General actually meant to kill Molo. Rinn dashed toward the combatants, and a pair of soldiers intercepted her. Kneeling in the dirt, Molo held out his hand for Rinn to stop.

"This is my fight." He cautioned. The General gave him no quarter, raining down blows with his mammoth sword. Molo deftly blocked them, moving quicker than a man his size should be able. The two giants traded blows, with ear-splitting impact. The ground rumbled as the titans clashed, hammer versus sword. They tore great ruts in the soil and split the air as their weapons collided. The General gripped his sword in both hands and brought the pommel down in a brutal strike. Molo blocked, but the blow shattered the handle of his hammer. The General flung the unbalanced hammer head from Molo's off hand.

Rinn would not stand by and watch her friend die. There was not enough growth to summon Lucus' magic, nor did she want to risk Tenebra's darkness—it might imperil Molo as much as it helped him. Rinn saw movement out of the corner of her eye, Cat standing behind the General, ready to strike. Before she could, Molo swung Clive around and delivered a powerful blow to the General's head, sending his gleaming helmet flying. Beneath it was a giant woman with cropped brown hair. She sank to one knee, clutching her head. A trickle of blood ran down her cheek. Molo stood over her, Clive held high.

The giantess snarled sarcastically. "Hello, father."

Molo lowered Clive, heaving a sigh. "Hello, Lea."

The General ordered her troops. "Take this traitor away and put him in chains." Soldiers surrounded Rinn and her friends, weapons drawn. This charade had gone on long enough. Rinn jerked away from the guards restraining her and planted herself between Molo and the strange General. Cat joined her at her side. The General was unimpressed, she lifted her helmet from the ground.

"Out of the way, foolish girls." She aimed her sword at Rinn.

"I wouldn't do that." Molo cautioned.

"What's this about?" Rinn demanded, arms held wide in protest.

The General pointed to Molo with her blade. "That beast is wanted for murder. He will stand trial. And he will be executed."

"You will do no such thing." Rinn showed no signs of fear. She could hear ripples of laughter from the troops. Her friends were surrounded by soldiers, hopelessly outnumbered, and Rinn did not even have a weapon.

"Don't be an idiot, Lea." Molo protested. "You don't want to fight her."

The General scoffed. "The only idiot here is you. Did you think I'd let you leave here alive, after what you did?" Rinn could see the hatred in the giant woman's eyes. She did not know what had transpired between Molo and the General, but Rinn suspected there would be no reasoning with her. The only thing she would understand was force. So, without weapons or armor, Rinn rushed her.

Chapter 38

The General was momentarily stunned by Rinn's ferocity. She attempted to swat Rinn out of the way like a pesky fly. Good, Rinn thought, she's using the flat of her blade. She's not actually trying to kill me. Using her small size to her advantage, Rinn ducked under the woman's blade and planted a hand on her metal breastplate. She yelled "scieppan", and the General's armor became liquid in her hand. Rinn pulled away, shaping the metal into a perfectly-formed spear. She settled into a fighting stance, weapon in hand and her opponent stripped of her chest piece.

The General was not amused, feeling her exposed torso. "You will pay for that." She lunged forward and swung a mighty blow at Rinn's midsection. Rinn lit her spear with green fire and sliced through the General's sword. Broken chunks of metal clanged to the ground. The giant woman stepped back, vexed by Rinn's fighting prowess. She threw down the remains of her ruined sword. "Spear. Bring me a spear." She demanded. An auxiliary brought forth a spear the size of a horseman's lance. The weapon was three times the length of Rinn's pilum—getting into striking range was going to be a problem.

"We don't have to fight." Rinn tried to appeal to the General's sense of reason. The General answered with a war cry. She lashed out at Rinn, forcing her to summon her shield. The General's massive spear deflected harmlessly off Rinn's green, glowing barrier. Rinn could sense the freshness of the wood in her opponent's weapon, it must have been harvested recently. With a crazy plan in mind, Rinn advanced. She thrust low several times, causing the General to block. Rinn trapped the giant spear to the ground with her foot and yelled "weaxan". The wooden shaft sprouted roots and was planted firmly in place. The General tugged uselessly at her weapon turned plant, giving Rinn just enough time to close. Rinn threw down her own spear and grabbed the giant woman by the legs. "Ahebbe" she shouted, and she lifted the alarmed giant off the ground. She kicked and screamed as Rinn held her high.

"Now, shut up and listen." Rinn ordered. She could hear Cat laughing in the background. "No one is going to be killed. You will stand down and let my friends go." The giant woman stopped struggling. Rinn let her drift down to the ground and backed away, retrieving her spear.

The General gaped at Rinn in disbelief. "Who are you?"

"I'm Rinn. And I'll not let you harm any of my friends." She swore.

Molo laid a conciliatory hand on his daughter's shoulder. "I told you not to fight her. You had no chance of victory."

Lea brushed off her father's hand. "What is she?"

"She's a Sigillum." Molo answered. All eyes turned to Rinn, a resolute blond teenager with a flaming spear. The senior officers seemed particularly interested.

The General flexed her fists. "By the gods, father, what have you done?"

::

Rinn and her companions were given quarter in a secure corner of the encampment. They were free to move about, but soldiers followed them everywhere and reported on their actions. Their weapons and supplies were reluctantly returned, and a meager meal of porridge with salted pork was provided. Lutra and Grus explored the tent city, eager to see the workings of a large military machine. Haril and Onager and the other guards had served enough time in the Legion and knew what to expect, they spent their time caring for Dempsi. Mafic and Felsic busied themselves repairing armor and weapons. Dora joined them, even though she did not know how to stitch leather or pound metal. Cat pestered her escort by repeatedly vanishing and reappearing nearby. And Sionne entertained soldiers with games of chance, which he typically won.

Night came to the camp, bringing with it near-complete darkness. Evening campfires were strictly forbidden. Rinn sat outside her assigned tent with her father and Molo. They had scarcely spoken since the events of that afternoon.

"Is that really your daughter?" Rinn opened the conversation.

"Yes." Molo admitted, staring up at the stars.

"Why does she want to kill you?" There was no good way to ask the question.

Molo replied with a grunt, and nothing more.

"He'll tell us when he's ready." Marshal assured Rinn. The three sat quietly in the dark until a messenger came to collect them.

"The General wants to see you." He reported. Rinn, Marshal, and Molo followed grudgingly along. The General's tent was an elaborate pavilion draped in heavy cloth to dampen illumination. Inside, Officers pored over a table with rough maps of their surroundings. Rinn could see that this camp was stationed just southeast of Messis.

Lea did not bother with introductions. "You lot must've caused quite a commotion. An Imperial Legion is prowling the Plains of Messis. My guess is the Curia want to find you before you find us." The General finally raised her eyes to meet Molo's gaze. "They will be upon us by tomorrow."

The four senior officers in the room began discussing plans of engagement. They seemed like capable military officers, but Rinn did not like their recommendation: send in a suicide unit to allow the bulk of the army escape. Lea, herself, was also not satisfied. She turned to her father.

"Well." She said, venting her anger. "You're good at killing people. What do you think we should do?"

Molo's head turned bright red. He slammed his fist down on the table so hard it splintered into pieces, maps flew everywhere. The commanders drew their swords in offense. Molo bellowed at his daughter. "She was my wife, too!"

"Then why did you murder her?" Lea yelled back, just as red.

"You have no right." Molo paced like an enraged bull.

"I have every right. She was my mother!" Lea's hands balled into fists. Confused officers backed away from the belligerent pair. Marshal cast Rinn a plaintive look: please help. Before the giant's fight could escalate, Rinn intervened. She inhaled and breathed out "acwin". The tent interior was cast into absolute darkness. Lea's officers yelped, and Molo groaned in anger. Rinn could see Clive's purple eye in the dark. She could feel her sister standing beside her.

"Do you want me to get you out of here?" Cat whispered.

"No." Rinn answered. "I need to see this through. Something feels off about this whole situation."

"Trust your instincts." A new voice added from the darkness. Yallakh emerged from the shadows. Slowly light returned to the tent. Soldiers relit the interior lanterns.

"What's the meaning of this?" One of the officers snorted. He was shocked into silence when he saw the ominous figure in the room with them.

Molo barked. "What's he doing here?"

"Helping." Rinn sassed. "Unlike you two." Molo and Lea shot each other furtive glances. Rinn took control of the situation. "Now, we're going to sit down and talk this out like adults. You can't be at each other's throats, not if there is an Imperial Legion on the way." Lea and her officers moved to one side of the tent, sheathing their swords. Molo, Marshal and Cat remained on the other. Yallakh hovered alone near the shadows.

Rinn played arbitrator. "We will start with introductions. I am Rinn Amali. This is my father Marshal and my sister Catherine. Yallakh is an associate working with me. You apparently know Molo already." Rinn paused to let the other side have a turn.

One by one, the senior officers introduced themselves: Iam, first centurion; Brachus, heavy infantry; Tectus, cavalry; and Pirum, the quartermaster. Lea attempted to wrestle control of the conversation from Rinn. "You're a capable warrior. Fight with us against the Curia. Together we could crush them."

"I'm not here to fight." Rinn countered.

"Then why are you here, Sigillum?" Lea challenged. Rinn was taken aback by the giant woman's intensity and mannerisms. Everything was a fight to her, she had no concept of backing down.

"Killing the Curia would change nothing." Rinn asserted. "Sevria would be no safer from the forces that are trying to destroy it."

"The Curia must be eliminated." Lea slammed her fist into her palm for emphasis. "Once they are defeated, the Empire will be liberated."

Rinn shook her head. "It is not that easy. We already killed one of their number, and it has not shaken their resolve."

Iam's jaw dropped. "You killed one of the Curia?"

Rinn squeezed her sister's paw. "Yes, we did. It was the right thing to do at the time, but I don't think the Curia all need to die. I fought with Serpio and he seemed like a reasonable man, once some sense could be knocked into him."

Lea raised a skeptical eyebrow. "You fought Serpio, the High Paladin?"

Cat's laughter filled the tent. "She knocked him on his behind. It was hilarious." She put a paw to her chin. "But that was after he knocked you on your behind."

Rinn squeezed her lips. "Cat, you weren't even there."

Lea's officers began to grumble and debate among themselves. Lea had to move to placate them. Marshal nudged his daughter's arm.

"Did you really fight Serpio?" He asked in hushed tones.

"Yes. Near Caminus' Forge." Rinn admitted. "He's a tough opponent, but I think he's a good person." Her father made no reply, but Rinn could see the awe in his eyes. Even Molo regarded Rinn with renewed respect.

"With the power of a Sigillum, we could easily overtake the Curia's forces." Iam argued. "We should attack at once."

"We have Molossus the Giant." Brachus proclaimed. "He can lead the troops to victory."

"I am Molossus." Lea insisted, losing control of her anger.

The four officers banded together. "We appreciate everything you've done for us, but your father's here now, the last living general of free Sevria. He was the first to raise a hand against the Curia. He's legendary."

Lea's jaw stiffened. Rinn thought she was going to strike her officers dead on the spot. Instead she turned on her heel and headed out of her own tent. Molo grabbed her by the arm before she could leave.

"Let go of me." She jerked away, tears in her eyes. "You stole my mother, my home, my life. And now you want my army, too. Fine. I'm done with all of you." She stormed out of the tent. Molo chased after her, leaving Rinn, Marshal, and Cat alone with the officers.

Yallakh cracked no smile. "As entertaining as this has been, this army is clearly doomed. You should depart while you can."

Rinn tried reasoning with the commanding officers. "We are doing exactly what our enemy wants. Nothing would be more satisfying to them than two Sevrian armies destroying each other." She added with a hint of sarcasm. "They would like that. Gadiom was their finest hour."

"Who?" Iam's curiosity was piqued. "Whose finest hour?"

"The Elves." Rinn replied with unshakable certainty. The officers wore incredulous scowls, clearly unconvinced. Marshal spoke up.

"I know it sounds incredible, and I had a difficult time believing it at first." He confessed. "But there's vile magic at work. We've witnessed it firsthand at Viburna and again at Peleon. The Curia are in over their heads, and they don't even know it."

Brachus straightened gruffly. "Can you show us proof of this magic?"

"The puppets want to see their strings." A hoarse voice jeered. Yallakh drummed his fingers together. "If you bring me the giant and his daughter, I can arrange proof."

The officers objected to Yallakh's tone, but they agreed to go along with his demonstration. Locating Molo and Lea was easy, their tirade could be heard halfway across the camp. Marshal and the officers managed to calm them long enough to return to the command tent. A new table had been brought in. Yallakh arranged for the pair to sit on opposite sides of it. He laid two of his black glass daggers between them.

"What's the meaning of this?" Molo huffed.

"A demonstration of the Elves' goodwill." Yallakh hissed amicably. Lea creased her brow dubiously. Yallakh motioned to the knives. "If you would each merely prick the end of your finger." Neither giant moved.

"Please, Molo." Rinn begged. With a sigh he picked up the dagger and pressed it to the tip of his finger, a single drop of blood welled there. Lea refused to use the assassin's blade, so she poked her finger with her own knife.

"Now, merely touch your fingers together." Yallakh instructed. Molo and Lea looked at their own fingers, a dot of blood on the ends of each. They reluctantly reached out to each other. Yallakh cautioned Rinn. "Be on your guard, my Queen. The result may be quite unpredictable." Unconcerned Molo and Lea touched fingers, their blood intermingling. Lea pouted so severely, Rinn thought she might stick her tongue out at her father.

"Is something supposed to happen?" Lea sneered.

"Give it a moment." Yallakh grinned. "The blood must mix." Sweat began to bead on Lea's forehead. Her breathing became rapid and deep. A guttural growl rose from her chest. She grabbed the table with her free hand, ripping a corner off. Her muscles tensed, veins bulging. Even her hair flexed, growing thicker, coarser, stiff as needles. Lea rose from her chair and let out a feral cry that shook the tent. Yallakh pried their fingers apart. Lea flew at Molo, but not before Rinn could trap her inside her barrier. Like a penned animal Lea beat and clawed at the restraining sphere. Her officers cowered in fear.

"What did you do to her?" Molo grabbed Yallakh by his black felt collar.

"She has tasted the poison in your veins." The assassin wheezed.

"In my veins?" Molo released Yallakh. He stared at his enraged daughter, a monster in a cage. She bit at him from behind Rinn's shield. Understanding finally came to Rinn. The monster she saw in her vision was not Molo but the poison inside him. The real Molo was the gentle man holding the monster's hand, restraining it.

Molo pointed a finger at Yallakh. "Turn her back."

"The effects will wear off momentarily." He replied dismissively, though his eyes watched Lea with keen interest. Rinn struggled to keep the raging giantess contained within her barrier. She knew she had no choice, if she faltered, Lea would maul her father and probably everyone inside the tent. Eventually, Lea's rage did subside. Her body seemed to relax, her breathing quieted, and her features returned to normal. She sat down on the floor of Rinn's barrier, head in her hands. Rinn released her magic cage.

"What did you do to me?" Lea moaned, rubbing her face.

"That was Ifreann." Yallakh paced the tent like a tutor among pupils. "A potent elvish elixir designed to heighten battle reflexes and speed. Too strong a dose would be lethal, of course, robbing its victim of their sanity."

"Poisoned." Molo breathed, more in relief than anger.

"I saw it, too." Rinn added. "The beast inside Molo. This is the work of the Elves."

"Why him?" Lea asked as her officers assisted her to a standing position.

"After their defeat at Messis, the Curia was weakened." Marshal deduced. "If General Molossus were to seize Peleon, the Curia's power would be lost. It was necessary for the Elves to intervene, to maintain control of Sevria."

For the first time in decades Lea and Molo looked at each other, not as adversaries, but as father and daughter. Lea took two hesitant steps and then threw herself into her father's arms, squeezing him tightly. "Daddy, I'm so sorry."

Molo's beard was wet with tears. "I know, little lion. I know."

Chapter 39

Rinn stayed awake most of the night, listening to stories from Molo and his daughter. The more she learned about Lea, the more she liked her. Lea had come to the war reluctantly. She was working in the mines of Saxitum when she was approached by revolutionary officers. Their movement was floundering, the people losing their will to fight. Everyone wanted to get back to their families and normal lives. The officers convinced Lea to return to Messis, disguised as General Molossus, to be a rallying point that could reinvigorate the populace. It worked. But the officers did not count on two things: Lea's fighting prowess and her sharp mind. Within a year, the army was firmly under her control. After a series of successful battles against the Curia's forces, the cities of Saxitum and Campis pledged their allegiance to her cause.

Lea in turn listened to Rinn as she recounted her adventures in the Rustic Lands. Rinn described her flight from Sevria, meeting Cat and Molo, and her clashes with Clanmorris. Her father embellished Rinn's tales with vivid accounts of her battles against magical beasts. Yallakh reclined on a pile of cushions in one corner, passively taking everything in. Eventually the story-swapping came to the uncomfortable subject of Lea's mother. Lea described the heart-rending experience of arriving home to find her mother butchered and her father missing. At first, she refused to believe her father was guilty, but the evidence against him was staggering. Lea was sent from relative to relative, but no one wanted the giant daughter of a known murderer. Eventually, she made her way to Saxitum and the mines. Her strength and size earned her a living, a chance to rebuild her life.

Even knowing Molo was not really to blame, Rinn still found it difficult listening to Lea's story. Molo had scant recollection of the events and the years that followed, he was aware it happened, but not much more. Rinn added the details of how she and her father found Molo living alone in the Rustic wilderness. She described Molo's hideous cave of bones, much to his chagrin. Rinn knew it was further evidence that Molo was not in his right mind.

"What I don't understand is how you survived the poison and regained your sanity." Rinn pondered. "Did it wear off over time?"

"The effects of Ifreann are permanent." Yallakh commented from his pile of pillows. He sipped a greasy black liquid from a flask.

"Then how did I recover?" Lea argued.

"You adapted to it, accommodated it." Yallakh explained. "The Ifreann is still there, inside you." He sank deeper into his pillow throne. "You will thank me the next time you are in combat." Lea stared at the tiny scab on her finger as if it were a tumor. Molo did the same.

"So, Uncle Molo adapted to the poison inside him?" Rinn deduced.

"Not exactly." Yallakh yawned. "The dose he received was meant to be lethal, even for a giant. He should not have survived, and if by some chance he did, his mind and will would be broken beyond repair."

"Clive." Rinn guessed.

"Very good." Yallakh nodded in approval. "I often wondered how such a brute was able to get his hands on a Soul Stone. Then it occurred to me, he trapped his own soul. Somehow, he buried his humanity inside that rock where the poison could not corrupt it. Quite ingenious, really."

Molo, Lea, and Rinn all stared at Clive, his purple eye seemed to be gazing back, acknowledging the truth. Yallakh rose and stretched. "Morning is coming, and I should be going. But I want to thank you for the conversation, it has been most enlightening." He bowed to Rinn and pulled his black cape about himself, vanishing into the shadows.

"Does everyone around you disappear?" Lea muttered.

Cat had been sleeping in the middle of the floor the entire time. She perked up her ears at the mention of disappearing, and with a pop she was gone. Marshal and Rinn snickered, Molo guffawed heartily. Lea looked around perplexed. Wiping the laughter from her eyes, Rinn excused herself, anxious to find some semblance of sleep before the day began.

::

Rinn felt small hands shaking her. "Rinn, Rinn. Wake up. It's going to rain." The sleeping Sigillum rolled over with a grumble, tangles of blond hair in her face. Dempsi yanked Rinn's blankets away, rousing protests from both her and Cat. "You have to come outside and see."

Bleary-eyed and mussy-haired, Rinn poked her head outside. The entire camp city was a whirlwind of activity. Teams of soldiers deconstructed rows of tents while others hastily stuffed supplies into waiting wagons. A central command center had been erected where senior officers supervised the dismantling of the encampment. Lea stood with them.

Dempsi tugged urgently at Rinn's sleeve. "Look at the clouds." A line of dark gray was gathering on the western horizon. The sunless morning sky was tinted a faint shade of green. A cool wind blew through the camp, tasting of moisture and smelling of loam. Rinn recognized the warning signs: a summerstorm was on the way.

"That does not look good." Rinn told Cat. Her feline sister stuck her head out the tent flaps, flattened her ears, and retreated back inside. Rinn pulled a homespun dress on and marched to the command center. The four senior officers were drawing battle lines on a map. When Rinn realized what they were doing, she admonished them. "You can't go to war now, a summerstorm is coming."

Lea took Rinn aside. "Curia scouts discovered our camp last night. Their main force is on the way as we speak. Evacuation is our first priority, but a small force will have to stay behind to delay the enemy's advance."

Rinn appreciated the severity of the situation, but something about the summerstorm vexed her. The timing was too convenient—two armies colliding exactly as a violent tempest ripped through the land. Here on the open plains the casualties could be catastrophic. The only ones who would profit from this would be the Elves. Rinn needed to find some way to avert the battle. She left Lea and the commanders and raced through the camp, searching for Molo and her father. She found them loading supply wagons with the other soldiers.

Rinn shouted over the wind which was whipping up in gusts. "Dad. Uncle Molo. We need everyone to stop what they're doing. A summerstorm is coming."

Her father called back. "Now's not the time. The Curia's Legions are on their way."

"I know." Frustration boiled inside Rinn. "Stop for a minute and think about it. The Curia find our location exactly when a summerstorm's about to strike. This is not a coincidence, it's a trap! This is elven treachery." Marshal and Molo exchanged glances, the weight of Rinn's words clearly sinking in.

"We need to get everyone to shelter." Marshal dropped what he was carrying.

"There is no shelter out here." Molo argued. "Just miles of flat farmland."

"Trenches." Marshal proposed. "To protect us from the winds. It's the only way to ride out a summerstorm. Also, we have to get far away from camp, flying shrapnel could kill us."

"I'll leave you to it." Rinn was relieved they believed her. She knew she sounded anxious and paranoid, but she did not want a repeat of Gadiom.

"What about the Curia's Legions?" Molo asked, shouting over the wind.

"I'll delay of them." Rinn promised. She scanned the chaotic encampment. "I need to get back to Dempsi and the others."

Marshal strapped on his sword belt. "I'm coming with you."

"No." Rinn insisted. "Stay here, see that the troops evacuate. Leave the rest to Dempsi and me."

"You can't take a little girl into a warzone." Marshal cautioned.

"She's not a little girl. She's a rain bringer." Rinn assured him. Her father did not seem any less worried, but he let her go. By the time Rinn returned to her friends, hail had started to fall, small stinging pellets bouncing off the tents. Dismantling the tent city had ceased, and soldiers started to abandon their positions—the severity of the storm was undeniable. Rinn found her friends huddled together under an awning. Niveus was playing mother to them. Lutra and Feena seemed particularly distressed.

"What is this mad weather?" Feena fretted.

"It's a summerstorm, a bad one." Rinn did not have time for lengthy explanations. "You all have to evacuate, now.

Dad is leading people away from camp." Rinn looked around. "Where's Dempsi?"

No one immediately answered. Sionne finally confessed. "She went outside to see the rain."

Rinn cried in exasperation. "You let her go outside alone in a summerstorm? What were you thinking?"

"I'm not her parent." Sionne quarreled. "Besides, she likes rain."

Rinn cursed as she rushed outside into the storm. The winds had kicked up fiercely, toppling tents and scattering supplies. Stinging hail intensified into clumps of ice the size of her fist. Rinn actually summoned her shield to fend off the painful icefall. She raced through the camp, her green barrier the only source of light in the twilight of the storm. Rinn cried out Dempsi's name, but nothing could be heard over the deafening wind. She ran straight for the cloudburst about to unleash. Standing alone in a field, staring up at the sky was Dempsi.

Rinn ran to her, encasing them both in her protective shield. "Dempsi. You have to stop this storm."

"I can't." Dempsi sobbed like a child with a guilty conscious. "The rain didn't want to come, but it didn't have a choice. It has to rain, right here, right now."

"What do you mean?" Rinn held the black-haired girl by the shoulders.

"There's too much pressure." Dempsi raked her fingers through her hair in distress. "If I stop the storm, it will tear holes in the sky."

Tornadoes, Rinn thought. Damnable elves, they wanted her to stop the rain, baited her into doing it, knowing it would create a worse disaster. By stopping the storm, she would cause the deaths of thousands. In frustration and rage, Rinn let her shield fall. The stinging hail buffeted her and the chill in the air bit through her flimsy dress. Howling into the storm Rinn cried. "Catherine!" A moment later her sister appeared beside her, quaking in fear. Rinn wrapped

Cat, Dempsi, and herself in a dense barrier, protecting them from the winds and hail. She yanked her mother's pendant off her neck and laid it in Cat's paws.

"Cat. Take my shield. Get Dempsi to the eastern edge of camp." She closed her hands around the pendant.

"I can't do that." Cat tried to scamper away, but Rinn held her fast.

"You can, and you must." Rinn insisted. "Dempsi needs to talk to the rain, coax it to gently pass over the camp."

"Where are you going?" Cat pined.

"The Curia's Legion is almost here." Rinn looked east. "I have to stop them."

"But you'll need your shield." The hurt in Cat's eyes pained Rinn. "It belongs to you."

"Sweet sister." Rinn brushed her feline whiskers. "I've seen the real you. This is not my power, it's ours. We can do this. Everything will be fine." Rinn centered her barrier on her mother's pendant and then backed away, leaving the shield in Cat's hands. It felt like losing a limb—an excruciating sense of being torn apart, racking knowledge that a permanent part of her was gone. Rinn gritted her teeth and ran into the violent hail and winds. The rain started falling in sheets, Rinn worried she was too late. She ignored the stinging hail, the biting winds, and the agonizing hole where her shield should be. She sprinted to the tent where her friends were gathered, only to find it blown away by the wind. She was in a panic until she spotted Niveus and the others with a group of soldiers in a nearby trench, heads down and faces covered. Rinn forced her way through the soldiers to her friends.

"Everyone, come with me." She yelled, not sure if they could hear her. Regardless, Tavin followed along, shielding his face from the stinging hail. Lutra and Grus trailed behind him with Feena and Calder bringing up the rear. Sionne remained behind, cowering in the trenches. Rinn kept low to the ground forging her way to the eastern edge of camp. Lightning flashed and thunder followed, Feena yelped. Rinn pushed on, ignoring the elements. Ahead she could see her own shield, a pleasant green glow in the slate gray rain. Inside Cat and Dempsi huddled together, staring up at the sky. The little rain bringer was talking to the clouds.

When Rinn entered her own shield, it felt amazing, like waking after twelve hours of sleep or finally shaking off a protracted illness. Cat skittishly forced Rinn's pendant back into her hands, and the warmth of her magic settled home. She felt complete. With a sigh of relief, Rinn expanded her shield to enclose all her friends. Outside, the roar of winds and the tumult of rain battered against her barrier.

Chapter 40

I n the quiet of her shield refuge, Rinn caught her first glimpse of the Curia's Legions. A brilliant flash of lightning illuminated the force, thousands of shields, each held at precisely the same height, advancing forward. They maintained strict military formation in spite of the weather. Orderly rows of cavalry flanked the main column of soldiers, their horses unphased by the thunder and gale-force winds.

"How do we stop that?" Grus' teeth chattered. Even Calder seemed apprehensive about a force of such size.

"I'm more worried about the storm." Rinn declared.

"More worried about the storm?" Grus ranted. "A little wind and rain aren't going to hurt you, but those soldiers will."

"Summerstorm winds can flatten buildings. Their floodwaters can sweep away towns." Rinn's anger rose. "We're on an open plain with no high ground. If this rain falls for very long, we'll all be underwater. Do you really want to drown in an endless lake of mud?" Grus made no response, but he was clearly stung.

"Could Dempsi talk to the storm, tell it to go away?" Lutra questioned.

"She says it needs to rain." Rinn tried to quell her temper. "If we try to stop it, the storm may get worse."

"What could be worse than this?" Lutra paled.

Rinn quieted herself and reached out a hand to Dempsi. She was wedged between Cat and Feena. Dempsi shied away from Rinn after her emotional outburst. So, Rinn knelt down to the girl's level. "Dempsi, can you talk to the clouds? Tell the storm to slow down until it's between our camp and the army?"

"You're not trying to hurt anyone, are you?" Dempsi asked coyly.

Rinn squeezed the little girl's hand. "Absolutely not. I want the rain to fall between us, to keep the armies apart. I don't want anyone fighting. Would you please help me do that?"

"Ok." Dempsi's cheeks dimpled. Rinn released her hand and watched the black-haired girl walk to the edge of her barrier. Outside the sky was slate gray, and the rain fell in sheets. Dempsi lifted her head and began to sing, softly at first. The song reminded Rinn of a lullaby she once heard, a forgotten melody from long ago. Dempsi's tiny voice was pure, unwavering. She repeated the simple melody over and over. Lutra picked up on the tune and accompanied her on his flute. Dempsi's lullaby filled the air, gradually growing louder than the rain. No, Rinn realized, the rain was getting quieter. The sky was still dark, but the rainfall was stopping. Even the winds quieted down. Dempsi continued to sing, keeping the storm at bay.

A hopeful cheer went up from Rinn's companions. Rinn did not celebrate, she watched the Curia's Legion creeping steadily closer. She let her shield dissipate, so long as Dempsi kept singing, the weather did not pose much danger. She turned to Tavin. "Do you have that list of words?"

The scribe reached into an oiled leather pouch at his side. He produced a cylindrical scroll case bound in dark cord. As he fished the parchment from the tube, Rinn wished she had spent more time studying these words. But they were unpredictable and dangerous, and she was not sure she wanted to harness the power they contained. However, her present need outweighed her reluctance. Tavin unfurled the list. "I've only deciphered a few of them."

"Do you know which word calls Imber?" Rinn needed to know.

"No." Tavin waited for his scolding.

Rinn suppressed her frustration. "Okay, which ones do we know?"

Tavin rattled off the list. "Gifan, beorgan, ahebbe, scieppan, weaxan, acwin, onlithe, and soth." The words danced in Rinn's head like the names of close friends or family members. She knew them intimately, but they were not the right key to this lock. She was too afraid to see the words, lest she release their power unintentionally.

"Read the remaining words to me." Rinn closed her eyes.

Tavin recited the list. "Merian."

Rinn. "No."

Tavin. "Broga."

Rinn. "No."

Tavin. "Scyldigc."

Rinn. "No, and yuck."

Tavin. "Ith."

Rinn. "No."

Tavin. "Hefige."

"That's it!" The word rattled around in Rinn's head. She knew this word, she had felt its power before, pulling at her, weighing her down. The Vallum. This was the force that sundered that defensive wall. She could pull the rain right out of the sky with it. Rinn would need to call on Onero the Burden, one of the Forsaken Gods. She knew what her father would say, but something about this felt necessary. Rinn turned to address her friends, astonished to find they had been joined by many others. The winds and rain had ceased, and soldiers emerged from their trenches. Felsic, Mafic, and Sora mingled with the teenagers. Onager and the palace guards assembled behind them.

A shout like the blare of a trumpet broke the silence. "Paladins!" A panic seized the camp. A line of armored knights advanced on their position. Commanders called for calm, but the sight of the holy warriors broke the army's resolve. The blue glow of the paladin's shields reflected off their polished armor. A single paladin could tear through an army like a plow churning soft ground. A line of forty was an unstoppable force, a natural disaster encased in steel. Behind the largest blue shield, leading the advance, was the unmistakable metal porcupine Serpio.

The rain started to fall. Rinn watched Dempsi collapse into Lutra's arms, the little girl's energy spent. Rinn shouted to Onager. "Get my friends to safety." She pointed northwest, away from the advancing Legion and their paladins. "Everyone. Get as far away as you can." Rinn yelled to those who remained. In what could be the most foolish decision of her life, Rinn walked out to meet the enemy. She had no weapon, she had no plan, she was not even wearing her dragon-feather armor. She was one girl, alone against ten thousand. She was not alone, she could feel her sister nervously padding behind her.

Rinn stopped halfway between the line of paladins and fleeing revolutionaries. Her blonde hair and dress whipped in the wind. The line of paladins closed the distance. Serpio himself came within thirty paces. Rinn pointed to the sky. "Praetor. Look above you."

The paladin line slowed their advance, but Serpio stubbornly pushed forward. "I will not be deterred by your witchcraft."

Rinn shook her head. "This is not my doing. It's elven treachery, a storm designed to decimate both our forces. Floods and tornadoes will come to destroy us all. We've both been deceived."

Praetor Serpio did not stop. "Why would I trust a criminal?"

How could she make this stupid man believe? Rinn yelled until she was red in the face. "If I wanted to kill you, I would've brought a weapon. I'm not here to fight. I'm soaking wet in a flimsy dress. Do I look like your enemy?"

Serpio was within striking distance. "Then you are a fool."

"I could've killed you in Peleon." Rinn's voice cracked in frustration. "But I didn't. I'm trying to save the people of Sevria, not murder them."

"What about Quivis?" The Praetor growled. "Your pet murdered him right before my eyes."

Rinn reached back to restrain Catherine. She hated being called a pet. "My sister is not as forgiving as I am. Why do you think she singled him out? We'd never met most of you before that meeting. But that man had captured her, tortured her, tried to break her bond with me. And that is unpardonable. The gods put us together, no one will dare to tear us apart." She squeezed her sister's paw.

Praetor Serpio did not speak, but his paladin guard encircled Rinn and Catherine cutting off any route of escape. The rain started to fall in sheets. In the sky, the clouds were beginning to twist like unspun fibers of cotton. The churning of the wind was deafening.

"Please." Rinn begged. "Before the storm kills us all."

The Praetor did not have time to answer. The attack commenced, two hundred hooves thundering toward the paladins. Leading the fray, on the back of something that was not a horse, was the giantess Lea wielding a two-and-a-half hand sword in one hand. Gods no, Rinn blanched. She's coming to rescue me. With the paladin's attention and shields focused on Rinn, the cavalry's charge was unexpectedly effective. They skewered ten of the holy warriors before the remainder could regroup. Once their magic shields were set, lances and even charging horses bounced off them.

"Traitorous witch." Praetor Serpio lashed out at Rinn so quickly she did not have time to react. Rinn should have been mowed down like wheat, but her sister blinked them both away. In the chaos of the battlefield, Cat could not find a safe place to emerge, so Rinn ended up only a few paces behind the raging Serpio. "Come back and fight, you wretched monster." He swung wildly at the air.

In the torrential rain, bodies clashed as the revolutionary guard collided with Serpio's Legions, spear against shield, sword against sword. The violence of war surrounded Rinn, and instead of feeling enraged, she felt sickened. All this senseless death and destruction was exactly what the Elves had wanted. The first funnel cloud dropped out of the sky like a wrecking ball, where it landed, dirt and bodies flew. But the fighting did not stop, soldiers intent on killing each other continued to wage war. Tears streamed down Rinn's face in the rain as she walked up behind the mad Praetor. She laid a hand on his metal armor.

"I never wanted this." She choked out between sobs. Before Serpio could turn around, Rinn spoke the word "scieppan". The Praetor's swords bent around him like a cage, a straight-jacket of steel. He fell to the muddy ground thrashing like a beast, cursing and swearing at Rinn. A second twister plunged from the sky, into the heart of the battle. The devastation was unfathomable, hundreds of screaming soldiers ripped from the ground. Rinn's heart broke as she witnessed the carnage, two armies that should not be fighting in the first place, both being annihilated. Dempsi had warned her, and Rinn did not heed her advice. Now there was only one way to stop the storms, an unthinkable choice she would have to make.

"Cat." Rinn croaked. "Find Dad." Find Molo, Lutra, Feena. Find Tavin. Save everyone. But she couldn't say it. No one was going to be safe. Cat nodded and disappeared. Eyes wet with rain and tears, Rinn surveyed the area, searching for her friends. They had not been far. In the madness of the battle, she could see a dark shape with a spear. Niveus. She was fighting off several Legion soldiers on her own. Grus and Calder fought by her side. Rinn ran to them. Seeing her approach, Niveus tossed Rinn her spear. The weapon lit in Rinn's hands, she did not stop to think, just survive and keep her friends alive. With ruthless efficiency, Rinn dispatched five soldiers around her friends.

"Go." She pointed to where Praetor Serpio lay. Cat had returned with her father sitting on one very nervous horse. Rinn pushed deeper into the warzone. She found Onager and Velle effectively fighting off Legion soldiers. Rinn carved through their opponents like weeds. She motioned to the place where the others were gathering. Her heart pounded in her ears above the cacophony of the battlefield and the deafening oscillation of the tornadoes. She needed to act, but she could not let her friends get caught up in the disaster she was about to unleash. Two more twisters were forming in the sky, beginning their descent. Sounds of fighting turned to cries of anguish. Then Rinn's eyes saw her, Feena laying crumpled on the ground. Standing over her, wet with blood were Lutra and Sionne, guarding her fallen form.

Chapter 41

Bloodlust overtook Rinn like an addiction. With unnatural speed she decimated the warriors assaulting her friends. Her violence was so absolute, the bodies of the fallen were nothing more than a smear on the grass. She did not pause to see if Feena was alive, the carnage propelled Rinn forward. Swords, shields, and armor all succumbed to her rampage. She would slice through the tornadoes so long as she could keep on killing. She was lost.

"Rinn." A voice called out to her. "Rinn." It insisted. A male voice, kind and gentle. It was not her father, but it was someone she did not want to kill. Rinn's racing heart stuttered and quieted down. Rinn shook off the fog of bloodlust. "Rinn." The voice called once more.

"Tavin." Rinn wailed as she fell to one knee. He came and draped a cloak over her shoulders.

"We have to get out of here." He steadied her with one hand, and he held a spear in the other. Its tip was wet with blood and rain. Good, Rinn thought to herself, our training helped keep him alive. Tavin led the wobbly Rinn to where the others were gathering. Lutra and Sionne carried Feena between them. Calder ran to his sister. The Praetor was still struggling, cursing Rinn and his metal cage. Onager, Velle, and Marshal faced off with a group of Paladins intent on rescuing their commander. Cat was harassing their backsides, confusing their advance.

Rinn ignored them. The battle was over. Rinn reached a hand down to the ground, feeling the water and the trampled wheat. "Weaxan." She commanded. Grow as tall as you can. Broken stalks straightened and thickened, longing to obey. Plants pushed up from the ground, an acre of fresh wheat in the midst of a battlefield. "Grow damnit." Rinn demanded. The wheat stalks thickened into trunks of tangled wood, the wheat flowers into bushes. Weeds grew with them, giant monstrosities of green and pink. "Grow!" Rinn yelled. The plants begged for roots. You don't need them, just grow. Rinn berated the plants like children. The sudden eruption of plant life terrified Rinn's friends, a jungle of tangled stalks pushed them away from the ground. Cat climbed above the branches, helping to pull the others up. Marshal's horse was so spooked it bucked him off and darted for freedom. Rinn had never seen her father fall from a horse.

More tornadoes were threatening, surely goaded on by the elves' magic. Rinn had to end this now, no matter the cost. She threw her hands to the sky and felt her own heart break as she commanded the clouds. "Hefige." She knew the destruction would be intense, but she was not prepared for the catastrophe that followed. The heavens opened like a sluice and water poured from the sky. A single great sheet plummeted to the ground. Where it impacted, there was no survival, thousands were swept away in the initial surge. In a matter of minutes, the plains of Messis were transformed into a sea, ten feet deep and rising. As the deluge drained the clouds, the waters rose. As the clouds dispersed, the tornadoes dissolved into mist. Rinn and her companions clung to their wheat-wood refuge as the floodwaters swept below them. Onager extended a hand to one of the paladins he had been fighting moments ago.

Rinn saw Lutra and Sionne struggling to lift Feena higher onto the branches.

Good gods, Feena was still alive. Lutra cradled her head and Sionne attempted to hold pressure on a bleeding wound at her side. Rinn scrambled to reach them, but her father arrived first. Like a skilled medic he triaged her wound and tore strips from her skirts to staunch the bleeding. Rinn knew Feena was in good care. She scanned her surroundings. Cries of the drowning were all around her. Rinn had done this—she had unleashed the flood. But she did not have a choice, if she did not stop the storm, the tornadoes would have only gotten worse. Stragglers clung to her island refuge like driftwood. Sora appeared, hauling two waterlogged dwarves behind her: Felsic and Mafic. She tucked them between stout branches and went back down for more. Niveus dragged victims out of the water with the blunt end of her spear. Rinn did not have time to feel sorry for herself and the horror she created. She climbed down to Felsic and Mafic, and heaved them to higher ground.

Soldiers, Legion and revolutionary alike, reached for hands in the water, attempting to pull survivors to safety. More than a hundred people were already on the wheatwood island. Rinn threaded her way through the branches, determined to find more to help. Velle and Onager hauled coughing victims from the water. Tavin and Grus urged them up to the higher branches. Survivors stubbornly clung to wagons, crates, salvage, anything that would float. A thoroughly drenched Cat corralled a group of wet children. What were children doing at a battlefield?

Rinn spotted a group of soldiers scrambling on a sinking wagon. She dove into the water and swam to them. She was not a strong swimmer, but they were not far away. When she reached the struggling refugees, she breathed out the word "ahebbe". The wagon lifted above the water, buoying everyone. Two minotaur swam by and pulled the group to the island. Apparently, minotaur were excellent swimmers.

Over the next hour Rinn worked to save as many lives as she could. She expanded the island and tried in vain to create a second refuge nearby, but there was not enough life under the water to grow. Sora dragged fifty people to safety herself, still heading back for more. The minotaur struggled to keep pace with her.

Eventually, all that could be done was done. The water settled into a placid sea spreading to every visible horizon. A thousand survivors squeezed onto Rinn's acre-wide island, like a tribe of monkeys cowering in the treetops. Rinn wandered through her silent world of wood and water. The refugees did not speak, they were too numbed by the loss of friends and loved ones. They clung to the branches, waiting for the water to recede. Someone determined that the giant wheat grains were edible, which helped quiet the crying children. Rinn stumbled across Serpio, tangled in the branches. Legion soldiers were attempting to pry him out of his metal cage. Rinn quietly crawled down and released him from his prison. There were no thank-you's. The Praetor's eyes burned with hatred.

"I hold you responsible." He seethed at Rinn. "For the deaths of thousands."

Rinn did not want to argue, this man was beyond reasoning. "You brought an army against a Sigillum. What did you think would happen?"

"You're a monster." Serpio reached for a sword that was not there.

"And you're a puppet." Rinn rebuffed. "When will you stop being pulled by the Elves' strings?"

Serpio pursed his lips. Rinn knew he wanted her seized, brought to justice. But on this isolated island, he had nowhere to take her. Rinn knew he would not risk the lives of his remaining soldiers in a senseless conflict. As Rinn departed, he called after her. "I'll never stop hunting you."

"I know." Rinn softly replied as she picked her way to the other side of the island. She found her friends together under a giant wheat blossom. They looked lost and forlorn, except Dempsi. She wore a new emotion: betrayal. The dark-haired girl sat with her back turned, jaw clenched, and brow knit tightly together. Rinn sat near her father, a safe distance away from Dempsi.

Tavin offered Rinn a serving of soggy wheat grain. She silently thanked him. "Any sign of Uncle Molo?" Rinn tried to sound hopeful, but no one had seen the giant nor his daughter since the deluge. Rinn even chanced using her magical vision to try to find him under the water. What she had seen was not pretty, but it contained no hideous beasts, alive or dead.

Mafic tried to reassure her. "A little water won't stop that lug. He'd swim across the Pernic Sea if he had to." Rinn faked a smile, but fear and self-loathing swarmed her like mosquitoes.

Velle attempted to lighten the mood. "Did you see Sora? She's the real hero today. She must've saved a hundred people."

Sora shivered under a wet blanket. "The minotaur helped." A pair of horns turned her direction. Three minotaur were speaking quietly among themselves in a language of grunts and snorts.

Rinn drifted over to them. "Thank you." She hesitated.

"Ziata." One of the minotaur snorted in response. "I am Ziata." He was the largest of the three, his head shaped like a bull with broad horns and a small mouth. Fine fur of dappled brown and black covered his body. His frame was large and powerfully built, but he was not the size of Molo. The memory of him stung Rinn. "Thank you, Ziata." Rinn bowed her head. "All of you. You saved many lives."

"What did you do to the sky?" The lead minotaur brayed. No easy answer came to Rinn. Her intentions were pure, she wanted to stop the war before it started, but in the end, she caused more damage than she prevented.

Her father leaned forward on his branch. "Rinn, help us understand what happened." Compassionate eyes were all around her, but so was the pain, the anguish of witnessing so much death.

"I made a mistake." Rinn could not bear to look up. "Dempsi warned me and I didn't listen." The black-haired girl made no sign of motion. Rinn sighed deeply. "The Elves sent that storm, and told the Legion right where to find us. They wanted a second Gadiom. It didn't matter who won the battle, the storm would finish off the victor. Sevria's armies would be severely weakened, and we'd both blame each other."

"But the flood." Marshal pleaded. "Why?"

"It was the only way to stop the tornadoes." Rinn confessed. "I tore a hole in the Elves' spell to relieve the pressure. I had no idea how much water was up there." She hugged her knees. "I should've listened to Dempsi." The little girl shifted on her tree branch, but made no other motions.

Tavin settled on a giant leaf near Rinn. "I'm sorry."

"For what?" Rinn pouted.

"I'm sorry you had to make such a difficult choice." His voice was as soft as a caress. "It's not fair." He said no more, but sat quietly with Rinn. Broken clouds marred the sky overhead, a colorless sun sat in the afternoon sky. At the lowest levels of the island, people began to murmur. The water was receding. Survivors began to stir, spurred on by a glimmer of hope. Dempsi began to cry, loud. Rinn looked down, the water level was falling fast.

"No." She rose to her feet in anger and despair. "No!" The water fell faster, and people began to scream in alarm.

"Dear gods." Onager's face blanched as he stared at the western horizon. A wall of water was rising out of the sea, a tidal wave a hundred feet tall. And it was headed straight for Rinn's refuge.

"Rinn." Marshal nervously asked. "What is that?"

"Rinn?" Cat anxiously tugged on Rinn's dress.

The island teetered as survivors scrambled for the far side of the refuge, bodies moving over bodies in a panic. The few paladins that were left moved toward the wave, instinctively trying to protect the masses. Serpio led them.

"Rinn!" Marshal shook his daughter, but she could not hear him. She was transfixed by a voice as ancient as the mountains and as wide as the sky. It seemed to come from everywhere.

Let this happen.

No. Rinn fought back. I will not let these people die.

Their lives are meaningless, they will not survive the coming war.

"Rinn, don't listen to him." Cat begged.

Let the water take them and you can start anew. You will have the world at your fingertips. No one will have any memory of this place.

Liar. Rinn fought back. Sora cannot drown. She will know. She will tell others what happened here. You cannot win.

Damnable dwarves.

Rinn laughed, almost maniacally. That's right, dwarves. They are my closest allies, they craft the weapons I use against you. I know who you are, and I know where you are. And I know this: I'm coming for you, Elf.

You'll have to survive first. The voice broke off and Rinn could hear the cries of terrified refugees and the thunderous approach of the tidal wave. But fear could not touch Rinn, she would endure this and she would save these people. Then, she would finish what she started.

Chapter 42

T he paladins pressed their blue shields together, locking them into one solid magical wall with Serpio in the center.

"Hold, men." The Praetor braced himself against the barrier, his powerful legs pushing off thick wheatwood trunks. The fifteen paladins that remained imitated him, preparing for impact. Calmly, Rinn walked to their shield wall accompanied by Cat and Tavin.

"Stand down." She ordered.

Serpio growled. "Stupid girl, get back. We're trying to save lives."

"I'll stop this wave." Rinn asserted.

"I don't trust you." Serpio's loathing blinded him even more than his thick single eyebrow.

Rinn's muscles tensed. "When are you going to wake up? We are five hundred miles from the sea and there's a tidal wave. This is magic, Elf magic meant to kill us. When will you stop trusting the one who sent you into this trap?" Rinn could feel the mist from the wave that was towering over their heads.

Serpio clenched his teeth.

"I'm trying to save us, all of us." Rinn pleaded.

Serpio lowered his shield. "Paladins. Let her through."

Rinn mouthed thank you. She walked to the edge of the island. All she could see was a wall of water, a wave as tall as the Vallum. The top had begun to curl, ready to crush the island.

"I really hate water." Cat reminded Rinn.

Rinn smiled to herself. She had one chance at this, she would have to trust Tavin. He had been working to decipher the Sigillum words. He believed he had worked out the word to summon Inrigo, the god of oceans. The word was "ith", an ancient word the Cibeans used to mark time. Tavin believed it meant "tide". Rinn hoped he was right. She held out her hands as if she was going to stop an approaching wagon. Her voice rang with fury as she yelled: "Ith!"

Rinn cleaved the massive wave in two, as if it had struck an invisible mountain. Seafoam spray rained down on the island, but the split tidal wave passed on either side of it, harmlessly crashing into the sea. Rinn's refuge bobbed in the resulting shockwaves, but the people remained intact, though many grains of giant wheat where shaken loose. Rinn breathed out a sigh of relief. Cheers of joy erupted across the island. Cat joined in with them, swinging Tavin around in a celebratory dance.

Exhausted, Rinn climbed her way back to her father and friends. She did not expect any thanks from Serpio and his paladins, but the Praetor's voice called out to her.

"Gentris." He said. "That is the man you want."

Rinn turned her head back. "I know. My aunt told me." She continued to thread her way back to her companions. She received praises and pats on the back from her friends and a huge hug from her father. Rinn went to check on Feena. She was still unconscious, but stable. Lutra and Calder kept careful watch over her. Evening was falling and the stars were coming out. Refugees settled onto broad leaves and crooks in branches for the night. Velle came and brought Rinn a blanket, which was almost dry.

"Velle?" Rinn asked as she laid down. "Could you find Sora for me?"

"Sure." Velle replied.

Cat came and snuggled next to Rinn, stealing most of her almost-dry blanket. The dwarves lit their collapsible lanterns, one of the few sources of light available. They hung them in high places around the island. Tavin gave his portable oil lamp to a group of children. Sora came and found Rinn.

"You needed me, m'lady?" She bowed.

Rinn fought sleep. "I wanted to thank you."

"Thank me?" Sora asked.

"You saved everyone on this island." Rinn confessed.

"No, m'lady." Sora denied. "I just pulled a few people from the water."

Rinn shook her head. "The Elf spoke to me, tempted me. He wanted me to wipe Sevria clean, start it over anew. He promised that no one would ever know except me."

"You can't do that." Sora pleaded.

"I know." Rinn smiled drowsily. "I told him his plan would never work. There was one person he couldn't drown—you. He was quite perturbed."

"I wish I could've been there." Sora chuckled.

"I thought you should know." Rinn closed her eyes. Sleep found her, deep, restful sleep. She dreamed of a city of glass in the distance. Rinn reached out a hand and felt her sister's paw. Together they walked to the city, not in urgency or fear, but casually, happily, as if they were taking a stroll to the city market.

::

By the time Rinn woke the next morning, the level of the water had dropped considerably. Tracts of muddy ground were visible in the distance. People stirred on the island, scrounging for food and drying out their belongings. The refuge was still very polarized, revolutionary guard on one side and Legion on the other, but there was no bickering or fighting. Serpio and one of his paladins even came to visit Rinn. Onager and the revolutionary guard tensed at his arrival. Out of his armor, he looked less like a brute, and more like a human being.

Serpio nodded to Marshal. "Theodric."

"Praetor." Marshal nodded back.

"I thought I was doing you a favor when I assigned you to the palace guard." Serpio reminisced. "I never believed it could turn out like this."

"There are forces greater than all of us at work here." Marshal admitted. "You did exactly what was needed of you."

"I never meant for the girls to be harmed." Serpio stated.

"I know." Marshal accepted the apology. "It had to happen this way. It was the only way to bring Tabitha and I together, to carry on the Sevrian line." Marshal extended a hand to Rinn. She squeezed it happily. Catherine refused to be left out, crushing his other hand in her paws.

Serpio addressed Rinn. "What is your plan, Sigillum?"

"I make for Farann Fada." Rinn confessed. "I know Gentris is there. He's holding Sidus prisoner, somehow turning her magic against us. I need to free her, before he can unleash any more calamities."

Serpio seemed vexed by this news. "How is it possible to capture a goddess?"

"I'm not certain." Rinn answered. "But I have it on very good authority." Serpio lowered his massive eyebrow but said no more. He bowed and returned to the far side of the island, head full of thoughts. Rinn's friends gathered around her, everyone except Molo. The giant and his daughter were still missing. Dempsi still sat alone, singing a sad tune to herself. Lutra assured everyone that she was okay, she was trying to make the water go back into the sky. Whatever she was doing, it was working. By midday, refugees started leaving the island, wading through the muddy morass searching for bodies of loved ones. The ground swallowed most of the corpses, leaving behind the flotsam from the tent city.

In the late afternoon, Rinn ventured out of the island onto the drying land with Cat and her father. A navigable walkway had been found leading north. Soldiers and noncombatants alike solemnly processed down the road of muck. Some carried children on their shoulders, most hauled equipment and armor. Serpio led his troops away in an orderly double column. The island refuge was depopulating, only Rinn's companions and a few stragglers remained. Rinn surveyed the somber battlefield, a muddy grave for thousands. She did not want to, but she could not leave without scanning the area one last time.

Rinn opened her mind and spoke the word "soth". The sky turned orange and pink and green, the water stone gray, and the mud yellow and blue. Rinn could see the bodies, thousands laying quietly in repose under the quagmire of mud. She could see their lives, youth through adulthood, she could see their families. Families that would never hold them again. Rinn wanted to cry, so much unnecessary death, but her tears burned into rage. Gentris would pay. Rinn glanced one last time over the battlefield, and she saw a figure, not laying down in the mud with the others, but standing upright. He turned and looked at Rinn with his penetrating purple eyes. Rinn dashed out into the mud.

"Rinn, wait!" Her father called out. Rinn ignored him, pushing further into the muck. It was at her waist now, but she did not care, she pressed on. The man stood patiently, watching her approach, but saying nothing. Rinn's friends came splashing after her, but she had too much of a head start. She arrived at the man, who gave her a sober smile. His eyes pointed down to the ground. Rinn reached into the mud with two hands, she could not feel anything. She submerged her entire body, clawing her way into the ooze. Hands pulled at her, lifting her up, but Rinn resisted. She had to get to him. When they pulled her from the mud, Rinn coughed and gasped for breath, but she would not let go. In her arms, she cradled a round rock with a purple eyeball on it: Clive.

::

"He's not dead." Rinn demanded.

Her father was not convinced. "Rinn, we've been searching for hours. He's not here."

"I will never give up." Rinn's stubbornness bordered on insanity. "There must be some sign of him."

"What exactly are we looking for?" Onager asked, standing waist high in muck. Rinn's able-bodied companions spread out like a search party.

"I told you, a beast, a giant beast." Rinn's frustration cracked her voice. "That's why he left Clive behind, it's the only way he could survive. He had to abandon his humanity and become the monster inside him."

Marshal took a cleansing breath. "Okay, if he did become this monster, what do we do once we find him?"

Rinn held out Clive. "Give him back his humanity."

Niveus reminded everyone. "Nightfall is coming. We need to get to dry land."

"Of course." Rinn's eyes widened. "Yallakh can find him. He can track anything. We'll just wait until nighttime."

Marshal scolded his daughter. "Rinn, we can't stay in this swamp at night. Feena's hurt and the rest of us need food and shelter."

"I'll stay." Rinn clutched Clive.

"No." Her father crossed his arms. "We are getting out of here while we can. There has been no sign of Molo or his daughter. If they are out there, we'll have better chances of finding them on dry land. Now, let's go while we can still see the way." Rinn could not argue. It would be impossible to follow the muddy causeway in the dark. Reluctantly, she agreed to let the search party be called off. Sora led everyone down the muddy causeway with Felsic and Mafic close on her heels. Onager helped Marshal navigate the muck. Lepas let Dempsi ride on her shoulders. Lutra and Calder carried a splint bearing Feena. She mumbled occasionally. Rinn trudged through the muck with Clive's extra weight. Catherine was nowhere to be seen.

After almost an hour of walking, Rinn's army came to dry ground, a gentle upland the water never reached. Some of the stragglers had built a meager camp on the site, hasty tents of mildewed canvas and salvaged poles. They were still on cultivated farmland, and a few farm families joined the refugees, their homes caught up in the flood. Food was scarce, but what people had, they shared—it reminded Rinn of the squatter's village. A few remained greedy and selfish, but by and large, people were decent to each other. Rinn and her companions stayed overnight. Catherine eventually showed up, disgruntled and covered in mud. It took Rinn an hour to towel her off using a blanket designed for a horse.

Rinn waited up half the night, calling Yallakh's name, but he never came. She even wandered away from camp and summoned magical darkness, but she could not hail the mysterious assassin. She gave up and slid under a blanket with Catherine, cradling Clive like a doll. In the morning, the refugee camp dismantled itself and began to trek north. There were reports of a small village that direction. Marshal asked his daughter. "Which way do you want to go?"

Rinn had been thinking about this all night. She loved being surrounded by her friends, but there were too many tasks that needed to be done at the same time. "We need to split up."

"Are you sure that's wise?" Her father cautioned.

"Yes." Rinn was certain. "Feena needs medical care. Calder and Lutra will take her to the nearest town. I'm giving Clive to Onager and Haril. They will have to track down Molo and return his humanity."

"What about you?" Marshal asked.

"I'm going to Farann Fada." Rinn stated.

"Alone?" Marshal inquired.

"No." Rinn replied. "I'm taking Felsic, Mafic, and Sora." She added. "Oh, and Tavin."

"And Catherine?" Marshal raised an eyebrow.

"Duh." Rinn grimaced.

"I'm coming with you." Marshal strapped on his swordbelt.

"No." Rinn said. "I didn't recognize it at first, but I am finally starting to understand. We're all here for a purpose. Your job is to take Dempsi to the Temple of Imber at Messis. Lepas and Velle will accompany you."

"Okay. But you should take Niveus with you." Marshal offered. "She's a formidable warrior, might come in handy."

"Alright." Rinn nodded. "I'll ask her."

And so, it was arranged. Rinn's army divided into four teams. Grus opted to follow Onager and Haril on the hunt for Molo. Sionne joined Lutra and Calder to find care for Feena. Niveus warmly agreed to accompany Rinn, as did Tavin. The rest travelled with Marshal and Dempsi to Messis. What little money the party had, they pooled together and allotted to the four teams based on need. Calder got the most, to pay for Feena's medical care. Rinn accepted what they could spare, not enough to buy passage to Farann Fada, but at least a start.

Hugs and handshakes were exchanged. Everyone wished each other luck. And like that, they departed. Rinn lingered for a moment, then she called out to her father. "Stay safe!"

He called back. "No heroics!"

Rinn chuckled to herself. She lifted her pack and headed south and east, on her way to Farann Fada. Her assault force followed behind.

Chapter 43

Rinn's assault team reached the Macellum River four days later. Its banks were overflowing with water trying to escape the plains of Messis. Cat was saddened they would not be able to hunt for crayfish, their muddy dens had been washed away with the floodwaters. The river ran swift with choppy waves.

"We'll have to have Cat take us across." Rinn stated.

"I'll swim, thank you." Sora started removing her things. Felsic and Mafic disrobed along with her.

"I don't see what's the big deal?" Rinn sulked.

"I feel safer in rough water than her crazy magic realm." Felsic snubbed.

"You are aware we're heading to a city of magic?" Rinn pointed out.

"Yes." Felsic pulled off his shirt. "But that's different." Rinn did not know what she could do with him. Dwarves were stubborn to the core. Niveus and Rinn gathered up their things.

Niveus whispered. "Is it really that bad?" She had never been transported by Catherine. Back in Peleon, she found her own way into the sewers, a situation she never fully explained.

Tavin whispered back. "It's best if you close your eyes the first time."

Rinn glowered at them. She piled the things in front of her sister. "Would you rather go one at a time or all at once."

"One at a time." Cat insisted. "I'll take the stuff first." With a pop she was gone, appearing on the other side of the river with the packs. A moment later she was back. She laid a paw on Rinn and was gone.

"See." Tavin told Niveus. "Nothing to it." Cat came back, and tagged him next. He disappeared with a smile. By the time Sora hauled a waterlogged Felsic and Mafic across the river, Niveus still had not recovered from her second-long journey.

"You lied to me, boy." She trembled as she sat on the soggy riverbank.

"It's worse if you're scared." Tavin hefted his pack. "I was just trying to help."

"I was not scared." Niveus pulled herself with her spear defiantly.

South of the swollen riverbank, farmland gave way to rolling hills covered in thin forests of beech and birch. The woods were a welcome sight, offering shelter from the heat and plentiful hunting. Sora was not exactly comfortable in the forest, but she adjusted to it. Felsic and Mafic found edible oyster-shaped mushrooms growing on birch trees. Cat dined on every variety of bird, rabbit, and mouse. Conversation was light as they traveled, a distraction to keep them from thinking about where they were going. On their third day in the woods, Niveus brought up the topic.

"Explain to me this Farann Fada." She opened. "I have never been there."

"Few have." Rinn confessed. "It's so unlike Sevria, it's almost another country. I think at one time it may have been. Tavin would know more about that."

"It was." The scribe demonstrated his formal education. "At one time the Empire was divided into three nations, Farann Fada was the smallest. But they had magic, and no army or navy dared to invade their peninsula. Eventually, Sevria was reunited and Farann Fada was brought back through treaties instead of warfare."

"They still have considerable autonomy, even their own code of laws." Rinn added.

"And the reason for our journey?" Niveus questioned.

"To kill an Elf." Rinn's words were as sharp as a knife.

Niveus raised a curious eyebrow. "To kill an immortal is not a small thing."

"This one has it coming." Rinn stewed in her anger.

"What has he done to deserve this fate?" Niveus asked.

"The flood at Messis, for one." Rinn's ire was so fierce, her skin prickled with gooseflesh. "The Battle of Gadiom for another. The Sevrian Civil War. He's orchestrated the deaths of 50,000 people, and probably many more. My mother and grandmother were among his victims."

"I see." Niveus chewed on this information for the next few days, asking no more questions.

::

In the weeks of travel that followed, Rinn and Tavin worked together deciphering the Sigillum commands. They connected three more words with their sources: "Maegen" with Iugo the Mountain; "Broga" with Timor the Fear (Cat helped with that one); and "Merian" with Imber, the goddess of Rain. Rinn could not determine exactly what Imber's power granted her, but it seemed harmless. She was reluctant to tempt Iugo's abilities, she did not want to cause a rockslide or a ground tremor. She tried calling upon the power of Fear, but its effect worked so much better when Cat used it.

Tavin unfurled his scroll, which was fading and crumpled from excessive handling. "Okay, we've narrowed the list down to only two gods: Aedis and Metus."

"That's an odd pairing." Rinn remarked. Aedis was the god of ceremonies, and Metus was the Bringer of Dread. Rinn scanned the list. "Why are there three words left?"

"We've been over this." Tavin complained. "There are fifteen words, but only fourteen gods." Rinn screwed up her face in mock confusion. Tavin rolled his eyes. "Look, I didn't make the rules. That's just the way it is."

Rinn put her finger on her chin, imitating Catherine. "Well, I'm going to guess that my magic weapon does not come from Metus. That means it's a gift from Aedis."

"I'm not so sure." Tavin surmised. "Your weapon is pretty formidable, dare I say, dreadful."

Rinn socked him in the arm. "No, you may not."

"Okay." Tavin yielded to Rinn's physical argument. "We'll assign 'gifan' to Aedis. That leaves two words: 'scyldigc' and 'acendoer'. Any clues?"

"I'm not the one who speaks Cibean." Rinn protested. "But if I had to guess, I really don't like the sound of the first one. I'd wager it goes with Metus."

"Alright." Tavin scribbled notes on the parchment with his quill. "That just leaves one final word: 'acendoer'." Rinn puzzled over it for the rest of the day. She dared not call upon the powers of a god nobody knew. Felsic proposed the idea that it might call upon a non-human deity. Tavin argued that the word was Cibean, not dwarvish, elvish, nor orcish. It had to be somehow associated with the Sevrian Empire. Rinn let it go, but the notion of an unknown god haunted her.

::

On their third week of travel through the forest, Rinn and her friends stumbled across a woodland home. Niveus recommended caution, but Rinn was undaunted. She walked up and knocked on the wooden door. It was opened by a gruff-looking man with a hatchet. Rinn introduced herself and her friends.

"We're travelers looking for shelter." Rinn put on her most innocent face. The man wanted to refuse, but a feminine voice from inside scolded him.

"Let them in, Vimur." A young woman holding an infant pushed her way to the door.

"I don't think it's a good idea, Didi." Her husband argued.

"Nonsense." The pleasant woman eyed down her husband. "They're not Legion, just ordinary folk. Now, be a decent neighbor and let them in."

Reluctantly, the doorman let them in. The lodge was home to two brothers and their families. Small children played near a stone hearth. Vimur and his brother were trappers, selling furs to the coastal villages south of the forest. Rinn offered to chop timber for them in exchange for room and board for the night. The men easily agreed, chopping wood was not a task they enjoyed. Rinn and her friends were shown out back to a stand of forest being cleared for firewood. They got to work at once.

A few hours later, Vimur came out to check on their progress. A stout pile of neatly trimmed logs filled the space between two trees. "Wow." The trapper exclaimed. "You all are good at this."

Rinn wiped sweat from her brow. "I was raised in Viburna."

"That would explain your skill with an axe." Vimur smirked to himself. In exchange for their hard work, Rinn and her friends were treated to a homecooked meal. The house was noisy with all the children and there was no table large enough to hold everyone, so the guests sat where they could. Rinn leaned against a wall, not caring that she sat on the floor. She was savoring a slice of warm, buttered bread—she had not eaten bread in over a month, a culinary tragedy. Cat entertained the children, chasing after strings of yarn. And the dwarves reclined near the hearth.

"How far is it to the coast?" Felsic asked over dinner, always practical.

"Two day's travel at most." Vimur responded. "Funis is the closest fishing village. Where are you headed?"

"Hyalos." Rinn replied honestly.

Didi dropped a plate. Her husband moved to help her clean up. The young woman urged. "You must not go to Farann Fada. It's cursed."

"I know." Rinn admitted. "That's why we're going."

Vimus straighten, helping his wife up. "That's madness. Any boat foolish enough to stray near their shores does not make it back. You'd be safer sailing to Migalia."

"Yeah." Rinn grinned. "Already been there." Vimus and his wife blanched. The kids jumped up and down, begging for stories about the monsters of Migalia. Rinn shied away, she was no bard.

"That's it!" Tavin exclaimed. "Monsters."

All heads turned to him. Rinn raised an eyebrow. "Monsters?"

"'Doer'." The scribe explained. "It's Cibean for monster. I remember now, the Pernic Sea is called Ythandoer, the Waves of Monsters."

Rinn sat up on her knees in breathless anticipation. "The final word. What do you think it does?"

"I'm not sure." Tavin knitted his brow. "But I'm sure it has a connection to monsters."

Vimus stared at the teens. "What are you talking about?"

Rinn chuckled nervously. "Trust me. You don't want to know."

::

The fishing village of Funis was quaint. It still smelled of brine and rotting fish, but the homes were tidy and the sandy shoreline picturesque. Rinn and her friends had to wait while Catherine took another sand bath. Tavin shielded his eyes as she stripped down to nothing but fur. Rinn wanted to hurry her sister along, but she seemed to be enjoying herself so much, she made everyone wait. Afterwards, they headed for the town tavern; all fishing villages have taverns. Finding a ship willing to travel to Farann Fada was impossible, local folklore forbid any journey to that mythical land. Rinn pressed her case, surely someone must trade with Hyalos, the capital city of Farann Fada. Only sailors from Amne Dua dared to make that voyage.

So Rinn booked passage to the port city of Amne Dua, using a gold hairpin as payment. The trip aboard a small ocean skiff was arduous. The captain had to fight foul winds the entire journey and the tides of the Aspero Sea were unkind. Halfway through the two-week journey even Niveus began to complain.

"It would have been faster to walk." She grumbled as she gripped the side rail of the boat while it pitched and tossed in the wind-turned sea. Sora was the only one unperturbed by the voyage. Rinn really missed Dempsi, she hoped the little rain-bringer was doing okay. She should have made it to Messis by now. Marshal would be with her. Rinn's heart ached at the distance between her and her father. He had been a constant everyday of her life, like the sun in the sky or the ground beneath her feet. This last month she had woken every morning expecting to see him, only to be reminded he was far away. The boat crashed down hard on a rolling swell. Rinn wiped her eyes and went below to be with her sister.

Chapter 44

To say Amne Dua was a grashel nest would be a compliment. Even the boarded-up, burnt-out streets of southern Viburna were an improvement over this cesspool of a city. The buildings looked like something straight out of a squatter's village, and the smell was so fierce Rinn wondered if the streets were paved with rotting fish. Boats of all shapes and sizes docked at piers that were nothing more than floating ladders.

Niveus declared as she disembarked. "We are not staying here."

Holding her nose Rinn concurred. "Only long enough to secure transport to Hyalos."

"We're going on more boats?" Cat whined. She had her head and face wrapped in a towel against the ghastly smell. With her long robe and hood it made a reasonable disguise, though her whiskers did poke out a bit.

Sora suggested. "We should find the custom house."

"Why?" Rinn questioned.

Niveus pursed her lips. "All shipping in and out of the Empire must be cleared by customs. They keep extensive records."

Sora explained. "The tax officers will know which boats are bound for Farann Fada. If we get lucky, we might find one headed to Hyalos itself."

They did not get lucky. The custom officer on duty was a thick-necked bureaucrat, all regulation, no exception. He would not divulge the destination of any ship in his ledgers. Cat offered to sneak in and steal them, but Rinn decided against it.

"We'll scout the local taverns." She proposed.

"Is that really a good idea?" Mafic queried. "Harbors can be dangerous places, especially at night."

"We can handle it." Rinn pshawed. "We're warriors."

::

The three dwarves roared with laughter as they slammed their empty mugs on the table and called for more. Rinn and her companions had been in the tavern for three hours waiting for a captain named Levo. Apparently, he was the only sailor foolish enough to travel to Farann Fada. Rinn sulked in a corner, nursing a cup of room-temperature coffee. The tavern, simply known as Scuppers, was not the cleanest dive in town. Mugs stuck to the grime on the tabletops and windows were smeared with soot, but Mafic swore they served the best malted ale in the Empire. Niveus sampled it. She was not particularly impressed, but she did finish her glass. Tavin shied away from the strong brew. On a dare, Catherine gulped down one swallow before spitting it back up. Margot and alcohol do not mix.

Tavin nudged Rinn. "Let's get out of here."

"Where would we go?" Rinn pouted.

"We could go visit the Temple." Tavin stood up and held out his hand. Normally, when a young boy invites a young girl to the Temple, he only has one thing on his mind: marriage. Rinn flushed at the thought. She liked Tavin, but a thousand misgivings ran through her head. She was too young. He was too young. They did not have income nor any place to live. And there was that other stuff that went along with marriage, Rinn was definitely not ready for that. She stammered as she made excuses.

"Don't you want to see where you were initiated?" Tavin asked with a hint of chagrin.

"Initiated?" Rinn wondered.

"This's Amne Dua." Tavin reached down to take Rinn's hand. "Your father brought you here when you were a baby."

"My father?" The dam of heartbreak Rinn had been holding back started to crack. She missed her father so much. "He must've been traveling from Migalia." Rinn could not imagine what the journey had been like for him. He had just lost his wife and he was forced to return in secret to the Empire that killed her—all for the sake of his two-year-old-child. He had given up everything for her, endured the ravages of Migalia, lived in secret for over a decade in Viburna, pretending to be a simple town guard. And when danger threatened, he left it all behind once again to whisk Rinn away to the Rustic Lands. He had sacrificed everything for her.

"It's how I found you, or at least records that you existed." Tavin explained. "You were initiated into the Sevrian faith right here, at the Temple in Amne Dua."

"Let's go." Rinn jumped up. Cat followed her motion.

Niveus raised an eyebrow. "Where are you headed?"

"Tavin and I are going to see the local Temple." Rinn snapped, eager to leave.

Niveus rose from her seat. "I'll go with you."

"No." Rinn insisted. "Someone sober needs to stay here to watch for Levo and keep an eye on our drunken friends." Mafic and Felsic raised their mugs in salute. Sora was face down on the table, asleep. Niveus reluctantly agreed. "We won't be long." Rinn headed for the door.

Rinn, Cat, and Tavin strolled the stinking streets of Amne Dua. The town was not large, and the Temple should not have been hard to find, but Rinn could see no white spires jutting above the shipyards and shanty homes. They would have to wander around until they stumbled across it. Rinn could sense unease in her sister, she had been on a ship for days, subsisting on ocean fish and dried rations.

"If you want to go hunt, it's okay." Rinn acknowledged. "We won't be long at the Temple. Just meet us back at the tavern." Cat bobbed up and down smiling. With a blink she was gone. Moments later Rinn could feel her sister chasing seabirds. Then she found out what one tasted like. The sensation was so awful, it churned Rinn's stomach. Cat moved on to hunting rabbits and mice in a field outside town.

"Are you okay?" Tavin asked, seeing Rinn's face turn all different colors.

"Yeah." Rinn struggled to maintain her composure. "Trust me, never eat seabird."

Tavin hinted at understanding. "You know what your sister eats?"

"Only when it's really gross." Rinn stuck out her tongue in disgust.

"That's some bond you two have." Tavin's stone grey eyes pierced Rinn.

"It's worse than you could imagine." Rinn admitted. "Sometimes I know exactly what she's thinking, as if they were my own thoughts."

"What's she thinking now?" Tavin asked playfully.

"Fresh rabbit tastes amazing." Rinn smirked. "Margot need fresh meat or they get weak. The time we spent on the boat was hard on her. Hunting helps."

"Oh." Tavin seemed resigned. He spoke no more as they explored the jigsaw streets of Amne Dua. The town had grown in random clusters, like lichen on a large stone. In some places, buildings stood shoulder to shoulder, in others, alone on a patch of sandy soil. Finally, they found it, the Temple to Aedis. The building was so nondescript they almost walked right past it. A thick-walled mud and stone structure with a simple dome roof. The only thing identifying it as a Temple was the crude statue of Aedis next to the front door. The nondescript figure held a bar and rod, the scales that symbolized balance and neutrality.

"This is it." Rinn announced. Tavin grimaced almost imperceptibly. Rinn was surprised when she found the front door locked, Temples were always open. She rapped loudly on the door with her walking stick, but no one came. She softly uttered the word "onlithe", and the door creaked open. Rinn felt pangs of guilt about breaking into a Temple, but it should not have been locked in the first place. She pushed the heavy door aside and braved her way in. The Temple was as dark as a basement. A single candle illuminated the altar at the far end of the sanctuary. The walls and ceiling were supported by beams of dark wood, the bones of old sailing ships.

"Hello?" Rinn called, but no answer came. She walked down the central aisle, feeling her way between the rows of pews with her free hand. She came to the foot of the altar, a single slab of polished stone.

"What now?" Tavin whispered.

"I'm going to see if this is the place." Rinn asserted. The initiation rites included laying the infant on the altar while prayers were said. If Rinn had been here, memories of her may be retained in the stone. Rinn closed her eyes and issued the command "soth". When she opened her eyes, the inside of the Temple was a violent array of images. The beams in the walls were entire ships and the floorboards were live trees. Rinn turned to the altar, knowing that it came from the marble mines of Saxitum. When she concentrated, she could see thousands of initiates laid out on the table, enough faces to fill the Great Amphitheater in Peleon. Rinn knitted her brow as she struggled to look through all the faces. After several minutes, she found herself, a toddler with curly hair so blond it was almost white. A priest was standing over her, speaking the words of initiation, she was crying, wanting her father to hold her.

Rinn tore her sight away from the altar. "This is the place." She covered her eyes with her hand and steadied her nerves.

"Are you okay?" Tavin touched her lightly.

"Yes." Rinn lied. "You were right. I was here when I was young." Rinn let Tavin lead her to a front row pew. Rinn sat down and waited for the effects of Sidus' magic to wear off. After a few moments her head cleared, and her vision returned to normal. Rinn took a deep cleansing breath and stood up. She pulled the metal spear tip from a pouch at her side and clicked it into place at the end of her walking stick.

"What are you doing?" Tavin fretted.

"I have to know." Rinn audaciously walked to the altar and imbued her spear with magical fire. She reached out to touch the altar with it.

"Wait, Rinn." Tavin said in alarm. The moment her spear touched the altar, a resounding noise shook the Temple, like a shrill note from a trumpet. The altar glowed a dazzling shade of green, illuminating the Temple interior. Rinn raised her spear above her head.

"I know you can hear me." She cried out. "Why are you helping me? After everything I've done, why?" Grief, anger, and frustration surged through Rinn. "Answer me, Aedis!"

An echo like the sound of rolling thunder responded. "Annihilation is not justice. Death is never the solution."

"But I can kill with a thought." Rinn argued, pleaded. "Why?"

The resonant voice returned. "So you are free to choose mercy." The light from the altar began to fade.

"Wait!" Rinn sobbed. "Don't go. I have so many questions." The noise in the Temple was dying down when an angry, elderly vicar burst in.

"What in the blazes?" He demanded, hastily fastening his ceremonial robe. Rinn recognized him, the same priest who performed her initiation rites.

"You." She said.

"Who are you people?" He berated Rinn and Tavin. "What are you doing in my Temple?"

The thundering voice echoed one last phrase. "Remember, mercy is the only way." Then, with one word, Aedis ruined the rest of Rinn's life. "Empress."

::

"Stop." The elderly priest shuffled after Rinn. "Please, wait." He was wheezing and turning red. Out of pity, Rinn let him catch up, but she was in no mood for pleasantries. She wanted this all to be over with. She wanted to go home, wherever that was. She wanted her father. Catherine had laughed in Rinn's head when Aedis said the word Empress, souring Rinn's mood even further. The priest reached Rinn, leaning on his staff like a crutch. "I heard a voice in the temple."

Rinn wanted to fabricate a good cover story, but Tavin interfered. "We were having a theological discussion."

"There was something else." The priest quivered.

Rinn replied bluntly. "That was the voice of Aedis."

The priest traced a triangle over his head and chest, a benediction to Aedis. He fell to his knees and mumbled a prayer of forgiveness. Rinn shook her head and walked away. The priest called after her. "He called you 'Empress'." Rinn paused then continued to walk. The priest would not let up. "Who are you?"

Rinn turned back to the elderly vicar. "I came here with my father. I was two years old. You initiated me."

The priest's mouth fell agape. "You're her—the Sevralis child."

Rinn came back and helped the priest to his feet. "My name is Rinn. But I am also known as Sabrinn Sevralis."

"My Queen." The priest went down on his knees again.

"Empress." Rinn corrected, rolling her eyes. She and Tavin struggled to keep the elderly man off the ground. The priest started to prostrate himself, but Rinn resisted. "Get up."

"Whatever you say, my Queen." The priest bowed before Rinn, his head held low.

"Stop that." Rinn chastised him. "Save it for your Temple services."

The priest cast his eyes downward. "The Divine said, 'Mercy is the only way.'"

"Yes." Rinn was irritated. "I don't understand what it means any more than you do." She felt uniquely unqualified to interpret the will of the gods. She had no idea what to do with Lucan's staff, she was not sure why she trusted Tenebra, and she made an absolute mess of Imber's rain-bringer. But the priest waited, hanging on Rinn's every word. She had to say something. "Just, be kind to people, okay?"

The priest traced the divine symbol once again and repeated Rinn's words to himself. Before she could do anymore damage, Rinn excused herself and walked away.

Chapter 45

W hen Rinn and Tavin returned to the tavern, they found a very drunk sea captain singing off-key with three inebriated dwarves. Cat danced around on table tops, with her belly full she was feeling much better. As it turned out, a sober captain was not needed to get a sailing vessel underway. The oarmaster called the strokes as the helmsman piloted the craft out of the harbor. Once they were in open sea, riggers ran up the sails and the oars were stowed. The merchant ship was a wide-bodied freighter called "Audacia". She rode steadily through the foamy waves of the Aspero Sea.

Captain Levo sat at a small deckside table drinking water and sucking lemons. The dwarves were sleeping off their liquid conquests in the decks below. Catherine perched atop a mast, as far away from the water as she could get. Niveus stood in the prow, staring out at the open ocean. Rinn maneuvered through the busy sailors and joined up with Niveus.

"Hi." She said.

Niveus leaned on the railing. "I once sailed these waters, before the Curia's taxes strangled my business."

"You've been to Farann Fada?" Any information about that mysterious land would help Rinn.

"No." Niveus answered. "I sailed west, to Brigantum. I traded with their largest cities, Sulia, Isca, as for north as Coria. I made a fortune delivering goods to Peleon." She gazed at the sea wistfully.

"What's Brigantum like?" Rinn's father never talked about his homeland. He never talked about much of anything from his past.

"It's a beautiful country." Niveus described its rolling pastures and rocky hills. The largest island was almost a small continent, home to over a million inhabitants. The capital city Sulis was renowned for its hot springs and fine horses. Brigantines were fine fisherman, but they did not venture into the open seas. Only foreign traders like Niveus braved those waters.

Captain Levo overheard the conversation and staggered over. "Sulis is a jewel of a city." He steadied himself against taut rigging ropes. "Tough negotiators, though." He hiccupped.

"Captain, how long will it take us to get to Hyalos?" Rinn asked.

"About two weeks, if the winds favor us." Levo looked for a moment as if he was going to be sick, then he recovered. "We'll make port at Sera, to the west. The cliffs of Hyalos offer no safe harbor."

::

Two weeks on the open seas passed uneventfully. Rinn's party kept busy with sparring drills and helping the sailors out where they could. Audacia's crew were decent men, mostly chest-hair and bravado, but they took a liking to Rinn and her party, especially Niveus. When the captain was sober, he was brash and authoritarian. Fortunately, he was not often sober, and the ship ran autonomously without him. His tall first mate, a calculating man named Flavus, controlled most of the ship's operations. Rinn found him discussing sea routes with the captain. Tavin was with them, browsing their nautical charts.

"We must turn back." Flavus insisted.

"We're two day's sail away." Levo rebutted. "We're not turning around now."

"There are storm clouds gathering over Hyalos." Falvus clenched a fist. "I think you know what that means." Levo glowered at his first mate, but made no reply.

"Excuse me, can I help?" Rinn asked.

Flavus curtly regarded Rinn. "I'm sorry, I did not get your name."

"I'm Rinn Amali." She smiled in reply.

"Amali?" The captain cursed. "I hate that clan."

"I have a clan?" Rinn boggled.

"Always lording over us, like they're better than everyone." Levo grumbled. "They should be run out of Brigantum."

"My father's from Brigantum." Rinn added.

"Probably from Rosswiede, one of those damn horse-lovers." Levo spat.

The first mate tried to be respectful. "I am sorry, Ms. Amali, but we will not be completing our voyage. Farann Fada has barred our landing."

"I suspected they might." Rinn revealed. "It's okay, I can handle it."

The first mate was not impressed. "I don't think you understand. The oceans and the skies are playthings to these people. We must turn back."

"I got this." Rinn oozed confidence.

Tavin concurred. "She can handle it. She has powers."

Falvus grabbed the captain bruskly. "You let a sorceress onboard?" The captain pleaded innocence.

"Technically, I don't do magic." Rinn confided. "But I can stop theirs."

Falvus released the captain and vented at Rinn. "I will not have this boat caught up in some wizard's duel. At the first sign of witchcraft, we'll throw you and your friends overboard."

"Won't do any good." Rinn met his hostile stare. "Our water dwarves can swim for days. Cat can teleport. And none of you could touch Niveus if you tried."

The first mate threw up his hands in frustration. "Accursed girl. You're going to get us all killed."

"No, I won't. I swear to protect this ship." Rinn promised. "Just keep her heading straight for Hyalos. And have a little faith."

::

Felsic and Mafic met with Rinn below decks. Felsic's dour expression was extra dour. "The sailors are about to mutiny if we aren't thrown overboard."

Rinn explained the situation. "The mages in Hyalos will impede our arrival. We have no choice but to fight back. We can't exactly sneak into a city made of magic."

Mafic tried to be calm. "How can we expect to win?"

Rinn waved her hand dismissively. "They're going to send waves, maybe a few fireballs. Nothing I haven't handled before. Just keep the boat moving and I'll take care of the rest." Mafic did not seem relieved.

A feline voice called from above. "Uh, Rinn. You'd better get up here." Rinn hurried to the ladder and climbed up to the top deck. Sailors were derelict in their duties, readying to abandon ship. A massive wall of water rose in the distance, heading directly at them.

"This again?" Rinn sighed. She marched over to the captain and first mate, who were stuffing belongings onto a tiny life-raft. "Captain." He seemed embarrassed (and a bit drunk). Rinn raised a finger. "If I save your boat, will you believe me?"

347

"They're trying to kill us." Captain Levo stammered.

"No." Rinn corrected. "They're trying to find me. This is just a ruse. They know I can stop it. They're just making sure I am here."

Flavus cast an incredulous eye at Rinn. "Who are you again?"

"I'm Rinn." She feigned innocence. "And I'm the Sigillum."

The captain pointed at her accusingly. "She's an outlaw! I've heard stories about her. Murderer. Villain." He spat. The wall of water was getting precariously close.

"Excuse me gentlemen." Rinn pushed her way to the front of the vessel. A third of the crew was already in the water. Rinn sighed. She faced the tidal wave bearing down upon her. She prayed a word of thanks to Onrigo and then called out the word "ith". A counterwave rose off the prow of the ship and cleaved its way through the oncoming water. The tidal wave collapsed into the sea, the merchant ship bobbing up and down on its swells. A cry of relief went up from the sailors and crew members were fished out of the water.

Defiantly Rinn turned to the captain and first mate. "Do you believe me now? Stay on course for Hyalos. Let me deal with the rest."

Several more waves and a few fireballs were launched at the vessel, but Rinn handled them serenely. Her lack of concern lasted until a hail of fire rained down on the merchant ship.

"Firestorm!" A watchman called, and the crew panicked. The hull and the sails began to catch aflame as burning embers fell from the sky. Rinn summoned her energy and wrapped a barrier shield around the entirety of the ship. The crew was quick to douse the fires, and Rinn's barrier protected them from the flaming assault. When the head of a sea-serpent appeared out of the water, Rinn threw up her hands in frustration.

"Oh, come on!" She cried. If she distracted herself long enough to battle the sea monster, her barrier would fall and the ship would burn.

"We got this." Cat zipped by excitedly, three dwarves hot on her heels. Sora dove into the water with a fishing spear and Cat teleported Mafic and Felsic to the top of the massive serpent's head. They battered away at the beast with their hammers while Niveus hurled javelins from the deck of the ship. The monster fought ferociously, but it was impossibly outmatched and eventually fell to the four warriors. Again, a cry of relief went up from the crew.

"Land ahead." Called a spotter high on one of the masts.

A whirlpool opened between the land and the Audacia, threatening to swallow the ship and her crew.

Incensed, Rinn yelled at the seas. "You will not stop me." She slapped her hands down on the deck and growled the word "ahebbe", floating the boat inches off the water. In a second breath she unleashed the fury of destruction with a primal scream. Her violent "onlithe" shredded the whirlpool, the water crying out as it was cast into oblivion. The seas closed in around the void, the resulting wave propelling the boat forward. As the shore drew close, Rinn spotted a grove of scrubby pine trees. Using Lucan's gift, she coaxed the trees to grow into a living pier. The Audacia gently glided into the newly created port.

Flavus and Levo stood side by side, mouths hanging open. "What are you?"

Rinn hefted a heavy spear and answered them. "Deteremined."

The cliffs of Hyalos soared above, angry black rocks fractured by the sea. The assault team disembarked, and Rinn called back to the crew. "You should be safe for now, but I would remain here, at least until the battle is over."

"Battle?" Captain Levo whined.

Rinn's companions assembled at the base of the cliff. Cat rubbed what little sand was available on her fur. The dwarves outfitted themselves in their heaviest armor and wielded thick hammers. Niveus wore agile scale male and brandished a long spear similar to Rinn's. Tavin also wore thick leather armor and carried a spear, but less massive than the one Niveus carried. Rinn and Cat wore their dragon-feather vests. Rinn hefted a stout spear. Cat sharpened her claws on the pier. As she scratched, she pointed out to Rinn. "I think that thing we fought was a sea-dragon, so technically I'm a dragon slayer."

The dwarves all chuckled. Rinn patted her sister on the head. "Yes, you are. Catherine Dragonsbane." Cat smiled in her squinty, feline way.

"What now?" Tavin asked, peering up at the precipitous cliffs.

"We go to Hyalos and find the Elf known as Gentris. We put an end to his meddling in the affairs of Sevria." Rinn was singularly focused. Nothing would stand in her way.

"How do we get up there?" Tavin pondered.

"We climb." Rinn suggested meekly.

Mafic pointed to an incline in the rock. "There's a staircase hidden in the cliff face." Rinn could not see it, but when the dwarves started up the side of the rocks, she knew it must exist. She felt her way forward with her foot, planting it on a step so cleverly concealed in the cliff it was nearly invisible. She climbed, Tavin and Niveus trailing behind her. Felsic stopped several times to show her where the stairs switched back on themselves. The boat shrank below until it was only a toy in a sea of bathwater. The air became thinner, and fish hawks circled the skies nearby.

"We're almost there." Mafic panted. Weapons and armor weighed everyone down, making the climb arduous. Rinn was reminded of her trip up the Grand Staircase in Peleon. She knew she had to go back, face the Curia again after this was over. Maybe free from the influence of Elves they would listen to reason. Then she remembered Serpio, he would never stop hunting her. Rinn looked out to see the sun setting in the western ocean. Somewhere out there was Brigantum, her father's home, and Migalia. Her world was so much simpler when it was just a hilltop.

Felsic reached down a hand. "We're here."

Chapter 46

C alling Hyalos a city of glass was an understatement. The buildings were all crystalline, jagged angular shapes jutting out of the ground as if they grew there naturally. The slanting light of the setting sun refracted through them in shades of orange and yellow and red, like a city on fire. Bronze and gold instruments topped many of the structures like bizarre weathervanes. Silent streets of polished stone glistened between the buildings.

"Okay, circle up." Rinn's friends made a huddle, arms on shoulders. Rinn outlined her plan. "We make for the city center, to the Astrarium. The Elf Gentris will most likely be there."

"How can you be certain?" Niveus questioned.

"I think I've been getting help." Rinn brightened and then turned serious. "This may get very ugly, but remember, your mission here is to rescue Sidus. Don't take unnecessary risks. And leave the Elf to me. If we are in combat, do not get close to us."

Tavin asked. "How do we find Sidus?"

"I'm not sure." Rinn admitted. "But holding a goddess probably isn't easy. There must be some sort of magical prison in the city. It'll be big."

"I want to get a better look at those buildings." Mafic said. "They're fascinating."

"Don't get distracted." Rinn reminded him. "Finding Sidus must be your first priority."

"How will we know when we've found her?" Felsic asked. "I haven't seen too many goddesses."

Sora mumbled. "If she looks anything like her sister, I'll recognize her."

"Great." Rinn nodded to Sora. "Take your time, be cautious. There're likely to be magical traps everywhere. Trust each other. Be safe." Rinn addressed Tavin. "See if you can decipher any of their writing. There may be clues that'll help you locate Sidus."

"I'll do my best." The scribe turned warrior replied. Rinn gave him a peck on the cheek for good luck.

"Godspeed everyone. May you all be safe." The huddle evolved into a group hug. "And thank you for believing in me." Once their farewells were said, Rinn and Cat prepared their assault. Rinn donned her mother's pendant, it glowed faintly in the twilight of dusk. "Are you ready?" Rinn asked her sister.

"I could use a snack." Cat's tail swished.

"Here." Rinn held out her hands. "Have some magic instead." Catherine eagerly drank Rinn's green magic energy. Her eyes sparkled and her claws glistened.

"Okay." Cat grinned. "Let's go."

Rinn explained her strategy. "We'll head to the center of town. When they launch their first attack, I'll cast darkness. We'll enter into the darkness, but then teleport us away, somewhere stupid. Let them waste their energy looking for us. Then we'll make for the Astrarium." Cat nodded in understanding. Hand in paw, they walked into the crystal city. The gossamer-thin buildings were impossibly tall with quartz-like doors and iridescent windows. Rinn was admiring their beauty when the first magic attack came, a white-hot ball of something halfway between fire and lightning. Rinn's barrier was up in an instant, and she called for Tenebra's power. Darkness spread over the city center, drowning the crystal towers in the blackest ink.

A moment later, Rinn found herself high above the city, perched on the spire of the Astrarium. She had to quickly grab ahold of a brass antenna to keep herself from falling. The Astrarium was the tallest building in Hyalos. It stretched to the sky like a glass pyramid that had been heated and pulled. Its sides sloped sharply downward, tumbling hundreds of feet to the ground.

"Cat!" Rinn barked at her sister, holding onto an antenna for dear life.

Catherine calmly squatted on the peak. "You said stupid." She reminded her sister.

"I know." Rinn huffed. "But what're we supposed to do up here?"

Cat scratched her chin. "I thought we could float down."

Rinn laughed to herself. "You really like flying, don't you?" Cat nodded vigorously. Rinn shook her head. "Silly, silly Margot. Give me your paw." Cat reached out and Rinn invoked the power of Divum, the goddess of the sky. As they drifted lazily down like feathers, Rinn could see the magic battle on the edges of her summoned darkness. Flickers of light exploded, and smoke billowed up from the area. Mages darted between buildings like commandos, hurling flame and light. Rinn hoped her friends were far away finding Sidus.

Rinn and Cat silently touched down outside the door to the Astrarium. Cat put a paw to her chin. "Do we knock?"

"I don't think so." Rinn smirked. She whispered the word "soth" and the colors of the sky and ground twisted around. Surprisingly, the buildings of Hyalos appeared exactly the same, white crystalline towers with iridescent windows. Rinn studied the entrance to the Astrarium and found no lock or mechanism in the door, no one touched it at all. But on the ground in front of the door were traces of four precisely placed footprints. "Clever." She remarked, matching her feet up with the images. The crystalline door slid downward.

Rinn led Cat into the Astrarium, down a triangular hallway lit by some unseen source. Rinn held her spear at the ready as she crept deeper into the structure. As she walked, her magical vision returned to normal. After a short distance, the hallway opened to an immense atrium. The interior of the pyramid was essentially hollow, the space filled with a giant mechanical monstrosity. Massive gears whirled as brass and silver spheres orbited a golden sun. Two moons, one light and one dark danced around a planet bathed in blues and greens and yellows. Home, Rinn thought. She had never seen a globe of the world before. Sevria was just a small patch on her home world, covering a fraction of the world's surface. Edera, her continent, was one of many continents spread across the planet. To the west she could see the islands of Brigantum, maybe even Migalia. To the east she found the sands of Uurden Els, a vast desert the size of Sevria.

And then Rinn's eyes tracked north. She followed the planet as it rotated slowly around the room. To the north, across the Pernic Sea, was a continent the color of lush green leaves. The heart of this land was a vast waterway like the trunk of a tree, its branches extending into every part of the land. This was Tir Odigan, the home of the Elves. It was no wonder Gentris had to come to Hyalos, it was impossible to hide a continent from the moon.

"I know you are there, Gentris" Rinn paced around the room. "I've seen your homeland. I know how to get there, just like these priests of Sidus. That's why you had to silence them."

"You know nothing." A rich, resonant voice denounced her. A figure emerged from behind the orrery, tall and thin, dressed in a hooded blue robe. The Elf Gentris was pale, his gaunt hand holding a rune-covered staff. Gentris reminded Rinn of the half-elf bard that betrayed her years ago. He moved with an uncanny grace like Yallakh. Good gods, Rinn thought. Yallakh was an Elf—an Elf who murdered Elves.

Rinn inhaled, holding her resolve. She called out defiantly. "I know war, oppression, and death. You taught me well."

Gentris glided forward, his feet invisible under his long robes. "Your trivial lifetimes are a mere blink to us. You are insignificant."

"Then why go through all the trouble of coming here?" Rinn challenged. "The murders, the wars, why bother with us if we are so insignificant?"

"You cannot fathom the plans of the immortals." Gentris progressed closer to Rinn. She reached for a leather bag at her side.

"That is where you are wrong." Rinn quickly spoke to her sister in her head. Cat, get far away from me. Her sister was uncertain, but Rinn mentally insisted. Cat began to pad to the far side of the room. Rinn continued her soliloquy. "The gods of Sevria have been fighting for a thousand years, only one thing could bring them together. The threat of annihilation. You aren't fighting Sevria, you're trying to destroy our gods."

"Pretenders." Gentris trilled loudly. "There are no gods in Sevria, only charlatans and thieves." He closed the remaining distance with the speed of a striking snake. Rinn mentally yelled to her sister, catch! Gentris reached for Rinn with zeal in his glowing elven eyes. His bony fingers grabbed at Rinn's chest, wrapping around her ribs. He roared in frustration.

Rinn cracked a cocky grin. "Looking for something?"

"Impossible." Gentris cried.

Rinn. Cat whined. It's heavy.

Just hold on to it. Rinn pleaded. With a forceful push she shoved Gentris away. She struck the ground with her spear and it burst into flames. Rinn's magical barrier formed around her, a thick shell of triangles and spheres. "It's over."

Gentris scoffed. "Your petty magic cannot harm me."

"I know." Rinn admitted. "But yours can." With that she upended the bag of dirt at her side, scattering it across the polished crystal floor.

Gentris took a step backward. "What have you done?"

"Sealed your doom." Rinn lowered her spear. "This is soil from Gadiom. One scratch and you're dead."

Gentris growled. "I will not be defied." His rune-covered staff burst into azure light. Rinn did not give him a chance to strike, she lunged forward, swiping at his midsection. Her flaming spear point clashed against his staff, but it did not break. Gentris slashed Rinn's shield as if it were an apple peal, carving a circle-sized hole out of it. Rinn tried to seal the wound, but the gap would not close. She rotated her barrier so the injury was behind her, but her palms began to sweat. Her shield was a permanent part of her, without it, she was defenseless.

Gentris launched two more attacks, carving great lines into Rinn's barrier. She yelled out "acwin", and the room was plunged into darkness. A blue light flickered and the darkness evaporated. Gentris closed on Rinn. "I've had enough of your feeble tricks."

Rinn lifted the last of her father's tiny pottery jars in the air and smashed it on the ground. In an instant, the atrium was filled with smoke. Rinn evaded the coughing and cursing elf. She dashed around the orrery to find her sister cowering in a corner, shaking. Rinn bend down to her, Catherine peered up with terrified feline eyes.

"Can I have my soul back now?" Rinn reached out a hand.

"Take it." Cat pushed her paws forward to Rinn's chest. Rinn felt the hot, tingling glow of her soul settling back into its home, a sensation like dipping into bathwater that was a bit too hot. "Don't ever do that again!" Cat cried, literally cried.

"Soul magic." Rinn explained in a whisper. "It's the Elves' greatest power. Yallakh can manipulate souls. I was certain Gentris would try."

"How did you do it?" Cat shivered.

"If Molo could do it, I knew I could, too." Rinn explained. "I just pretended I was throwing you Clive."

"Well, it was horrible." Cat wailed. "You don't understand."

Rinn was a bit offended. "It couldn't have been that bad."

"Horrible." Cat grimaced.

And that's when Gentris found them, two girls sitting on the floor, arguing like sisters. He brought his staff down like a hammer, but not before Cat could teleport them both away. Rinn found herself sitting atop the golden sun, looking down at the bewildered Elf. He smashed his staff into the floor several times in frustration. Rinn's own shield was battered and torn. Her spear was already starting to corrode from her magic flames. She could not win like this.

"Cat, get us out of here." She moaned. Cat took three quick breaths then transported Rinn away. Right into a wall. Rinn hit her head with a resounding thud and fell to the floor.

Chapter 47

"Ow, ow." Rinn rolled on the ground holding her head. Her spear fell from her hands. When Rinn looked up, the sky was purple. Everything was purple. She was still inside the Mist, but she was also inside the Astrarium. Cat crawled over to the wall and knocked on it with a paw. Its reverberations echoed through the Mist.

"What's this doing here?" She wondered.

"I don't know." Rinn sat up to investigate. The entire building was here, including the mechanical planets. Rinn could also see the hallway leading outside. She wandered through the atrium, laying a hand on the rotating spheres of the orrery. They were solid and felt cold, like metal should. Before Rinn could explore more, Gentris' voice rang through the structure.

"Vile vermin. How dare you pollute this holy place!" Rinn could not tell where his voice was coming from. She could feel the familiar tugging sensation, the Mist was pushing her out.

"Cat." Rinn grabbed onto her sister. "How close can you get us to the door?" In an instant, Rinn found Cat and herself standing squarely in the doorway. "Good job." She scratched her sister's head. Together, they raced down the hallway to the exit. Outside, Rinn assessed the situation. Niveus and the dwarves ducked behind a crystalline wall while a group of mages lobbed fireballs at them. Between blasts, Niveus launched javelins. It was a standoff. Tavin knelt in a separate corner, deciphering inscriptions on the buildings. When he saw Rinn, he came running over.

"Any luck?" He panted.

"Not yet." Rinn answered. "But I think I know what's going on."

"What's the plan?" He asked.

"I need Cat to take me back to the Mist one more time." Rinn cradled her sister's paws in her own. "Please."

"Okay." Cat sighed. Rinn knew how hard frequent teleportation was on her sister, especially when she was dragging a passenger along. A blue light appeared in the doorway, and behind it, the enraged elf Gentris. Tavin tackled Rinn as the Elf lashed out with his glowing staff. An instant later, Rinn, Tavin, and Cat were all three in the Mist.

"What the blazes?" Tavin gazed at the buildings in astonishment. The entire crystal city was here, even the streets. Rinn's friends were gone, the other mages were gone, Gentris was gone.

Rinn pried her way out from under Tavin. "Quickly, I don't have much time." She pointed to her sister. "Cat, don't let him out of your sight."

"Where're you going?" Cat fussed.

"There's something I need to see." Rinn dashed into the center of the plaza. The sensation of running in a magical void was bizarre but successful. She did not need to explain the concept of ground to her feet. When she could see most of the city in one view, she called out the word "soth". Almost nothing changed: the Mist was the Mist, the crystalline buildings remained unaltered. But a bright white glow emanated from a distant structure. And inside the Astrarium, a deep red swirl appeared, like water spiraling down a drain.

Rinn pointed to the light in the distance. "There. That's where he's keeping Sidus. She's trapped in the Mist." Rinn called out to her sister. "Cat, can you get to her?"

"Maybe." She frowned at Tavin.

Rinn dashed back and grabbed Tavin's hand. "I'll take him out. You get Sidus."

"Oh." Cat smiled. "Okay."

Tavin stared at Rinn nervously. "You're taking me back?"

"Yes." Rinn reached out her arms to embrace him. He willingly went to her. "Don't let go." He held on much more tightly than he needed to, but Rinn did not stop him. She focused on the doorway to the Astrarium. She let the magic of the Mist shove her and Tavin back to the physical world. He was still holding her tightly when they landed. For an elongated moment he refused to let go. Rinn lightly tapped his back. "I need to go. I have an Elf to fight."

"Right." Tavin released her. He blushed at his own actions. Rinn was not offended, just now was not the right time. She backed up and surveyed the area. "Get somewhere safe."

"What are you going to do?" Tavin asked, voice full of concern.

"What I do best." Rinn promised. "Destroy stuff." She skipped her way through the door into the triangular hallway. Gentris had beaten her inside, he was standing at the orrery, siphoning power from it. Like the final piece of a puzzle clicking into place, Rinn understood what she needed to do. The Mist was the Elves' magical repository. If she could sever his connection to it, she could stop him. She danced her way over to the orrery, whistling a tune. "Oh, Gentris."

The expression he shot her was pickled with fury. Rinn did not care. His reign was over. Never again would he control Sevria, enslave her people, or orchestrate bloody massacres. Her country was going to be whole again. She was going to win. She was almost sad her father was not here to witness her victory. But he was safe in Messis with Dempsi. Rinn danced her way dangerously close to Gentris. She realized the tune she whistled was one of Lutra's original creations. It was uplifting, energizing.

Gentris lashed out with his glowing staff. "Shut up."

Rinn laughed as she brushed a hand across the orrery. "Scieppan." The outer ring shuddered and melted at her touch. She stretched a section of the metal into a long spear which burst into green flames. It felt comforting in her hands, like holding onto Catherine's paw, or hugging her father. Or Tavin. Gentris laid into her, but Rinn spun away, her joy unabashed. She parried and blocked his strikes, but his staff hacked Rinn's weapon to pieces. Rinn did not care, she brushed her hand against the orrery and pulled out another spear, this one curved like a scimitar. The second ring of the orrery faltered and jerked. Gentris grinded away at Rinn, destroying her second weapon, but Rinn did not care. She danced and sang. She could not shape the massive brass planets or dials, but there was enough iron in the orrery to keep her well-armed. She twisted the third ring into a spear, this one ridiculously long. Gentris howled in rage as he dissected her absurd weapon. Rinn made a fourth, and a fifth.

Rinn felt a faint tug, something similar to the magic-draining struma she fought in Viburna. This was it, the Elf's portal to the magical realm. Rinn threw down her weapon and reached for it. Gentris was not fooled. He lunged straight for her heart. Rinn dropped to the ground as his staff crashed through her barrier like an eggshell. Only broken shards of triangles and swirls remained. What was left Rinn positioned between herself and the Elf. She reached again to the core of the orrery, through the grinding gearworks. She could see the central mechanism, an intricate metal sphere notched with irregular grooves, some sort of three-dimensional gear. One of Rinn's fingers brushed the control mechanism. The metal was not iron, but it felt familiar.

"Morton thrane." Rinn whispered to herself. Her mother knew. Somehow, she knew about the Elves. She knew they were manipulating magic. She left behind a clue, Rinn just never understood it. Gentris hacked away at the broken machinery to get to Rinn. She reached around her neck and pulled off her pendant. It glowed faintly in the shadows of the broken orrery.

Gentris' rage ripped through broken metal. "You are nothing." He swore and he stabbed at Rinn with his glowing staff. She took the blow on her back, and it seared through her dragon-feather vest, burning into her skin. Rinn cried out in pain, but she refused to give in. "You and your pathetic gods will die like the vermin you are."

"We are stronger than you think." Rinn cried. "For my mother!" Gentris stabbed again, but it was too late. Rinn thrust her mother's pendant deep into the metal core of the machinery. The floor of the building shuddered. The rage in Gentris' eyes turned to fear.

"What have you done?" He backed away as the crystalline walls began to splinter and crumble. He produced his own blue barrier to shield him from the falling debris. The orrery heaved a great mechanical sigh and collapsed in a pile of broken gears and rails. The ground shook and the crystalline ceiling fractured. "What have you done?" Gentris yelled, trying to make for the door. Destruction rained down on everything. A great crack split the center of the building in a shower of iridescent shards. Giant chunks of crystal crashed down like icicles in a spring thaw. The Astrarium, the entire city of Hyalos was collapsing. Magic was the only thing holding it up, and that magic had been cut off.

The earthquake and devastation lasted more than fifteen minutes. Buildings toppled and great fissures opened in streets. Rinn's friends had enough time to get to safety, they were fighting on the edges of the capitol. By the time it was over, nothing in the city was left standing. A portion of the cliffs tumbled into the sea, narrowly missing a very nervous boat at the bottom. Hyalos was a complete ruin. Only outlines in the crystalline rubble suggested that a city might have once been here. No one fought. The grieving mages wandered through their city like lost children. Rinn's friends sifted through the rubble calling out her name.

Deep beneath the wreckage of the Astrarium, Rinn lay alone in the dark. It was cold, very cold. Her breathing was shallow, and her back burned like fire. She could feel her life slipping away from her. A pale, silver glow joined her in the darkness. Not a person, just a glow. And a voice. "Thank you, Rinn."

Rinn tried to respond, but she was too weak, her air came in gasps. The silver glow departed and Rinn was left alone. She did not want to die by herself. In a last desperate thought Rinn cried to her sister. Help me.

Chapter 48

H ammering. Metal on metal.
Voices. A pinpoint of searing light.

"She's in here." A voice cried out. A deep voice, male. Dwarven. More hammering and the bending of metal. More voices, and then hands. "My god, she made a barrier out of iron." Rinn was lifted from the ground.

"She's bleeding." Another called out. Younger, a voice full of worry. Rinn was pulled into the light.

"Let me through." Her sister, Catherine. "Rinn. Rinn." Furry arms holding her close. Rinn wanted to lift her arms, to hug her sister, but they were too heavy. They would not obey. She could barely breathe. "Rinn don't die." Catherine commanded. "Don't die on me!"

Then commotion. Shouting. Blue light. Rinn wanted to get up. She had to protect her friends, she needed a spear. But she did not have the strength. It took everything she had to keep breathing. Rinn heard fighting. Violent clashes as dwarves and humans screamed. Then Catherine roared, and it was over. They had lost, Sevria had lost. Gentris would come over any moment to finish Rinn off. She waited as the last seconds of her life dripped away.

Something touched her face, something warm and soft. "I'm sorry, Rinn. I have to do this." Her sister squeezed her so hard it hurt.

::

Rinn woke up furry. She breathed in and out, and it came easily. Her back did not burn, and her head did not ache. Her fingers felt numb, and she was laying on something. She reached back to feel her tail. Tail! Rinn looked down at her paws. She was a Margot. She was Catherine.

"No!" Cat-Rinn cried out. She sat up in bed. Tavin rushed in to check on her. She tried to stand, but flopped on the floor like a fish out of water. Margot legs bend differently than human legs. Tavin lifted her up.

"Whoa, slow down, Rinn." He settled her on the edge of the bed.

Cat-Rinn held her head in her paws. Her voice was just a squeak. "Where's my sister?"

"She left." Tavin answered. "There's much to explain, but you need your strength first." He attempted to lay her back down in bed.

"Gentris." Cat-Rinn growled, an awful guttural sound.

"He's dead." Tavin assured her. He pulled a blanket over her.

"How?" Cat-Rinn struggled against him.

"Felsic killed him." Tavin propped up her head with pillows. "He's gone. We won. But right now, it's time to rest. I'll bring you some food in a bit. We'll talk about it later." Cat-Rinn quieted down, allowing her head to sink into the pillows. "There, that's good. Just rest. I'll come back to check on you." Tavin closed the door. Cat-Rinn was aware of the room for the first time. Wooden-beams, second story window, thatched roof. There were mice burrowing in the thatch. She heard voices, Tavin was talking to someone outside her door, or possibly downstairs. Niveus maybe. She heard other voices she did not recognize. The smell of freshly baked chicken wafted through the hallways.

Cat-Rinn crept out of bed. She crawled on all fours at first, to get used to her Margot form. After several turns around the room, she felt confident enough to try standing. It was wobbly, but the tail helped. A lot. Tails were really useful. They moved exactly where they were needed, no thinking required. Rinn walked around the room on her hindlegs, holding onto the walls for support. She knocked into a pitcher of water on a table, but she caught it before it reached the floor. Her reflexes were amazing, if she could control them.

Once she was able to walk across the room unassisted, Cat-Rinn made for the door. Paws were terrible for grabbing things, but the claws compensated. She hooked a claw under the latch and lifted. The door swung open and she padded out into the hallway. She made no sound as she moved, her fur silenced her actions and her footpads muffled her steps. She moved like a ghost to the stairs. She was not sure if she was ready for them, but she took them slowly, easing herself down one at a time. The smell of chicken was getting stronger. More voices mixed in with the rest. New smells assaulted her nose: horse, ale, leather, something burning.

Cat-Rinn spotted Niveus and Sora sitting at a table talking. She lumbered across the room to them. They looked up in shock when they saw her coming. "Where's my sister?" She squealed. Niveus supported her and Sora pulled out a chair. Other patrons at the inn murmured and gossiped about the strange goings-on, eyeing her warily. Cat-Rinn could hear and understand every word. She hissed at them.

"Calm down, Rinn." Niveus seemed restrained, but Cat-Rinn could smell the fear on her. Niveus' fingers twitched nervously near her blade. "Go get Tavin." She instructed Sora. The silver-haired dwarf ran off. Her smell was like fish and seawater.

"Where is my sister?" Cat-Rinn uttered. It was more of a command than a question. Niveus tried to pacify her, but she had no answers. Finally, Tavin appeared. He took over.

"It's okay." Tavin pulled up a chair opposite the feisty Margot.

"Where is my sister?" Cat-Rinn repeated. By this time, the tavern guests were starting to leave. The bartender glowered as he polished his glassware.

"Do you feel up for a walk?" Tavin asked. When he got no answer, he said. "There is someone outside who wants to talk to you." He held out a hand. Cat-Rinn refused it, standing on her own power. She clumsily padded her way to the doorway. Patrons moved aside as she passed by. Tavin held the door open for her. Outside it was as bright as daylight, except there was no sun. Only a moon. Cat-Rinn looked up at the moon, and it smiled down at her.

"Hello, Rinn." The moon said. "I want to thank you for rescuing me. It was my own arrogance that allowed me to be captured. My sister told me all about you. We are forever in your debt."

"Where is Catherine?" Cat-Rinn mournfully howled to the moon.

"She's alive." The moon answered. "She made a tremendous sacrifice for you. She took your body and locked herself in the Mist. My prison became her refuge."

"Why?" Cat-Rinn mewed.

"You were dying Rinn." The moon replied. "She saved your life."

"Get her back." Cat-Rinn demanded.

"I can't." The moon sighed. "Not without killing you in the process. You need to find a way to repair your body before your souls can be swapped. My sister said she will help you, but it will not be easy." The moon disappeared behind a bank of clouds. Cat-Rinn cried tears of frustration. They dribbled down her furry cheeks and rolled off her whiskers. Tavin threw his arm around her shoulders, and escorted her back inside.

Cat-Rinn sat alone at a tavern table. She could hear the barkeep making demands to Tavin. "Get that monster out of here. She's driving away my customers."

"She's not a monster." Tavin fought back. "She's a person. She's just having a rough day."

"I want her gone." The barkeep spat.

"Fine." Tavin spat back. "When everyone finds out who you've insulted, I don't think you'll be bothered with customers anymore." Tavin came to collect Cat-Rinn. Their simple room was cleaned out and a coach hired. Sora and Niveus appeared and joined them in the coach.

"Where are Felsic and Mafic?" Cat-Rinn asked. Her speech was still weird, but it was becoming more natural.

Sora answered. "They went on ahead, to get things ready."

"Ready?" Cat-Rinn questioned.

"We're going back to Peleon." Niveus answered.

Sora explained. "Tavin thinks it's the only way to help your sister. We have to find the man who healed your mother and bring him to Hyalos." His idea seemed sound, but Cat-Rinn did not know the man who brought her mother back from the dead. She had only seen him once and she could not even remember his name. The only person who knew him was her father.

What would her father say when he saw her? Cat-Rinn started to make a high-pitched whining noise. The coach driver turned back to see if everything was alright. Sora made excuses. "Everything's fine. She just needs sleep. Once we get underway, she'll settle down." She shot an expectant glance at the emotional Margot, who quieted herself.

Tavin came out of the inn and loaded the last of their things on the coach. With a whip crack they departed. Traveling by carriage did not agree with Cat-Rinn. The horses stank and the bumpy motion made her dizzy. She tried concentrating on the roadside. She was in a small village somewhere near the sea, she could smell the salt in the air. It was the middle of the night, but she could see perfectly well. The colors were a bit muted, but the detail was amazingly clear. She looked up at the moon, it was just the moon, distant and quiet. She scanned the skies and saw Tenebra, the invisible moon. She could see it, almost the same size as her sister, a dark disc moving through the night sky.

Cat-Rinn wanted to call out to Tenebra, to talk to the invisible moon, but her friends already thought she was crazy. She did not want to give them any more reason to think that she was out of control. She sat quietly in the coach, eventually napping off. She remained behind when they arrived at the docks. Tavin and Niveus haggled over passage to Peleon. Cat-Rinn dozed again until the transaction was completed. Then she was escorted onto a two-masted sailing ship bound for the capital.

Boats and Margot were the worst possible combination. The rocking motion messed with Cat-Rinn's feline equilibrium, and endless water in every direction felt like a deathtrap. She barely ate or drank, clinging mainly to the tall mast. When the ship encountered rough weather, she clawed her way to the prow to yell at the waves. Surprisingly, they listened to her, quieting down. The captain and the crew gossiped about her constantly, and Cat-Rinn heard every word. Even soothing reassurances from Tavin could not placate her. Once a day, Sora would dive into the sea and bring back fresh fish. This did help keep her strength up. After a few days, she stopped waiting until they were cooked and just ate the fish raw. They were soft and salty-sweet.

By the time the voyage ended, three weeks later, Cat-Rinn was better adjusted to her body. She could walk steadily and even run short bursts. Her voice was more under her control, as was her temper. She no longer hissed and snarled at everything that perturbed her. Her fur was still straw stiff and needed constant brushing. Occasionally, she would find herself absent-mindedly licking her fur. A habit that she tried to quash, the taste of fur in her mouth was despicable.

Waiting on the docks of Peleon, were the dwarves Mafic and Felsic. Cat-Rinn jumped off the boat before the first mooring line was cast. Solid ground felt so good beneath her feet. Sand would feel even better. The dwarves bowed to her in unison. "M'lady."

"It's just me." Cat-Rinn protested. She gave them feline hugs. They were a bit stiff, but the smell of fear on them was not very strong. "What's happening in the capital?"

Mafic reported. "The Curia are divided. Half of them still want your head and this rebellion crushed, but they are meeting with strong resistance. Serpio is leading the opposition. He wants your name cleared and a cessation of hostilities."

"That's a switch." Cat-Rinn put a paw to her chin. "I wonder what caused his change of heart?"

"No one knows." Felsic stated. "But he has swayed three members of the Curia to his side. It's a deadlock and nothing is getting done."

"How are the people of Sevria?" Cat-Rinn asked.

Mafic chuckled. "Life goes on, m'lady." He led her to a waiting carriage. Sora stepped off the ship and threw her arms around Felsic. The two exchanged an uncomfortably long kiss. Niveus had to walk around them to get down the gangplank. Tavin waited patiently on-board until they were through. Cat-Rinn wondered if she would ever kiss Tavin that way. She liked the way he held her, but kissing seemed so unnatural. Maybe she could lick him instead.

Everyone piled into the carriage. Compared to travel by boat, horse drawn carriages were nothing. Cat-Rinn peered out at the buildings like an excited child. The streets of

Peleon were packed with thousands of people and millions of smells, all unique. The crowds did not bother her so much, although some people did point and comment as she passed. She paid them no mind. She stuck her tongue out at a little boy who was doing the same to her. They both laughed. The carriage rumbled down familiar streets to a nondescript warehouse.

Cat-Rinn recognized the place. Niveus pulled out a key and unlocked the main door. Her storeroom was filled with merchandise. "What is all this?" She demanded.

Mafic explained. "In the last few weeks, a wealthy investor has taken a keen interest in your business. It is rumored that you might have pulled his only son from the water at Messis." Niveus did not know what to say, so she went to work, checking shipping ledgers and inventory lists.

Felsic pulled out several cots from a closet. "We thought you might want to stay somewhere familiar."

"What, no room at the Palace?" Cat-Rinn joked.

Felsic grumbled. "It's still pretty dodgy up there. The Curia's militias are fighting each other, trying to hold on to what little control they have left."

Mafic amended his brother's statements. "The Curia's days are numbered. The rebellion will likely march into Peleon unopposed. There's talk of finding the missing princess and putting her on the throne."

"I need to save my sister. She comes first." Cat-Rinn's whiskers twitched in agitation.

Tavin intervened. "That's enough for today. We should turn in for the night, tomorrow will be a big day. Rinn, your father will be here in the morning."

"Really?" Cat-Rinn's tail waved madly.

"Yes." Tavin handed her a pillow and a blanket. "Now get some sleep."

Chapter 49

U nder the best circumstances, Margot only sleep a few hours at a time. An excited, easily distracted Margot that could not wait to see her father got no sleep at all. Being able to see perfectly well in the dark made it worse. Cat-Rinn watched scurrying mice dart across the warehouse floor. She was not hungry enough to eat them, but chasing them seemed like a good past time.

When morning arrived, Cat-Rinn looked awful. She had big bags under her feline eyes and her fur stuck out in every direction. Sora brushed out her coat with a horse grooming kit. Cat-Rinn had to restrain herself from purring. Several hours and several fish later, she was ready. Everyone loaded into a new carriage and headed west to the Emmer Gate. Cat-Rinn remembered this place, she had escaped here during Tenebra's eclipse. She recalled pulling two bars of the portcullis off. Someone had welded new bars in place.

A line of soldiers waited at the gate, wearing green palace guard sashes. A choice few sported small triangular medallions. Cat-Rinn did not recognize any of them, but she knew they must be Onager's men. Sora greeted several with hearty handshakes and hugs. She introduced Felsic and Mafic to them. One guard was holding the reins of a very familiar horse.

"Bayard!" Cat-Rinn ran over to her old friend. The horse stamped and whinnied nervously, the smell of fear was intense. "Oh, right. Sorry, boy. I forgot who I was." The horse nickered in protest. She backed away a safe distance.

A watchman called out. "Troops approaching."

An officer called. "What colors are they flying?"

"Red on grey." The watchman replied.

"Stand down." The officer ordered.

The column of soldiers approached with a line of cavalry leading the way. There were over a thousand men, wearing matching gray military uniforms. Many carried tall lances with long streaming pennants. They marched like an army on parade, with carefree strides and smiling faces. The horses were in good spirits, prancing proudly. And sitting atop a black roan was a familiar-smelling man in a bright military uniform.

"Daddy!" Cat-Rinn squealed. She ran to him, crossing the vast plain in less than a second. Before his horse had time to react, she jumped up into his arms. He awkwardly caught her. Cat-Rinn purred and rubbed all over him. He smelled so good. She lifted her chin for scratching, which he obliged.

"Hello?" His voice was a mixture of relief and confusion. "Which one of my daughters are you?"

Cat-Rinn looked up at her father plaintively. "It's me, Daddy. It's Rinn."

"I see." He stroked her head. Other soldiers riding in the column regarded her with suspicion. Marshal glared at them. "It's a long story." Onager rode over and spoke with her father. Cat-Rinn did not listen to anything they said, she was curled up asleep in her father's lap.

::

Rinn's army assembled in a backroom of a Peleon tavern. It was richly decorated with finely carved wood panels and rich tapestries lining the walls. There were almost no mice at all. The tavern owner was a jovial man who was a friend of Onager. He was delighted to host a private party for the future Empress. He was a bit shocked when he met her, she bobbed up and down on her hindfeet and started sniffing around the room for playthings. When platters of roast chicken were brought out, Cat-Rinn happily joined everyone at the table. She squeezed on a bench between her father and Tavin. Grease dribbled down her chin as she devoured chicken meat in huge chunks. Everyone was happy to see her eating so well. Boiled eggs were brought out for her, and she ate those, too.

Marshal called the meeting to order. He banged a mug on the table for silence. "Thank you everyone for coming. I know many of us have traveled far in the last month, and much has happened all across the Empire. I think it's time we got together to tell our stories."

"Did someone say 'stories'?" Lutra burst into the room. The crowd gave him a round of applause. Cat-Rinn ran over and grappled him like a huntress. He smelled great, a different kind of great than her father, but absolutely great.

"Hello, Cat." Lutra smiled. He seemed older somehow, a bit more mature.

"I'm Rinn." Cat-Rinn complained.

"Oh." Lutra scratched his own head.

Marshal peeled Cat-Rinn off the bard. "It's a long story. We'll discuss it in a minute. Hello, Feena." Standing next to Lutra was a woman who smelled like Feena, but who looked different. She had lost a significant amount of weight and her rusty freckles were pale. She moved slowly, deliberately.

"Hello, Marshal." She said in a friendly but somber voice. "Hi, Rinn."

Cat-Rinn wanted to hug her, but she was afraid she might break her. Feena looked so fragile. Lutra helped Feena to a comfortable chair and brought her a small plate of food. Cat-Rinn realized there was another smell in the room, a repulsive one. She followed it to a smartly dressed young man with cropped red hair. She stifled a little hiss.

"Hello." Sionne said. "You're Rinn?"

"Yeah." Cat-Rinn sneered. "What of it?"

"Nothing." Sionne chuckled. "It's just, different, that's all." He extended a hand to shake. "Good to see you, Rinn." Cat-Rinn did not know what to do with it, if she shook his hand, she'd likely claw him. So, she bounded back to the tables and ate more chicken. Sionne raised a curious eyebrow.

Marshall confessed. "It takes some getting used to." Everyone settled down without introduction. Lutra took a central seat, like a performer on stage. He strummed an unusual stringed instrument, it made a pleasing accompaniment to his voice. He sang the Songs of Sevria, beginning with Rinn's flight from the Empire and her exile in the Rustic Lands. He let a single note ring high when she first picked up a sword and set it afire with magic. He counted all her deeds, the slaying of dragons, defeating Clanmorris, and vowing to return home. His melodies changed as he recounted her adventures in the Empire, starting with the liberation of her hometown and her narrow escape from Peleon. He detailed her flight west and her struggle with the armies of the rebellion. His story ended at the great flood whose waters reached all the way to the gates of Messis. He sang bitter tears for friends lost along the way, and ended on a melancholy note. The room cheered and applauded his performance.

He bowed to Cat-Rinn. "Only you know the story from here." All eyes turned to her. She shrunk back into her chair. She barely had control of her voice as it was, singing was absolutely out of the question. Before she had a chance to speak, Tavin stood up. He did not sing, but he read from a sheaf of papers. He recounted Rinn's journey south to the coast, and her voyage to Hyalos. Sora helped explain the reason for her voyage, and their encounter with Tenebra. Tavin described the magical city and the towering Temple made of crystal. He made an account of the battle against the mages and the sudden destruction of the city. Niveus and the dwarves had fought ferociously against superior adversaries, but when the Elf Gentris emerged from the wreckage of the Temple, all hoped seemed lost. As he attacked, Catherine made one horrific roar. The Elf could barely stand in the onslaught of her fury. In that moment, when he was distracted, Felsic managed to stab him with a shard of crystal. The injury was small, but fatal. The Elf could not recover, he bled to death in the crystal ruins. Felsic saved Sevria. It was not known how he was able to resist the ferocity of Catherine's roar, and he was not talking. He merely squeezed Sora's hand silently.

Tavin turned to Cat-Rinn. "Only you know what happened inside that Temple." The room waited for her story. Lutra held his stylus and wax pad anxiously. Feena peered at Rinn. Marshal leaned forward in his seat. The dwarves watched. Onager and the palace guards dared not breathe.

"Mom." Cat-Rinn squeaked. "She saved me." Her father looked at her in disbelief. Whispers rippled through the room.

"Tell us what happened, Rinn." Her father implored. "Please."

Cat-Rinn fumbled her paws. "We were fighting Gentris. At first, I thought he'd win, his magic was so strong. When we were running, trying to escape, we jumped through the Mist. That's when I pieced it together, the Elves were drawing power from the Mist. It's their magical repository. If we could sever Gentris' connection to the Mist, he'd be powerless. So, we went back.

"I faced Gentris and Catherine left to free Sidus. The goddess had been imprisoned in the Mist. During our fight, I found Gentris' magic link, a great machine inside the Temple. At the heart of it was a master gear made of Mornton Thrane." The dwarves murmured. Cat-Rinn lowered her eyes. "I used my mother's pendant to break the gear. But I'd already been stabbed twice by Gentris' magic. As the city tumbled down around me, I could barely breathe. My barrier had been destroyed in the battle. I shaped a shell of metal around myself, hoping it would protect me. By the time Cat found me, I was dying. She swapped souls with me. She took my dying body into the Mist and locked herself in the prison Gentris built for the goddess." Cat-Rinn could not stop crying. "She sacrificed herself for me." Her tears turned to rage, claws raking across the table. "And I will not stop until my sister is rescued."

Her father limped over and threw his arms around his daughter, joining her in tears. "That's why we're here, to save Cat."

"I want to depart now." Cat-Rinn demanded.

"Yes." Her father agreed. "We'll go to the Great Temple immediately." Cat-Rinn cocked an ear sideways. "Cassinius is there. We've been granted an audience with him. He's normally cloistered, he doesn't speak to anyone. But there's this zealous priest from Amne Dua raving about you. Something about hearing the voice of Aedis."

"Oh, that." Cat-Rinn frowned with her whiskers, somewhat embarrassed. She had left the part where she yelled at a god out of her story.

"They're expecting us." Marshal escorted Rinn through the tavern with her entourage in tow. Everyone loaded into carriages, except her father who mounted Bayard. He wore such a contented smile in the saddle of his favorite horse, Cat-Rinn did not feel bad about not having him in the carriage. Tavin, Lutra, and Feena rode with her.

Conversation was light as they rumbled through the town. Faces in the crowds turned and stared at the procession, flanked by city guard dressed in their finest regalia.

The spires of the Great Temple of Aedis drew closer. It was the birthplace of Sevria. Its high altar built on the stones of the original temple constructed by Sevrius himself. The first altar, a venerable hunk of weathered stone, had been moved to a private chapel along with other artifacts from the founding days. The imposing building still made Cat-Rinn feel uncomfortable, but the person who could save her sister was inside.

Their carriage stopped at the main entrance, double arched doors below a menagerie of statues. The saints and heros of Sevria gazed down on everyone who entered. Rows of clergy filed out to greet them. The high priest, a balding man named Palpo, was not exactly happy to see Rinn, especially in her feline form. But, it was rumored that his days in the Curia were numbered. He was being replaced by an elderly priest from a remote temple who was telling everyone to be kind to each other.

Cat-Rinn gripped her father's hand tightly as she entered the Great Temple. The vast structure had no secrets to hide, her nightvision could see into every dark corner. The forest of alabaster columns was not frightening at all. The pillars were far too thin to be actually holding up the domed ceiling, they were merely decoration. A giant statue of Aedis dominated the far wall, a somber man dressed in robes bearing the rod of justice. This imposing visage exactly matched the resounding voice Cat-Rinn had heard in Amne Dua.

A pleasant friar met the party halfway down the main isle. He was dressed in a simple red robe and the hair on his head dramatically tonsured. "Thank you for coming." He bowed to Cat-Rinn and her father as he traced a triangle across his head and chest.

Marshal returned the gesture. "Thank you for arranging the meeting."

"Brother Cassinius usually does not accept visitors." The friar talked as they walked. "He has taken vows of silence and seclusion. He spends his time in contemplation and prayer." The friar lowered his voice. "But his health is failing. He has not seen sunlight in ten years nor stepped out of the confines of his cell." He stopped at a heavy door behind the altar space. "I was surprised when he agreed to see anyone."

"Cass and I have a history." Marshal explained.

The friar put a single finger to his lips. "He only agreed to see the girl. He gave no indication why. He only communicates in brief written notes." The friar jangled a large keyring, trying several keys before he found the correct one. The hinges groaned as the door swung open. A winding staircase led to the chambers below the sanctuary. Cat-Rinn hesitated, remembering the awful prisons below the Temple in Viburna. The friar respectfully addressed Marshal. "This is a private place. I'll have to ask you to wait here. I'll lead the girl the rest of the way. It is not far."

Marshal did not like it, but he let his daughter go.

"I'll be fine." Cat-Rinn insisted. He tried to hand her a small knife, just in case. She held up her paws and wiggled her claws. Marshal cracked a smile. She followed the friar into the staircase, he closed and locked the door behind them. Darkness was no obstacle as Cat-Rinn descended deeper into the tunnels beneath the Great Temple. It felt like a crypt, except there were no tombs or sarcophagi. The friar led her down confusing, twisted corridors. Cat-Rinn would be lost, but her nose could smell the way back to the surface. Finally, they arrived at a dead-end with one single dark oak door. The friar rapped on it several times.

"Brother Cassinius. Your visitor is here." He motioned for Cat-Rinn to go inside.

Chapter 50

C at-Rinn padded her way quietly into the cell. The stone room was devoid of decoration, its only furnishings were a straw mat on the floor, a simple table, and a kneeling bench. An orderly pile of devotional books filled one corner. Brother Cassinius knelt at the bench in prayer. Cat-Rinn waited for him to finish, but after several minutes of silence she finally spoke up.

"Thank you." She said.

The monk completed his private contemplation, and traced a benediction across his chest. He rose from his kneeler slowly, as if he was suffering from a grave illness. He wore a simple robe of undyed cloth and a rough-spun belt cinched around his waist. He was thin, like Tavin was thin after a year of being imprisoned. Brother Cassinius raised his eyes to meet Cat-Rinn's. If he was surprised that she was a Margot, he did not show it.

"Thank you." Cat-Rinn repeated. "For saving my mother's life."

Brother Cassinius folded his hands before him. "Not a day passes without thinking about what I've done." His voice sounded like dried bread.

Cat-Rinn could smell the sorrow. "You brought her back."

The monk spoke stoically. "I violated the natural law."

"What natural law?" Cat-Rinn challenged.

"The law of the gods." Cassinius did not waver.

Cat-Rinn planted a paw on her hip. "See here. I've met the gods, at least some of them. And they're not at all what you think."

"I raised someone from the dead." Cassinius remained detached, like a statue. "Thousands have suffered and died because of my arrogance."

"And millions would have died without it." Cat-Rinn's tail swished.

"I tore Sevria apart." The monk confessed.

Cat-Rinn's fur bristled. She berated the defenseless monk. "I didn't come here to listen to you feel sorry for yourself."

"Then why did you come?" Cassinius asked flatly.

"I came to save my sister." Cat-Rinn screeched.

The monk settled himself on his straw pallet. He folded his hands in his lap. "I will not raise anyone from the dead."

"She's not dead!" Cat-Rinn hollered. She followed it with the softly spoken phrase. "I am." For the first time, Cassinius looked at her with interest. "There is so much happening that does not make sense. The gods of Sevria are at war and they're losing. That's why I'm here. I'm the Sigillum, the protector of Sevria, all of Sevria. Even her gods."

"How can the gods be losing?" The monk wore the expression of a young child, lost and forlorn.

Cat-Rinn sat on her haunches, tail wrapped around her. "Our deities are fighting against the Elves of Tir Odigan. Somehow, the Elves have discovered how to interfere with the Sevrian gods' powers. They're ripping the Empire apart. They kidnapped the goddess Sidus and twisted the Curia with their promises. I've seen the truth. I must stop them, and to do that I need your help."

"I've unleashed enough death and violence on this world." Cassinius cringed.

Cat-Rinn grabbed the monk forcibly by the shoulders. "I don't care what you think. You will help me save my sister." Before she could throttle him to within an inch of his life, a bright glow appeared in the room. It coalesced into the shape of a young woman in a flowing, white dress. Cassinius threw himself prostrate to the stone floor. The figure focused into a form that Cat-Rinn recognized, long silver hair and bright white eyes. In a gentle, lyrical voice the goddess spoke.

"I am Sidus, the goddess of Light." The brightness of her being filled the tiny chamber. "Listen to this one, my child. She sacrificed herself to rescue me from my magical prison. She freed my brother Lucus from his certain doom. She is our greatest ally in a dark and trying time."

Cassinius cowered on the floor, eyes firmly clamped shut. "What must I do, revered goddess?"

"Do what it is she asks of you." The goddess sang. "We all have our parts to play in this celestial dance." She lifted off the floor and dissolved into a shower of sparkles.

"Yes, my goddess." Cassinius answered, but she was gone.

Cat-Rinn opened the door. "If you'll just give me a minute." She stepped outside into the lightless hallway. Her tail swished in agitation as she walked from Cassinius' cell. "I know you're out there. Why'd you do it, Tenebra?"

In a poof she appeared, dressed entirely in black. Her expression was all pouty. "How did you know it was me?"

"I'm a Margot." Cat-Rinn pointed to her own eyes. "You're not invisible to me. I can see you up in the sky."

"Oh, right." Tenebra seemed deflated.

"And you don't sound a thing like your sister." Cat-Rinn crossed her arms.

"But we do look alike." Tenebra noted. "We're twins."

"I figured that much." Cat-Rinn tapped her hindfoot in agitation. "So, why did you help me?"

"We need you." The goddess twisted a silver lock of hair in her fingers. "You are our best chance for survival."

::

Cat-Rinn emerged from the cellars beneath the Great Temple with the gaunt monk. Brother Cassinius had to shield his eyes from the candlelight in the cathedral sanctuary. Marshal had been waiting patiently for his daughter. He limped over to meet her, his cane making a hollow sound on the flagstone floor.

"How did everything go?" He asked. Cat-Rinn motioned to the monk accompanying her. "Hello, Cass." Marshal's voice was layered with complex emotion.

"Hello, Ted." Cass solemnly replied. Cat-Rinn stifled a giggle (unsuccessfully).

"It's Theodric." Marshal floundered. "No, Marshal. My name is Marshal. Everyone calls me Marshal now."

"Okay, Ted." Cass repeated. Cat-Rinn broke into feline hysterics.

"Let's go." Her flustered father led the way out.

When they reached the main portico, Brother Cass had to stop and rest. He was unaccustomed to activity, and the harsh sunlight was overwhelming. Marshal helped his friend lean on his cane until he had recovered some of his strength. Cat-Rinn whipped her head around, she could smell fear and anger. A home-baked militia stormed the steps of the Great Temple with swords and clubs.

"Death to tyrants!" They cried.

Cat-Rinn summoned her shield—she was not sure she could still do that—but it appeared. Her barrier looked like shards of broken glass floating in the air; however, it was enough to thwart her attackers' assault. She evaded backwards, jumping onto the head of a Temple statue. Marshal shoved Cass behind him and held several men at bay with his sword. Anger welled inside Cat-Rinn. She felt a sharp pain in her tail, a young man with a sword stabbing at her from below.

"We won't be ruled by beasts!" He yelled as he slashed. Cat-Rinn pounced on him, flattening him to the ground. His sword clattered down the Temple steps. She bore her claws and prepared to rip his throat open, then she remembered the words of Aedis: Mercy is the only way. She looked down at her assailant, he was not a soldier, just a man. Probably a common worker by his simple clothes. Where did he get a sword? The militia was regrouping and preparing to mount a second assault. Marshal had disarmed three of them, but more were coming.

"Dad!" Cat-Rinn yelled. "Ears!"

He disarmed one more combatant and then turned himself and Cassinius into the doorway, covering his ears. Rinn inhaled deeply and shouted the word to summon Timor the Fear's power. She had tried it before, but not while in Cat's body. The word "broga" came out as a roar, so intense the air rippled over the steps of the Great Temple. Statues shook and small trees were toppled. Cat-Rinn realized with enough intensity this word could kill, but she only wanted to scare her attackers, make them flee. She succeeded, along with everyone else outside the Great Temple. The streets of Peleon were in pandemonium as people fled in a panic.

The terrified workman Cat-Rinn pounced upon was white as a sheet. She hopped off him and went to check on her father and Brother Cass. They had sheltered themselves in the stone doorframe and avoided the brunt of her sonic attack. Marshal was talking loudly as he helped Cass up. "Everyone okay?"

"I am." Cat-Rinn licked her wounded tail. "How's Cassinius?"

The frail monk looked even more frazzled than normal. "What was that?"

"The power of the gods." Marshal explained. A contingent of town guard stormed onto the scene, swords and spears drawn.

"What's going on here?" The decurion demanded.

Marshal answered. "We were attacked by a group of thugs. And we defended ourselves." The decurion took him at his word, Marshal was wearing his full military uniform. City guard fanned out to secure the plaza outside the Great Temple. The decurion raised the trembling workman off the ground and held him at sword point.

"Is this one of them?" He questioned.

"Yes." Cat-Rinn answered. "But don't hurt him. He's not a warrior. He didn't know how to hold a sword properly. Someone put him up to this." She walked over to the frightened workman and peered deeply into his eyes. She uttered Sidus' magical command. At once her vision inverted, the sky turned green and the grass blue. The stones of the Great Temple became as clear as glass. Cat-Rinn could see the workman's family, his parents and children. And his murdered wife. She had been killed by a group of minotaur slaves trying to escape. She was an innocent nanny at a wealthy merchant's estate.

"I will find the ones who killed your wife and bring them to justice." Rinn promised. The workman's eyes changed from fear to awe. She directed the decurion to take him away for questioning, but not to charge him. Marshal backed up her instructions. Slowly, normalcy returned to the plaza. The entourage that accompanied Cat-Rinn to the Temple missed the attack, they had ventured into a nearby bakery for meat pies and sweet rolls. They came running once the commotion broke out.

Lutra found Cat-Rinn immediately. "Are you okay?"

She held out her tail. "I only got hurt a little." Lutra smelled so good. She half wished he would kiss her tail to make it feel better. When Tavin arrived, she pressed that urge deep down inside herself. Tavin smelled good, too. A different kind of good.

"What happened?" Tavin asked.

"Some locals attacked us." Cat-Rinn smoothed out the fur on her tail and scratched behind her right ear. "I think it was a set up."

Tavin put an arm around Cat-Rinn, escorting her back to the parked carriage. His warmth felt wonderful. "We'll have to be extra careful from now on." He loaded everyone into the carriage, including Brother Cassinius. Marshal rode point on Bayard.

"We'll take refuge at the warehouse." Marshal commanded as he led the carriage away.

::

Onager paced the warehouse with members of his palace guard. Marshal was preparing a simple dinner for everyone: bread, cheese, and soup. Lutra and Tavin were setting up cots.

"I can help." Feena offered.

"You just rest." Lutra insisted. "You've had too much excitement for one day already." Feena nodded, but she seemed a bit sad.

Onager had been going over the attack at the Temple all afternoon. Several of the assailants were captured and questioned, but none of them had any valuable information. "We can't have vigilantes running loose in the city."

Marshal passed out bowls of soup. "It doesn't matter. We'll be departing in the morning."

"Again?" Onager did not seem enthusiastic. "Where are we headed this time?"

"Hyalos. That's where my sister is." Cat-Rinn nibbled on a chunk of cheese. It was not fresh meat, but it did satisfy her hunger. "Catherine took my dying body and sealed herself in the Mist. We need to heal her before we can bring her out."

"What is this Mist?" Brother Cassinius asked as he slurped his soup.

"It's hard to explain." Rinn-Catt put a paw to her chin. "It's all around us, but it's not part of this world. Cat and I use it like a magical shortcut when we teleport."

"You can teleport?" The monk's spoon halted halfway to his mouth.

"She can do a tremendous number of things." Marshal assured his friend. "I wouldn't believe it if I hadn't seen it with my own eyes."

"Do you remember that time she punched a hole in the Vallum?" Lutra elbowed Tavin.

"No." He replied.

"Or when she made that flower grow really large?" Feena weakly offered.

"Not to mention all the buildings she's destroyed." Her father remarked.

"You should have been at Hyalos." Tavin muttered. "She leveled the city."

"Stop it." Cat-Rinn blushed. Apparently, Margot can blush, mostly in their cheeks and ears. "I only did what I had to."

"We know." Lutra joked. "We've just all learned to stand back when you do it." Cat-Rinn pouted, but she knew he was right. The rest of the evening was spent reminiscing with friends. Cat-Rinn let Tavin tuck her in for the night, though some part of her wanted to curl up at the foot of his cot. She slept soundly, dreaming of her sister and chasing mice.

Chapter 51

The sailing ship Audacia clipped through the waves of the Aspero Sea. Cat-Rinn still hated boats, but she was at least used to this one. She remained below deck most of the time, sniffing out rats. She knew better than to eat seabirds, their meat tasted so awful she became nauseated just thinking about them. Cat-Rinn was surprised that Captain Levo agreed to ferry her back to Hyalos, considering everything that had happened last time. But his first mate saw the size of the purse Onager was offering and strong-armed him into it.

Lutra accompanied her, though he had to leave Feena behind—she was not strong enough to make an ocean voyage yet. Velle and Lepas promised to take good care of her. Sora and Felsic also came along. It was strange to see Felsic without his brother, but Mafic remained in Peleon to try to help the dwarves that were still living in slave-like conditions. He was becoming somewhat of a celebrity among the oppressed.

And then there was Tavin. He quietly came along, asking no questions, tending to Cat-Rinn's little needs. When he was not helping the sailors or hanging around with Cat-Rinn, he spent his time reading. He smelled so good, Cat-Rinn wanted to curl up in his lap. Once, when she walked past him on the boat, she licked him. He was sitting on deck reading, his shirt off and his brown hair glistening in the sun. She did not know why, it just seemed like the right thing to do. Her tail swayed contentedly just thinking about it.

Marshal and Onager anticipated trouble as they crossed the sea, but nothing came. A light rain, some high rolling waves, and a pod of whales were all they encountered. Sora caught fresh fish and Felsic whittled nautical-themed figurines. With a favorable tailwind, the Audacia made good time and docked at the port of Sera two weeks later. The seaside town went about its daily routine, not knowing who had landed on its shores. Onager arranged for transportation to the ruined city of Hyalos. The cart-drivers initially refused to go, but with enough money Onager convinced them.

Cat-Rinn sat in the cart next to Tavin. She leaned precariously on him, absorbing his warmth. Tavin made a gentle inquiry. "So, Rinn, what's the plan when we get to Hyalos?"

"We save my sister." Cat-Rinn answered in a dreamy voice.

"Do you know where she is?" He asked.

"She's in the building Gentris used to imprison Sidus." She snuggled her chin on his chest. "Not far from the Astrarium."

"Is the city really destroyed?" Lutra questioned. Tavin nodded silently, not wanting to disturb the sleeping feline.

::

"Rinn." A hand shook her. "Wake up."

Cat-Rinn's ears perked up. Before she could open her eyes, she could smell the magic. She shot up from her spot on the padded carriage bench. "Who's there?"

Marshal and Onager stood warily at the head of the carriages, their swords drawn. The dwarves backed them up with hammers. Lutra had a sword and shield, Tavin a spear. The carriage driver was nowhere to be seen. Neither was Brother Cassinius. Cat leaped onto the edge of the wagon. They were at Hyalos, a graveyard of broken buildings in a desert of crystalline powder. And they were not alone. Bizarre, enchanted animals picked their way through the wreckage, hoofing at the ground and braying to each other. Marshal and Onager used their swords to hold at bay two beasts that looked like twisted, scaly gazelles.

"What are these things?" Cat-Rinn scrutinized the strange herd, their scent was unnatural, like lamp oil and decay. The beasts sifted through the remains like a hunting party, searching for something.

"The beasts of Farann Fada." Marshal called back in answer without interrupting his swordplay. Cat-Rinn heard a crashing of trees on the far side of the city. She could smell the intense rage and hatred. Cries of alarm came from her father and friends.

"Dragon!" Marshal called out. "Everyone get back." But no one did. They stuck with him, in a tight formation as the massive beast clawed its way through the wreckage of Hyalos. The dragon was the size of a two-story barn with legs. It reared its reptilian head and roared loudly, its breath searing the sky. The beasts were startled by its approach and they fled into the forest. Cat-Rinn could not fight her internal instincts—she attacked. On all four paws she sprinted for the gigantic dragon. It snapped its teeth at her, but Rinn was too quick. She scampered past and raked its front leg with her claws. Dragon scales were tougher than dragon feathers, and her attack did nothing. The beast twisted around, annoyed. He opened his mouth and exhaled a column of flame.

"Rinn!" Marshal shouted, beating his way through lesser beasts to get to his daughter. But she was gone.

Cat-Rinn looked down from the top of the dragon's head. She must have teleported. She did not remember being in the Mist, but in one instant she was on the ground ready to be scorched, and in another she was atop the dragon. She wrapped her claws around a scale on the dragon's head and tried to pry it away. Marshal dropped his sword and drew his bow. Onager did the same. Felsic and Sora kept monsters off them as they nocked arrows. Lutra and Tavin guarded their flanks. The dragon thrashed about, trying to dislodge the annoying pest on his head. Marshal and Onager pulled hard and took careful aim.

"Rinn, get away from the head." Marshal cried. Cat-Rinn leaped off and rolled to the ground. Marshal let an arrow fly, Onager did the same. "Don't aim for their eyes. Their lenses are as tough as their scales. The mouth is their only weakness." He loosed another arrow. Onager backed him up, timing his shots so the dragon was under constant assault. The beast breathed fire, scattering the archers and combatants. The dwarves recovered fast, but the dragon's massive tail swatted them aside. Marshal launched more arrows, but his limp slowed him down. Soon the dragon was nearly on top of him. It raised its horrible head like a snake about to strike and bellowed fire directly at Marshal. In that instant Cat-Rinn yelled "acwin". The dragon-fire was snuffed, and the beast encased in darkness, along with everyone else. The beast stomped and flailed wildly with its tail.

"Rinn, we're blind here." Marshal called.

"I know." She shouted back. "It was the only way to stop the flames." A rhythmic rumble and wind covered the area. The dragon burst above the dome of darkness on giant leathery wings. It circled through the sky prepared to breathe fire again. Real fear washed over Cat-Rinn. Her father could not win this battle, the dragon was too tough.

The only one who could defeat it was her, and she could not hold a weapon. A sudden realization struck Cat-Rinn, she knew what she must do.

Cat-Rinn appeared next to Tavin. He jumped in the pitch black when she laid a paw on him. "Tavin, it's me."

"Rinn." He gasped. "I can't see a thing."

"It will fade in a moment." She reached out her other paw. Good, he was still holding his spear. "Do you trust me?"

"Of course." Tavin replied.

"I might get us killed." Cat-Rinn said honestly.

"I'd die with you." He held her close. She wanted to kiss him, but Margot mouths do not work like that. She licked him instead, several times. And then, holding him tight, she blinked away into the Mist. This time she could see it, the purple place she traveled with her sister. Just like the buildings in Hyalos, the crystalline structure in the Mist had been demolished, leaving behind only floating shards of crystal. In the distance, she could see one intact prism. I'm coming for you Cat. But first, I have to kill a dragon.

"Whatever you do, don't let go." Cat-Rinn cautioned. Tavin nodded in understanding. She teleported them out, high above the ruined city, much higher than she intended, in fact. The air was cold and thin. She wrapped her arms around Tavin as they plummeted down. Tails were amazing, hers worked just like a rudder to steer her position as they fell. Tavin grit his teeth as the wind whipped around them. Below them, the dragon flitted around the city ruins, no larger than a fly.

"We'll attack from above." Cat-Rinn pointed to the dragon. "My paws can't hold a spear, so you'll have to do it." She was not sure if he responded, he was fighting the air currents. She laid a paw on his weapon and lit the spearhead into green flame. The dragon was nearing, still unaware of their presence above. Cat-Rinn's darkness was fading. Combatants on the ground took cover against the dragon's flame as the beast strafed the city ruins before darting into the clouds.

Tavin risked talking. "How can we hit that thing?"

"I'm going to ground it." Cat-Rinn replied in a guttural growl. On the next pass over the city, the plummeting pair were getting dangerously close to the dragon. It angled its head up midflight, noticing the mid-air targets. It changed course and sped straight for them. Before it could open its mouth, Cat-Rinn yelled the word "hefige", commanding the power of Onero the Burden. Like the water from the sky over the plains of Messis, a great weight took ahold of the dragon. It flapped its wings uselessly as it fell like a stone.

"When we're in range, throw your spear." Cat-Rinn commanded through the wind whipping past them. The ground was growing perilously close. The dragon smashed down first, Cat-Rinn and Tavin trailed behind it like a comet. "Now!"

Tavin launched his weapon at the beast's midsection, seconds before the ground met them. With a great cry, Cat-Rinn pulled them both back into the Mist. They splashed through a wash of crystal powder way too fast. Tiny shards cut deeply through them both. Cat-Rinn had to shut her eyes to keep herself from being blinded. She teleported them back outside among the clouds. This time she incanted the word "ahebbe" and their descent slowed. Cat-Rinn clung tightly to Tavin as they drifted down like feathers.

"Are you okay?" She asked, spitting out blood and flecks of crystal.

"Did we get it?" Tavin held his right side painfully, blood was seeping through his leather armor. Cat-Rinn could see the immobile body of the dragon far below them.

"Yes." She held him close. "You were perfect."

"Good." He smiled weakly. As they descended, he grew colder in her arms, blood pouring more freely.

Cat-Rinn berated him with angry tears. "Don't you die on me." Minutes passed as they drifted to the ground, it felt like a lifetime. When they touched down, Tavin's body fell limply to the crystal sand, blood staining his entire left side. Cat-Rinn screamed in frustration. "Tavin!" The boy she loved was dying in her arms. She could not deny herself any longer—she loved him. His curling brown hair, his storm-grey eyes, his genuine smile. She did not know if her hot Margot blood drew them together, or if deep down a part of her soul refused to live without him.

In the distance her father and the dwarves were finishing off the dragon. Cat-Rinn cradled Tavin's head in her furry lap, holding him in her paws. Through fits of tears she sobbed "weaxan". She wiped away the sting in her eyes. "Grow damnit. You will not die on me. Now grow!" She could feel the ground stirring beneath her, trying to obey her demands. "Grow, Tavin." She commanded, forcing her will into Tavin's dying body. "Grow!" Light poured from the wound at his side and his color stabilized. The tiniest of weeds shot up like bamboo stalks. "Don't leave me." Cat-Rinn wept.

Cat-Rinn could hear her friends calling out to her. She knelt in the center of a grove of weeds. Tavin's face grimaced and a soft moan issued from his pale lips. His storm-grey eyes opened. Cat-Rinn's tears turned to cries of joy. Tavin lifted a weak hand to touch her face. "I'd follow you anywhere."

Chapter 52

"Get his shirt off." Marshal ordered. Lutra was cutting and pulling away the bloodied fabric. Marshal sifted through his pack for bandages and healing salve. Onager helped position his body. Cat-Rinn watched as they worked. Lutra tore away the last bits of his shirt.

"Samria's tears." Lutra gasped, backing away.

Marshal dropped his things and came to the boy's side. "What is that?" Cat-Rinn did not want to look. When she raised the courage to open her eyes, she saw a hideous scar on Tavin's side, right below his ribs. The skin had grown through the crystal shards piercing him. She had not cleaned the wound, she healed the crystal fragments directly into his body. Marshal went back to his kit. "Don't move, we'll get them out."

"What've I done?" Cat-Rinn wailed.

"It's okay." Tavin sat up on one elbow. "I feel fine."

"We have to remove them." Marshal insisted.

Tavin scooted back defensively. "It's fine. They don't hurt. Besides, we need to rescue Catherine." It felt like a slap in the face. How could Cat-Rinn forget about her sister? She was wearing her body. She needed to find the monk. The lesser monsters had fled when the dragon arrived, but he was not out of danger. She must locate him before they come back. Cat-Rinn dashed through the crystalline graveyard. It was not her eyes that found Cassinius, but her nose. Even after three weeks at sea, he still smelled like a hermit's cell and old books.

"Let's go." She hauled him off the ground. He was prostrate, praying fervently, covering his head.

"Mortal men should not witness battles between the gods." He refused to open his eyes.

"That was no god." Cat-Rinn scoffed. "Just one big, angry lizard."

Brother Cassinius dared to squint at Cat-Rinn. "But I saw you fall from the sky in green flames, an arrow of god sent to smite the beast."

"I'm no god." Cat-Rinn flatly denied. "I'm only a person. And I've got bad news for your theology: the gods need our help as much as we need theirs." She pulled him out into the open. She had a sister to save.

::

Marshal and Rinn's friends stood in a circle. Felsic and Sora wore proud dragon-slayer smiles. Onager looked exhausted. Marshal turned to Brother Cassinius. "Are you sure you want to go through with this?"

"How can I deny a request from her?" He replied with all piousness.

"We've been over this." Cat-Rinn rolled her eyes.

Tavin stepped forward. He held his side absently, but did not seem to be in any pain. His color was better. "Be safe. Come back soon."

"I will." Cat-Rinn promised. "And then we'll talk." He squeezed her paw in understanding. "Thank you for staying with me, through it all."

"I wouldn't want to be anywhere else." His gray eyes smiled.

Cat-Rinn held out a paw for Brother Cassinius. "It's time." He reluctantly extended his hand.

Marshal behaved exactly like any concerned parent. "Are you sure you know where you're going?"

Cat-Rinn chuckled to herself. "Yes. I can feel her. She's right below us." With a curt nod of her head, her father and friends vanished. Cat-Rinn was bathed in the purple Mist. Brother Cassinius floated in the void mouth wide and eyes agape. Cat-Rinn pulled him down to the crystal prism that held her sister. "We don't have much time."

Seeing her body in the crystal prison was surreal. Rinn-cat had her eyes closed and her hands folded neatly across her chest, holding some precious object. She looked at peace. Cat-Rinn could not tell if she was breathing. She pointed to the prism. "When I open this prison, my soul will be sucked back into my body. That's when I need you to heal me."

Brother Cassinius bobbed his head slightly.

"Ready?" Cat-Rinn laid a paw on the crystal and breathed the word of destruction: "onlithe". Fine cracks appeared in the prism and it shattered into a thousand pieces. Cat, catch! Rinn said to her sister. The violent vortex pulling her home was stronger than the magic sucking struma in Viburna or the whirlpool in the Aspero Sea. It felt like falling into a pool of fire. Her paws were pried apart into human hands and her feline ears crushed into human ears. Her fur solidified into human skin. And what happened to her tail should not be described in words.

Rinn took a gasping breath, she was dying. The pain in her back was so severe she could not make words or concentrate on any thought. An echo rumbled across the Mist, a single resounding word spoken by Brother Cassinius. Four simple sounds wrestled with the forces of the universe. The first sound was like the letter "C" infused with the strength of mountains. "W" followed with the force and power of the wind. "I" burned as hot as a raging inferno. And finally, another letter "C" cooled the incantation like hot iron dipped in water. The word was spoken.

Rinn took a deep breath, a painful, human breath. Her head felt like a split melon and her back ached, but she was alive. She opened her eyes, too many colors and details flooded her vision. She was nearly deaf, and her sense of smell gone, but she could see perfectly. Hovering right in front of her, was her smiling feline sister.

"Hi." Rinn said.

"Hi." Cat replied.

Rinn did not know what else to say. "Hi." She repeated, tears flowing down her face. She dropped whatever she was holding and threw her skinny, human arms around her sister vowing to never let her go again.

"Uh, Rinn." Cat asked. "Who's the weird guy?"

"I'll explain later." Rinn laughed, squeezing her sister tighter. "Take us home, Cat."

Cat leaned down and picked up the dull object. "You might want this." She handed Rinn the cracked master gear with her mother's pendant wedged inside.

::

Sora proudly showed off the seven figurines Felsic created. He called the set "The Dragonslayers". A miniature Marshal drew his bow in a mighty arc. Onager slashed with sword and shield. Lutra stood in a proud fencing pose, sword in one hand, bardic scroll in the other. Sora swung her mighty warhammer, dwarvish battle-lust meticulously carved into her face. Felsic made a figure of himself (something he never did) which paired perfectly with Sora's. He also crafted an image of Brother Cassinius, the model of piety. But his seventh figure was his masterpiece. Tavin and Cat tumbling from the clouds, both holding a single flaming spear aimed at the ground. It was perfect. Studying the figure, Rinn could tell that it was her behind the Margot face.

"Tell him this is his finest work." Rinn told Sora. She smiled happily and carried the collection below deck. They had been at sea for three weeks. The Audacia agreed to escort them home—Captain Levo and his first mate were getting used to shuttling Rinn around. I'm going home, Rinn thought. She recalled her vandalized house in Viburna, the place she grew up. She remembered the ruined house in the Rustic Lands and its transformation into a fortress. She missed the people of Hilltop, but that was not her home. Not really.

Sevria was were she belonged. Here, with her father and with her sister. This Empire was home. The forests, the plains, the salty air whipping through her hair were all home. And she had saved it. When she set out more than a year ago, she had no idea how or if she would succeed. She only knew her home was in trouble, and it was up to her to set things right.

"What's that grin on your face for?" Tavin asked. He parked next to Rinn on a bench over the oar lockers. The crew of the Audacia were lazing in the midday breeze. On the gentle open sea, only the helmsman and a lookout were needed.

Rinn turned to Tavin. "I was just thinking. We did it."

"Did what?" Tavin asked coyly.

Rinn tapped his arm. "Saved the Empire, silly."

"Oh, that." He confessed. "I still only understand about half the story."

"You know more than you think." Rinn put her hands in her lap. "You knew how to decipher the Sigillum words. You let me drag you all over Sevria. You stood beside me so many times that I can't imagine what it would be like without you."

Tavin touched Rinn's face softly. "I would follow you anywhere." He delicately lifted her chin and their faces came together. Tavin closed his eyes in expectation. Rinn had no regrets, this was the boy she loved. Rinn leaned in close and licked him.

Embarrassed, Rinn jerked away. "I'm sorry. I'm so sorry."

Tavin rubbed his wet cheek, laughing. "It's okay. I'm kinda used to it." His laugh was infectious, before long Rinn found herself laughing, too.

Precisely, Catherine appeared. "What're you doing?"

"Hi, Cat." Rinn fought back giggles. "How are you feeling?"

"Fine." Cat peered suspiciously at the silly teenagers. She sniffed at Tavin curiously, examining his head, neck and side. "Oh, okay."

Rinn raised an eyebrow. "Are you sure you're alright? I know how you feel about boats."

Cat rolled her eyes. "I've gotten over that."

"And no after effects of being human?" Rinn asked.

Tavin interjected. "Rinn keeps licking people." She shot him a vexing glance.

Cat answered. "Not really. Though you do have strange dreams."

"Well, I miss having a tail." Rinn rubbed her backside. "And being able to see in the dark. And hear everything. And smell people's emotions."

Cat raised an eyebrow. "Did you want to switch back?"

Rinn waved her hands to stop. "No, I'm fine being me. I just think you're awesome, that's all." She reached forward and hugged her furry sister. "I love you, Cat."

"I'm hungry, Rinn." Cat replied.

::

The Audacia gently glided into port. The docks of Peleon were packed with Legion soldiers expecting her arrival. Crowds assembled to watch the spectacle. Onager and Marshal disembarked first. The soldiers parted to let them through. Rinn and Cat waited at the top of the gangplank. Rinn surveyed the area like a tactician. Her shield was still wrecked, but she could shape metal. If she could summon wave, she could disable most of the soldiers, and Cat could get her father and Onager to safety.

Her father returned and motioned for her to come down. He did not seem concerned at all. In fact, he wore a slight smirk. Apprehensively, Rinn walked down the gangplank with her sister. When she set foot on solid ground, all the soldiers knelt down—five hundred armed men and women. Only one man remained standing, a porcupine of swords and armor. Preator Seprio strode forward through the kneeling soldiers. In his hand he held out a scroll. He stopped several paces short of Rinn and unfurled his parchment.

"By order of the Imperial Military, the Curia have been disbanded. Those who resigned their positions were released. The others have been taken into custody. The time of the interregnum has ended."

Rinn looked around, unsure what was happening. She saw the four generals from the revolutionary guard kneeling with the Imperial soldiers. Even people in the crowds had joined them, merchants, fishermen, laborers. They all knelt down. Serpio himself took a knee and offered up the scroll to Rinn.

"All hail, Sabrinn Sevralis, rightful ruler of Sevria." He said in a mighty voice.

The soldiers and crowd chanted. "Sabrinn Sevralis."

Rinn could not find words. She stood stunned as the citizens of Peleon called her name. Chanting turned to cheers and applause. Rinn squeezed her sister's paw. Cat shrugged. The next few hours were a blur. Rinn's assault team was paraded down the Grand Concourse with all the pageantry Peleon could afford. The festival-like atmosphere lasted the entire journey to the palace. Rinn's ornate carriage stopped at the foot of the great staircase leading to the Royal Pavilion. She looked up at the daunting climb and saw her father sitting across from her in the carriage.

Rinn asked the driver politely. "Could we take the other entrance?"

Chapter 53

" A re you sure it doesn't hurt?" Rinn asked, helping Tavin into his formal toga. Her coronation as Empress was weeks away—officials needed time to travel from all parts of the Empire. But today was her first public audience.

"I'm fine." Tavin insisted, draping the heavy cloth over his shoulder and pinning it with a clasp.

"I can have the healers come again." Rinn did her best not to look at his side.

"I'm okay." Tavin assured her. "It doesn't hurt. We've seen no ill-effects. If I can avoid having surgeons cut on me, I'll learn to live with it." But Rinn would not stop worrying. She had been the one who asked him to fight the dragon. She had dragged him through the Mist, gotten him severely injured. And she healed him carelessly without cleaning the wound. The crystals had fused with his skin. Guilt gnawed away at her. Tavin detected as much. "Rinn, It's okay. I'm fine."

A palace official entered the chamber and bowed. "M'lady. They're ready for you."

Rinn straightened Tavin's toga and adjusted her own flowing gown, sapphire blue with long draping sleeves. It reminded Rinn of the dress she wore to the palace dinner. That was the first time Tavin had told her she was beautiful. She still did not believe it, but she loved hearing him say it anyway. Rinn peered around the room.

"Where's Cat?" She asked. Tavin shrugged. There was a small thud as Cat jumped down from whatever hiding place she found in the rafters. She yawned and stretched out her arms.

"Do I have to go?" Cat whined. Rinn knew how Cat felt about boring meetings, but she needed her for this one.

"Yes." Rinn straightened Cat's vest and pants, a fetching sapphire blue outfit that highlighted her human-like characteristics. Besides, Margot looked ridiculous in long, flowing robes. Cat smoothed the fur on her face and fluffed her tail, just a bit.

"Okay." She said. "I'm ready."

"Let's do this." Rinn took Cat and Tavin by the hand and led the way to the audience chamber. Well-dressed guests awaited her arrival, wealthy men in flamboyant togas and women wearing more jewelry than Rinn had seen in her life. The palace herald rapped his long staff on the ground.

"The true and honorable heir to the Sevrian throne: Lady Sabrinn Sevralis." The attendees clapped appreciatively.

Rinn ahemmed. She subtly motioned to her sister.

"And her companion: Catherine." The herald paused for a last name.

"Amali." Rinn finished. Cat purred in delight.

Rinn motioned to her other guest. The herald sighed. "And her friend."

"Tavin." He announced himself. Everyone waited for his last name. "Dumetella." Rinn raised a curious eyebrow. Tavin merely shrugged. The three of them were seated in chairs on a dais at one end of the room. A long line of wealthy merchants and statesmen took turns highlighting their own successes and outlining their vision for how the Empire should be governed. Rinn listened to them patiently, saying nothing. Cat mostly yawned and stared out the windows of the Royal Pavilion. Rinn could feel that she wanted to go flying again. Tavin actually took notes on a small scribe's pad which impressed many in attendance. When the high-profile petitioners had finished, two scruffy guests were allowed in. Rinn barely recognized the two men, one older with a black beard and the other younger with the beginnings of facial hair. They were clad in worn hunting armor and leather gloves.

"Haril!" Rinn rose in excitement. "Grus!" The two men knelt before Rinn, as was expected. Rinn daintily descended the dais steps as quickly as her dress would allow. She begged the men to rise. "What news do you bring?"

"We tracked the beast Molo as far west as Demisi, but he has proven to be a formidable opponent." Haril apologized. Grus opened a sturdy pack on his back and produced a round rock with a purple eyeball on it. Clive seemed to be studying Rinn. Members of the gentry murmured at the highly unusual intrusion. "We have good reason to believe Molo is alive, but we need help to bring him in."

"Certainly." Rinn agreed. "You can have whatever you need." Her statement caused general unrest among the wealthy. Heated discussion and arguments filled the chamber. Rinn climbed the stairs to her seat and had the herald call for order. The commotion in the room settled. "I have an announcement: I have no intention of reforming the Curia." The crowd clucked in shock and disbelief. A hundred opinions were voiced. Rinn spoke over them. "The Curia represented the selfish needs of men, petty and shallow. Research into our nation's history has revealed that the original Council called by Emperor Reno contained nine members, one from each faith. That was their original purpose, to represent the gods." Rinn squeezed Tavin's hand, he smiled proudly. Reverberations of displeasure spread through the room. "I vow to create a new council, one that brings Sevria and her gods closer together."

"And who will be on this new council?" A merchant challenged.

"Some are already known, chosen by the gods themselves." Rinn answered. "There is a boy called Reicio in the forests of Viburna. He holds the Druid Staff given to him by Lucus himself. In the city of Messis, a girl named Dempsi speaks with the voice of Imber, commanding the rains. And who could deny the authority of Serpio as the voice of Parma? In the most difficult of times, he remained loyal to the protection of Sevria and her people."

Gossip and chatter once again filled the room. A haughty voice in the crowd asked. "Will this council answer to you? Do you interpret the will of the gods?"

"No." Rinn confessed. "The council will not answer to me. I will be an equal member with no authority over their proclamations."

"And which god will you represent?" Another voice called.

"That will not be disclosed here." Rinn stated abruptly.

"And what about our businesses?" The merchantman asked.

"You will regulate yourselves. We can help you create charters for each industry." Rinn tread very carefully. "I don't think government should be dictating how you sell your goods or where you sail your ships." This statement met with a fervent round of applause. Rinn excused herself before the crowd could ask her any more questions. She was terrified of making a political misstep. The room was abuzz with speculation as she departed.

Back in their apartments, Tavin soothed her. "You did great out there."

Rinn unclasped the necklace Duke Kapros had given her. She wore it to every public function she attended. People had gotten so used to seeing her with it that knock-off look-alikes were available for purchase at every jewelry stall. Rinn rubbed her temples. "So many questions. I'm not cut out for this. Let smarter people than me worry about logistics."

"No more meetings?" Cat's eyes glistened hopefully.

"No such luck." Rinn slumped down on a padded sofa. "You and I are on the new Sevrian Council." Cat's ears folded down in a pout.

"Which god is Catherine going to represent?" Tavin settled gently on the sofa beside Rinn. He unlaced her sandals and began rubbing her feet.

"She is definitely the voice of Timor." Rinn made small noises of appreciation for the foot rub. "Any who doubt her can have a demonstration." Tavin chuckled at that.

"How about you?" He quizzed.

"That should be obvious." Rinn leaned back. "I destroyed the Vallum, wrecked Lucan's Grove, leveled a Temple of Aedis, and demolished the city of Hyalos."

Tavin cocked an eyebrow. "You do make a fair point. Reneo the Unraveller, then?" Rinn nodded wordlessly, enjoying her footrub. "So, you mean to put the Forsaken Gods on the council? People aren't going to like that."

"I know." Rinn concurred. "But without them, we would never have freed Sevria. We need the gods, all of them. It will take the public a while to come to terms with that, but it needs to happen."

"What about the other members?" Tavin asked. "The ones who haven't been called yet."

"I have faith. The gods will send us what we need." Rinn relaxed back into her sofa. Tavin started to open his mouth, but Rinn put her finger over it. "No more questions."

::

Every mouth in Peleon discussed the news of Rinn's proclamations. As expected, opinions were divided. Traditionalists approved of the returning to earlier days, but businessmen and traders were critical, especially those who dominated monopolies under the Curia. The day of Rinn's coronation drew closer. She fretted over every detail: her clothes, her hair, Cat's fur, Tavin's title. She lost track of everything in those whirlwind hours. Then a message came from the west. Molo had been spotted. Rinn dropped everything to go after him.

"You're going to miss your own coronation." Tavin cautioned.

"It can wait." Rinn strapped on riding boots and her dragon-feather vest. It had been meticulously cleaned and repaired, it sparkled like diamonds.

"I'm coming with you." Tavin left for his own apartment to pack. Catherine appeared with a huge feline smile on her face.

"Adventure time!" She clapped her paws. She was wearing her own dragon-feather get-up which had not been cleaned nor meticulously repaired.

"We're off to find Molo." Rinn nodded. "It will be dangerous."

"Yay." Cat bounced around the room.

"You're not scared?" Rinn cracked a grin.

"No." Cat answered honestly.

Tavin returned from his room, holding a piece of parchment. "Will we be passing by Gadiom?"

"Yes. Why?" Rinn questioned.

"I have a thought." He replied. "I've been researching the Sigillum words. And I think I know what Imber's command does, but we'll need Dempsi."

Rinn was stung by her past with the little rain-bringer, but she agreed. Messages were sent and by nightfall Rinn, Cat, and Tavin were loaded onto a barge bound for Gadiom. The dwarves Felsic and Sora arrived, decked out in fancy, new armor—tough plates carefully fused together in form fitting shapes.

"Wow, you two look amazing." Rinn recognized a faint hint of brown and green. "Is that?"

"Sure is." Felsic strutted. "Finest dragon-scale armor around. We weren't about to let a treasure like that go to waste."

Rinn tapped on Sora's plates. "Can you swim in that?"

"Absolutely." Sora grinned. "It's lightweight, otherwise dragons wouldn't be able to fly."

"And it's ten times stronger than steel." Felsic proudly patted his own chest piece. "And fireproof." Rinn's own dragon-feather vest seemed trivial compared to the dwarves' awesome armor.

"Do you think you could make a set for my dad?" Rinn asked.

Marshal boarded the ship behind the dwarves. "I don't think I could string a bow in all that platemail. Thanks, but I'm fine."

"Suit yourself." Felsic paraded off with Sora to show off their armor to the rest of the crew. Onager climbed the gangplank. He and Marshal traded handshakes.

"Good to see you." Marshal said. "Not sure if you'd want to come along."

"Are you kidding?" Onager dropped his duffle bag. "Ten years in the Legion did less for my reputation than a few months with your daughter." He bowed to her. "Hi, Rinn."

"Hi, Onager." Rinn chuckled. "Thanks for coming along." He gave her a thumbs up. Rinn surveyed the docks. "Anyone seen Niveus?"

Marshal smirked. "Suddenly, she's in high demand. Her business tripled overnight. She has become a very wealthy woman."

"And she has all the troubles that come along with it." Onager joked.

"Is that everyone?" Rinn asked.

"A few more are coming." Marshal noted. A thin young man in a finely cut merchant's robe and silver rings walked up the gangplank. His hair was cut tightly to his head, leaving only hints of red at the top. His green eyes sparkled.

"Hello, Princess." He inclined his head.

"Sionne?" Rinn coughed. "What happened to you?"

"He became respectable." Marshal shook the young man's hand. "Thanks for coming along."

"My pleasure." Sionne replied. "I owe you for all the trouble I've caused."

Rinn warned. "This is going to be a dangerous journey. Are you sure you want to come?"

Sionne slid back the folds of his robe revealing two fencing swords. "I've been taking lessons. Master Durus is an excellent teacher."

Onager cringed. "He's brutal."

Marshal added. "But effective."

The last party members arrived as the barge was preparing to launch: a long-haired swordsman, a bard, and his frail wife. Cheers went up for Calder, Lutra, and Feena. Rinn hugged them all warmly, exchanging tearful greetings with Feena. She looked stronger than she had in many months, but she was still the ghost of the vibrant person she once was. Her actions were slow, and her speech deliberate.

Rinn pulled Lutra aside. "Are you sure it's safe for her to come along?"

"We're only going as far as Messis." Lutra whispered. "Feena wanted to spend some time with you." Rinn understood, she missed her closest friend from the Rustic Lands. Ever since Feena and Lutra had started dating, she had seen very little of her. After their quiet marriage, Rinn saw even less of her friend. It would be nice to spend time with her and talk to her about married life. Strange thoughts about Tavin filled Rinn's head. She shooed them away. Rescuing Molo came first.

Chapter 54

Rinn's Molo Rescue Team sailed to Gadiom in record time, the waters of the Lenis Sea were calm and the winds favorable. From there, they were outfitted with horses for the journey west. Rinn was offered a carriage, but she declined. She could travel more quickly on horseback and she was comfortable in the saddle. Haril and Grus joined them at Gadiom. Together they rode the Imperial highway west to Messis. Without the threat of war, traffic was returning to the Imperial roadways. Merchant goods traveled by barge to Macellum, and then on to Messis. But travel upriver was slow, unless you had a rain-bringer along; the highways were quicker. Rinn's team followed a route paralleling the river, one that was nearly abandoned—it led dangerously close to the toxic battlefield.

At night Rinn and her companions stayed at waystations. The facilities treated them to the choicest rooms and best meals (for a waystation), honored to be visited by royal guests. In some small way, Rinn missed sleeping outdoors under the stars. Cat disappeared every night to hunt in the wildlands, and Rinn actually wanted to tag along. But she knew her father would scold her for slipping away unprotected. On the sixth day, the rescue team reached their first destination: the Battlefield of Gadiom.

Everyone dismounted a safe distance away from the tainted soil. Using her gifts, Rinn could easily see the demarcation where the malignant magic began. Tavin shuffled through his horse's saddlebags. "Where did I put that stupid thing?" He finally retrieved a leather scroll case. "Found it." He slid a parchment out and read its contents to Rinn. It sounded archaic and full of unnecessary language, like a merchant's contract.

When he finished reading, Rinn asked. "What does it mean?"

"It's a Cibean trade deal." He explained, more excited than he should be. "Two tribes agreed to swap wood for clean drinking water. Did you hear it? 'Merian waet'? It means purified water." Rinn knitted her brows in confusion. Tavin tried to explain. "Don't you see, Imber's word is 'merian'. It means purify."

Rinn tented her fingers together. "So, how does that help us?"

"If you had enough water, you could purify anything." Tavin could hardly contain himself.

"I don't mean to be dense, but I still don't understand." Rinn confessed.

"The battlefield." Tavin threw his hands up. "If you had enough rainwater, you could purify the tainted ground, undo the Elves' magic." Rinn's eyes widened in understanding.

"Tavin, you're a genius." Rinn leaned forward and kissed him. To be honest, it was not their first kiss. They had spent many unsupervised hours in the palace and found that kissing agreed with them both. However, they were both too young and too shy to attempt anything more.

Rinn explained the plan to her father. He was delighted. He called for everyone to make camp and wait for the contingent from Messis to arrive. An hour before suppertime, a throng of people was spotted traveling south, a procession of priests flanked by soldiers. Dempsi's entourage had taken a wide route around the loathsome battlefield. Rinn waited patiently as they paraded in with full religious pomp and ceremony. A blue carpet was rolled out and a carriage door opened. Attendants led a little girl with short cropped black hair forward, she looked like she had aged five years since Rinn saw her last.

"Hello, Rinn." Dempsi said. No bow, no curtsey.

"Hello, Dempsi." Rinn replied, equally uncomfortable.

"Hi, Marshal." Dempsi gave a wan smile to Rinn's father.

"Hi, Dempsi." Marshal looked like he wanted to pick the little girl up and hug her. Cat waved, but she did not elicit any response from the stoic rain-bringer.

"Do you remember Tavin?" Rinn pulled him forward. Dempsi nodded her head. "He has been researching the Sigillum words. He deciphered the command of Imber, unlocked its meaning. He devised an excellent way to use it."

Dempsi was a statue of skepticism. "Well?"

"Imber's power can purge the evil magic that is here." Rinn gestured to the battlefield. "We can bring life back to this place, but we will have to work together." Rinn wrung her hands nervously. "Dempsi, I'm so sorry for what happened on the plains of Messis. I should've listened to you. I did not understand how much water was in the sky. I regret all the terrible things that happened because of my recklessness. But this isn't about you and me, it's about healing the land."

Dempsi surveyed the empty countryside, rolling hills of idle, brown grass. No birds, no insects, nothing dared to venture into the poisoned wasteland. "What must I do?"

"Just ask the sky for rain." Rinn sighed in relief. Tavin did the same. "When the rain falls, I'll invoke Imber's command to purify the ground. The water does the rest."

"Okay." Dempsi consented.

"Thank you." Rinn wanted to pick the little girl up and swing her around, but it did not seem appropriate. Eagerly, she asked. "When could we start?"

Talking seemed to tire Dempsi out. "The clouds have gone to sleep for the day. I'll speak to them about it in the morning. You can have your rain then."

"I understand." Rinn nodded. "Thank you."

Dempsi turned and walked back to her carriage accompanied by her priests and honor guard. Rinn asked her father. "Will she be okay?"

"Being a rain-bringer is a huge responsibility for a little girl." Marshal explained. "When I took her to the high priest, he wanted to seal her away in a sacred chamber. I reminded him that she's just a child who needs to grow and play and learn. It will take some time, but she will come to terms with her new life."

::

The next morning, Dempsi's escort and Rinn's entourage assembled on a grassy knoll overlooking the battlefield. Rinn was dressed in a simple gown and soft leather shoes. Dempsi wore an elaborate mantle and shawl embroidered with mother-of-pearl raindrops. On her head she wore a fanciful headdress and veil. She looked miserable. Rinn walked with her to the verge of the tainted magic.

"You don't have to wear all that." Rinn whispered as they stood side-by-side. Both parties waited behind them, expecting to see something spectacular.

Dempsi straightened her headdress. "The priests say this sacred outfit helps me channel my abilities."

"Imber chose you, not them." Rinn added softly. "The happiest I've ever seen you was when you danced in the fountains at the Natatorium. You made the rain fall in nothing but a flimsy cotton dress. You don't need all those fancy clothes. Just be yourself."

Dempsi considered this for a moment, and then she pried the gaudy headdress off and set it on the ground beside her. "Okay." Rinn gave her a smile, and she wished the little girl would return it, but it was still too soon. Some wounds needed time to heal. Rinn looked to the sky, a blanket of clouds blocked out the blue.

"Can you ask the rain to fall over the entire battlefield?" Rinn requested. Dempsi raised her head to the sky and talked to the clouds, not in a harsh commanding voice, but a soft sort of cajoling, like she was coaxing other children to play a game with her. In the distance, the clouds responded with a peal of thunder. Gently drops of rain began to fall. The priests began to chant and praise the glory of Imber. Rinn rolled her eyes. Dempsi almost cracked a smile. Once the rain was falling in earnest, Rinn raised her hands and in a loud voice yelled out "merian". The power of the word rippled through the rain like a squall line.

Rinn quietly chanted "soth" and her vision inverted. The cloudy sky turned green and brown, the morning grass bright red. Rinn could see the blue taint in the soil dissolving like ink in rain water. The showers continued for nearly half an hour before they subsided. By then, the blue taint had been completely rinsed from the battlefield of Gadiom.

Rinn turned and faced the small audience. "By the power and mercy of Imber, this battlefield has been purified."

"May she rain forever." Dempsi added.

::

Camp was broken and horses saddled. Dempsi's entourage packed up their things and readied for the procession back to Messis. Marshal gave the little rain-bringer a warmhearted hug before she climbed into her carriage. Rinn offered a parting wave. Dempsi nodded back.

"I think she's going to be fine." Tavin commented.

"Yeah." Rinn agreed. "She just needs to do things her way."

"Are you still going to have her on the council?" Tavin questioned.

"That's not up to me." Rinn admitted. "That's up to the gods. But, yes, I think she's the best person to represent the kind, compassionate views of Imber. I asked her if she'd join us. She said she'd think about it."

"Have you talked to anyone else?" Tavin inquired.

"A message was sent to Reicio in Viburna. And also, to a zealous priest in Amne Dua who claims he heard the voice of Aedis." Rinn chuckled.

Tavin accepted her answer. "Some positions will be hard to fill. The Astrarium is destroyed, who will speak for Sidus?"

"I'm not sure." Rinn held his hand as they walked. "Some night when the moon is full, I'll have to ask her." She chuckled. Her mood changed abruptly. "I was thinking about having Sora speak for Inrigo, the ocean goddess."

"A dwarf in the ruling council?" Tavin raised an eyebrow in jest.

"Crazy, right?" Rinn smirked. "But it's about time dwarves had some say in the government of Sevria."

"Spoken like a true Empress." Tavin grinned proudly. Rinn wanted to punch him, but she refrained. Instead she threw her arm around his waist and held him close. Now was not the time to argue. They stopped at Rinn's mount, freshly saddled and ready to ride. She gave him a quick kiss and then set one foot in the stirrup and mounted up.

"Let's go find our giant." She grinned.

Chapter 55

Ten days of hard riding brought Rinn's rescue team to the banks of the river just north of Amne Dua. Haril, Grus, and Marshal led the way, Onager and Sionne rode behind them. Rinn, Cat, and Tavin followed with Felsic and Sora on rearguard. Lutra, Calder, and Feena departed separately for Messis. Lutra made Rinn promise to give him a full account of their adventure, he needed more material for his songs. The party followed the riverbank for several miles before they located a fisherman who agreed to ferry them across. He could only carry two at a time on his modest skiff, as horses were skittish on rivercraft. Rinn and Cat crossed together with their mount. Cat had gotten over her fear of horses, but she could not manage one by herself—paws and claws were not good at handling reins. Aboard the boat, Rinn made small talk with the ferryman.

"Any news of monsters in these parts?" She hinted.

"You come to slay the beast?" The ferryman trolled with his oar. "Was wondering what a band of warriors were doing in these parts."

"We're tracking the monster." Rinn kept her emotions in check.

"Killed a couple of farmhands outside Demisi." The ferryman rowed. "They were trying to protect their cattle from the beast."

"Oh, Molo." Rinn shook her head. "We'll find you and we'll fix this."

Two more hard days in the saddle brought Rinn to the edge of the Egredi Forest, a vast hardwood timberland in remote southwestern Sevria. There were no large settlements this far from the heart of the Empire, just a smattering of cottages and hunting lodges. Marshal stopped to ask about monster attacks. Molo had definitely been through here, a local shepherd found dead and his flock decimated. Several woodsmen reported sightings, but no one was foolish enough to confront the beast. By their descriptions, he was twenty feet tall with massive arms and terrible fangs. Rinn knew the truth was worse, she had seen his true form.

Haril and Marshal tracked him deep into the woods. The Egredi Forest was alive with animal calls, birds chattering nervously and wolves howling in the distance. Furry creatures dashed through the underbrush as Rinn and her party passed. The horses nickered and stamped at the ground. Haril pushed on.

"He's been here." Marshal pointed down a corridor of smashed trees, as if someone had rolled a giant boulder through the forest. Rinn was reminded of Clive. She hoped there was enough of Molo's humanity left in the magic rock to stop his rampage. Marshal followed the trail of destruction, but it ended at a rocky ridge cutting through the forest. Haril, Marshal, and Onager discussed how to proceed. The dwarves dismounted to stretch their legs and adjust their armor.

"He'll be in a cave." Rinn reasoned. "That's where he went last time."

"Last time?" Onager questioned.

"He turned beast before, right after the Elves poisoned him." Rinn explained. "He left a path of destruction all the way to the Rustic Lands. Somehow, he snapped out of it.

That's how Clive was born." Grus looked back to the precious cargo he carried in his rucksack.

Haril cracked his neck impatiently. "We can't search every cave in the Egredi."

Marshal asked. "Cat, can you catch his scent?"

Catherine shook her head. "He was here, but it was long ago. I don't smell him anywhere nearby."

Marshal frowned. "It's getting late. We'll camp here for the night." He chose a defensive position at the foot of a rocky ridge the cut through the forest. Tents were pitched and a crackling campfire built. Grus and Cat ventured into the woods to hunt dinner. Sionne sat by the campfire sharpening his swords. Rinn noted how he had changed, he carried himself with confidence and poise.

"Your new life seems to agree with you." Rinn commented.

Sionne grinned his crooked smile. "I've made some good friends. Quality people. They seem to think I'm useful." He set down his swords. "I did not belong in the clan, always kicked about from one place to another. I never thanked you for freeing me, giving me a second chance. I promise I'm making good on it."

Rinn was relieved. "I'm glad to hear that. We all need second chances."

Grus and Cat returned a short time later arguing.

"That was totally unfair." Grus grumbled.

"Why?" Cat argued, carrying eight freshly caught quail. "You have a bow."

"And you can teleport!" Grus moaned. Sionne and Rinn laughed.

Cat shrugged and plopped her catch next to the campfire. Marshal and Haril plucked the birds and Rinn roasted them on sticks. Soon, everyone was savoring a hot meal. Felsic and Sora added freshly picked mushrooms and berries to the menu. The veil of night descended on the forest and everyone bedded down to sleep. Haril stood first watch. Rinn lay on her bedroll with Cat, her head poking out of her tent flaps. She stared up at the nighttime sky, trying to catch a glimpse of the moon. She knew Sidus was up there and nearly full. She wanted to talk to her.

"My Queen." A voice hailed her from the darkness.

Rinn shot up, toppling her tent. Cat squealed in protest. "Yallakh." A dapper figure emerged from the shadows, clothed in the deepest velvet, a cloth mask covering his lower face and long brimmed hat on his head. "Where have you been?"

Yallakh bowed gracefully. "My goddess set me on a mission to find the lost giant. She is convinced you have urgent need of him."

"We are tracking him right now." Rinn insisted. The rest of the camp began to stir, awoken by the intrusion.

"I know where he hides." Yallakh conceded. "But approaching him is fraught with danger."

"I know he's holed up in a cave somewhere." Rinn surmised.

"You are correct, my Queen." Yallakh's red and brown eyes glowed with admiration.

"Can you take us to him?" Rinn inquired, readying her spear and armor.

"That would be unwise." Yallakh cautioned. "The beast hunts at night when his rage is at its peak. He retires to his cave at dawn. It would be best to confront him then."

"But daylight weakens you." Rinn countered. "I won't risk getting you hurt."

Yallakh smiled behind his mask. "The forest affords me some degree of freedom, and once inside the cave darkness will not be an issue."

Rinn understood. "Okay, in the morning then."

Yallakh bowed. "Goodnight, my Queen." And he melded into the shadows.

The whole camp was astir. Marshal limped to his daughter. "What did he say?"

"He's going to guide us to Molo's cave in the morning." Rinn related the events of the encounter. Marshal conferred with Haril and Onager and made plans for the following morning. After the excitement died down, everyone returned to their tents. Rinn lay awake for nearly an hour, listening to Cat's soft snoring. Finally, the sounds of the forest lulled her to sleep.

::

The entrance to Molo's cave was not natural. It looked as if rock rippers had gouged a hole into the rocky escarpment that ran through the forest. Outside, the woods were deathly quiet, no bird call or rustling in the underbrush to disturb the stillness. On Yallakh's suggestion Rinn and her companion's left their horses some distance away, not wanting the scent of their flesh to arouse the monster.

"That looks bad." Grus stared at the foreboding cave entrance. He adjusted the pack on his back.

"We specialize in bad." Tavin patted him on the shoulder. Grus glowered.

Marshal corralled everyone together. "Here's the plan. We don't know what's in that cave, but we go in together. We protect one another. If the beast does attack, we fall back. In a worst-case scenario, we rely on Rinn's shield."

Rinn fretted with her hair. "Um. I don't have one anymore. At least, not much of one."

Marshal's eyebrows shot up. "What?"

"It got destroyed in the battle with Gentris." Rinn confessed. "It's only broken shards now. It can't protect us."

Marshal sighed heavily. "Okay. Felsic and Sora will take point, we'll trust in their armor."

Felsic proudly patted his platemail. "Nothing'll get through this."

"Stick together, get out if we have to." Marshal reached into his quiver and pulled out four arrows with round ceramic tips. "I've laced these with sleep salts. Once we spot Molo, Onager and I will try to knock him out." He handed two arrows to his fellow cavalryman.

"Tricky." Onager studied the unusual missile.

Marshal cautioned. "Don't get caught in the smoke. This is an especially potent batch, meant to take down a giant. One whiff might kill any one of us. When we launch, retreat. Is that clear?" Everyone nodded in understanding. They lined up and readied their assault. Like cautious field mice about to cross an open patch of ground, they crept toward Molo's cave. Rinn's heart was aflutter.

"Stay with me, Cat." Rinn gripped her spear with sweaty hands. Cat did not need to reply, Rinn understood her intentions. Felsic and Sora held out dwarven lanterns, leading the way. Onager, and Marshal followed behind them, bows at the ready, Haril and Grus guarded their flanks. Rinn carried Clive with her sister at her side. Sionne and Tavin brought up the rear. Yallakh faded into the shadows.

I can smell him, Cat whispered in Rinn's head.

How far? Rinn asked.

Two turns, one right, one left. Cat showed her images of the passageways. Rinn could not understand how her sister could see with her nose, but she accepted her information. She signaled her father with hand motions, instructing him which directions to turn. He nodded and passed the information on to the dwarves. The passages were unnatural burrows of sharp rock and hideous claw marks, but at least they were not full of bones. After rounding two bends, the tunnel opened to a large, low-ceilinged room. Sleeping in the middle of the chamber was the hideous beast Molo.

Molo's back was covered in thick quills, like a grashel. Even at rest, his arms and legs bulged with hulking muscles. His head was half-buried beneath his quills, black horns curling out of his skull. The woodsmen had not been exaggerating about his size—beast Molo was twice the size of regular Molo. His chest rose and fell slowly as he slept. Marshal signaled for absolute quiet. He gingerly nocked a sleep arrow, careful not to make any sound. He nodded to Rinn. She passed the round rock to Cat and motioned to Molo. Cat blinked twice. She silently padded over to the monster and laid Clive near his head, purple eye pointing to the beast.

Nothing happened. Cat raised her paws in askance. An eye opened, red and blue, like magic and blood stirred together. Cat turned to see the monster stir and with an eep she vanished. Beast Molo rose from the floor of the chamber and bellowed, a thunderous noise that shook the cavern's walls.

"Arrows!" Marshal cried. He and Onager launched two perfect volleys of smoke arrows. They smashed into the beast and the floor nearby. The room filled with billowing smoke. "Fall back." Marshal ordered. Everyone retreated down the corridor, the dwarves and Haril guarded their withdrawal.

Rinn could hear the beast thrashing about in his hollow, he was not getting any quieter. Billows of smoke came dangerously close. Cat, Rinn called in her head. Get Dad out of here. Cat reappeared next to her father. They both winked out of existence. The beast's head broke through the smoke roaring. In a panic, Rinn summoned her shattered shield, fragments of it hovered in the air. Molo swiped with awful black talons at the dwarves, flinging Felsic against the cavern wall.

"Felsic!" Sora cried as she slammed her hammer into the head of the beast. The blow stunned him momentarily. She rushed to Felsic's side, and he rose to his feet.

"I won't be taken down that easily." Felsic snorted. He lifted his hammer and readied to attack. Haril fended off the beast with his spear, barely dodging a vicious swipe. The two dwarves stood in unison and blocked the beast. Rinn and her friends had retreated almost to the entrance. Molo roared and collided with the dwarves. Felsic hammered furiously, beating back the ferocious monster. Sionne, Tavin, and Grus exited the cave. Rinn was about to follow when she saw Molo grab Felsic and fling him deep into the cavern, right into the billowing smoke.

"No!" Rinn cried. "Felsic." Sora did not hesitate. She dashed into the smoke after him, leaving only Haril and Rinn to face the monster alone. Molo lashed out at Haril, who tumbled free and stabbed with his spear. Rinn was racked with indecision. Her shield was useless, there were no plants to grow, no metal to shape. She was loathe to cast darkness, not with Felsic, Sora, and Haril still in the cave. Molo raked his claws along the walls, flinging hunks of stone. Haril took a glancing blow to his shoulder, but he remained focused. Rinn caught the largest chunk against her shattered shield, but smaller stones struck her, cutting into her leg and arms. Molo stampeded forward, head down and horns lowered for the kill. Haril lunged to the side, spearing the beast in the head. It roared in anger.

"Get out of here." Haril barked.

"I'm not leaving you." Rinn stubbornly held her spear. Then she saw blood pouring down Haril's torso. Molo's horn had impaled the warrior through his chest.

"Go." He wheezed, driving his spear forward. Molo whipped his head side to side, wringing the life from Haril's body. He tossed the broken warrior lifelessly to the cavern floor. Rinn screamed out in grief and disbelief. Molo reared his head, and with a snort he charged.

Chapter 56

T he beast Molo thundered towards Rinn at full speed. In the close confines of the cavern tunnels, she barely had time to react. "Hefige!" She cried out, summoning the power of Onero the Burden. The monster froze as the cavern ceiling crashed down, burying everything. Rinn tried to use the fragments of her shield to block the rockfall. Before she was smothered by stones, a darkness enveloped her. Rinn was disoriented as she was ripped away from Molo's cavern. She floated in the inky night. She could feel a hand holding hers, it was warm and comforting. Rinn looked over to see Yallakh gliding through the blackness. Rinn tried to talk, but the liquid night stole her voice.

"Shh." Yallakh put a finger to his mask. "My Mistress warned that Molossus was a formidable opponent. She tasked me with protecting you." Rinn opened her mouth again, and she started to choke. This was not the Mist, she could not breathe this inky blackness. "Be still." Yallakh soothed her. "We are almost out." Rinn's head rolled back and her tearing eyes caught a glimpse of the moon overhead, bright and silver. Somehow, she recognized it was not Sidus, but Tenebra the Queen of Night. The darkness faded and Rinn felt the uncomfortable forest floor materialize beneath her. She could hear her father calling her name. Tavin and the others as well.

Cat appeared beside her in a panic. "Where were you?" She cried soggy feline tears. "I couldn't find you."

Rinn groggily lifted her head. "Yallakh."

Cat threw her arms around her sister and squeezed her tight. "Don't ever do that again." She sobbed. "I couldn't feel you. I thought you were dead." Rinn's body ached fiercely. Shouts called louder and louder. Catherine yelled in reply. "She's over here."

Tavin and Onager burst through the underbrush. Marshal, Grus, and Sionne followed a few steps behind. Tavin helped Rinn sit upright. "What happened?" Marshal wiped rock and dirt from his daughter's face.

"I collapsed the tunnel with Molo inside." Rinn groaned.

"What happened to the others?" Her father asked.

"I'm not sure." Rinn winced. "Molo killed Haril." She cast her eyes down. Gasps came from everyone except Grus. The boy warrior balled his hands into fists and contorted his face in rage. "The dwarves got trapped in the smoke. I'm not sure if they're still alive."

Tavin lifted Rinn to her feet. "We have to get away from here."

"We can't leave like this." Rinn resisted. "We have to save Felsic and Sora. We have to turn Molo back to normal." The ground shook, the beast was digging his way out. It was only a matter of time before he broke free.

"He's too strong for us." Her father's words stung. "We don't have any sleep salts and you don't have a shield. We can't win against him. We must flee."

"No. I'm not leaving my friends." Rinn flatly refused. "The gods sent me here for a reason. Tenebra said it was urgent. I have to save him."

"You can't trust the Goddess of Darkness." Marshal yelled. "She's evil."

"I don't have a choice." Rinn fought back. "I need her, and she needs me."

"You're going to get the rest of us killed." Marshal's sour tone made Rinn's chest tight. She did not mean for any of this to happen. She did not intend for anyone to die. She could not believe Haril was really gone.

Catherine laid a paw on Rinn. "We should go."

"I won't leave them behind." The lump in Rinn's throat felt like a vice.

"They're gone." Her father's voice was thick with regret. "Once he's free, Molo will kill all of us. He has no remorse, he's a mindless beast now."

Remorse. Guilt. The words clicked inside Rinn's head. The only reason Molo was on a rampage was his utter lack of remorse. That was what separated humanity from wild beasts: guilt. It was not an evil emotion, it was necessary, a vital part of being human. Rinn knew at once how to stop him, but she needed Clive to truly return him back to normal. The tremors and roaring were getting closer, Molo had almost dug his way out.

Rinn rose to her feet. "I know what I have to do."

"Rinn." Marshal seethed.

"I can stop him." Rinn contended. "But I need Clive. Cat, can you retrieve him?"

Cat fretted with her paws. "You know I can't teleport Clive. He won't go through the Mist."

"He's buried under tons of rock." Marshal chided his daughter.

"I'll figure it out." Rinn's armor was determination. Her weapon was bold action. "I will bring Molo back. I'll find Felsic and Sora." She hurried to the entrance of Molo's cave and started climbing the rocky ridge. The tremors and underground howls grew louder until the beast burst from the rock-filled cave opening, sending stones flying in every direction. Molo snorted and thrashed on the ground. Rinn called for vines on the forest floor to entangle him and she splashed darkness over him using Tenebra's power. It would not delay him for long, but every precious second counted. Rinn had to stay focused, the others would have to hold him off until she returned. She ignited her magical vision with the word "soth". Clive's magical energy was easy to see, even buried deep underground. She also spotted Sora holding Felsic close by. They were in Molo's chamber room. Rinn climbed to a spot directly over their resting place. In the distance she heard Catherine's roar, waves of pure terror cutting through the forest. She could feel her sister's fear poured into her voice. The ferocity of it slowed Molo down, but did not stop him. Hold on, Cat. I'm coming.

Rinn bent down and selected a sapling pushing through the leaf litter. She touched the infant tree and spoke the word "weaxan". Dig deep, get me what I seek, and I'll make you the tallest tree in the forest. You will have all the sunlight you can drink. The small plant begged to grow. Down, Rinn demanded. Grow down, split open the earth. Open a passage and you'll be the largest tree in the world. The ground shuddered as Lucan's power took hold, the sapling's taproot burrowed deep. More, it demanded. Rinn chanted Lucan's word a second time, and the growth accelerated. The little sapling thickened until it was as wide as a carriage. More, it cried. Rinn called out "weaxan" a third time. Tendril-like roots spilled out across the forest floor rending the ground apart. Rinn scampered backwards, dodging the tangle of wood and destruction. Smoke billowed out from a fissure torn deep into the ground. Now, the tree pleaded. Throwing her hands to the sky, Rinn yelled. "Up!" The tree shot skyward like an avalanche in reverse. Massive boughs split from the trunk and stretched over the forest canopy, tree limbs larger than ship masts. Branches exploded in a conflagration of greenery.

Rinn sat on the forest floor stunned. The tree she created was a mountain of wood, overshadowing the entire forest. When the smoke cleared, she climbed down the colossal roots into the great fissure. An acorn the size of a barrel smashed into the ground next to her. Rinn scampered down before she was crushed. She landed in the heart of Molo's chamber. Sora sat on the floor, holding Felsic in her arms.

"Sora." Rinn called in the near darkness. "Are you okay."

"I'm fine." She replied. "I can hold my breath for hours."

"What about Felsic." Rinn asked.

"Asleep." She held him close. "His stubbornness kept him alive."

"Have you seen Clive?" Rinn begged.

"Here." Yallakh stepped from the shadows, Clive in his arms. Rinn rushed to him, rescuing the round rock.

"Thank you, Yallakh." Rinn exhaled in relief. "Now, can you get me out of here?"

Yallakh reached his arm around her waist. "Yes, but it will not be comfortable."

"I'm ready." Rinn assured him.

"Hold on." He said. Then, in a fit of unnatural strength he threw her straight up, out of the fissure. Rinn sailed halfway up the enormous tree. She had to mutter "ahebbe" to keep herself from being crushed by the fall. She let herself drift down toward the battle below. Her companions squared off against the beast Molo. Grus and Onager formed a two-man shield wall with Tavin as their spearman. Sionne struck at the beast's backside with his swords, and Marshal harassed it with arrows. Cat perched on the monster's head, scratching furiously at his tough hide.

Rinn floated into the center of combat. "Molo. You will heed me."

The beast whipped its head around and bared its glossy, black fangs, teeth as sharp as broken glass. Fearlessly, Rinn landed and stepped forward with Clive. Her father let another arrow fly, striking the beast in the side. Molo snarled. Rinn held forth an empty hand, palm outward. "You have lived as a beast for too long." She shouted the

Sigillum word "scyldigc", calling upon the might of Metus the Dread. A cold shockwave of guilt shook the forest. Marshal, Onager, Grus, Tavin, Sionne, everyone except Cat, fell to their knees. The unaffected feline bounced down and took her place next to Rinn. The beast Molo was afflicted the worst, shriveling and howling in pain. Rinn ardently walked forward with Clive, his purple eye glowing. "I return your humanity, Molossus."

The beast's voice was a strangle of emotion. "No."

"You must." Rinn commanded. "You cannot stay a monster."

The beast shuddered in pain. "Please. No."

"I know what it means to suffer, to be racked with guilt, to not want to go on. I never wanted to be a Sigillum, a killer, a destroyer, a weapon. But I never turned my back on what I needed to do." She touched the glowing soul-stone to the beast's head. "The gods need you—the whole you, good and bad. I need you, too. Come back to us."

The beast quivered and Clive's purple eye glowed brightly. The stone floated out of Rinn's hand and expanded into a ball of searing light. Rinn had to shield her eyes, retreating several steps as the monster was encased in a shell as bright as the sun. The forest floor crackled and nearby trees withered. The blinding light ended in a flash, and Clive dropped to the forest floor. Lying next to him, naked and dirty, was Molossus the Giant. Deftly, Marshal unclasped his cloak and spread it over his friend's exposed body. Molo raised a massive hand to his head and groaned in pain. Rinn wiped her eyes as Catherine clapped her paws together. Everyone cheered for Molo's return, except Grus, who fumed silently. Sora and Yallakh hauled the sleeping Felsic from below ground, reuniting everyone.

Marshal helped ease the giant into a sitting position. "Easy, friend."

Molo's voice cracked. "You should've killed me."

Rinn lifted Clive from the forest floor. "We could never do that."

"I butchered so many people." Tears of rage poured from his giant eyes. "I murdered Haril. I don't deserve to be alive." Grus gripped his sword tightly.

"No." Rinn refuted. "That was never your decision to make. You have been given another duty. The gods have chosen you to speak for them."

"I don't understand." Molo furrowed his brow. All the others exchanged puzzled glances. Rinn knelt down next to the giant.

"Rise, Molossus the Dread." She handed him his rock. "You are the voice of Metus, the god of guilt. You will be our conscience, the deciding vote when our council cannot agree."

"What are you talking about?" Molo struggled to his feet.

"I'll explain everything on the trip home." Rinn leaned to her father's side. He wrapped an arm around her. Cat rubbed against his other side, demanding attention, too.

"Wait." Molo stopped. "Where's Lea?"

A figure in the shadows answered, the well-dressed assassin Yallakh. "She is safe, for the moment. My Lady charged me with rescuing her from the dark waters of the flood."

"What did you do with her?" Molo demanded.

"My Lady bid me take her north to Tritica." Yallakh politely spoke. "From there she traveled on to Saxitum."

"Why?" Rinn asked.

"She bears the mantle of General Molossus." Yallakh showed no emotion. "She is leading the defensive efforts."

"Defense against what?" Marshal questioned.

"The Elves have invaded Sevria." Yallakh answered. "They landed on the northern coast two days ago."

"They crossed the Pernic Sea?" Marshal said with disbelief.

"They created the Pernic Sea." Rinn explained. "I now see why Tenebra said it was urgent. We have to gather our Legions and meet the Elves before they destroy the Empire."

Onager was aghast. "Fighting one Elf nearly killed all of us. How can we stand against an army of them?"

"We can, and we will." Rinn vowed. "Besides, we have the gods of Sevria on our side. And this time, I know we're going to need them."

Glossary

Language of the Sigilla

acendeor: meaning not known
acies: magic focused into a blade or point
acwin: shroud of Tenebra, 'extinguish'
ahebbe: embodiment of Divum, 'float'
beorgan: manifestation of Parma, 'shield'
broga: cry of Timor, 'fear'
gifan: instrument of Aedis, 'gift', used to summon an acies
hefige: weight of Onero, 'burden'
ith: force of Inrigo, 'tides'
maegen: might of Iugo, actual meaning undiscovered
merian: purity of Imber, 'cleanse'
onlithe: destructive power of Reneo, 'unravel'
scieppan: craft of Caminus, 'forge'
scyldigc: chains of Metus, 'guilt'
soth: insight of Sidus, 'vision'
weaxan: breath of Lucus, 'growth'

Gods of Sevria

Aedis: god of ceremonies
Caminus: god the forges
Divum: goddess of the skies
Inrigo: goddess of oceans
Imber: goddess of rain
Iugo: god of the mountains
Lucus: god of forests
Metus: god of dread
Onero: god of burdens
Parma (*the Shield*): god of protection
Reneo: god of destruction, also known as 'The Unraveller'
Sidus: goddess of magic; also, the visible of the two moons
Tenebra: goddess of darkness; also, the unseen moon
Timor: god of fear

Non-Human Races

Dvalinn: dwarven race with exceptional stone carving skills
Dverg: craftsman and artisan dwarven race
Elves: mysterious, immortal race from Tir Odigon
Giant: towering humanoid race from the mountains of Fendu
Margot: rarely seen humanoid race with feline features from the deserts of Uurden Els, known to exhibit an affinity for magic
Minotaur: humanoid with bull's head and shoulders; contrary to common belief, minotaur can be any gender, a female minotaur is a minotauress—do not call them 'agelada'
Náin: water dwarves, a race once thought to be extinct

Geography

Amne Dua: southwesternmost port in Sevria, not a nice place
Aspero Sea: large inland sea separating the peninsula of Farann Fada from Sevria
Brigantum: island continent west of Edera, renowned for its well-bred horses
Coram: port city opposite the capital of Peleon
Edera: continent south of the Pernic Sea, its western half the Sevrian Empire and eastern half an untamed wilderness known as the Rustic Lands
Farann Fada: mystical land in southern Sevria governed by the priests of Sidus
Fendu: large continent northwest of the Pernic Sea
Gadiom: port town on western Lenis Sea, closest city to the great battlefield
Hyalos: capital of Farann Fada, home to the Astrarium of Sidus
Lenis Sea: serene land-locked body water in central Sevria

Messis: large city in western Sevrian plains, home to Temple of Imber

Migalia: a savage archipelago west of Sevria populated by monsters, the Empire launched a series of unsuccessful invasions to the islands

Murstein: northernmost region of Uurden Els, ancestral home to the dwarven race

Peleon: capital city and founding location of the Sevrian Empire, home to Great Temple of Aedis

Pernic Sea: vast ocean north of Sevria populated by hostile sea monsters

Roinn Mountains: snow-capped mountain chain across northeast Edera

Saxitum: mining town in northern Sevria

Sevria: a dynastic Empire in western Edera spanning more than 500 years of history

Tir Odigon: mythical continent that is home to the Elves

Uurden Els: large continent east of Edera, known for its endless inhospitable deserts

Viburna: Rinn's childhood home, a city in Sevria, home to Lucus' Grove

Creatures

Caedes: (rock-rippers) large, fearsome beasts that bore into mountainsides with their fierce claws

Feathered Dragons: (bobs) large, flightless reptiles covered with feather-like scales

Clive: a rock

Floefang: creatures made of living ice with snouts resembling a wolf and long, flexible bodies like a ferret

Grimalkin: demonic familiars associated with witches

Grashel: burrowing pests with spiny, poisonous quills

Struma: immortal magic sucking beast of unknown origin

Bibliography

It is my privilege to call attention to these excellent books that helped me craft the world of Sevria:

Complete Encyclopedia of Elves, Goblins, and Other Little Creatures, Pierre Dubois 2005

The Dragon Keeper's Handbook, Shawn MacKenzie 2013

SPQR: A History of Ancient Rome, Mary Beard 2015

An Invitation to Old English & Anglo-Saxon England, Bruce Mitchell 1995

Medieval Europe: A Short History, C. Warren Hollister 1990

Everyday Life in Medieval Europe 500-1500, Kathryn Hinds 2009

How to Draw Fantasy Art & RPG Maps, Jared Blando 2015

Emotions Explained with Buff Dudes, Andrew Tsyaston, 2018 (some days I need to laugh)

The Belgardiad, *The Malloreon* and all the over novels by David and Leigh Eddings. Their careful and complex world-building has been an inspiration to me.

About the Author

Patrick Basil lives in southern Indiana with his wife, three teenage children, and two cats. He is a graduate from Purdue University with a degree in Biology. His debut novel, *Spear of the Sigillum* was published in 2019. Patrick enjoys exploring the outdoors, music, history, and finding new fantasy and science fiction series to read.

Find him on facebook: Patrick.Basil.98
He occasionally posts goodies for his readers to enjoy.